IN THE SHADOW

of

GOTHAM

IN THE SHADOW
of
GOTHAM

Stefanie Pintoff

 Minotaur Books ♔ New York

IN THE SHADOW OF GOTHAM. Copyright © 2009 by Stefanie Pintoff. All rights reserved. Printed in the United States of America. For information, address St. Martin's Press, 175 Fifth Avenue, New York, N.Y. 10010.

www.minotaurbooks.com

The Library of Congress has cataloged the hardcover edition as follows:

Pintoff, Stefanie.
    In the shadow of Gotham / Stefanie Pintoff.—1st ed.
        p. cm.
    ISBN 978-0-312-54490-4
    1. Police—New York (State)—Fiction. 2. Murder—Investigation—Fiction. 3. Criminologists—Fiction. 4. New York (State)—History—20th century—Fiction. 5. Westchester County (N.Y.)—Fiction. I. Title.
    PS3616.I58I5 2009
    813'.6—dc22

                                                                    2008045676

ISBN 978-1-250-00054-5 (trade paperback)

Second Minotaur Books Paperback Edition: June 2011

10 9 8 7 6 5 4 3 2 1

For Craig and Maddie

ACKNOWLEDGMENTS

No book, especially a first one, comes about without the support of many people. First and foremost, thank you to everyone at Minotaur Books and Mystery Writers of America for giving me what is truly a unique opportunity.

Special thanks go to Kelley Ragland, who has been a wonderful collaborator and terrific advocate, and to those at St. Martin's Press who helped to bring this book to publication.

Thanks to David Hale Smith for excellent advice and guidance.

This novel was tremendously improved by those who read portions of it as a work in progress: Marianne Donley, Gita Trelease, Karen Odden, Barbara Fischer, and especially Natalie

ACKNOWLEDGMENTS

Kapetanios Meir, whose ready encouragement and keen insight were invaluable.

Thanks to all my family—but to no one more than Craig, who always believed this day would come. He is a tireless and dedicated creative partner, without whom this book would not have been possible.

Finally, in grateful memory of Elaine Flinn, who first discovered me. No one could have been more generous and encouraging.

While nothing is easier than to denounce the evildoer; nothing is more difficult than to understand him.

—attributed to Fyodor Dostoevsky

IN THE SHADOW

of

GOTHAM

Dobson, New York
Tuesday, November 7, 1905

CHAPTER 1

The scream that pierced the dull yellow November sky was preternaturally high-pitched. Its sound carried effortlessly, echoing through a neighborhood of Queen Anne Victorians into the barren woods beyond, fading only as it descended toward the Hudson River. Those who heard the sound mistook it for that of an animal—perhaps the call of a screech owl, maybe the shrill cry of a loon. No one believed it to be human.

I did not hear it myself. I can only describe it as others did, after the fact.

But memory can be an odd thing. The report of that inhuman sound, relayed countless times, took root in my mind. It played upon my imagination, creating an impression so vivid it came to seem authentic. I know all too well that memory sometimes refuses to let die what we most want to forget. But now, I also know that memory can create something that never really existed. That is why this particular scream haunts me as surely as though I had been present, then and there, to hear it with my own ears. And I cannot mistake its origin: I know it is Sarah Wingate's dying cry, sounded just before her brutal murder.

News of her death came as the oversized grandfather clock in our office chimed five o'clock. My boss, Joe Healy, never one to stay a minute late, was putting on his coat, ready to leave for the day.

"You'll lock up when you're done?" Joe tucked his scarf around his neck.

I was at my desk finishing the paperwork for an arrest I'd made that morning. Thomas Jones had shown up for work at the Conduit and Cable factory with a hot temper and liquor in his belly, an unhappy combination that led him to sucker punch his foreman.

"Of course," I said, turning over the final page in the file. "Only Tuesday and our third assault this week." I blotted my pen before I signed and dated the report. "At this rate, the local paper will proclaim it an epidemic and we'll have the women's temperance union on our doorstep. Though I'd say it was lucky the assailant in each case was drunk. Men who can't see straight rarely land a solid punch."

We were interrupted by the sound of footsteps clattering up the short flight of stairs that led to our office at 27 Main Street. I stiffened with a flash of foreboding, for no one ever rushed toward our headquarters. After all, the sort of serious crime that might lead anyone to need a police officer in a hurry tended to circumvent the sleepy village of Dobson, New York, at the turn of the century.

Charlie Muncie, the young man who served as village secretary and had taken charge of the building's sole telephone
downstairs, brought a terse message from Dr. Cyrus Fields. He
needed our immediate assistance at the Wingate home.

"Mrs. Wingate's home on Summit Lane?" Joe asked, frown-
ing in puzzlement.

There was only one Wingate family in town but I understood why Joe was perplexed. The Wingate home was in the
estate section of town, and Dr. Fields was not the preferred doctor of Dobson's wealthier residents. One of several local physicians
who served in rotation at the county morgue, he also treated the
blue-collar factory workers in neighborhoods along the waterfront. He partnered closely with us on calls involving domestic
disputes or drunken brawls since, if the altercation were in
progress, we could intervene more effectively than the portly
but diminutive doctor. The affluent classes of Dobson preferred Dr. Adam Whittier, who catered to their whims with
absolute discretion. While rumor had it their homes were not
immune to violent disputes, they tended to handle such matters behind a wall of secrecy. The police, certainly, were never
involved.

"Did Cyrus say what's happened?" Joe asked. A stout man
in his early sixties with bushy white hair and a normally pleasant, ruddy face, today he glared at the young man as though it
were his fault Joe's dinner would get cold.

"He says there's been murder done." Charlie whispered the
words as though he were frightened to utter them.

In an instant, I recalled the reason why. His mother had
worked for Mrs. Wingate as a housekeeper for years. He would
have practically grown up in the Wingate household. In fact,
the one time I had met the elderly Mrs. Wingate, she had come

by the village offices to vouch for Charlie's character and recommend him for the secretarial job he now held.

"Who's been murdered?" Joe's voice thundered more loudly
than he must have intended.

"The doctor said it was a young lady. A visiting relative. But
he gave no details." Charlie's face blanched. For a moment, I
worried he might faint.

"He told you nothing more because your mother is fine.
Not to worry." I patted his shoulder and tried to smile reassuringly. I knew Charlie was eighteen already, but right now, he
seemed little more than a boy. "And not a word to anyone, okay?
Not yet."

He nodded in agreement as I grabbed my coat and worn
leather satchel. Joe and I then sprinted to the corner of Main
and Broadway, where we hailed one of the waiting calashes that
hovered near the trolley stop. It was not far to the Wingate house.
However, it was situated at the top of a steep hill—and we were
in a hurry.

Once we were seated, I glanced over at Joe, the "chief" of
our two-man force. Tight lines framed his mouth as he drew his
oversized black wool coat closer to him in a futile attempt to
ward off the icy gusts of wind from the Hudson River that buf-
feted the carriage.

"When did you last see a murder case in Dobson?" I asked.
My voice was quiet so the driver would not hear.

"Why? You're worried I'm not up to it?" He bristled and
gave me a withering look that I did not take personally. My hir-
ing five months ago had been the mayor's doing, part of his plan
to modernize Dobson's police resources by adding a younger
man with newer methods. I was thirty years old and a seasoned
veteran of the New York City Police Department's Bureau of

Detectives, specifically the Seventh Precinct. But Joe had been Dobson's sole police officer ever since the police department was first created. After twenty-seven years on his own, he did not welcome the addition of a new partner, believing I was the replacement who would force him into retirement. His dark suspicions often strained our relationship.

It was several minutes before he spoke again, and when he did, his answer was grudging.

"In the winter of '93, a farmer was shot dead," he said. "We never solved it." He shrugged. "But we also had no more trouble of that sort. Always figured the culprit was someone from the man's past with a personal score to settle."

Then he looked at me sharply. "I'm sure you've seen your share of murder cases in the city. But maybe I should ask if you're sure *you're* up to it? You look a bit out of sorts."

I searched Joe's expression, looking for some indication that he knew more of my recent past than I had thought. But there was no sign. His question had reflected his own concerns; he had not expected it to hit a particular mark.

I swallowed hard before I said, "I'm fine," with more confidence than I actually felt. I had a weak stomach, especially for certain kinds of cases, and I feared this would prove to be one of them.

What Joe did not know was that I had come here this past May in search of a quieter existence with fewer reminders of Hannah, a victim of last year's *General Slocum* steamship tragedy. I was not alone in my grief; nearly every family in my Lower East Side neighborhood had lost someone that awful day—June 15, 1904. For almost a full year following Hannah's death, she haunted me, particularly in cases where other young women met tragic, violent ends. I had planned to marry Hannah and build a life with her—but I had no desire to live with a ghost. That was why this job in Dobson, a small town seventeen miles north of the city, had seemed just the right opportunity: I could grieve quietly and rid myself of unwanted nightmares in a place where murders and violent deaths were not to be expected.

But still they came . . . and this one would test whether my rusty skills—and my weak stomach—were up to the task.

Behind us, the cragged cliffs of the Palisades loomed large over the Hudson River, colored in the faded oranges and yellows of late fall. The character of the neighborhood changed with each passing block; "hill and mill" was how the local townspeople described the division between the row houses and apartment flats nearer the riverbank and the imposing estates situated at the top of the village's rising landscape. Church's Corner marked the dividing line, an intersection with three churches—all Catholic, each distinguished solely by ethnicity, with one church for the Italians, one for the Irish, and still another for the Polish.

As the hills became even steeper, the homes became noticeably more capacious and ornate, some characterized by elegant stonework, others by latticed wood trim and dentil molding. The Wingate house was one of the statelier of these homes, situated on a particularly large expanse of land. It was a magnificent stone Victorian with a pink and gray mansard roof and an angular wraparound porch. On past occasions when I had visited this neighborhood, I had admired its majestic lawn and gardens. Today, it scarcely resembled the place I remembered, for the scene surrounding the house was one of complete chaos.

Dr. Fields was certainly inside, for Henry, the son he was grooming to take over his practice, was keeping several agitated neighbors off the Wingate porch. Two small white terriers were leashed to a stake in the middle of the lawn; they protested their restraints with ear-piercing yaps. And Mrs. Wingate herself, now approaching eighty years old, was seated on a straight-backed wooden chair in their midst. She looked cold, despite the fact that someone had brought her a warm wrap to protect her from the evening's increasing chill. She repeated a series of questions to no one in particular in an anxious, petulant voice. "Why can't I go inside my own home?" "Won't anyone tell me what sort of accident there's been?" And most frequently of all, "Where's Abby?"

Joe and I rushed past all the confusion, hurrying toward the main porch and front door, where Henry acknowledged us with a brief, grave nod. Inside the entry hall, we found Dr. Fields organizing his equipment. Cyrus Fields was a short, middle-aged man who seemed to have boundless energy and a remarkable enthusiasm for each case he encountered. His wide face usually held a jovial expression, even when tending to the dead or dying. But today he appeared unsettled. Heavy lines marked his forehead and his full head of salt-and-pepper hair was uncharacteristically mussed.

He looked up, and when he recognized us, his relief was palpable.

"Thank God you're here," he sputtered. "In all my years, I've never seen anything quite like it . . . I just can't imagine why . . . or what kind of person . . ." And the normally garrulous doctor trailed off for lack of words.

"It's all right," I said calmly. "Why don't you take us to her?"

"Of course. Where are my gloves?" He didn't mean ordinary winter gloves, but rather the cotton examination gloves he used for each new patient. They were behind him, on top of the black bag he had set on the floor. "Oh, yes, here they are. Come then. We're headed upstairs."

We followed him as he began to ascend the giant staircase that rose in a half circle above the entry hall.

"Is anyone else in the house?" I asked, adding, "We saw Mrs. Wingate outside."

"Yes, and her maid should be with her," he said. "Her niece, Miss Abigail, is resting in the library. I didn't want them to overhear us, or worse yet, disturb anything. No one has touched anything. I know that's always your preference even with our, ah, less serious cases." He fumbled before he found the words that would do.

We continued to climb. The stairs creaked under the weight of our steps, despite the plush carpet runner designed to cushion the wood. Upon reaching the first landing, I detected an unmistakable odor—the sickly-sweet smell of blood. I cleared my throat before commencing the next set of stairs. But death's odor is a singular one that, once detected, manages to pervade all the senses. With each step, my awareness of it—and my revulsion to it—grew more intense. I could taste it, feel it, almost see it by the time we reached the top.

I had to pause for a moment. I gripped the banister, fighting to suppress the wave of nausea that welled up, threatening to overwhelm me.

Dr. Fields pointed toward the bedroom immediately on our right, facing south toward the street.

We followed with hesitant, slow footsteps.

When he reached the door, he stepped aside, allowing me to enter first.

I took two steps inside before I halted—for there she was.

I stared woodenly, at once repulsed and transfixed by the scene of ghastly carnage before me. The victim lay propped against the bed, her body precisely positioned, hands folded together in a demure pose. Her head had been so badly battered that I no longer recognized the features of her face. Splattered on the blue toile wallpaper nearest the bedpost, intermingled with red blood, was a gray substance I knew to be brain. I swallowed hard, again fighting the sensation of nausea that threatened to resurface.

"What is her name?" I asked.

"Sarah Wingate. She has been visiting since Friday," the doctor said. His voice was even, but the beads of sweat on his forehead and the way he averted his eyes from the figure by the bed belied his apparent composure.

"And she is a relative of Mrs. Wingate's?"

"Yes. Her niece."

To refocus my wits, I forced myself to survey the undisturbed portions of the room. It was apparent it had been decorated in a tasteful and pleasing style—a fine dark blue and red oriental carpet complemented a pale blue bedspread and curtains, and two delicate Chinese vases adorned matching mahogany tables at either side of the bed. It was an atmosphere that suggested wealth and privilege. Yet today, it was nearly impossible to see past this senseless display of violence. I drew closer to the swath of blood on the wallpaper. Not yet dry, I noted as I came close enough to touch one stain, which indicated her death had occurred within the last few hours.

I breathed deeply through my mouth, vowing not to be sick. Such a response to the sight and smell of blood was a liability in my profession, and I never failed to be frustrated with my body's visceral response. The hollow pit in my stomach was a familiar physical reaction, though it had been nearly six months since I was last summoned to a murder scene. That was in May, just before I left the city. There, I'd seen more than my share of the squalor and crime endemic to my native Lower East Side, not to mention the official indifference to it. Yet my stomach had never gotten used to it. Once again I forcibly willed my nausea to subside.

The doctor and Joe had already begun talking about the case. "When I arrived, her face was covered by that blue cloth," Dr. Fields said as he pointed toward a crumpled, bloodstained material that lay atop the bed. "I removed it so I could check her identity."

"Is that cloth from her dress?" Joe asked curiously, walking a wide perimeter around the body to get a better look.

It took a moment for the meaning of his question to register, but I soon understood. The killer had slashed the victim's dress in haphazard strokes from the bodice down, and the blood-stained cloth was of the same material.

"How old was she?" I asked.

Dr. Fields paused before offering his opinion. "I'd say she was in her mid-twenties. And, judging from the bloodstains, her body temperature, and the fact that rigor mortis has not yet set in, I'd guess she has not been dead long—two hours, maybe three at most." He sighed and wiped his brow with a knotted handkerchief. "I've lived in this town for thirty years. That I should live to witness something like this . . ." He shook his head.

"Were the others home at the time? Did anyone hear anything?" I asked, drawing his attention back to details and descriptions. It was the doctor's analytical skills that this victim required now, not his empathy.

"You'll want to speak with Miss Abigail, Mrs. Wingate's other niece. She's the one who found her cousin's body." Dr. Fields mopped his brow. "She told her aunt to call me before she fainted. No one else is aware of the murder. We still haven't told them. At this point, it's probably best if you do so." His voice was soft as he added, "It has been quite an ordeal for Miss Abigail. I for one can understand how difficult it is to walk into this room unprepared."

But of course no one could ever be prepared for violence such as this. As I tried to refocus on the important details of the crime scene, one inconsistency stood out. The victim had a deep throat wound and multiple slashes on her upper arms, in addition to the battery done to her head. Yet there was not a single mark apparent on her hands or forearms. I knelt down next to her to check more closely. But no—there was nothing. Had she even tried to resist? It would have been a natural instinct to raise her hands to protect her face from the crushing blows. And I did not think she had been restrained, for in that case, her wrists would show signs of bruising or chafing.

The only rational explanation—one the autopsy could confirm—was that she had been incapacitated first, perhaps by a blow to the head. In that case, my picture of her assailant changed entirely. What sort of person would beat and slash a woman who was certainly unconscious, possibly dead? There was no fight in that; only brutal savagery. Was her killer so filled with anger that he had lost all control? Or had he been deranged by bloodlust? Just as I had an instinctive visceral repulsion to it, I knew others experienced a strange attraction to it. They enjoyed its sight and smell, as may have been the case here, where Sarah's cumulative injuries were more than was necessary to kill.

I got up and circled to her left, where I noticed something else so odd I could not believe it had escaped my attention earlier. Part of her hair had been cut and—had it been *removed*? I searched the room quickly to ascertain it had not been placed elsewhere, but it was not to be found. I took out my notebook and made careful notes of what I observed: Sarah's long blond hair had originally been pulled back in two neat braids; however, the braid by her right ear had been cut off at the level of her earlobe. I examined the shaft of hair nearest the cut and observed that while the exterior of the braid was encrusted with blood, the inner part was clean, which suggested her hair had been removed postmortem. I had seen cases before where bizarre acts were done to a corpse as a message or sign, but the missing braid defied explanation.

Fortunately I had remembered to grab the camera as we left. I breathed deeply and began to take slow, certain photos. What my mind could not grasp now, I would revisit later, when the black-and-white of the film had muted the red blood that covered the room and overwhelmed my senses. I only hoped the record would not be marred by the slight shaking of my hands. As always, that shaking was made worse by the aching pain in my right arm, which had intensified with the first cold chill of autumn. Its dull throbbing these past eighteen months was an ever-present reminder of Hannah's death. Or perhaps more accurately, it was a reminder of the incompetent doctor who had botched my treatment after I was broadsided by falling timber from the collapsing deck of the *Slocum*. As if I needed anything more to remind me of that horrible day.

From every angle, and varied distances, I photographed the

victim and the scene surrounding her. At my insistence, we had acquired a fine Kodak. Even though Joe had seen little practical justification in this expense, he had reluctantly allowed me to outfit the department with what I considered to be an essential tool for recording forensic evidence. While at the detective bureau in the city, I had become fascinated with the latest technology, especially cameras and basic fingerprinting equipment—though admittedly, the latter remained controversial and was not yet accepted by the courts. But earlier this year, London had sent two murderers to the gallows after gaining convictions based on fingerprint evidence alone. And our prison system in New York already used fingerprints to identify inmates. So I expected it would be only a matter of time before fingerprint evidence made its way into New York's courtrooms. Perhaps it would even be evidence I had collected.

Joe remained skeptical that Dobson had any use for all this equipment, but after the mayor supported my request, Joe had acquiesced. No doubt he feared his refusal would give the mayor additional ammunition to force him into the retirement he so dreaded. He waited patiently until I had finished photographing the crime scene; then he and Dr. Fields examined the body while I began dusting for latent prints.

I took out my kit containing the two kinds of fine powder that would make invisible prints appear: black and gray. I used the gray powder on dark surfaces, and the black powder on light ones. Print after print appeared, most smudged and partial, but a few were complete, with each finger ridge delineated. I photographed them all, drawing as near as my lens would allow. I stayed clear of Dr. Fields, though I knew his initial exam would not take long. The bulk of his work would be done at the morgue.

"Will you be performing the autopsy?" I asked.

"I expect to. While it's not my turn in the rotation schedule, I suspect they will honor my request given the circumstances."

To my relief, Joe announced he would go downstairs to break the news to Mrs. Wingate, who remained unaware of Sarah's death.

"We'd better call in help on this one," he said, explaining he planned to call our neighboring police department in Yonkers for additional resources.

"Do you want to telephone Mayor Fuller, as well? He will want to hear about this," I said.

He scowled. "No. He'd only bother us with useless questions that we've got no answers for."

I shrugged. "It's your decision."

But the repercussions would affect us both. The mayor and Joe intensely disliked one another, and I had come to understand why. When problems arose, Joe was practical in his approach to tackling them; he had little patience for the mayor's preoccupation with political expediency. For his part, the mayor had long ago lost patience for what he viewed as Joe's frequent insubordination.

We discussed how the Wingates might retrieve some personal items from the house for their immediate needs this evening, for I did not want them walking past this bedroom—certainly not until we had finished a thorough examination, and the more gruesome signs of death had been scrubbed away. Joe pointed to the area at the opposite end of the hall by the guest bath. "There's a back stairwell off the kitchen that takes them up over there," he said. "I expect the family uses it more regularly anyway, since it links these bedrooms with the kitchen."

"Good. Then let's cordon off this room and the front stairway; we can examine it again tomorrow, in first morning's light."

We were lucky to have light at all this evening. The Wingates had been among the first families in the area to install electric lighting in their home, but each individual light was placed so sporadically as to offer little real advantage over the ever-growing darkness. Still, I continued my work until well past seven o'clock.

After the county coroner's wagon arrived, and Dr. Fields removed Sarah's body, I finished my examination of the room in haste, for the blood splatters on the walls and bed were almost as unsettling as her corpse itself. Her possessions were spare, typical of a visiting guest. Opening the small wardrobe, I discovered three shirtwaists, each plain with large cuffs. They were next to two dark-colored skirts and a pair of boots that buttoned up the side. There was a modern Hammond typewriter at the desk, next to which was a notebook. On its cover, Sarah Wingate had written her name, as well as a title—THE RIEMANN HYPOTHESIS. Inside, line after line was filled with mathematical symbols and equations that resembled mere gibberish.

At the nightstand by the bed, there were two books: *The Ambassadors* and *Dracula*. At the bottom of the stack was last month's serialized installment of Edith Wharton's *The House of Mirth* as well as the September issue of *Harper's*. Sarah appeared to share popular literary tastes. Ten dollars was shoved into the back of a drawer, as was a pamphlet entitled *Common Sense for Women's Suffrage*.

I checked between the pages of each book, in each drawer, and even in the pockets of each piece of clothing hanging in the closet. But I found no letters, diary, or notes—in short, no personal item that connected Sarah with anyone, much less the person who had wanted to kill her.

I went on to explore the first floor of the house, checking whether anything appeared to be amiss. In the kitchen, I lingered a few moments; amid the odors of mulled spices and baked fruit, I could almost forget the stench of death that seemed to cling so tenaciously to my skin and clothes. I was so preoccupied with my thoughts that I was startled to hear Joe's voice calling me, insistent and loud.

"Ziele!" His voice echoed through the back hallway. "We need you over here. You've got to take a look at this."

I followed the sound of his voice to a rear exit near the back porch, where I became aware once again of the coroner's wagon as it rumbled over the cobblestones of the Wingate drive, departing for the county morgue. Through the door, I saw a full moon gleaming in the stark November sky. A number of glowing lights bounced up and down in the yard; they were lanterns carried by our neighboring police reinforcements, who had recently arrived and were searching the grounds outside the house.

Joe met my gaze, and I noticed how his lined features reflected the grim events we had endured this day. With a flash of foreboding, I had the unsettling sensation that we were being drawn into an even more complicated case than I'd originally thought—one that would draw upon our every power of deduction to unravel.

CHAPTER 2

"We've found something outside." Joe motioned to me, pointing toward the rear porch as I approached, indicating that I should follow him. He opened the door and gestured to what appeared to be a number of muddy footprints, each consistent with the tread of a man's boot. The prints were remarkably clear: well defined at the toe, if slightly smudged near the heel. One set led into the house, while another led back into the yard.

"Large enough to be a man's footprint," he explained. "And they are not yet dry, so they can't have been here long." He stepped back so I might see more clearly.

"Maybe these were left by the killer," he said, stating the obvious, "but how is it possible that there are no prints inside the house?"

"He removed his boots, I'd say," I commented dryly.

I was far more interested in the smudges around the heel of each print, which could indicate that the man had a limp or some other walking impediment. Or perhaps the heel was simply so encrusted with mud that the tread was wholly obscured. I glanced into the expanse of wooded forest behind the house, which was certainly as muddy as the walking path that I had taken to work this morning. Though today had been dry, the past several days had seen heavy rain and the ground was saturated.

Leaving that issue aside for the moment, I noted how unusually large and wide the prints were. "We should do our best to measure one of these. Not an easy thing to accomplish in the dark," I said, with a glance toward the evening sky, "but important in case someone should disturb this area overnight."

Joe nodded in agreement as we stepped back into the house. "I also need to show you this," he said quietly. "We found it outside, as well."

He pulled a small item out of his breast pocket. He was careful to use his handkerchief, and I realized that—despite his own skepticism about fingerprints—he was trying not to jeopardize whatever evidence the object he held might provide. Nestled within the cloth lay a silver locket that was threaded onto a pale blue ribbon. The ribbon was slightly mottled with what I took to be smudges of blood and dirt. As I carefully lifted it, also by means of the clean handkerchief, I noticed it was of superior workmanship, with a filigree pattern bordering its smooth body. On the back, I could barely make out finely engraved letters, which appeared to identify the name of the craftsman. Above this unintelligible writing was an inscription: *For S.W.*

"And inside?" I asked.

"See for yourself," Joe said.

My fingers were thick and clumsy as I pried open the locket, still making use of the handkerchief so as not to touch the silver myself. Inside were two small portraits: one man and one woman. I presumed the woman pictured on the left to be Sarah. Although I had seen her only after her brutal death, the person in the picture seemed familiar. Even in black-and-white miniature, it was apparent she had been a handsome woman. Straight hair that I knew to be blond was pulled back, revealing a perfectly oval face with strong, high cheekbones. I also noted wide-set eyes that stared forward with forthrightness, while her smile, though pleasant, was restrained. I could clearly sense her reserve around the photographer.

The picture opposite Sarah's was that of a man. He stared into the camera, his broad features half hidden by the large handlebar mustache that had been the fashion in recent years. The soft hues of the small black-and-white photograph suggested a light hair color—perhaps gray, or even white, given his age. He appeared to be much older than Sarah, easily in his fifties I would guess, at the time this picture was taken.

"I expect that's her father," Joe said.

"Seems likely. We'll ask the Wingates to confirm it." I continued to stare at the locket. "Where did you find it, again?" If Joe had mentioned it, I didn't remember.

"On the lawn another ten feet beyond the back porch, heading toward the woods. Do you suppose the killer dropped it?"

"It's possible," I said. It was certainly the most plausible explanation. I placed the necklace in my pocket, nestled within the handkerchief. I would check it for fingerprints, but given its small size and the amount of dirt on it, I was not optimistic any clear prints would be found.

Yet I could not shake the troubling sensation that something was not right. If the man pictured were Sarah's father, then where was her mother? It seemed odd to carry a photo of one in a locket, yet not the other. And it was odder still to carry a picture of oneself.

As I made my way back through the house, intent on retrieving my equipment, I heard a discreet cough as I passed by the library. I had almost forgotten about Abigail Wingate, Mrs. Wingate's other niece. She was sitting on an uncomfortable-looking, overstuffed gold sofa in a room of dark walnut bookcases, heavy red velvet drapes, and a plush oriental carpet. The two terriers I had previously noticed outside were with her; completely exhausted, they lay at her feet and took little notice of me.

A petite woman with brown hair and blue eyes that were accentuated by a navy blue dress, she looked much younger than I had expected. I did not think she could be more than twenty-five, twenty-six years of age.

"Simon Ziele . . . or, Detective Ziele, isn't it?" When she spoke, it was in a smooth, modulated voice, and I immediately recognized the precise diction I associated with New York's upper classes.

"Yes," I said, as I noted the lines of dried tears on her face. Although it was part of my job, I was keenly aware as I stepped into the room that I was intruding upon someone's private grief. Often, I was able to brace myself beforehand, but she had taken me by surprise.

"My name is Abigail Wingate. Dr. Fields said you would have questions for me. And I have some questions for you—" She broke off mid-sentence and gestured toward the small reading chair directly across from her.

"I'm sorry to meet you under such unfortunate circumstances." I took the seat that she offered, and was struck by how formal my voice sounded. "We are finished upstairs for tonight," I said to reassure her as I collected my thoughts. As the first person to have discovered her cousin's body, she would be an important witness—and given that she seemed coherent enough to talk, it would be best to interview her now, before her memory became muddled by time. Or by the relief offered by one of Dr. Fields's sedatives—for there was a small container of bromide salts on the end table.

"Have you found Stella?" Her voice was hushed but her tone was urgent.

"Stella?" The question caught me by surprise.

"Stella, our housemaid. Didn't Chief Healy tell you she's gone missing? No one has seen her since Dr. Fields first arrived. And her suitcase as well as all her clothing are still here."

"Had she been told of your cousin's murder?"

"I don't think so," she said. "But it's possible she overheard something."

Or she could have seen something, had she ventured upstairs during the confusion.

"Perhaps she has friends in the area to whom she has gone for the night?" I suggested. "It would be understandable, if we assume she knew what happened here today."

"No, she has only been here a few months, and she has no friends nearby." Rising panic was evident in her voice. "Something's terribly wrong, if she's not here."

"But she was here for a period of time after you discovered Sarah?" I asked.

"I think so," she said, though uncertainly.

Probably the girl had simply become so upset she ran away.

"No need to worry yet, but we'll check back first thing tomorrow to make sure." I tried to sound reassuring. "Stella was with your aunt this afternoon?"

She nodded yes, explaining that Stella had been helping her aunt prepare the garden in the backyard for winter by digging up bulbs to store in the basement. "Aunt Virginia has quite a fine garden each summer. She takes fastidious care of each plant."

"And this would have been around what time?"

"Three o'clock." Her reply was certain.

"And no one else was home at the time, other than your cousin?"

She confirmed it, going on to explain that Maud Muncie, their cook and general housekeeper, had been shopping in town; she herself had just taken the dogs for a walk.

"Do you think your aunt or Stella would have heard a noise in the house from where they were working?"

"Certainly not my aunt—she's half deaf. Stella may have heard something. But when I'm outdoors, I never hear any sound from inside the house. Especially when it's cold enough that our windows are closed, like today."

As one terrier nuzzled closer to her, a thought occurred to me. "Miss Wingate, do you walk your dogs around the same time every day?"

"I try to," she said. "Unless the weather is awful."

"And how does your aunt usually spend her late afternoons?" I spoke casually, trying to sound as though my question had no real significance. If Sarah's killer had been watching the Wingate house, tracking their comings and goings, I'd rather Miss Wingate not suspect that fact.

If she followed my logic, she did not betray any anxiety.

"Most weekday afternoons around three o'clock Aunt Virginia takes her tea with Mrs. Stratton, our next-door neighbor in the yellow Colonial. Today, she didn't, since Mrs. Stratton planned to join us for dinner."

"Right." I wrote the name in my small notebook. The assisting officers from Yonkers would be questioning Mrs. Stratton, as well as all the other surrounding neighbors, this very evening.

"Did you notice anything out of the ordinary while you were walking? Any sight or sound unfamiliar to you?"

"There was a man," Abigail said. "He was unfamiliar to me, and strangely dressed, so of course now I wonder if I saw . . ." She took a moment to compose herself. "But he did not act suspiciously."

"Can you give me any more detail?" I asked. "Where he was, what he was wearing." My attention was fully focused.

"One of the dogs became distracted by a squirrel on our way back to the house at the end of our walk. She raced toward the trees near the ravine that runs by the south corner of our property. She kept barking and would not leave the area, so I leaned down to leash her. And when I did, I saw a man walking below, heading deeper into the woods." Abigail caught her breath a moment before continuing. "To be honest, I didn't notice much about him. I had no reason to, then. All I recall is his hat, which was odd given today's weather. It was large and bushy, made of fur."

I thought I could picture it: almost cylindrical, made of brown or black fur, and rounded so as to cover one's ears. Such hats were common in the bitter cold of a New York January, but they seemed out of place in the slight chill of a November afternoon. Yet Abigail maintained that apart from the man's hat, nothing else about him had seemed remarkable: He had walked briskly, but not hurriedly, and had appeared to know exactly where he was going.

"And you heard nothing unusual while you were out?"

She considered her answer a moment before she responded.

"Now that you mention it, there *was* a really loud sound soon after I began to walk, but it was just some animal in the woods. Actually, it terrified the dogs. It sounded like the wail of a loon—though of course it couldn't have been. There are no loons around here."

"It definitely originated from the woods?" I studied her carefully. I wanted her to be sure, for the timing alone rendered the sound suspicious to me.

"Definitely. Humans do not make noises like that."

I determined to move on, and somehow I managed to elicit the facts of twenty-five-year-old Sarah Wingate's life with relative ease. Her upbringing had been comfortable, typical of a New York upper-middle-class family. The family had moved to Boston when she was thirteen, the result of an opportunity for her father, a banker, to start a new branch in that city. But she had returned to New York to pursue her studies. Gifted in math, Sarah had just begun her fourth year in Columbia's graduate program in mathematics, having finished her undergraduate degree at Barnard. She was apparently doing well in her work, and had even published two papers—the primary criterion for succeeding in academic work. According to Abigail, Sarah had seemed content and happy, and while certainly she had experienced the usual difficulties one would expect a woman to encounter in graduate education—especially in a man's field such as mathematics—Sarah had never complained.

"Of course, I'm sure she was the target of an occasional

snub or rude remark," Miss Wingate said, "but she was very confident in her abilities. I think she just ignored anyone who tried to belittle her ambitions or achievements. Such people were simply not worth her time."

"Did your cousin ever mention anyone she disliked? Or anyone who may have sufficiently resented her—"

"Enough to do *this*?" Miss Wingate broke in, horrified. "Oh, no . . . I would hardly think so. Certainly people begrudged her; some may have felt that she was taking a place at Columbia that properly belonged to a man, or that well-bred young ladies belonged at home. But from all Sarah told me, she encountered nothing that amounted to more than petty jealousy or resentment."

And yet, it was possible that Sarah may have been uncomfortable discussing such matters with her family, so I took Abigail Wingate's opinion with a grain of salt. Sarah's classmates or professors could well offer a different estimation.

"Was there perhaps a gentleman?" I asked, trying to phrase the question of any romantic interest discreetly.

Miss Wingate's answer was absolute. "I'm quite certain she had no beau. Her parents often introduced her to suitable young men, hoping she would make a good match. But Sarah was uninterested."

In response to further questions about Sarah's family, it became clear that Sarah had been closest with the Wingates. Abigail and her aunt constituted Sarah's only family nearby, for Sarah's parents split their time between Boston and Europe, where they were now.

Miss Wingate went on to describe Sarah's activities during the past few days in detail. Sarah had arrived unannounced in Dobson late Friday night, surprising Abigail and her aunt.

Sarah had apologized for the lack of advance notice, explaining only that she needed a quiet place to study; her subsequent time had been spent working, and she had joined them only for meals and the occasional brief walk.

I glanced at my watch, and realized time was growing short, for we would need to escort the Wingates to friends for the night. I had learned all I could about their daily habits; now I broached the toughest part of the interview and asked her to describe what she had seen upon returning home. It was painful to listen to Miss Wingate describe the harrowing experience: She had entered the kitchen, unleashed the dogs, and put away her coat in the hall closet. As she turned on a few lights in the kitchen, she had heard the smaller terrier whining upstairs. Perplexed as to why, she had gone upstairs to check out the source of the dog's concern and discovered her cousin's horrific murder. The rest, I already knew.

"One final question," I said, standing. "Would you please take a quick look at this necklace?" I gently opened the locket for Miss Wingate, holding it within its protective handkerchief close enough that she might see.

"We believe this to be Sarah's," I said, implicitly asking her to confirm it.

She nodded with a numb expression I initially mistook for sorrow.

"And the man opposite is her father?"

She did not answer immediately. When she looked up at me, her eyes were filled with tears and bewilderment. "He is old enough to be her father. But no, I've never seen him before." Her brow furrowed, creating deep lines across her face. "Why would she have a picture of this man in her locket?"

It was a rhetorical question, for how could I know, but I

answered her anyway to keep her from worrying unnecessarily. "It may be someone she spoke of, whom you would recognize by name."

"Maybe," she said. She sounded unconvinced.

"Was she wearing this locket when you saw her earlier today?"

"I don't think so. She rarely wore jewelry at all, except on special occasions. Or, at least, that used to be her practice." She looked at me with heavy, brooding eyes. "Seeing this picture makes me wonder how much I really knew about Sarah's life."

I did not answer her; there was little I could say. Under the close scrutiny of a crime investigation, all manner of private details became public knowledge. And it was the rare person who did not harbor some secret, be it large or small. No one's life was ever quite what it seemed.

We became aware from the noises at the back of the house that Joe had brought the others inside. Amid the general uproar, we heard an agitated, querulous voice. "But of course I'm sleeping here tonight! This is my house, and my things are here."

Mrs. Wingate, it would seem, strenuously objected to our suggestion that she and her niece spend the night elsewhere. Most people whose homes are invaded by crime—any crime, even a lesser one than this—prefer to spend time away. After a murder, many choose never to return at all. But such emotions were apparently foreign to Mrs. Wingate. Joe carefully placated her in reply: it was "only for one night," and "wouldn't she be more comfortable with neighbors after such a harrowing afternoon?" The response was a vehement no, coupled with a firm statement that she intended to sleep in her own bed that night and would not hear otherwise.

As Abigail Wingate went to reason with her aunt, I bid Joe

good night. I had one task still to accomplish in town, and a brief walk in the cold night air would help to restore my senses.

As I walked beyond the cobblestone driveway and down the hill toward the village, I found myself increasingly disturbed. Despite my assurances to Abigail Wingate, Stella's disappearance was worrisome, another piece of a mystery that was becoming more puzzling the more we uncovered. It was possible Stella had seen or heard something important, especially since it now appeared she had run away. And so many details of this case were confounding. What was I to make of a braid of hair taken from Sarah's head for unknown reasons? Or the locket she kept with an unknown man's picture inside? But it was Sarah Wingate herself who bothered me most. She was an unlikely victim, her aunt's home an unlikely setting. Why had someone killed her with such ferocity?

All these unanswered questions so troubled me that even the sight of the Hudson River below, shimmering from the reflection of light from the full moon above, did little to calm the turbulent disorder in my mind.

CHAPTER 3

Well past eleven o'clock, I found myself at O'Malley's having a late dinner with Peter Voyt, the local photographer I had asked to develop the crime-scene pictures. He had agreed to do so immediately, so long as I paid for his dinner afterward. "Come and join me," he had said, adding, "I daresay you've eaten nothing yourself for dinner."

It was true, for even had there been time, what I had seen earlier this evening had entirely ruined my appetite. But there was an unrelenting pounding in my head that would not go away unless I ate something, so I agreed. And because it would have been inappropriate not to include my boss, I stopped by the in-town Colonial Joe shared with his wife and found him ready and willing to join us. Joe had just eaten a cold dinner, but he was never one to turn down a pint of ale.

At this late hour, O'Malley's was uncrowded, with only a handful of men clustered near the bar. It was well past their official dinner hours, but they were always willing to make something from the kitchen for regulars like me, who ate there most nights. I had been told when I first moved to Dobson that, come dinnertime, everyone went to O'Malley's. By "everyone," people of course meant unmarried men like myself with little time or inclination to cook for themselves. O'Malley's food was decent and their comfortable tables made it easy to linger and talk— even when the subject of conversation was as terrible as ours that night.

Peter, Joe, and I sat at a table by the fireplace where the searing warmth was a comforting reminder that we were safe and alive. As we reviewed the photographs, Joe assured me that more interviews were being done even as we spoke, for the Yonkers police department had assigned a junior detective to help us with the case; he was continuing to interview the neighbors that very night. Still, we were frustrated by the initial lack of evidence or witnesses, and the photographs displayed in front of us did little to allay our concerns as we tried to imagine possible scenarios for how the killing had occurred.

"Sheer butchery." I grimaced in disgust, sliding the photographs back into a plain envelope. "He's a monster, whoever did this."

"You've referred to the killer as a 'he' all night. Are you quite sure the killer is a man?" Peter had directed his question to me. He leaned back and peered at me through small wire-rimmed glasses. He was a slight man with a remarkable eye for evaluating those he photographed, and the unusual assignment

I'd given him had more than piqued his interest. "You've found some footprints that appear to be from a man's boot, but there's no way of knowing for sure they were left by the murderer. And, ludicrous as it may seem, you can't rule out the possibility that a woman could have worn thick socks and men's boots."

I took a large spoonful of the lentil soup that had just been placed before me. Though not as good as I remembered at Mc-Sorley's in the city, it was piping hot, which was exactly what I needed. "I would suspect the killer is male in part because most killers are," I said, "but in this case, I am convinced of it because the crime was so brutal."

Peter listened intently as he pushed his empty glass of ale to the side.

I went on to explain, "When women kill, they usually choose methods that are less messy, like poisoning, or that require little physical strength." I leaned back and gazed into the fire; the image of Sarah Wingate's battered, lifeless face seemed to lurk within the flames. "To put this murder in practical terms, I don't think even a strong, muscular woman would have had the strength to accomplish what was done to Sarah Wingate."

Joe nodded in agreement. "You didn't see the victim in person, Peter, but even judging from how she was injured . . ." He shuddered at the memory. "I agree with Ziele that it had to be a man who did it, and a large or heavyset man at that."

"Have you found the weapon used?" Peter asked.

"No," I replied. "We'll have to search the grounds—and the woods—more thoroughly tomorrow."

"Any idea what you're looking for?"

"Something with a broad, blunt edge," I said.

I had begun to recognize my own habit of mind in Peter's questions. Like me, he attempted to sanitize the horror of this crime by reducing it to base analytical terms. Today, in the midst of so much blood, I had trouble facing up to the Wingate crime scene. But tomorrow I would have no difficulty reviewing and analyzing the autopsy report. It was always far easier to deal with the violence of murder when it was reduced to words and facts on paper.

We ate and drank in silence, each of us absorbed in our own thoughts, until Peter interrupted us. "Let's look sharp, boys. We've got company."

I turned around and saw a tall, lean figure purposefully striding toward us. John Fuller, our mayor, was sputtering with anger, and we were fortunate that his respect for our fellow diners—not to mention his own self-interest—kept his voice civil and controlled when he spoke to us.

"Good evening, Chief." His icy stare was directed at Joe. "You've got time for socializing, but no time to inform your mayor about the first murder this town's seen in twelve years?"

Joe responded evenly, his voice filled with gravity. "If you've heard about the murder, then you've also heard what a horrific scene it was. Can't think you would begrudge a spot of dinner to men who have worked such a tough case."

"Dinner?" The mayor looked pointedly at Joe's empty pint glass before continuing to complain. "I had to hear the news from Mrs. Keane."

I groaned inwardly; the interference of the village busybody certainly would not help matters. I had seen her among the group of neighbors clustered on the Wingate property. Since she could know only the barest of details, she no doubt embellished them with whatever her fertile imagination could invent.

"She had quite a tale to relate," the mayor said, continuing to berate us for not notifying him. Because he had known the

Wingates so well, he was personally offended, but his true concern involved how the public would react.

"This kind of news can cause widespread panic if we don't handle it right," he said. He rambled on in terms that ignored the loss of human life we had witnessed today; he was more concerned with how Dobson's business community would react. If businesses were scared away, tax revenues would be lost. But once he finished saying his piece, he bid us good night. "I'll be keeping a close eye on this one, men. I expect to see regular reports—and solid progress, mind you. We need this case solved straightaway." He walked away with a confident step, as though his command alone could accomplish the task at hand.

Of course, I knew better. For every murder case I solved in the city, there were at least ten I didn't. Merely *wanting* to solve a case wasn't enough. And neither was political pressure. You also needed sufficient skill, intelligence, and more than your fair share of luck. But a man like Fuller—who was less concerned with the murder itself than he was with its political fallout— would never understand that.

"Did you have any thoughts about the locket?" I asked quietly after the mayor left, for I had asked Peter his opinion about the two miniature photographs it contained.

"I can make some inferences from these photographs," Peter said, "though whether they'll help you is another matter."

"Go on," I said. I certainly hoped something he had discovered would help, for the locket otherwise seemed a dead end. While Peter had developed our photographs in his darkroom, I had dusted the small locket for prints. I found none that were usable, unsurprising given how dirty the locket had been.

He pulled the locket photographs gingerly from his pocket and turned the two pictures toward us. "As to the type of print, though the photographs are small, I was able to determine that they are what we call Woodburytypes."

Joe and I simply listened, knowing Peter would go on to explain what that meant.

"The Woodburytype is a process that reproduces a high-quality photograph and, to the untrained eye, may look exactly like a gelatin silver print. And both processes have much in common: This process is used when the photographer wants to produce a print that will last for years without any loss in quality. And it allows photographs to be enlarged with no loss of detail whatsoever."

He sighed, closed the locket, and returned it to me.

"But the fact remains it is a Woodburytype—which for your purposes is significant in two respects. First, I would expect there to be other, much larger prints of these photographs in existence. Most photographs made with this process are large prints suitable for gluing into luxury albums. You wouldn't normally choose a sophisticated development process like this if your only goal was to create small photographs."

He paused a moment. "And second, because these photos are Woodburytypes, we know they were taken at least five years ago. The Woodburytype process was discontinued in 1900 because its cost had become too high. I myself stopped doing it even earlier."

Joe breathed a soft, low whistle, as he settled back in his chair. "So she has known the man in the locket for at least five years—and yet her closest cousin could not identify him!"

"Looks that way," Peter said.

I suspected I already knew the answer to my question, but I had to ask anyway. "Both photographs were taken at the same time, by the same photographer?"

"In my opinion they were," he said, and his opinion was unequivocal. "You'll notice the backdrop, the lighting, and even what I call the tone of each picture seems markedly similar. If they were taken in the New York area, it may be possible to locate the photographer, since the expensive nature of the process would necessarily limit the number of photographers offering it."

Our conversation continued along these lines, exploring different possibilities, until we were interrupted by a commotion near the front of the bar. After a moment, I heard my name called. I hastened to join Mrs. O'Malley by the door, where a delivery boy waited with a telegram for me. He had attempted to come inside, but had been hindered by Mrs. O'Malley's inflexible idea that boys should be at least sixteen years old before they were permitted to enter a bar. After giving the boy a coin—well earned for tracking me down at this time of night—I returned to the table, where the three of us read the telegram together.

Received news of murder in Dobson. Must meet immediately.
Know suspect.
Your office 7:30 A.M.
—Alistair Sinclair, Esq.

"Alistair Sinclair." Joe tried out the name, practically snorting as he chuckled. "And the man paid good money to sign himself 'Esquire'! Either he's so rich he doesn't care about the expense, or he's that full of himself. How do you know him?" He looked at me, one eyebrow arched, obviously suspicious that I had gone behind his back and contacted Alistair Sinclair about our case.

"I don't," I said. "I have never heard of the man—and I have no idea how he has heard of me. I can't even imagine how news of the crime itself could travel so fast."

It was the truth, though Joe would think what he would. Others repeatedly told me that Joe was a good-hearted man and would come around in time. But he perceived me as a younger, smarter man destined to take his place. I did not dislike Joe, but I did chafe under his constant questioning of my motives and habits.

I glanced at my watch; it was now almost half past midnight. I made my excuses and left Joe and Peter talking quietly, for there was unfinished work I wanted to complete before the night was over.

I folded the telegram into my pocket, stopped by the office to make a brief telephone call, and then caught the trolley home straightaway. But I could not stop thinking of Alistair Sinclair's strange message as the ache in my arm pounded unrelentingly and kept me from sleep well until dawn began to show its earliest light.

Wednesday, November 8, 1905

CHAPTER 4

After a fitful night's sleep, I rose early and headed toward my office, buying a cup of coffee and the morning *Times* on the way. I skimmed the paper before beginning my own work. *MCCLEL-LAN REELECTED MAYOR—HEARST WILL CONTEST* was its headline, and multiple stories about yesterday's election fraud filled its pages. The Tammany machine toughs had intimidated would-be Hearst voters, meting out terrible beatings to keep them from voting. One Hearst supporter had actually lost a finger in such an altercation, the *Times* reported. And multiple boxes of ballots had ended up in the East River rather than the election office. All disgusting, but unsurprising. Anyone who knew Tammany boss Silent Charlie Murphy knew he would do whatever it took to ensure his candidate won.

But the case at hand was what demanded my attention this morning. I read through the contents of a report left by Jimmy Meade, the detective from Yonkers who had taken charge of the grounds search and interview efforts last night. As I tried to focus upon his summary of interviews with the Wingates' neighbors, questions about my strange appointment with Alistair Sinclair continued to unsettle me. Why had he contacted me? By all rights, he should have reached out to Joe, my boss. And what made him think he knew anything about who may have murdered Sarah Wingate? There had been no similar murders in the city in recent months. I had placed a call to Declan Mulvaney, my former partner in the city, late last night to check. Mulvaney had been working late at the office because of the unrest surrounding yesterday's city election, but he had nonetheless taken the time to search the department's files for me.

I forced my attention back to the interviews, ascertaining that no information of importance had come from them. The Braithwaites next door had been home at the time, but did not remember hearing or seeing anything unusual. Elderly Mr. Dreyer across the street, who spent all his waking hours in the rocking chair on his wraparound front porch, had noticed a strange man at the Wingate house in the recent past. But that had been at least three months ago. I resolved to follow up with Mr. Dreyer and the Wingates about the sighting, but given the time lag, it did not seem the sort of detail that would crack open the case.

The common theme in each interview was that around half past three, almost everyone had heard the strange wail Miss Wingate had described. It was an interesting coincidence, but not evidence. Generally speaking, no neighbor had offered any detail of substance—only a composite picture that verified the whereabouts of all concerned, including the Wingate household help. We had proof no one lied, but little else.

I hoped Joe would have better luck discovering information that would help us. He was attending Dr. Fields's autopsy of Sarah Wingate, which had been scheduled early, at five o'clock this morning. With a sigh of frustration, I turned to place the folder in my file cabinet when the steady sound of footsteps on the stairwell informed me that my visitor had arrived.

In stepped a middle-aged man with a meticulously trimmed mustache and dark hair just beginning to gray around the temples. He was fashionably dressed; his expensive leather shoes were polished to a high gloss and his coat was made of fine, soft, dark wool. He immediately took full measure of me with intense blue eyes, and flashed a charismatic smile that revealed perfectly white, even teeth. When he spoke, his voice was very smooth and cultured, reflecting a muted European accent.

"Detective Ziele, I presume?" He gripped my right hand and shook it firmly—too firmly. Through sheer willpower, I forced myself not to wince. "I am Alistair Sinclair. You should call me Alistair."

In manner and voice, he seemed far more cosmopolitan than his English name had led me to expect. I would learn in coming days that he had traveled extensively in addition to spending part of his childhood in Rome.

He removed his coat and hat. "May I?" He gestured toward the wooden coat rack by the door.

"Please," I said.

"It was good of you to meet me on such short notice; I can

imagine how busy you are after yesterday's events. I promise to take up no more of your time than necessary."

I made a polite reply, even as I reflected that his telegram had given me little choice in the matter.

"Shall we sit?" Although he claimed the guest chair across from my desk, Alistair conducted himself as though the office were his and not mine. Yet once we were seated, facing one another, he regarded me silently and seemed unsure how to proceed.

"I admit—I was surprised to hear from you last night," I began. "Never mind your claim to have important information about a suspect, I can't make out how you got word of this murder so quickly."

"Ah, yes." He leaned back easily, having anticipated the question. "I've found it very useful over the years to develop good sources of information—among the police, the press, the fire wardens. In this case," he confided, "it was one of my newspaper contacts at the *World* who came through with news of the murder last night. Amazing, given how preoccupied they were with yesterday's election." He nodded to the *Times* article on my desk. "But those fellows are unstoppable when it comes to newsgathering." He smiled congenially, assuming we understood each other.

"True enough," I said. News reporters could be downright predatory. I knew not all of them were so single-minded in their pursuit of a story as to behave indecently, but I did not hold them in high regard.

"How much did you learn about yesterday's murder?" I asked. I wanted to be sure he knew what he was talking about and was not wasting my time.

He folded his arms in front of him and recited the facts of

the case. "A young woman, mid-twenties, was killed late after-noon at a local residence. She suffered multiple lacerations and bruising." He went on to detail other relevant facts that allayed any doubts I had about his being fully informed.

"And what about this local case attracts the attention of a professor from Columbia Law School?"

He looked at me with both surprise and respect, for he had told me nothing of who he was or what he did for a living. "It would appear you have cultivated your own sources of informa-tion. Those individuals who described you as exceptionally smart and resourceful were quite right."

I never would have put it that way. And I was very curious as to whom he had spoken about me. But I could not give Alistair the satisfaction of knowing it.

My own inquiry into his background had been rather sim-ple: A brief telephone call last night to the Seventh Precinct had produced a basic outline of Alistair Sinclair's life. Personally, he had recently celebrated his fifty-second birthday; socially, he was from a wealthy family who counted themselves among Mrs. Astor's New York Four Hundred; and professionally, he held advanced degrees from both Harvard and Columbia, where he had spent the past ten years as part of their law faculty with a specialty in criminal law. Mulvaney had dug up those facts for me and even remembered one thing more, since it was the tough Irish cop's guilty pleasure to follow the society pages in the *Journal*. He recalled that Alistair was separated from his wife, who had moved abroad after their only son died tragically two years ago.

"Can't remember how the son died, though," Mulvaney had said. "I do recall the obituary mentioned he died while on an archeological expedition in Greece."

These scraps of information had sated some of my curiosity about the man, but they could not explain his interest in this local murder case. I pressed him once again to explain himself.

"As you've already learned, I am a teacher of criminal law," he said, stretching his long legs out to his side to become more comfortable, "but I consider myself a criminologist. Do you know the term?"

"It means you study crime?" I hazarded a guess.

"Yes—but with a specific focus on criminals and their behavior." He leaned in closer toward me, and I grew uncomfortable under his direct gaze. "When you arrest a man for a particularly heinous crime, don't you often wonder why he did it?"

I had to confess I did not.

"Most of the time there's a pretty simple motive," I said. "Revenge, jealousy, greed . . . those are the reasons why most criminals kill or steal."

"Yes, you're absolutely correct in a general sense. But have you never wondered specifically—*why him*? To put it a different way, suppose fifty men are in dire economic straits, equally desperate for money. But only one will kill to get it. Fifty women may find themselves unhappily married. But only one of them will poison her husband. Why? What makes him—or her—different from the forty-nine others who don't resort to criminal acts?"

He continued to talk. "I'm taking part in a broader research effort pioneered by criminal scientists in Germany, France, and Italy to further our understanding of criminal behavior by using the collective wisdom of different fields, including sociology, psychology, anatomy, and, of course, law. Together with like-minded colleagues, I've established a research center at Columbia to answer some important questions. Why do criminals behave as they do? What motivates them? What deters them? What actions are necessary to redirect their behavior, or rehabilitate them?"

His hands gesticulated to emphasize his words as he talked. "Imagine the good we could do if only we understood the answers to these questions. If we could identify those people who were predisposed—or simply more *susceptible* than others to committing crimes—then perhaps we could intervene before they ever committed their first criminal act. Or, if we could take a repeat offender and figure out how to rehabilitate him, then you can imagine how much more efficiently our courts and penal systems would operate."

I did not mention how strongly I disagreed with some of his assumptions, which were grounded in a view of human nature I did not share. I believed some people were capable of doing bad things, plain and simple. Sometimes even otherwise decent people were quite capable of behaving criminally when pushed far enough. Unbidden, my mind filled with images from the *Slocum* disaster, where with rescue efforts under way, I had witnessed normally law-abiding men shamelessly trample over women and young children in their efforts to save themselves. If this were evidence of the human nature of the more civilized among us, then what hope could there be for violent offenders?

But this was not the time for such discussion. A young woman was dead, and her murderer had yet to be identified, much less apprehended. Alistair was beginning to take our conversation in a direction more theoretical than was useful for my purposes. I needed to hear only what practical information he might offer to solve this case.

"This is well and good, but today I am investigating an

actual murder committed by an unknown assailant. I need to know how, exactly, you can help me," I said.

Alistair spun his chair forward. "It is likely I hold the key to your murder investigation. I know the man responsible. It is someone I have interviewed as part of my research." He placed a small black-and-white picture on my desk. "It is this man. Michael Fromley."

I stared at him in silence for a few moments while I thought about what he had just said. I half glanced at the photograph before I pushed it back toward him.

"I'm sorry," I said, and shook my head, "but I think we misunderstand each other. The murder I'm investigating happened just yesterday. Late yesterday. So any incriminating information that came out of one of your past interviews could not possibly be relevant."

"You do misunderstand," Alistair said, "so please bear with me a moment while I explain." He folded his hands and asked, "Are you familiar with Eugene Vidocq and his way of thinking about the criminal act?"

He continued talking—almost lecturing, really—before I had a chance to think, much less answer his question.

"Vidocq was a notorious French thief. After his last arrest, the police made him a unique offer: if he wished to avoid jail, he might put his skills to good use and join the police. He eventually became chief of the Sûreté, and you may have heard of him in your line of work because he is responsible for so many of your modern practices, such as having policemen work in disguise. Or 'undercover,' as you would say."

Alistair got up to pace, once again gesticulating with his hands. "He is also famous for creating a filing system—but no ordinary filing system. For each criminal his department arrested, he recorded information about their age, appearance, and background as well as the details of their crimes. Vidocq showed us that every criminal has a certain kind of behavior pattern—or style—that remains consistent in each crime he commits. It could be a certain kind of weapon or a specific kind of victim. It might even be a habit of choosing a particular place or time of day."

Alistair sat down again. I began to perceive that his constant alterations between sitting and pacing were a sign of his boundless energy, which was difficult for him to contain.

"So do you mean to imply," I asked, trying to understand, "that what you've heard about the murder here in Dobson is similar in style to criminal behavior that you've previously encountered?"

"That's exactly it!" Alistair beamed at me, pleased to have gotten his point across.

I had to admit that Alistair's argument made some sense. I had not heard of Vidocq, but I knew from experience that the gang-style murders I had previously encountered all followed certain patterns; each gang's handiwork was unique.

I reached for the small photograph that still lay on my desk. It showed a young man of about twenty or so. From underneath a full shock of wavy blond hair, he stared insolently at the camera. He had high cheekbones, wide eyes, and full lips twisted in a half smile. I gazed into the picture searching for a sign of that peculiar brand of evil that turned an ordinary man into a murderer. But of course I wouldn't see it. I never did. Some people said it lurked in a man's expression. I knew better—for whatever it was that led someone to murder, it was concealed deep within the soul.

Yet Alistair's resolution sounded too simple.

"If your suspect has committed this type of murder before, then how did he avoid the electric chair, much less prison?" I was filled with disgust that a murderer should have ever been given a chance to repeat his crime.

Before he could answer, though, my frustration began to grow, and I reversed myself, determined to get to the point. "That doesn't matter now. Do you know where I can find this man?"

Alistair responded with frustration. "We have been trying to locate him ourselves for over two weeks—and we have failed."

"You mean he was in prison, but escaped?"

Alistair shook his head.

"Even so, there should be a case history on him." I began thinking of alternatives, saying, "I'll need the background you have on his past arrests."

Alistair looked at me oddly. "It's not as simple as that, I fear. You won't find any help in his arrest records—at least, not the sort you seem to want." He rubbed his chin as he explained. "Our man has a police record, to be sure: assault, battery, even petty theft, if I'm not mistaken. But it has not—at least not yet—included murder."

"Then how can you even think he may be responsible?" I sputtered. I could hardly control another flash of anger, as I thought of the valuable time I had lost pursuing this entire conversation. I would have said more, but Alistair responded to my frustration immediately.

"Please—a moment's patience. Let me back up, and tell you the story. Then you will see why I believe he is responsible, and what I am telling you will make perfect sense."

I glanced at my watch: near half past eight already. I had

promised Joe I would return to the Wingate house this morning.

"I must get back over to the crime scene. You're welcome to
accompany me; we can talk on the way."

I hustled Alistair out the door, and after we had settled ourselves into a waiting cab, I leaned back and tried to listen with
an open mind to a tale that grew stranger, and more disturbing,
with every new detail that emerged.

Our driver whistled loudly to himself, oblivious to our conversation. Nonetheless, Alistair leaned in toward me to ensure the
driver could not overhear his words.

"Are you capable of rehabilitating a monster?" Alistair demanded. His eyes locked into my own, blazing with intensity.
"That challenge is one Michael Fromley's older brother Clyde
Wallingford—half brother actually—granted me right after Michael's first serious arrest, three years ago." He paused dramati-
cally before continuing. "The boy had been in trouble before, to
be sure—but not like this time. There had been barroom fights,
petty thefts, and more property damage than you would care to
pay for. But no harm was done that money could not fix. And
his behavior was not so extreme that it couldn't be sugarcoated
within the Wallingfords' social circle as simply that of a young
man sowing his wild oats." His tone became sober. "The incident three years ago was different, and Wallingford was beside
himself with worry."

I listened, becoming more interested in spite of myself.

Alistair gripped the sides of his seat to keep his balance as
the wheels of the cab rattled violently against the cobblestones.
Dobson's steeper roads were all cobblestone, which helped the
horses to keep their footing, but made for a bumpy ride.

"Michael is the youngest son of Louise Wallingford Fromley by her second husband." He shook his head and grimaced. "Awful woman—so domineering and loud, both husbands undoubtedly hastened to the grave just to get away from her. She nonetheless did a fine job raising her four oldest children, whose father was Earl Wallingford. But for some reason, it was difficult with Michael, right from the beginning. 'Even in the womb,' she told me, though of course she was being typically melodramatic. Still, as a small child, he so terrorized the nannies who cared for him that none lasted more than a month or two."

"How did he get on with his father and his older siblings?" I asked.

"His father died a few months after he was born, and when Fromley was very young, his older siblings were all out of the house. Certain problems arose when his half brother took over the family home and moved back with his wife and two young daughters. Louise of course lived there until her own death, and initially Wallingford was quite willing for Michael to stay on. But Michael began to exhibit disturbing behavior. For example, he had strange moods, in which he would climb into a closet and sit as though in a trance. He also set fire to the drawing room curtains. It was only by good fortune that the house was saved from burning to the ground. Wallingford was horrified, and adamant that the boy should not come in contact with his young daughters."

Alistair sighed before continuing. "Young Fromley was sent to live with Louise's spinster sister, a Miss Lizzie Dunn, until a suitable boarding school could be found; when it was, he returned to his aunt during school vacations. She was a timid, mousy woman unprepared to give him the kind of discipline and structure he needed. But then again, perhaps we cannot fault her too much. Neither his overbearing mother nor a succession of strict boarding schools boasted better success. He amassed quite a disciplinary record for starting fires and assaulting others. He was expelled after he menaced another student with a knife. It was terribly embarrassing for the Wallingfords, but they hoped he would eventually grow out of it. They hung on to that hope right up until Michael was arrested in October 1902 for attempted murder, accused of knifing a prostitute named Catherine Smedley and setting her room ablaze."

"I see. Now he had done real harm and was facing serious jail time."

"Exactly. As far as the prosecution was concerned, it was a weak case with considerable doubt as to Michael's guilt. While he was the last person identified as talking with the victim before the attack, no one could swear he was the man who accompanied her up to her room. Though the victim recovered, the experience had affected her memory, and she was never able to identify her attacker." He looked at me with what appeared to be genuine regret. "Quite frankly, even if the witnesses had been able to testify with greater certainty, it would have made little difference. You might not need a choirboy to put someone like Michael Fromley away, but you need a witness more credible than you'll find in a brothel."

We continued to talk as we arrived at the Wingate home, and I was relieved to find the house and grounds were empty. Although the Wingates had spent the night there at Mrs. Wingate's insistence, they were gone this morning; their note directed us to look around as we wished. I showed Alistair around the perimeter first, alert for anything that might appear unusual. The light this morning was good, and I hoped we would uncover something that had gone unnoticed in last evening's twilight.

After finding nothing out of the ordinary outdoors, we returned to the house and searched Stella's third-floor room, for she had not yet returned. According to Miss Wingate, all her clothes were accounted for but her purse was gone. That meant she had taken money, probably as a means of travel, which supported my theory she had sought out friends after yesterday's tragedy.

"In terms of the Smedley woman, I take it you believe Michael Fromley was, in fact, guilty?" I asked.

"Of the assault, yes." Alistair was matter-of-fact. "He later admitted it to me, and he said as much to his brother. Given the weakness of the case, the prosecutor and judge were willing to dismiss the attempted-murder charges. He faced lesser charges, as well, but for those, I convinced the prosecutor to accept a plea bargain involving supervised probation. Wallingford was eager for Michael to enter a plea and save the family from an ugly trial—but only if something could be done to rehabilitate Michael. It did the family no good to keep him out of jail this time, if it meant he would only go in for something worse next time. That was where I came in."

We made our way back to the second floor and the room where Sarah had been murdered. There, I took additional notes, measuring each individual bloodstain with particular attention to its distance from where Sarah's corpse had been positioned. Alistair watched me silently for some moments before he continued his story.

"For me, it was a chance like no other." Alistair's face was flushed and animated, and his voice reflected his passionate feeling. "I had long envied Lacassagne, the French criminologist who succeeded in getting jailed criminals to tell him their most intimate thoughts. He was interested in all manner of criminals, however, whereas I wished to focus upon violent offenders. Following his example, I went to Sing Sing and Riker's and interviewed the prisoners there. I even spoke with death row inmates in the hours before their execution. But you're well aware how quickly New York executes its violent offenders once they are convicted and their appeals exhausted. Remember when Leon Czolgosz assassinated President McKinley? He was convicted at trial near the end of September, and he died in the electric chair only a month later."

Of course I remembered, for President McKinley's death had elevated Teddy Roosevelt into office. "But surely," I interjected, "that was an unusual case, given the circumstances?"

He conceded as much. "It was exceptionally fast, I agree. But even normal cases proceed quickly. If there's to be no appeal, most convicted offenders are executed within months. And once they lose an appeal, their life is measured in days and weeks. That is barely enough time to gain their confidence, much less scratch the surface of their minds. Not to mention that some death row inmates would rather spend their final hours doing something other than talking to me." He flashed a self-deprecating smile before he continued talking. "But with Michael, I had a living, breathing research subject who was mine to keep. I needn't yield him to the executioner in a matter of months. It was a chance—and a chance like no other—to look into a violent mind still very much in formation. How did Michael's mind work? What motivated him? Why had he developed so differently from his siblings? And was there a way we could intervene and rehabilitate him before he actually crossed the line?"

I looked up from my examination of a three-inch blood splatter.

"Wait a minute." I was certain I had heard something incorrectly. "Did you say that his criminal tendencies were still 'in formation'? If he tried to murder this woman—if he slashed her with a knife, set her room afire—then it is no credit to him that she survived. It sounds as though he did everything to kill her, and it is merely by the grace of God that she lived!"

I stood up to face him. "Surely in the mind of this man, there was no difference."

Alistair was unfazed by my eruption. "Yes, I used to think so, as well. But what my colleagues and I have discovered is that there is a progression in the criminal's mind that leads to the escalation of violent activity. I'm talking of course about premeditated stranger murder, you understand, not the kind of murder you would call a 'crime of passion.'" He was careful to clarify the legal distinction, for he seemed to sense my next objection before I voiced it. "No murderer, even the most vicious, even that notorious Lew Burdick your police are so proud of having captured earlier this year, simply wakes up one day with the desire to kill. Rather, his desire develops over long periods of time, through tremendous imaginative effort."

This sounded idiotic and I told him so plainly. "I don't see Lew Burdick as having made much imaginative effort." The man had been convicted of butchering his victims in their beds, even as their immediate family members lay listening in terror in nearby rooms.

"In the end, there is nothing imaginary." Alistair corrected me. "By then, it is too late—there, you are right. But in the beginning, as we've discovered from our interviews with so many others, even a man like Burdick would have first started with nothing but a picture in his mind." Alistair walked around the room, using his hands emphatically to help me visualize what he was saying.

"He must have liked the picture he imagined. He probably experienced sensations of power that were new to him, and these sensations proved intoxicating. But this imaginary stage I describe is still just that—an act of the imagination—and he would have no serious thoughts of killing anyone at this point."

His tone suddenly became more somber. "What our interviews have shown, however, is that the more he mulls over this imagined violence, the more he creates his own need for it—and then he constructs this violent fantasy more and more often. One day, his imaginary victims will not satisfy him, so he will begin to imagine real people he has seen, even his acquaintances, in the role of the victim. It's at *this* point he begins to consider real violence against real people. And from there, it is simply a matter of time until . . ."

He didn't have to say it. All we had to do was look around us. Alistair, in fact, seemed to be registering the aftermath of yesterday's violence for the first time.

His theory was an interesting one, but I still had difficulty understanding how it pertained to Michael Fromley.

"Even if you are right," I said, challenging him, "what you describe with Catherine Smedley was not merely a fantasy. It was real, and it had terrible consequences. " I shook my head. "By your own theory, his would no longer be a criminal mind *in formation*. He had committed a criminal act."

"Well, it's true that Fromley had begun to cross from the imaginary realm into reality, in that he was dealing now with real victims," Alistair said. "But he didn't mean to kill the girl—not yet, anyway. He was still experimenting with how it might feel."

"How can you know that?" I demanded.

"Because despite his many problems, Michael was always very candid with me. That's what he claimed, and I believed him." He paused. "He was, and *is*, a dangerous man. And I knew the imperative." Alistair's voice grew thick with emotion. "I knew that if we didn't succeed with him, that he would try again—and the next time he would kill. So we put in place certain safeguards, all financed by Wallingford. We hired a bodyguard to protect both the public and ourselves. Plus, we implemented rigorous interview sessions with the goal of understanding Michael and rehabilitating him. We worked incredibly hard, and I thought we'd done it. As he told it, his daydreams were becoming less frequent and less violent. He had interviewed for a job at the Fulton Street docks, and he seemed to be more content than ever before. All was proceeding very smoothly until the day he vanished. And we have seen no sign of him for the past two weeks, until last night when I received word of the murder that happened in this very room."

"But you still haven't explained why—*exactly* why—you believe Michael Fromley is Sarah Wingate's killer?" I countered. "I understand he is dangerous and has brutally assaulted a young woman in the past. And it's worrisome that he's now missing. But I see no particular reason to suspect him in my case."

Alistair swallowed hard. "You are right, to a point, but there is more—which only you can confirm. Because from what I've heard about your crime scene, it exactly mirrors the fantasies Michael has nursed these past years. Read this"—he handed me a piece of paper—"and tell me if you do not share my concern. It is just one of my many case notes. There are more that will say the same thing."

A strong November wind whipped around the house and rattled the windows in the room. I took the paper from Alistair, quickly scanning his words.

Thursday, March 18. Today he reported another incident of his daydream. This is the fifth time this month. The trigger was a young woman of about twenty who boarded his car on the El downtown. A blonde, she wore a blue dress and was exceptionally pretty. He imagined her to be a seamstress and conjured many sordid details about her life. Then he began the process I have noted before:

1. Objectification: He degrades her until he no longer views her as a human being worthy of respectful treatment.

2. Imagination: He envisions himself interacting with her with the same result: a rush of excitement when she obeys him after he displays his knife; a pleasurable feeling of control as he decides where and how she will die.

3. Method: He cuts her dress away from her body into long strips of ribbon. Finally, he plunges his knife into her heart, before he slashes her skin at random. When she is dead, he describes the impulse to take some part of her as a remembrance. The remembrance varies; in today's version, it is the tiny signet ring she wore.

4. Effect: The experience is so intense he loses track of time and space. Here, he travels on the El two stops beyond his destination.

I felt physically ill, my stomach lurching as I thought of Sarah Wingate's battered corpse. I could distinguish the cases and focus upon their differences. But the similarities were striking: Sarah Wingate was a blonde; she had been slashed multiple times; she was wearing a blue dress that had been cut into ribbons. And even if I managed to dismiss that evidence as mere coincidence, there was no getting away from the remembrances he had taken. The killer had taken a braid of Sarah's hair and likely attempted to take Sarah's locket, dropping it as he left the premises. The similarities were far too compelling to disregard. I shuddered as I remembered the crime scene. Any man who could do such terrible things was deserving of nothing—not Alistair's help, and certainly not the limited freedom he had enjoyed.

My response to Alistair was accusing. "How could you in good conscience have helped someone with these kinds of thoughts? Couldn't you see—the moment he began telling you such vile things—that you had made a terrible mistake and he should be locked up?"

"But I judged there to be no imminent danger, for even his daydreams were a tangible sign that he was still working himself up to it. And my hope was that, with conscious effort, he could begin to change the direction of his thoughts and fantasies. Besides, the bodyguard provided us a measure of protection."

"And why did his bodyguard not prevent this recent disappearance?"

Alistair looked uncomfortable. "We felt Michael was making such significant progress the bodyguard was no longer necessary. We dismissed him last summer."

Botched private justice was what it was—no more and no less. And I didn't understand it. To strive to learn why a man succumbed to a life of crime was well and good, but only when the stakes were hypothetical and no lives were at risk. Here, it seemed an innocent girl had died as a result of this failed experiment, and nothing Alistair Sinclair had learned could be worth that cost.

"Tell me more about what happened two weeks ago, when he vanished," I asked quietly.

"There is no more. He simply disappeared. We last saw him October 22," Alistair said.

"Did he have friends or other family he could have sought out?"

"None that we know of." Alistair rested his chin on his hand. "His aunt was the only person he seems to have contacted regularly, and she has not heard from him."

He stepped over to the bed and looked at the large bloodstain on the floor. He leaned down, examined the area more closely, and pointed to the mattress. "May I?"

I nodded in agreement, and watched unbelievingly as he pulled out what appeared to be a cloth—but was actually a heavily bloodstained envelope. Hidden underneath the mattress, it had seemed part of the stained bedclothes and thus escaped our attention. As Alistair opened the envelope to expose its contents he let forth a low whistle. "Twenty, forty, sixty, eighty . . ." He continued counting the wad of money now uncovered. "There's enough here to buy one of those newfangled Model T cars that just came out."

Or to pay my salary for a year, a few times over, I thought silently. Aloud, I asked, "Assuming this money is Sarah's, what could she possibly be doing with so much cash?"

Alistair shrugged, rewrapped the money, and handed it to me wordlessly.

I paused for a considerable time. "I suppose I should see more of your files on Michael Fromley. Are you available to take me to your offices now?" Although I phrased it as a polite request, my tone made clear that it was a demand.

"Absolutely," he responded eagerly.

I stopped by 27 Main Street to deposit the money into the village safe and make the appropriate calls to clear my schedule for the day. Joe, returned from the autopsy, was more than happy to manage the investigation in Dobson without me. I took with me his scribbled summary of the autopsy findings. I would review what he and Dr. Fields had learned on the trip into the city.

The next Manhattan-bound ferry was already boarding when Alistair and I approached the landing.

I had one last question for Alistair as we took our places on the top deck of the ferry. "You mentioned earlier how the killer's mind often progresses from first imagining his crime to then actually committing it. If you're right, and Michael Fromley has just killed for the first time, does that make him even more likely to kill again?"

Alistair's mouth set in a firm line. "I'd say it's good odds."

"Then we'd better find him straightaway," I said.

I gazed onto the rocky banks that lined the Hudson's shores, and I couldn't help but wonder whether Alistair's solution was not too simple, however compelling it might be. Was I chasing a red herring while the real murderer only slipped farther away? But no—the coincidences Alistair had mentioned were remarkable. They were coincidences of the sort that in good conscience I could not ignore. Not when the cost would be measured in human lives.

CHAPTER 5

Thick gray clouds overhead threatened rain but never produced it. Fog cloaked the Hudson River in a heavy shroud, entirely obscuring not only the Manhattan skyline but also the other ferries, barges, and transport boats that regularly journeyed between the city and points north. I could barely see the approach of other vessels, even when their foghorns sounded, so I turned away from the railing rather than anxiously mind what only the captain could control. I was always discomfited traveling on a boat of any kind. While I did not fear water, or even the experience of being on a ship itself, I did have a profound distrust of those who operated such vessels. With good reason, I might add: Accidents were common enough, given that greedy owners and captains seemed more concerned with their profit margin than their passengers' safety. Alistair also seemed restless and tense, and we said little to one another during the short half-hour trip.

Alistair's Center for Criminological Research was located at Columbia's new Morningside Heights campus at 116th Street, which I'd never visited. I had spent two brief years at Columbia on scholarship until family circumstances forced me to leave. But that was over ten years ago, when the college still occupied cramped quarters downtown.

Alistair's research center, a small, redbrick house from the early 1800s, had lingered untouched even as McKim, Mead, and White's buildings of columns and marble sprang up around it. We approached by way of a brick walkway covered with wet, slippery leaves. Following Alistair, I pushed open the black-painted door and made my way up a narrow, steep staircase with a faded blue carpet runner to the second floor where his office was located. Two men and a woman were there already, conversing quietly—for Alistair had telephoned ahead to convene this meeting. They sat around a massive oak table in the center of the room, covered by stacks of papers, files, and books.

"Ziele," Alistair directed, "do come in and take a seat." He gestured to indicate where I should hang my coat. I placed my satchel on the floor beside it as a large dog with golden fur emerged from under the table to nuzzle my hand briefly.

"Oban, back here!" The woman ordered the dog back to his former spot under the table.

"I'd like you to meet my associate in sociology, Tom Baxter." Alistair drew my attention to an unassuming man in his mid to late thirties, lanky and lean with a firm handshake.

"Tom came to us just last year from Harvard," Alistair explained. "We're lucky to have him join us."

He continued with more introductions.

"Fred Ebbings, professor of psychology." I turned to greet a stooped, rail-thin man with hunched shoulders. He appeared to be older, well past sixty.

"And my assistant, Isabella Sinclair—who is also my daughter-in-law," Alistair added with a warm smile.

I turned to the slim woman in her mid-twenties with smooth dark hair. Exceedingly pretty, she wore a white shirtwaist and tailored dark green skirt. "A pleasure, Mrs. Sinclair," I said.

"Likewise." She offered a friendly smile, and her demeanor was refreshingly straightforward. "Professor Sinclair has already told us about you. It will be nice working with you."

In the days to come, I would learn that Isabella had been widowed two years prior. As Mulvaney had discovered, her husband Teddy, Alistair's only son, had died tragically during one of his frequent trips to Greece. Teddy's death had forged an odd partnership between Isabella and Alistair, as grief redirected her interests from the social pursuits considered normal for a young woman of her station toward Alistair's criminological research. And, in an arrangement of which the extended Sinclair family highly disapproved, she continued to live alone, with only an old housekeeper and the dog as chaperones, in the apartment adjoining Alistair's—living space Alistair had procured for the young couple at the time of their marriage. In short, her life revolved around Alistair's domestic and professional interests in a way that was considered unhealthy, if not wholly improper.

"Shall we begin?" She immediately took charge. "I see we're finally all here." With a glance to the area behind me, she made a final introduction. "Detective Ziele, also joining us this morning is Horace Wood, Professor Sinclair's research assistant."

I turned sharply, for standing beside me was a slightly balding, pudgy man in his late twenties with thick brown spectacles, worn-looking trousers, and a rumpled shirt that was not fully tucked in. I scarcely registered his clammy handshake or awkward greeting, for I could not help but stare at the large purple lump on the left side of his forehead. It was a nasty injury.

"What happened, Horace?" Isabella asked.

"Tammany toughs tried to discourage my vote yesterday." He sidled into the room and slouched into the chair next to Isabella. It may have been my imagination, but I thought I saw Isabella flinch, ever so slightly, as he brushed against her while reaching for his chair. "They knew I was a Hearst supporter." This last was muttered almost under his breath.

"Sorry to hear that, Horace," Alistair said, adding for my benefit, "Of course, we don't discuss politics here as a rule."

"We are all here to collaborate in a large effort." Isabella picked up Alistair's cue; his nod of encouragement was barely perceptible. "Our effort will be twofold. First, we want to find and question Michael Fromley. As you know, he has been missing for over two weeks now, and we are faced with a new, urgent reason to locate him. Detective Ziele"—she nodded toward me—"is investigating a case involving the unfortunate killing of a young woman named Sarah Wingate—a student here at Columbia, actually—and Professor Sinclair has reason to suspect Michael may be responsible. If this is true, then we need to help find him and establish his guilt."

Horace Wood spoke up; he had a nasal-sounding voice, and his words were fast and clipped. "But we are not detectives. Isn't what you describe a job for the police—in fact, for our detective, Mr. Ziele? I don't see how we can help."

"Of course you are right," Alistair interjected smoothly, "in that Detective Ziele will provide the greatest expertise here, in terms of the murder investigation. But he has already confirmed enough information to establish a strong probability of Michael Fromley's involvement; suffice it to say that the crime scene in Dobson almost perfectly embodies one of Fromley's recurring fantasies. That makes Fromley the most likely suspect in the detective's case."

Horace raised an eyebrow. "Does this mean you've given up on the idea of rehabilitating him, Professor?"

"One never gives up when something is important," Alistair replied firmly, his tone admonishing, "but we have larger responsibilities now that will take precedence. It's our duty to help find and apprehend Fromley. Because of our work these past three years, no one else knows as much about his habits and behavior as we do."

"Professor Sinclair believes we should begin our search for the connection between Michael Fromley and Sarah Wingate here, at Columbia," Isabella continued. "Would you agree, Detective Ziele?"

"It's a worthwhile avenue to explore," I said noncommittally. I wanted to learn more about Fromley and their work with him here at the research center before I made up my mind for certain.

She went on to explain, "At the moment, it is the only common point in their lives that we can identify: She was a student here, and he of course came to the research center each day. At least, until recently."

Alistair added, "Of course, we cannot know whether the connection we are looking for is a formal one or not. They may have crossed paths on neighboring streets or ridden the same subway car."

I involuntarily shuddered, thinking of the case notes Alistair had shared with me.

"I take it Sarah Wingate was a blonde?" Fred Ebbings said in a weary tone.

Alistair nodded and then summarized the same material he had shared this morning with me, aiming to refresh their memories. I listened, taking stock of the differing personalities in the room. Alistair had assembled a diverse group of people for this project—so diverse, in fact, that I wondered how they managed to work together productively on a daily basis. Alistair, an ebullient personality who enjoyed being the center of attention, seemed an odd partner for Fred Ebbings's dry wit or Tom Baxter's common sense. For his part, Horace seemed to be a typical overanxious graduate student. And I could not yet figure out what to make of Isabella, whose quick intelligence probably helped Alistair more than he seemed to realize.

As I listened, I experienced a brief pang of conscience: To approach a murder case in such a backhanded way was contrary to everything I had learned about proper procedure. In a textbook investigation, I would work to learn as much as possible about the victim herself. After all, some facet of her life—some circumstance or some connection still unknown—had inevitably led to her death. But Alistair made a convincing case that Fromley *was* that very connection I sought.

"I believe if we analyze the crime-scene behavior we find evident during Sarah Wingate's murder"—Alistair gestured to the large chalkboard that dominated the left side of the room—"then I can allay any remaining doubts the rest of you may have about his guilt."

"Most of us know Fromley's history, and I assume you've

told Detective Ziele the relevant details," Tom Baxter said. "But have you fully explained your theory about crime-scene behavior? If you haven't, the rest will make no sense."

"That's a good idea," Horace Wood said, for no apparent reason other than wanting to be included in the discussion.

"Tom, I appreciate the reminder. That's exactly where we should begin." Alistair seemed genuinely relieved to have other minds helping him. "Could you summarize our views?"

"Sure," Tom said. "And then I'd like to hear more about the evidence that convinces you Fromley is the man Detective Ziele seeks."

Tom walked to the front of the room. "Even before criminological theorists like Alistair's mentor, Dr. Hans Gross, began to spell it out for us in journals such as *Kriminologie*"—he tapped a large line of journals on the bookcase shelf immediately behind him—"I think even regular police officers like Detective Ziele recognized that different criminals commit crimes in ways that reflect their unique identity. The detective can correct me if I'm wrong, but suppose we found a dead body in an East River warehouse with a bullet to the back of the head. I'm sure he would immediately suspect Paul Kelly or Monk Eastman."

These were—or had been—the leaders of two notorious street gangs, the Five Points gang and the Eastman gang. Though now that Monk Eastman was doing time in Sing Sing, it was Kid Twist Zwerbach who headed the Eastman gang. What Tom had just described was an execution-style murder, and he was correct that the police would suspect an organized crime figure, not an individual offender.

Tom went on. "On the other hand, if we found a man shot or stabbed to death on the street, we might suppose that he died following an argument that got out of hand; in that case, the detective would look for someone with a quarrel or grudge against the victim." He took a deep breath before offering his final example. "And if we found a man poisoned to death from arsenic, we might look to the victim's wife or another woman in his life." Tom looked to me for confirmation.

"That's right," I said, "because the method itself suggests something important about the culprit. Certain personalities are likely to choose particular methods, as your last example suggests."

"Criminals are best understood through their crimes," Alistair clarified, with a slight smile. "But you can flip it around, and say that crimes are best understood through criminal behavior at the crime scene. The idea is not a new one—if you would like to understand more, you should read my former teacher's seminal work here." He thumped a worn copy of Dr. Hans Gross's *Criminal Investigation, A Practical Textbook for Magistrates, Police Officers, and Lawyers*, which occupied a central spot on his massive desk.

Apparently worried that Alistair was about to launch into a long theoretical lecture, Tom interrupted, explaining that while law enforcement officers have made these kinds of judgments for years, what he and his colleagues had tried to do was to refine and extend this type of analysis. He went on to detail how the behavior Fromley had exhibited during past assaults suggested something important about his personality and motivation. For example, where Fromley had caused extensive wounds to his victim's face, it suggested that Fromley harbored intense anger toward the victim for a reason real or perceived.

"Let us consider this in the context of the Dobson crime

scene, then," Isabella said, redirecting our focus to the task at hand, "if Detective Ziele will be so good as to describe it for us."

"Of course." I cleared my throat, and walked over to the giant black chalkboard. "Sarah Wingate's autopsy this morning shows she was killed by an eight-inch wound to her throat in the guest bedroom of her aunt's house. But she was extensively injured after her death. Postmortem, she suffered blows about the head and upper torso. Then"—I slowly placed a handful of selected crime-scene photographs on the board, each picture displaying some part of yesterday's horrific murder—"she was posed by the side of the bed as you see in these pictures."

I moved slightly to the left so everyone might see better, pulling the autopsy notes out of my folder. I had given the report a cursory review during our trip; Joe, writing for Dr. Fields, had efficiently rendered the brutal injuries Sarah had sustained into medical terms. The official cause of death was the incision across the throat, which extended from just below the left ear to within two inches of the right, penetrating the trachea, or windpipe. But I explained to the others that her secondary injuries were also sufficient to cause death. Her skull had been shattered; or, as the autopsy described it, her occipital bone (which is located at the back of the head) was fractured, her nose was broken, and there were several contusions around her forehead.

As I was speaking, Isabella joined me by the blackboard and began to list the main points in neat capital letters above the pictures that rested on the ledge. I had expected we would be uncomfortable discussing such material with Isabella present, but she appeared nonplussed.

Alistair asked, "Did the doctor who performed the autopsy indicate what type of weapon caused the throat and head wounds?"

"Yes," I said. "Because the throat wound was a very clean incision, with no extraneous tearing, Dr. Fields believes an extremely sharp weapon was used, such as a razor. Moreover, a large weapon was used to effect the head injury, and Dr. Fields goes so far as to suggest it would be some kind of metal object, such as a crowbar or pipe." I quickly scanned the report to find the relevant margin note he had written for me. Tapping the report with my pen, I explained, "In his opinion, a different material, such as wood, could not have lacerated the skin as cleanly as was done in this case."

"I see," Alistair said. He was staring at the list of injuries on the board, apparently absorbed in thought; he barely looked up as Horace excused himself and left the room.

"Do go on," Fred Ebbings urged, and I noticed they were all listening attentively.

"There were traces of chloroform in her body. From that, in addition to some peculiar bruising on Sarah's heels, and the fact that she has no defensive wounds on her hands or wrists, it is the doctor's opinion that she was incapacitated elsewhere in the house and dragged to the guest bedroom. There, her killer arranged the room to look as we found it." I went on to describe the other details apparent in the photographs: how her long braid of hair had been cut, and how her blue dress had been slashed, with one fragment of cloth used to cover her face.

"Part of his plan revolved around blood. As Dr. Fields has explained it, her throat was slit first, and it bled extensively as she died. But bleeding stops within a few minutes of death, so the postmortem wounds to her head generated less blood than would otherwise be expected. To compensate for this, her killer appears to have struck the same head injuries—over and over, using his metal weapon—in order to create the blood-spatter effect we saw."

Tom Baxter leaned forward against the table, brow furrowed, trying to make sense of it all. When he spoke directly to Alistair, his tone was carefully measured. "You know, I admit many of these elements fit what we've learned about Fromley's murderous fantasies. But the use of chloroform does not. And neither do the postmortem injuries to her head. How do we explain the inconsistencies?"

"Those discrepancies initially bothered me, too," Alistair conceded. "What I have concluded is that, given the environment in which Fromley confronted his victim—with her aunt and the housemaid Stella nearby on the grounds—he subdued her with chloroform as a method of control. Otherwise, she might have made too much noise and commotion. But to make the experience emotionally satisfying for him, he needed her injuries to mirror what he had imagined. So that is why he inflicted the wounds that Detective Ziele might describe as 'overkill.'"

"Yes," Fred Ebbings said. "Putting aside Fromley's possible involvement for the moment, what we need to remember when we look at this crime scene is that it reflects the mind of the killer. He has killed in the first place because his distorted thinking led him to believe he needed to. And when he killed, he did so in *this* manner because it made the experience satisfying in a way that no other method could."

"By that you are referring to the blood spatter?" I asked. I recollected I had had a similar thought at the scene last night.

"Yes, that's definitely part of it," Ebbings said. "But it's also about fulfilling his fantasy. The fantasy is something he has replayed countless times in his own mind, and he is finally at the point of making it a reality. To change some aspect of a scenario he has so long imagined would disappoint him."

I did not mention it to the group, but I thought briefly of a recent visit paid to the police department by Detective Abberline of Scotland Yard, the senior detective involved in the still unsolved "Jack the Ripper" case in London some fifteen years back. While discussing a number of new procedures and techniques such as fingerprinting, he had also revisited the case of George Chapman, one of the chief Ripper suspects. Chapman had been in London during the time of the Ripper murders, but then he returned to the New York area and proceeded to poison three different women. Abberline had wondered why a killer whose method had been "mutilation" would suddenly turn to poison—and questioned whether it was even possible. It led him to have serious doubts about Chapman. By analogy, I worried whether we should have similar doubts about Fromley.

"What about her facial wounds?" I asked. "You mentioned earlier that the shattering blows to her head may suggest her killer was angry with her. But that implies a personal relationship, and there's no indication such a relationship existed between Sarah Wingate and Michael Fromley—right?"

"Strictly speaking, you are right," Alistair said. "But we must remember that he perceives the entire world around him in a distorted manner, and within this mind-set, a 'personal relationship' means something altogether different to him than it would to you or to me. He may have built the relationship entirely within his head, with little or no participation from his victim. Or she could be a stand-in for someone else, since Sarah Wingate shares some of the same characteristics as the women in Michael's fantasies."

Ebbings picked up Alistair's thread of reasoning. "And what we learned from our interviews with Michael was that before he killed in his fantasies, he first dehumanized his victims so as to make his own actions easier. The brutal facial injuries are a way of dehumanizing her, since with each blow, she less resembles a real person."

"I agree," Alistair added. "Our killer in this scenario wants two things. First, I read him as wanting *control* above all else. Through killing he exercises the ultimate control. First, he determines whether she lives or dies. Next, he determines exactly how she dies."

"And the locket?" Horace asked. "Why take her jewelry?" Horace Wood had rejoined the group, though at what point I could not say.

"It provides a tangible way for him to remember the experience," Ebbings said. "It serves as a memento, to put it another way. In this case particularly, since the locket contained a picture of her, I can see why it would appeal. He would have wanted to take it out, look at her photo, and fantasize yet again about the experience of killing her."

"So it sounds like it's safe to assume Fromley is the guy who did this, right?" Horace voiced my own question for me. "It's hard to imagine another criminal who thinks and behaves like him."

"Well," Tom replied, "while I may have some lingering doubts, the fact that the actual crime scene so closely mirrors the fantasy that Fromley described seems too coincidental to disregard."

"I do have one last question," I interjected. "Why do you believe the killer covered Sarah's face with part of her dress?"

Alistair's eyes lit up, as though he had been waiting for just this question. "Your question has just, in a nutshell, hit upon why I held out such hope for Michael Fromley's rehabilitative potential. Covering his victim in some manner was always part of his more violent fantasies, and I read the act as signifying remorse for what he has done. At the very end, he felt a flicker of shame, so he covered the victim and left her with some dignity. To put it another way, he rehumanized her at the end of a long process of dehumanizing her."

"Do we know anything yet that would suggest why she was chosen?" Tom asked. "If Fromley is her killer, what would have led him to pick her, specifically, as his victim?"

"I can't say for sure," Fred Ebbings said. "But her physical profile does resemble a woman in one of Fromley's recurring fantasies. I'll check my case notes."

My mind was churning, trying to make sense of so many ideas at once. I could not see how Alistair and his colleagues could claim to know everything they had just suggested. And yet, they each spoke with a comfortable authority and spun a narrative that was both cohesive and logical.

"From all you have said, Michael Fromley certainly is a suspect who must be thoroughly investigated—and I appreciate the help you can give me toward that end," I said. "Alistair, can you arrange for us to meet with whomever of Fromley's family and friends you believe might help us locate him? Meanwhile, I can begin to talk with some of Sarah Wingate's acquaintances to learn more about her. I want to pursue this investigation on both traditional and nontraditional fronts."

"I asked Horace to speak first thing this morning with Richard Bonham, a professor of mathematics here, to get some basic information about Sarah. He knew her both as a graduate student in his department, and also as his daughter Mary's closest friend," Alistair said. "We discovered Sarah actually lived with the Bonham family at their town house on 113th and Riverside."

"Yes, well," Horace said, "I did speak with Richard Bonham first thing this morning—in fact, I got there within a half hour of the policeman who broke the news about the murder." Horace beamed with satisfaction, clearly pleased with himself. "Professor Bonham was quite a help. He thought the girl had tremendous academic potential. But from what he said about her activities, I'd say she was also a troublemaker. Apparently Sarah was one of those rabble-rousing feminists desperate for the vote, always marching in one demonstration or another," he said. "Last month she led the group that demonstrated on the president's steps for granting women admission to the undergraduate program."

I happened to glance at Isabella. For an instant so brief I was convinced I must have imagined it, I saw disapproval in her eyes as she looked toward Horace—who was by now again seated immediately to her right. Once more, I had not noticed him move.

"Horace, isn't your fiancée a member of one of those feminist groups?" Isabella asked. "You'll have to change your tune once you're married next summer!"

"She's not in *that* kind of feminist group," Horace snapped, flushing with embarrassment.

"Enough of this," Tom interrupted. "It's not what got Sarah Wingate murdered, after all."

"Actually, we can't know that yet," I said. "We don't know

what her connection with Michael Fromley was—if indeed that's what led to her murder. And until we've solved her murder, nothing about her life is unimportant."

"Ziele is right," Alistair said, his expression unreadable. "Horace, please continue."

"Yes, well," Horace continued, "Sarah was determined to get her doctorate in mathematics, and had just started her fourth year of graduate work this fall. According to Professor Bonham, she was in good academic standing and performing well. He also mentioned that she had a part-time job at the dean's office. Just some filing, simple clerical work."

"Thank you, Horace," Alistair said. "Perhaps some of Sarah Wingate's friends can offer more detail about these matters."

"I actually have a list of Sarah Wingate's friends," Horace said, producing a grimy, wrinkled piece of paper from his pocket. "Do you want me to follow up?"

"I would like to," I said, and he handed me the list wordlessly. While the extra efforts of these people were well intended, the success or failure of this investigation was ultimately mine—and I disliked relying on the opinions of others. This was especially true in interviews, where I had to evaluate the information I learned in light of the credibility of the person speaking.

Alistair must have understood, because he immediately delegated other assignments—but all entailing simple background research. Tom and Fred, as senior faculty, would visit the registrar's office to get a list of Sarah Wingate's courses and talk with the faculty about her performance. They would also visit the dean's office to determine the length of her employment there and the scope of her duties. Horace would visit the offices of the student paper, *The Spectator*, to view back issues and gather any past articles mentioning Sarah Wingate. Alistair would try to reach Fromley's family, the Wallingfords, to arrange an immediate meeting. Meanwhile, I would interview the Bonham family as well as Caleb Muller, her academic advisor. Alistair promised to meet me at 113th Street and Broadway at one o'clock; he was confident he would have reached the Wallingfords by then. Then, he took me aside to offer an additional suggestion.

"You may want to take Isabella with you to the Bonhams. She will be able to put Miss Bonham at ease—and that will enable your interview to proceed more smoothly."

"Understood. But first, I need to check in with the office; may I use your telephone?" I asked.

He directed me to his private office next door, where I closed the door and dialed Joe. It was some moments before Charlie, our secretary, brought Joe to the telephone. I filled him in, omitting nothing.

"You trust everything this professor says?" he asked. After hearing my tale, he sounded incredulous.

"Not for a moment," I said. "But it bears looking into, wouldn't you say?"

Joe's answer was a loud grunt.

He went on to tell me that Peter Voyt had scored a breakthrough of sorts. His calls to a number of the more successful—and thus expensive—photographers in the city had yielded results. After discovering a photographer who promised to be the right match on the telephone, Peter had straightaway gone to examine the photographer's files. The tiny photographs in Sarah's locket were indeed part of a larger series of portraits, completed in December 1899, and paid for by an A. MacDonald. The photographer barely remembered the couple, since almost six years had passed. But he was able to confirm Peter's suspicion that the photographs were part of a larger series, typical of couples sitting for engagement pictures.

"It was very unusual to have photographs like that reduced for a tiny locket," Joe explained.

But Sarah had wanted to keep the photographs secret— and that would have been impossible with a large photograph. The other photographs were no doubt within the possession of A. MacDonald.

Now that we had a name, Joe would follow up by attempting to locate as many A. MacDonalds as he could identify in the New York City area.

"What's your plan if you find him?" I asked.

"To figure out what he had to do with Sarah Wingate and her murder. I'll just ask him."

Of course. That always worked.

I hung up before I said something I would truly regret.

CHAPTER 6

The brownstone near the corner of 113th Street and Riverside Drive where the Bonhams lived was newly built, marked by ornamental iron filigree combined with patterns of red, yellow, and tan brick. Similar buildings throughout the Upper West Side were going up as fast as construction would allow, each one more elaborate than the last, in a real estate boom that seemingly had no end in sight. The city was expanding northward, and its growing economy enabled more and more people to afford what was being so rapidly built.

Once inside the Bonham home, Isabella and I were taken through a passage behind the stairwell to a large, comfortable library to wait for Sarah's friend. Floor-to-ceiling bookshelves dominated the room, each filled with old books stuck in at odd angles. No doubt they were the source of the room's musty smell. Mary Bonham did not keep us waiting long. A short and plump young woman, she had brown hair, a round face, and red, puffy eyes behind thick glasses. I noticed that she visibly relaxed upon seeing Isabella, and I silently thanked Alistair for his foresight in suggesting Isabella as a companion.

"Our condolences," I offered gently, after we had made the necessary introductions. "We appreciate your talking with us this afternoon; we realize this is a difficult time for you."

She nodded insensibly, but remembered her manners and asked if we cared for coffee or sandwiches. Though I was famished, I declined. I always felt it was inappropriate to eat or drink in these circumstances, as though this were a social visit. It was not, and I disliked having any pretense about that.

I began by asking Mary a few simple questions about her family and the duration of her friendship with Sarah. Her responses—even to such simple questions—were so reluctant that I signaled Isabella to try. Perhaps she would have better success with this shy young girl. The risk, of course, was that she might not formulate the right questions, but I soon found myself appreciating her natural instincts. She first asked when Sarah came to live with the Bonhams.

"Just over a year ago," Mary said, pulling a green shawl tightly around her. "She came to us soon after last fall's robbery."

"Can you tell us—"

I cut off Isabella's question with my own. "What robbery?"

But I was too abrupt, and Mary recoiled from what she perceived as a rude reply. "I'm sorry," I said, modifying my response, "I'm not familiar with that incident, and it could be important." Then I waited, annoyed that I had overreacted.

"Well," she said, "it happened a year ago September, right after Labor Day. It's the reason why Sarah moved here, since the Wingates wouldn't hear of her living alone after the robbery." She corrected herself quickly. "Of course, Sarah had never lived *alone*; Mrs. Gardner runs a respectable rooming house for young ladies who attend college. But it's not the same as living with a family."

"We understand," Isabella demurred before prompting her to get back on point. "And the robbery?"

"Oh, yes," she said, almost breathlessly. "Sarah returned to her room one night and surprised a stranger rifling through her personal things. She screamed and the man left, but he made off with money and some jewelry."

"This man was caught and identified?" I asked.

"Eventually, yes," she said, "and Sarah recovered the jewelry, but not the money. That was long spent by the time the police arrested him."

"Do you remember anything more about the incident? Perhaps the man's name or occupation?"

"He was German, I think," she said, trying to remember. She frowned. "I believe he was a vagrant who took advantage of an open window. Sarah described him as having long, unkempt hair and wearing soiled clothes."

"Did the experience change her behavior in any way?" I asked.

"Apart from changing her living arrangements, I don't think Sarah thought much of it at all."

September 1904. I jotted the date down in my notebook. I would have one of my contacts at the department pull all arrest records from the Morningside Heights precinct to try to locate the case.

Mary looked down, her fingers playing with the fringe on her shawl.

"We understand you last saw Sarah on Friday, when she left to go visit her aunt in Dobson. I wonder if you could describe her mood for us?" Isabella's tone was friendly, as if she were merely chatting with a friend she had known for years. When Mary did not answer immediately, she offered further help. "Was she happy and excited about her weekend with her aunt?" It was just the right approach to help Mary relax and talk more comfortably.

The girl shrugged. "Sarah was out of sorts, I'd say. She hadn't been sleeping well. She was up most nights with terrible insomnia. I think that's why she decided to visit her aunt." She looked up from the fringe. "We had a row about it, actually. We had opening-night tickets to go with my parents to see Maude Adams in her new musical, *Peter Pan*. I couldn't believe Sarah would cancel plans like that." Her voice was husky as she fought back tears. "I didn't understand why she chose to go to Dobson and miss seeing it."

"When did she change her mind?" I asked.

"Thursday night." Mary hiccupped a sob.

"She must have given you a reason why." Isabella tried to encourage her.

But Mary shook her head. "She said she had a great deal of work and couldn't concentrate here. But her next dissertation chapter draft was not due for another month, and just two weeks ago, she claimed it was almost done. Her excuses made no sense."

I mulled over this information, wondering what to make of it. Something had troubled Sarah, giving her insomnia and prompting her abrupt decision to go to Dobson. It was an altogether different picture than Abigail Wingate had painted when she described Sarah's visit.

"Do you have any idea what may have troubled her?" Isabella asked. "Was she having any academic difficulties?"

"Of course not," Mary said. "Sarah's studies came very easily to her."

"And her classmates liked her?"

Mary wrinkled her nose. "I suppose most liked her well enough. There was jealousy, of course."

"Could you give us an example?"

"Well, only one incident comes to mind," she said. "During Sarah's second year in the graduate program, she briefly considered changing her focus to medicine. She enrolled in an organic chemistry course, and when she received the highest grade in the class, her classmates—most of them doing premedical studies—were up in arms. The professor used a bell curve standard and Sarah's doing so well affected their performance. One of them filed a formal challenge, alleging that she had not done the work herself. She had to meet with a panel of three professors and submit to an informal oral exam, just to prove she knew the material." She sighed and returned to pulling at the fringe of her shawl. "But if her classmate's strategy was to disparage her abilities, then he failed miserably; she performed even better in that scenario than she had in her written exams. Still, she hated having her abilities doubted."

"What about afterward?" I added. "Did she encounter that sort of suspicion elsewhere, perhaps in the math department?"

"I don't know," she replied. "I never heard about it."

"And what about her women friends from Barnard?"

Mary thought for a minute before answering, which in itself was telling. At last, she said, "Sarah generally got on well with people, but she had a strong personality and could be argumentative. It was a trait she developed over time, since every success she achieved had to be defended against the argument she hadn't really earned it."

"What was her area of research?" Isabella asked.

"I know her dissertation was about the Riemann hypothesis; Sarah was fascinated with it. But I can't begin to tell you much more than that, since I've no head for math myself."

"Whom should we talk to about her research, besides her advisor?" Isabella pressed.

"Mmmm," Mary thought aloud. "You might try Artie Shaw. He was the same year as Sarah, and they were quite friendly, talked through a lot of research issues together."

"Quite friendly?" Isabella asked for more explanation, though her tone remained casual.

"As classmates, nothing more," Mary clarified, before confiding shyly, "I do think she had a beau, honestly, but it wasn't Artie."

"Why do you think so?" I asked. Sarah's cousin Abigail had been convinced Sarah had neither the time nor the inclination for romantic attachments.

"Because Sarah used to visit Princeton on the sly," she replied, "always pretending she was going somewhere else."

Mary Bonham had our full attention now, but we waited to see what further information she would volunteer. Sometimes simply letting people talk—in their own time, in their own way—yielded the most useful information.

"I found out the first time because I saw a baggage claim check in her room marked 'Princeton Junction' following a weekend when she claimed to have visited her aunt. I almost said something to her about it, but I didn't. The next time she supposedly returned from a weekend in Dobson, I checked her room and found more ticket receipts from Princeton."

"Would she have had a research-related reason for visiting Princeton?" I asked. "Maybe Sarah needed to consult their library."

"Then why would she lie about going there?" Mary countered. "Whatever her purpose, it was a reason she didn't want to share. Don't misunderstand me: I'm not trying to suggest Sarah was involved in some sort of tawdry affair. She had too much sense, and was too dedicated to her research to risk something like that. I'm sure any relationship was entirely proper, but it was something she nonetheless kept secret."

I drew the locket out of my pocket. "Have you ever noticed Sarah wearing this?" I asked, handing it to her. She studied it, murmured, "No," and then slowly opened it. She appeared mesmerized by the two photographs inside.

"Do you know who the man is?"

"No," she answered, wide-eyed, "I've never seen him—or this picture of Sarah."

"Not even as a larger print?" I wanted to make sure.

She shook her head.

"What about this man?" I pulled out a small photograph of Michael Fromley that Alistair had given me for such purposes. My fingers fumbled awkwardly, for I had double-wrapped the picture inside an envelope.

She paused a moment as if to say something, then shook her head. "I've never seen him. He is closer to her age, though; perhaps he is her secret beau at Princeton?"

"I don't think so," I said as I returned Fromley's photograph to my pocket.

A glance at my watch showed we had spent over half an

hour with Mary Bonham, so I moved on to my last line of questioning. "We've been told Sarah was involved in the suffragist movement. Is there anything you can tell us about her activity there?" I tried to be as open-ended as possible to see what information Mary would volunteer; this was a sensitive political issue for some and I had no idea where her sympathies lay.

Mary's response was quick and to the point, however. "Sarah became involved with a local suffragist group our senior year at Barnard, but she did not become truly active until she completed the organic chemistry class I just mentioned to you." She sighed. "That marked the turning point when Sarah became . . ."—she paused for a moment before she found the right word—"embittered. She was frustrated by the fact that her accomplishments and research were undervalued, simply because she was a woman. Another fellow student sympathized, invited her to a suffragist rally, and ever after that, she was an active member."

"Did you ever attend any rallies with her?" Isabella asked, her curiosity apparent in her tone.

"No." Mary shook her head sheepishly. "I may agree with Sarah's political goals. But going to rallies and marches wasn't something I was interested in doing." I could well imagine that such events and the crowds they drew would not appeal to such a shy and awkward girl.

Isabella and I finished our conversation with Mary, obtaining little more information that was helpful. Before leaving, we looked through the contents of Sarah's room. It was a spartan room—even more so, perhaps, than the guest room she had occupied at her aunt's home. We found few possessions suggestive of her personality other than the collection of mathematics textbooks and papers on the simple wooden bookshelf by the bed.

I had expected to see Alistair waiting for us on Broadway; he had promised to be at the corner of 113th Street by one o'clock. I glanced at my watch again; it was a quarter past one. Where was he—and what could be taking him so long to arrange a meeting with Fromley's family? I disliked delegating this task to Alistair, but I knew that Alistair's relationship with them—and not my police badge—would make this meeting far easier.

"What next?" Isabella asked.

"We wait," I said.

I looked up and down Broadway. No sign of Alistair.

Isabella made a suggestion. "We could visit the math department. It's nearby; we can leave a message at Alistair's office."

I agreed, and we quickened our pace as we headed back up the three blocks to 116th Street.

"What's your opinion of all this?" I asked her. "Do you think Alistair has it right?"

She smiled. "I think my father-in-law is brilliant. And that you have probably never been given so solid a lead, so early in an investigation."

I laughed, saying, "You may be right about that."

Alistair had pointed me toward my prime suspect, using reasoning and simple logic. But I was growing doubtful that he would be able to deliver Fromley himself with similar ease.

CHAPTER 7

As soon as we arrived, Professor Richard Bonham, the chairman of the Department of Mathematics, convened an impromptu meeting in his office. His quarters were pleasant, though less amply furnished than those at Alistair's research center. Since Columbia supplied little in the way of office furnishings, most professors had to procure for themselves whatever items they wanted: furniture, plants, even carpets. But the office's best feature was a large window that offered an artist's view of Low Memorial Library's granite dome rising into the sky.

Professor Bonham did his best to make us feel welcome. "No need to call me professor," he said, waving off our formal greeting. "That's for my students; you should call me Richard."

He was an older man, near sixty by my guess. A dark gray suit that was at least two sizes too big enveloped his rail-thin body. He had lost significant weight since he bought that suit, which made me suspect he was—or had recently been—quite ill.

"This is Caleb Muller, Sarah's advisor."

I shook hands with a much younger man who was probably nearer my own age. He had the rugged features and strong build of an outdoorsman, and were it not for his tweed jacket and black-rimmed glasses, he would look out of place in this company.

"And one of our graduate students, Arthur Shaw." A young man with tousled hair and ruddy cheeks came over to shake hands.

"People call me Artie," he said shyly.

Richard sat at his desk after directing us toward his paisley-covered armchairs with stiff backs, while the others sat across from us on borrowed wooden desk chairs. We soon found ourselves deep in conversation about the academic dimension of Sarah's life.

"Yes," Caleb was saying, "Sarah officially became my advisee when she began her dissertation proposal, but I have unofficially advised her since well before her matriculation here, even while she was an undergraduate at Barnard. Her research centered on the Riemann hypothesis, a mathematical problem that has resisted every attempt to prove it since Riemann first published it in 1859. Even," he added with a self-deprecating grin, "my own best attempts."

"In layman's terms"—I returned his smile—"can you explain what the hypothesis is and Sarah's approach to solving it?"

"Of course. Generally, the hypothesis involves our understanding of prime numbers. To be precise . . ." He rose from his chair and wrote an equation on the blackboard, talking all the while. It made no sense to me, but as Caleb continued to explain, I tried to follow the larger point of what he was saying. ". . . so the unproved Riemann hypothesis is that all of the nontrivial zeros are actually on the critical line."

He looked at us hopefully, even expectantly. But when he registered only blank confusion, he clarified his point. "I suppose the details are of no use to you. What is important for you to know is that either to prove—or to disprove—the Riemann hypothesis is considered one of the most interesting problems confronting mathematicians today. David Hilbert, one of the world's most eminent mathematicians, has listed the Riemann hypothesis as one of twenty-three problems he believes will define twentieth-century mathematics. And Sarah was attempting to tackle it. She was building on the work of another mathematician, named von Koch, who had made an important breakthrough four years ago. If she could have done it, well then, not only would it have been a first rate-dissertation, but it would also have radically altered her future prospects."

"Altered them how?" I asked, puzzled. It seemed an understatement in light of Sarah's talents.

"As I daresay you know, there is inherent prejudice in this profession against women. Most women Ph.D.s go on to teach at the high school level. The best of them—and make no mistake, Sarah was among the best—have a shot at a position at one of the women's colleges. Perhaps Bryn Mawr, or Smith. If she had managed to solve this"—he tapped the board with his fingers—"she would have made history within mathematics. Even our most prestigious universities may have considered her."

"Did others in the department know the nature of her work?" I asked.

He shrugged. "I suspect most people knew her general focus, but she was a private person. She would have been loath, I'm sure, to share her successes or her failures. Perhaps Artie can speak better to that, however."

We all looked to Artie Shaw, who had hung back until this point. He flushed when he perceived he was the focus of our attention.

"I'm not sure how much people knew about her specific research. The general opinion was that she was brilliant, certain to write an exceptional dissertation." Artie shifted uncomfortably. "And that didn't sit well with a lot of them. They didn't want to believe she could do it. They didn't like being upstaged. And they especially didn't like the possibility—however remote— that she just might land a position that more properly belonged to them. In their view, of course," he added.

"And why was that?" Isabella asked. She had been bristling for the past few moments in light of the men's general disregard of her presence.

"Well, because they'd have families to support, but she presumably would not," Artie admitted.

His tone conciliatory, Richard Bonham explained further. "It's one of our greatest ideological barriers to admitting women to graduate education, and from the time she entered the program, Sarah knew she would have to face up to it. Since most women Ph.D.s find the responsibilities of academic life and family to be mutually exclusive, they tend to pick only one—usually the latter." He was stopped by a coughing fit—a rough, hacking cough that revived my suspicions he had recently been very ill. Then he added, "Though I wouldn't have expected that choice from Sarah. She was unusually ambitious."

"Did any of her fellow students seem particularly envious of her talents? Or particularly irritated by her inclusion in the program?" I asked.

Richard and Caleb exchanged a quick look.

Finally Caleb spoke. "I am hesitating, because I am aware my answer will cast undue suspicion on a handful of students who don't deserve the scrutiny. I can certainly give you their names, but you must bear in mind that, however much these young men may have complained about Sarah Wingate, there is not one of them I believe capable of her murder."

He carefully wrote down four names and handed them to me; I scanned them quickly: John Nelson, Louis De Vry, Sam Baker, and Alonzo Moore Jr. known as "Lonny." Caleb's reluctance to mention these individuals was obvious, but I discounted it. If it were not for the more obvious signs pointing toward Michael Fromley, then this list would offer much in the way of real suspects.

Experience had taught me, time and again, never to believe the protestations of friends and family who declared an accused man "could never do such a thing." "I know my son," a father of a murder suspect had once said to me. He had been adamant, sincerely convinced of his son's innocence. But what the father did not understand—no, not even after his son was convicted and sentenced to die—was that we only see those around us from one perspective. His son was one person at home, still another with friends, and still another when brawling at the corner bar. "I know my son *at home*," is what the father meant, though he did not realize it. It was impossible for him to know more.

"Richard," I continued. "Your daughter mentioned a housebreaking incident last fall; I understand it is the reason why Sarah Wingate came to live with your family. Are there any additional details you could tell me? I'm interested not only in hearing about the burglary, but also your experience of having Miss Wingate living under your roof."

"Of course, of course." Richard Bonham cleared his throat. "My daughter Mary had become friendly with Sarah when the two were at Barnard, and they kept up the acquaintance. Even before she came to stay with us, she was a frequent dinner guest. Quiet, polite—and a good influence on Mary, who tends to be a natural homebody. It did her good to be with Sarah, who took her to the occasional poetry reading or tea social. I'm not certain how well I remember the details of the burglary, but shortly after the incident occurred, I was contacted by Mrs. Wingate, Sarah's aunt. Apparently she took quite a fright after the incident, and put tremendous pressure on Sarah to leave the program unless a better living arrangement could be found. So we agreed on terms: She would live with our family, up on the third floor with Mary, during academic term; for that, she paid a modest sum merely to cover the additional expense we would incur by having her."

He sighed, sadness etched in the lines of his face. "She is—was—a fine young lady, and we will all feel her loss. Not just my daughter." He stumbled over the words. "And mathematically, what a mind! When she was in our home, she was more often than not in her room, puzzling over some problem. It was what interested her—what she found to be fun."

"Did you often discuss research with her?" I asked.

He shook his head. "Her research was not in my field of expertise, I'm afraid." He added wryly, "Even within the same department, we each become isolated within our own specialty, wouldn't you agree, Caleb?"

After Caleb assented, I determined to pick up a thread from our earlier discussion with Mary. I asked the three men in the room, "To your knowledge, was Sarah ever romantically involved with anyone in the department?"

"No," Artie replied, adding clumsily, "If any of us had gotten spoony with her, she'd have been certain to put us in our place. She wasn't interested in that sort of thing—not with my classmates, and certainly not with me."

"Never?" I asked. But their opinions were a unanimous no.

I brought up the fact that Sarah had visited Princeton frequently.

"Oh, yes," Caleb said, chuckling, "that was just one more indication of Sarah's talent; she presented her first important academic paper four years ago at Princeton, with most of our nation's best mathematical minds present. The paper she presented about functions of the critical line was brilliant. Positively brilliant. She had been working on it, actually, ever since she was a sophomore at Barnard. It even attracted the attention of a colleague of mine known for his cantankerous personality— Angus MacDonald. When I learned she was interested in the Riemann hypothesis, I introduced her to him."

His answer was as perfect a lead-in as I could have scripted. The photographs in Sarah's locket had been paid for by an A. MacDonald. "And Angus MacDonald is another mathematician?" I asked, trying to sound casual.

"A professor emeritus at Princeton, obsessed, like Sarah, with the Riemann hypothesis. In fact, it has been his life's work, trying to solve it."

"Did Professor MacDonald have significant contact with Sarah that you were aware of?" I asked.

"I wouldn't describe it as significant," Caleb replied. "Yet during my meetings with her, it was clear she had exchanged substantive ideas about her proof with him."

I pulled out the silver locket and handed it silently to Professor Muller.

His initial shock of recognition was quickly replaced by a look of unease. He handed it back, shaken. "Yes, that's Angus."

"This locket certainly implies that he was involved in more than a purely collegial relationship with Sarah, wouldn't you say? And yet, you were unaware of it?"

"I was unaware." He shook his head sadly. "Otherwise, I would have discouraged it. *Strongly* discouraged it." He was adamant as he voiced his opinion. "Such an association would have done neither of them any good professionally, and possibly much harm. Sarah already fought people's misguided assumptions that a woman could not produce the sort of mathematical work that she did. A number of people believed that a brother or father must do her work for her. A romantic association with one of this country's most gifted mathematicians would not have helped her to rebut such presumptions."

"What about you, Artie?" I turned to the earnest young man, who was occupied staring at his feet. "Did she ever tell you anything about her relationship with Professor MacDonald?"

"Not that kind of relationship." He flushed again. "I knew she corresponded with him, even met with him on occasion. Every time she had a breakthrough of sorts, she seemed to talk with him about it. But I supposed it was because he understood her research so well." He slouched deep into his chair.

Isabella asked, "You mean you were aware she went to visit him?"

Artie seemed surprised. "Why, yes. She wasn't secretive about it. He lives with his mother, so it was all quite aboveboard. I suppose that's the main reason I never suspected her relationship with Professor MacDonald was anything but professional."

Yet Sarah had been secretive about the visits with both the Wingates and her friend Mary. Why had she openly told Artie about her visits, yet concealed them to the Bonhams and the Wingates?

"You said the Riemann hypothesis was Angus MacDonald's life's work. Would he have been angry—jealous possibly— if Sarah had solved it?" I asked.

After another bout of coughing, Richard Bonham answered me deliberately. "I have known the man some twenty years, and I cannot believe he would react badly to another person's solving the proof. I would remind you, there have been a handful of people over the years who *thought* they solved the Riemann hypothesis, only to find their proof did not hold up under the scrutiny of other mathematicians. Angus never reacted badly to those attempts, however disappointed he may have been. And, do not forget: He was actively helping Sarah with her work on the hypothesis."

"And yet, you also would not have suspected MacDonald of pursuing a romantic relationship with Sarah, either," I reminded him. He looked away in embarrassment.

"What about this man?" Isabella asked. "Do any of you recall having seen him before?" She passed around our now dog-eared picture of Michael Fromley.

Caleb and Artie both glanced at the photograph briefly before replying no, but Richard looked at it long and hard before answering. He finally said, "There is something about the boy that looks familiar, but I can't place him. What is your interest in him?"

"He is our prime suspect," I said. "We have circumstantial evidence linking him to Sarah's murder."

But no hard evidence, I thought silently. And that was what I desperately needed.

Where was Alistair?

"Did your suspect attend Columbia?" Richard asked, puzzled.

But we answered no and imparted no further information. We thanked them for their time and left, the noise of Richard's hacking cough following us all the way down the stairs until we were nearly out of the building.

Across the quad at the research center, there was no word from Alistair. While Isabella assured me this was typical and not to worry, I was impatient, with so much still to be done. We had learned a great deal from this afternoon's interviews, and Sarah was beginning to take human form in my mind. But the more she became real to me, the more I felt an urgency to find her killer. Michael Fromley remained at large, and that was—unacceptable.

I made use of our wait to telephone Joe, filling him in about Angus MacDonald; then I left a message at Princeton for the mathematician himself, requesting him to telephone or come to the research center in person.

Why was Alistair taking so long?

Ten more minutes passed.

I suggested to Isabella that we walk over to Broadway to see if there was any sign of him. Perhaps we would even find him waiting to meet us at 113th Street, as originally planned.

A street vendor was selling bags of roasted peanuts at the corner of 116th and Broadway, and the moment I smelled their aroma, I became aware that I was ravenous with hunger. I purchased two bags, which Isabella and I devoured as we walked.

"You know, I think I met her once before. It would have been a little over a year ago." Isabella's comment was entirely unexpected.

"Her?" I asked her to clarify, though I assumed she meant Mary Bonham, the young woman we had interviewed.

But she surprised me further with her reply. "I mean Sarah Wingate."

"You've previously met Sarah?" I stopped walking and turned to face her. My disbelief was evident in my tone. "Why didn't you say so?"

"I only just remembered—and I'm not positive that I'm right. But I believe I met her last fall at a ladies' committee meeting held in support of Seth Low's mayoral reelection campaign. Many people, especially here at Columbia, were hoping we could persuade our former college president to run against Mc-Clellan again."

"What was Sarah like?" I asked.

"Intense." Isabella glanced up at me through thick black eyelashes. "By that, I mean she didn't engage in small talk. It was all highbrow political jargon. Sarah came to just one meeting. I got the impression," she said, smiling ruefully, "that we were not quite her style. And from what Mary has said today, I think I understand better; the ladies' committee approach would have been too conciliatory for her tastes."

I voiced my confusion as we began walking again. "I'm sorry. I've no idea what a ladies' committee meeting *is*, much less why it would not be to Sarah's taste."

She laughed at my bewilderment, her brown eyes flashing with humor. "Oh, dear—how discouraged our organizer Mrs.

Rodin would feel to hear that! You see, ladies' committees are essentially political groups made up of women who get together and plan how to influence the male vote! You must have heard their slogan," she gently chided, "'One Man, One Vote; One Woman, One Throat'? It's meant to remind women that their one opinion can influence the vote of many men."

"Never heard of it," I admitted candidly. "I take it this is part of the suffragist movement Sarah participated in?"

"Only loosely." She laughed again. "First, you must realize I am a relative newcomer to these efforts, which actually were started many years back by a group of women who were disgusted by the political graft and scandal that pervade the Tammany machine."

"Fair enough," I said, and waited for her to continue as we crossed the next block, sidestepping a man with a pushcart. As yesterday's election had once again illustrated, Tammany Hall was remarkably effective in putting specific candidates in office—and controlling them once there. They were largely motivated by their own interests, not those of their constituents.

Isabella went on. "I joined the group back in 1901, to support Seth Low's campaign for mayor as well as generalized reforms in education, tax, and sanitation. The larger goal, of course, was to break the hold of Tammany on local politicians that kept such reforms from actually happening. That's why the ladies' group supported Low again in '03, and Hearst this fall."

But Low hadn't won a second term, and even Hearst's money and popular support hadn't been enough to break the Tammany stranglehold. Reform came in cycles, while Tammany maintained consistent political control.

Still, I empathized with Isabella's sentiments. I had to, on some level, for I owed my profession itself to President Roosevelt's reform efforts ten years earlier. When he took over as police commissioner, he had mandated that rookie police officers be hired on the basis of admission tests, not political patronage. I had passed the test with ease, whereas I would have lacked both the money and connections necessary to gain admittance through patronage.

"General reform is a positive goal," I said mildly, "but it sounds as though Sarah was exclusively interested in gaining the vote."

"Yes. And reading between the lines of what Mary said, I suspect Sarah would have felt my group's methods were ineffectual. I'm not sure but that she wasn't right," Isabella said. "The ladies' committees want to effect change—but only within our current system, as it is currently set up. Someone like Sarah thinks our existing way of doing things is untenable. She didn't want to work within the status quo; she wanted to create a new social and political order."

Isabella tossed her empty bag into the garbage as we crossed to the other side of Broadway and turned around once more as we searched for Alistair.

"The group Sarah eventually joined has always been more radical in their goals as well as their methods: They believe women deserve their own vote, and they're not afraid to put on a demonstration or occupy a campus building to publicize their cause."

"What's your opinion?" I knew this question was in no way related to the case. I simply was finding myself more and more curious about Isabella Sinclair.

"As you might guess, I'm no radical," she said. "But I also like the practical appeal of women's club work to change our surroundings right now, not five or ten years down the road when suffragist activity may eventually gain women the vote. I joined a ladies' committee and supported Seth Low because I wanted cleaner streets *now*."

"And would you say his administration effected much improvement?" I couldn't resist teasing, for we had just passed one of the legacies of Seth Low's brief tenure in office two years ago: a whitewing, one of the city's street sweepers who wore a uniform that was completely white from hat to trousers. This man seemed to be moving at a snail's pace, picking up garbage by hand and dumping it into the large wooden barrel that he wheeled. He was ill equipped to combat the heavy litter and horse manure covering Broadway.

"Well, at least Low tried to do something when he was mayor," she said, laughing in response, "but there's still lots of room for improvement, wouldn't you say?" More soberly, she added, "In the end, no real change was accomplished. That's why I don't attend the meetings anymore. That, and the fact that Alistair's projects can demand so much of one's time."

"Yet I gather that working with Alistair is your choice," I hazarded. The question of why she was involved with Alistair's research was an intriguing one, representing something I did not yet understand.

"I needed something to do after Teddy died," she replied, and from her tone and the way her face closed down, I knew the reason was both complicated and deeply private.

It was the perfect opportunity to ask her more about the details of Alistair's work as well as her general opinion of the man. But those questions would have to wait, for as we approached the main entrance to Columbia at 116th Street, we became aware of Alistair's voice calling out to us from across Broadway.

"Ziele—over here!" I turned to see Alistair getting out of a new Ford Model B motorcar, which had just sputtered to a halt. As he approached the hand crank to restart it, he called out, "Come on, get in—I've arranged our meeting downtown."

I looked toward Isabella, but she smiled and motioned me to go along. "If you've no objection, I could go ahead and speak with Sarah's classmates." She gestured toward the crumpled list of names that poked out of my left pocket.

"I won't go alone," she promised. "I will get Horace to help me."

I finally agreed, handing her the paper. "You might speak with Dean Arnold, as well, to find out more about Sarah's work in his office."

Then, before I knew it, I found myself a passenger in Alistair's Ford, filling him in on all we had learned.

"The burglary is an odd coincidence, to be sure," Alistair said in response. "But even putting what we know about Michael Fromley aside, I don't see a vagrant housebreaker as the sort of murderer who killed Sarah Wingate. I wouldn't waste precious time on that lead while Fromley is still at large."

Of course he was right, but I would check into the incident nonetheless. Certainly Michael Fromley was the priority, given what Alistair knew about him. But I couldn't bring myself to ignore a decent lead, however unpromising it seemed at the moment.

We continued to talk of such matters as we journeyed downtown, passing horse carts and pedestrians at the speed of about seventeen miles per hour. It was testament to how focused my mind was upon the case at hand that I did not take note of the fact, until much later, that this was my first ride ever in an automobile.

CHAPTER 8

The Wallingfords were not industrial magnates like the Schermer-horns and Rhinelanders, and their financial success had been far less spectacular. But still they had amassed significant wealth, as their family home on East Sixty-seventh Street just off Fifth Avenue in the increasingly exclusive Upper East Side neighbor-hood made clear.

Clyde Wallingford was what one would call a true eccen-tric. That I determined within five minutes of meeting him in his second-floor library. Though it was well into the afternoon, he still wore a morning dressing gown, and he chomped on a cigar for the duration of our interview. Though not yet forty, he seemed much older than his years: His thinning hair was fully gray, and his pink puffy skin was creased and wrinkled around his brow. What was most off-putting, however, was his decidedly abrupt manner.

"So what's this about Michael gone missing?" he demanded of Alistair. "Thought you were going to be responsible for him, and take all necessary measures to ensure we had no more trouble."

"Ah, yes." Alistair was caught off guard for a brief moment. But he recovered his composure and managed to summarize the story of Michael's disappearance—in addition to our suspicions of Michael's involvement in the murder of Sarah Wingate—before Wallingford's apoplectic anger interfered. He alternated between pounding his fist on his massive wood and leather desk and berating Alistair for abrogating his duty to Fromley and, more particularly, the Wallingford family. I suspected that Alistair was not normally the type to take such treatment without objection. But since we needed Wallingford's help, I predicted Alistair would not risk further alienating him. When Wallingford's tirade was spent, Alistair continued talking politely, as though nothing had happened.

"When was your last contact with Michael?"

Clyde frowned, grinding the cigar into the heavy crystal ashtray. "Must have been about a month ago. He stopped by the house with his usual request for money. Of course he disappeared as soon as I gave it to him."

"Which was exactly what you wanted," Alistair said. This reminder prompted Clyde to snort in response.

"How much did you give him?" I asked.

He jerked his head up in annoyance. "Why does it matter? That's my private business."

"I am conducting a police investigation into a murder," I replied evenly, refusing to be bullied. "That means where any suspect is concerned, there's no such thing as private business."

He grew red in the face and glowered at me. I thought at first he would refuse to answer, or reply with another rude retort, but he reconsidered and answered, though his tone was gruff. "I gave him $500. It was a ridiculous amount, of course — but I hoped it would be enough to keep him away for a few months."

"So you had no indication that anything might be wrong? No signs of any sudden changes in Michael's mood?"

"Mood?" Clyde scoffed. "When has Michael's mood ever been anything but surly? You know I was never concerned about his moods. It was his actions that caused trouble. He needed discipline to keep from acting out."

"It was never as simple as that," Alistair began wearily, but Clyde cut him off.

"Yeah, yeah, spare me your ideas about—what do you call it?—'distorted thinking.' Nothing but poppycock. The point is, you need to find Michael, and with as little fanfare as possible. Don't want to see our family name dragged through the papers."

"Can you tell us where Michael was living?" Alistair asked. "I checked with the landlady at the last address I had for him; apparently he left there six months ago."

Clyde merely chortled. "Sounds like you haven't been keeping on top of the boy as you promised. Last I heard, he had rented a room somewhere in the west Forties. Maybe Lizzie will know. She always had a soft spot for the boy. Though I can't imagine why."

He cleared his throat and got up, ambling toward the door.

"Well, I believe our business is done, and I trust you'll take care of this situation quickly and discreetly. I summoned Lizzie over here after you telephoned because I thought, given her relationship with Michael, she would have more information to give you than I do. I'll send her in."

And without a word more, he shuffled out of the room and we did not see him again, although we almost immediately heard him berating someone with respect to a household task left undone. Apparently it was the man's nature to be disagreeable toward everyone he encountered. As Alistair later explained, Clyde Wallingford was an egalitarian in one respect: He was rude to everyone alike.

Clyde's aunt, Lizzie Dunn, was exactly as Alistair had described her earlier this morning: plain and mousy in both appearance and demeanor. It was easy to see why Clyde had prevailed upon her to take charge of a troublesome young boy; she was so excessively amiable she appeared unable to refuse any request.

"Miss Dunn?" Alistair stood politely and made the introductions as she came across the length of the room toward us; we had moved from the area near Clyde's desk to a sitting area by the fireplace. As I took her hand to greet her, I noticed it was icy cold, despite the general warmth that pervaded the house. She took the seat nearest the fire, sitting on its very edge.

"Please, can you tell me what's happened with Michael?" she asked nervously. "I know something awful has happened, or Clyde would never have asked me to come here. But he's told me nothing."

I watched her face blanch as Alistair explained what we

knew about Fromley's disappearance and suspected role in a murder. It seemed the news would overwhelm the woman, and I prepared to summon help in the event she fainted. She recovered, but as I observed their exchange, I decided Alistair's initial assessment had been remarkably precise: Lizzie Dunn meant well, but if Michael Fromley had anything of his half brother Clyde's domineering personality, she could never have stood up to it.

"No," she was saying, "the last time I saw Michael was in early October for his birthday. I'd put together a little birthday dinner for him, and he humored me by coming by to eat it." She smiled wanly. "You know, he doesn't come around the way he used to when he was a young boy. I suppose that's natural now he's grown-up."

It was incongruous to hear this woman talk about Michael Fromley as a favored nephew—and yet, I had seen this phenomenon before, where a mother or grandmother described men I knew to be depraved criminals in the most endearing of terms. I supposed it was because they clung to loving memories of what the child had been—even when the man became something far different. And, as Alistair explained later, Fromley was capable of presenting a charming demeanor when it suited his purposes. Apparently he was always pleasant with his aunt Lizzie, for it led her to indulge him with money and gifts. It was also, as I would soon learn, the manner he initially employed with the women he terrorized.

To Lizzie Dunn, Alistair merely said, "We both know Michael has had his share of problems. Was he in any particular trouble when you saw him last?"

"Well," she admitted, "he owed people money. I gave him

what I could, but it didn't cover even half his debts, so he probably went to Clyde for the rest."

"I see." Alistair retained an easy, nonjudgmental tone. "Did you talk about anything else?"

"He mentioned his new job at the docks, which he appeared to enjoy, though he wished it paid better. We also talked about a trip he was hoping to take to New Orleans in February for Mardis Gras."

I looked at Alistair with raised eyebrows.

He shook his head almost imperceptibly in reply. He later reminded me that Fromley had merely applied for the job on Fulton Street; he hadn't actually been hired. So Fromley had lied to his aunt, perhaps wanting her to think well of him.

I asked, "Is there anything you can tell us about his routines? The friends he socialized with? The places he frequented?"

Her response was automatic. "He loved all kinds of entertainment. You might check some of the dance halls down in the Bowery. I don't know the names, but I know that's where he went most weekends. But I can't help you with regard to his friends; he never brought them to the house, or even mentioned anyone in particular."

"So I take it you never saw this person?" I showed her the picture of Sarah Wingate.

"No," she replied, after taking a dutiful look at the photograph. "As I said, he never brought any friends around."

"When did he move out of your home?"

"After the incident," she said, and from her gesture toward Alistair, I knew she was being euphemistic about the assault on Catherine Smedley that had first brought Michael Fromley to Alistair. "I wanted him to stay," she added sadly, "but Clyde insisted. Said he was too dangerous. After he stopped staying full-time at your research center, I still let him stay the occasional night, whenever he asked, but by and large I think he moved from one rooming house to another. He probably stayed at nicer ones or cheaper ones depending upon how much he'd won or lost at gambling that week."

"Do you have the address where he is living now?" I asked.

Lizzie shook her head sadly. "No. Michael never stayed in one place for very long before he wore out his welcome, usually by not paying the rent. I helped him when I could, but . . ." She looked at us helplessly.

It lasted only a moment, but in that look, I saw a flash of fear. And I recognized the truth: Despite all outward appearances of a doting aunt, she was afraid of him.

After we finished our conversation with Miss Dunn, Alistair and I lingered on the sidewalk just outside.

"I suggest we visit your former precinct on the Lower East Side," Alistair said. "Michael's taste ran consistently to dance halls and gambling houses. Maybe someone there has seen him recently. Do you know the most likely ones to visit?"

I was familiar with them. To be honest, I knew them all too well. My own father had been a habitual gambler, for as long as I could remember. It had kept our family in debt my entire childhood—in fact, until one night when I was nineteen years old, a sophomore at Columbia, and he finally succeeded in gambling away our life's savings and running off with another woman. His failings had devastated my mother and sister and radically altered my own future. With my family looking to me for financial support, my college days had ended.

I did not share any of this with Alistair at the time—although

I soon learned he knew it already. I was the man with whom he was prepared to entrust his larger secret, if it came to that. And so he had learned everything he could about my life history, even before he had shown up in my office this very morning.

CHAPTER 9

Despite some trepidation about parking his new Ford Model B in a tough neighborhood, Alistair drove us downtown. The Bowery in lower Manhattan could be a rough area, especially inside the entertainment halls and saloons of the sort we planned to visit. During the last reform administration, Mayor Seth Low had closed the saloons in hopes of improving the neighborhood. But as soon as the Tammany-endorsed McClellan administration claimed office, they reopened, and the Bowery filled once more with opportunists anxious to relieve the too drunk and the too naïve of their wallets and more. To be fair, one could find several more or less respectable saloons in the Bowery. But a man doing a job like mine was less familiar with them.

Our first stop this evening was the Fortune Club on Pell

Street, where the Bowery adjoined Chinatown. I had chosen it because I knew the manager—assuming he still worked there. When we entered, a young man was earnestly straining to master the high tenor of "In the Shade of the Old Apple Tree." Although the effect was slightly ludicrous, I made no sign that I thought so. I knew Nick Scarpetta was trying to emulate Mike Saulter's Pelham Club and John Kenny's Chatham Club, where singing waiters were the latest innovation in entertainment. Big Nick hoped one of his waiters would manage to attract as devoted a following as a young singer named Baline had done at Saulter's. But I had trouble thinking of the place as anything other than a gambling joint—which, admittedly, was all it ever pretended to be. Unlike surrounding saloons where additional vices like prostitution and opium could be found in back rooms and on upper floors, Nick Scarpetta stuck with what he knew best: cards.

"Does Nicky still manage the place?" I caught the ear of the first waiter who came by. The fellow nodded and gestured toward the back room, where a raucous poker game was in progress.

Alistair, completely out of his element, simply followed as I made my way to a black door at the far left of the room. Inside, Nicky Scarpetta was seated at a large table, cigar in mouth, a pile of chips stacked high to his left. Clearly, he was having a good night.

He looked up and recognized me instantly. "Well, I'll be damned, if it isn't Simon Ziele. How're things going, old boy?" He got up and lumbered over to clap me on the back, careful to avoid my weak right arm. "Haven't seen you in a dog's age. What brings you back to the neighborhood? You here on official business, or just for old time's sake?"

There was a searching concern in his drooped, baggy eyes

that he would never overtly acknowledge. I had not spoken with him personally since my loss, but of course he would have heard about the deaths—so close together—of both my mother and Hannah.

"Good to see you, Nicky," I said warmly. He was a large man with a gruff demeanor, but it obscured a kind heart. Nicky always took good care of his friends, and I was lucky to count myself among them. I'd known him for as long as I could remember. Though he frequented the same gambling circles as my father, he possessed two qualities my father had forever lacked: a talent for cards and a sense of his own limitations. On countless occasions, he had visited my mother after a night at the tables with my father and pressed an envelope into her hand with a few brusque words. Waving away her tearful thanks, he always left muttering, "A man with young children's got no business betting two weeks' salary on a pair of aces."

Still, I never forgot for a moment that Nicky had another side—one more commonly reserved for those who crossed him—that was dangerous and unforgiving.

"I'm here on business," I answered him, "but not department business. I'm not with the precinct here anymore. Instead, I'm investigating a murder that happened north of the city; this is Alistair Sinclair, who is assisting in the investigation." I nodded toward Alistair, whom Nicky acknowledged with a grunt.

"Hey—Moe," Nicky called to a man lurking at the back of the room by the liquor cabinet. "Fill in for me and finish the game, will ya?"

"Sure, Nick," the man said, and took the vacant place at the table.

Meanwhile, Nicky led us to his office, where we could talk in private.

"So what do you need to know?" he asked, as he lowered his large frame into an oversized leather chair and offered us his cigar box. We declined, and settled ourselves into the two chairs opposite him. Alistair pulled out his photograph of Michael Fromley.

"We're wondering," he asked, "if you've ever seen this man?"

Nicky grabbed the photograph and lifted it to the light, turning it first one way and then another, studying it intently. "What's his name?"

"Michael Fromley," I responded.

"I've seen him around," Nicky said. "He's played the back room, but not in a long time. Maybe six, nine months ago? Couldn't hold his drink, and started trouble at the table—accused one of my guys of stacking the deck. Never let him in the game again after that. And I spread the word."

That meant Nicky had blackballed Michael Fromley among the Bowery's other gambling hells, as they were called. With good reason, I might add, for when caught in the game, many men were tempted to sell their very soul to the devil. But while New York was filled with places catering to poker, stuss, or faro, it was far more expensive to get in a game anywhere outside the Bowery.

Nicky took a final draw from his cigar before grinding its stub into an ashtray. "Still, you'd see him come in on occasion to the bar, usually with some dame who fancied herself an actress. What d'ya want him for?"

"He's the main suspect in our murder case," I said. "We're trying to find him for questioning, but it's tough going—he disappeared a good two, three weeks back. Think anyone here would have seen him?"

Nicky got up and went over to open the door; his steps were

heavy on the worn wooden plank floor, causing it to creak loudly. His voice thundered out, "Hey, can someone tell Izzy I need him in here?"

No one ever kept Nicky waiting, so almost before he was seated again, a heavyset middle-aged man with large eyes and drooping jowls had joined us. From the white towel hanging from his waist, I assumed he was one of the bartenders at the Fortune Club.

"What can I do you for, boss?" he asked, his voice deep, soft, and accented in the unique style of a native New Yorker.

"You seen this guy in here lately?" Nicky thrust the photograph of Fromley into the bartender's hands. "A friend of mine needs to know."

It was an implicit authorization to talk. Otherwise, I had no doubt Izzy would have passed the photograph back to us with a flat denial and opaque expression.

Izzy studied the photograph a full minute before handing it back. "Yeah, he was in here about two weeks ago. It was a Saturday night. He came in with one of those actress types. You know, I think it was Clara Murphy."

Nicky grunted. "You don't say."

"She's a regular?" I asked.

"Yeah," Izzy said. "Fancies herself a Broadway chorus girl, but probably generates her rent doing private shows."

Izzy's euphemism implied Clara Murphy was a prostitute rather than an actress—although there were some, I knew, who would maintain there was little difference between the two in the first place.

"Did either of them talk with you?" I asked. In a neighborhood such as this, a bartender like Izzy was often a confidant to customers, especially the regulars.

Izzy shuffled his weight from one foot to another, and replied slowly, "Well, I talked with Clara when her fellow left her alone for a minute. She asked me if I knew whether the rumors were true about him."

"The rumors?" I shook my head. I'd heard any number of unsavory facts about Michael Fromley, but it was unclear which of them Izzy had in mind. From the look on his face, Alistair was also unsure.

"Yeah," Izzy said, "lots of rumors fly around about that guy. He always has a wad of cash and can show 'em a good time, so the ladies don't want to believe the rumors, see? I always tell 'em to stay away, that he is bad news. But mostly they listen to the money, not to me."

"So what did you tell Clara when she asked?"

"I said steer clear and find yourself another fellow—that this one'd got a reputation for getting rough with the ladies." He cleared his throat and continued in an even quieter voice. "Some people said he roughed 'em up real bad, using . . . well, stuff that ain't fit for polite conversation." He eyed Alistair suspiciously as if uncertain how much detail to give. When he spoke again, he merely said, "She left the bar with him not long after that, so I'm guessing she did like most of 'em and listened to the money."

"Have you seen her since?"

"Naw, she ain't come in since."

"And no news about Fromley?"

He just shook his head.

"Do you happen to know where Clara lives?"

"Think Clara's got a place up on West Twenty-eighth Street. It's a building where a lot of singers and actresses live, a block over from Tin Pan Alley proper. You might check there."

It was more substantive information than we'd gotten from our last couple of interviews, and with only a few more inquiries, we found the specific address of her flat. I thanked Nicky for helping us out. "Anytime," he had said, and his gravel-toned voice managed to sound soft as he added, "Your mother was a fine woman, Ziele. A damn fine woman." And with another clap on my shoulder, he returned to his game.

Alistair was some moments ahead of me leaving the Fortune Club. When I caught up with him, he was strangely preoccupied, staring at a nondescript building across the street.

"Everything okay?" I asked, wondering if anything had happened to the Ford, since he was not cranking his engine as expected.

"Just fine." He smiled reassuringly and walked toward the front engine crank. "I thought I saw—" But he stopped himself. "Never mind. I'm sure I'm mistaken."

But as the engine revved to a start, I looked over to that nondescript building. I caught a glimpse of a tall man who glanced around furtively before entering. Maybe it was detective's intuition—or mere idle curiosity—but I kept watching as an array of gambling toughs cycled in and out of the building.

Alistair climbed up into the driver's seat, and I called him on it.

"It's not a gambling den itself," I said, pointing. "But it's related to the business. It may be a place where owners keep and manage their money. Or where a bookie or a loan shark operates. But it's not a legitimate business. Are you sure"—I eyed him carefully—"that you didn't see Fromley entering?"

"I'm sure," he said, though a troubled look crossed his face.

I waited, making clear I expected him to say more.

"I was mistaken," he said. "A man I saw going in resembled Horace enough to make me look twice."

"Your research assistant?" My tone was skeptical. I believed I had just seen the same man as Alistair, and he in no way resembled Horace.

Alistair nodded. "A trick of the mind inspired by our visit to the Fortune Club, I'm sure—and because Horace developed a slight gambling problem this past year. I've had to loan him money on occasion. But Horace's weakness is for low-stakes card games at houses farther uptown that cater to students." He was firm as he added, "Not a place like this."

I accepted him at his word and knew he was right. If a man like Horace were to gamble, it was unlikely to be here. And if he needed money to pay some debts, obviously Alistair was willing to provide. But I resolved to speak with Alistair about it later, because he was wrong on one count: There is no such thing as a *slight* gambling problem. That lesson was one my own father had taught me well. Time and again I had seen him break down in tears, promising my mother he would never gamble another cent. But he never kept his promises. And he never won a single game. It had been a blessing when he finally left.

We made our way back uptown to Clara Murphy's building. We had no trouble locating Clara's flat on the fourth floor of a building that obviously catered to musical and theatrical types—not surprising, for its location on Twenty-eighth Street between Sixth and Seventh Avenues was by the heart of the music-publishing district known as Tin Pan Alley. When we knocked on her door, however, there was no answer. We asked several people in the lobby, and they not only recognized Michael Fromley's picture, but they had also seen Clara often in his company. What was troubling, however, was that no one could recall seeing Clara herself within the past week or two.

We were stalemated once again.

Some fifteen minutes later, after Alistair whisked us twelve blocks south, we found ourselves at Luchow's, overlooking Fourteenth Street from a small table by the window. I had objected, but Alistair insisted. "You've got to eat something, old boy," he had said.

"What are you drinking?" he asked.

I glanced toward the bar, where the beer selection was sketched out on a long chalkboard hung underneath an impressive collection of beer steins. The choices were overwhelming. "Whatever you recommend," I said absently as I perused a menu of sauerbraten and wild game.

The strains of a Strauss string quartet sounded over the general din of restaurant noise. The musicians performed in the back of the restaurant, and we could not see them from our vantage point. Apparently the practice of offering live music to diners had caught on, even this far north of the Bowery. I was not a fan of it at the Fortune Club, but here the classical tones calmed my frayed nerves

"Prosit!" Alistair raised his glass after the waiter brought two oversized steins of pale ale to our table.

I reluctantly raised mine to join his, although I was not in the mood for toasting with Fromley on the loose.

"Say," Alistair said, looking at me reflectively as his fingers traced the green and brown painted coat of arms on his stein. "Ziele is a German name, isn't it?"

"Originally it was German, I suppose. I've been told the spelling has been corrupted over time." I deliberately sidestepped the intent of his question.

"But you are German? Obviously your family settled in the Lower East Side, which I know to be heavily German." Alistair's curiosity was not easily deflected.

"My family was German, and Russian, and even French Canadian. But I am American," I said emphatically. On no account did I want Alistair delving into my own past; he had already learned more at the Fortune Club than I would have liked.

"You don't quite trust me, do you, Ziele?" Alistair said with a hint of amusement. "No, no." He waved off my feeble protests. "You are trying to be polite. I can tell that you don't. And I'm not offended. I suppose it is natural in a detective—a good detective, anyway—to develop a healthy sense of skepticism."

I was saved from inventing a response by the arrival of our food. Our waiter placed a steaming plate of Wiener schnitzel in front of Alistair. I had chosen the sauerbraten, which, despite my initial reservations, looked delicious.

I changed the topic some minutes later, after giving Alistair a chance to begin enjoying his meal. "Where do you suggest we go from here, Alistair?" I asked. "We have spoken with Michael Fromley's family; they have no idea where he is. He's been seen in the Bowery, but no one there can offer a specific address, either. But someone must know something. The man lives somewhere, he eats someplace, he buys coffee and a morning paper—" I stopped myself as I felt my frustration building.

"I'm at a loss, just like you, Ziele," he said. "I'm not hiding anything."

"But he was central to your research," I said. "I would think during your time with him, you would have learned *everything* about him: who his friends were; what he ate for breakfast; what time he went to bed."

"No, Ziele. You're thinking like a detective, not like a criminologist," he explained. "My goal was to learn everything about how he *thought* and how he made decisions about his *behavior.*" Alistair emphasized those words, enunciating them too clearly. "He had no friends to speak of, and I could not have cared less about his daily habits."

Alistair regarded me for a moment as though we were speaking two different languages—and perhaps we were. "But I am trying to think of these things now, in order to help you," he offered lamely.

"I need you to think harder," I said. "And to review your files, this time to search for any reference to the minutiae of Fromley's life. You may have noted something that, at the time, was unimportant to your research but could now prove important as a means of locating him."

"All right," Alistair agreed, seeming somewhat surprised. "We can return to the research center after dinner and I will search. But first, old boy, you've got to try their apple strudel. It's exquisite, especially paired with their Rheinlander coffee or perhaps a Brandy Alexander."

I resigned myself to following this suggestion, for clearly Alistair did not share my own sense of urgency about the case. I could have argued with him, but I had the sense that he would be more helpful in our search if he first satisfied his discriminating palate.

CHAPTER 10

With the day nearly ended and my energy completely sapped, only sheer determination kept me alert as we headed back uptown. We continued to work at Alistair's offices until near ten o'clock, comparing notes and discussing our options. It had been a strenuous day. I always found interviews to be exhausting—and frustrating—though the initial phase of any investigation was necessarily spent gathering and evaluating information. The best detectives did so with amazing efficiency; they separated solid leads from weak premises and arrived at what appeared to be effortless conclusions.

I had learned a great deal about Sarah Wingate, enough that I could now imagine what she must have been like. And I continued to learn more about her presumed killer, Michael

Fromley. But I had no conclusions to show for it. I had only a manhunt in progress, marked at either end by two missing women: Stella Gibson, who may have witnessed a murder, and Clara Murphy, who was last seen with Michael Fromley.

We were working in the meeting room with the large table, the better to spread out our notes.

"Here's July 1905," Horace said, struggling under the weight of seven thick folders as he entered the room.

"Thank you, Horace," Alistair said.

"Professor, it's getting late." Horace leaned heavily against the table. He had been working with us all evening, bringing us file after file from Alistair's copious case notes.

"Of course. Why don't you go on home? You've been a terrific help, but we've everything we need. We won't be much longer ourselves." Alistair spoke absentmindedly, for he was already skimming through the first folder Horace had brought.

Horace nodded in relief. "Good night, Professor. Detective." He shuffled out of the room, and even without the weight of the files, I noticed that he seemed drained of energy. His head injury had swollen in size and now had a particularly nasty appearance.

Once I was certain he was gone, I mentioned it to Alistair. "I don't recall Horace's injury looking so severe yesterday."

"What?" Alistair looked at me in confusion for a moment; then my question registered. "Oh, that. Yes, it happened during his altercation at the polls yesterday, but it's giving him more trouble today. Horace has been very active in the Hearst campaign for the past month. Rough day for supporters yesterday all around, wasn't it? Beat up at the polls, literally and figuratively. I hear Hearst is taking charges of voter fraud and intimidation to the courts. It'll be interesting to see what they do,

IN THE SHADOW OF GOTHAM

although however dirty the vote, I can't imagine them overturning the reelection of a sitting mayor." And his focus turned once again to his case notes. His interest in the mayor's race was only a passing one. I would have found it more interesting myself, were I not consumed by the hunt for Sarah's killer.

Several minutes later, we were interrupted by a knocking noise downstairs. Alistair went to the door and called out into the hallway. "Horace, are you still here?"

We heard more knocking and shuffling sounds.

"I said, is anyone there?" Alistair asked, much louder this time.

The answer came from a man on the stairs. "Your message said you would be working here late tonight. So I came." His voice—a rich low voice with a thick Scottish burr—grew louder as he came closer. "Though, until I saw your lights burning strong, I had my doubts I would still find you here."

Alistair stepped back to admit a burly man with thick gray hair and beard, and large, mournful eyes. He was an older man, but his voice and mannerisms were energetic. I sensed that his normal personality was lively, even jocular, though his mood tonight was somber. And I recognized him immediately from his picture. Standing before us was Professor Angus MacDonald.

After we took his gray and brown tweed coat and invited him to sit, he explained that he had not received my message until well after dinnertime, but had determined to take the train into the city immediately on the chance we would be here as promised. He had learned of Sarah's death almost immediately from a mathematics colleague, but my telephone message had been a surprise. Apparently he had—overoptimistically in my view—believed his relationship with Sarah to be entirely secret.

But then again, I knew better than most how quickly secrets vanished once a murder investigation began.

I first asked the professor to confirm for us the details of his relationship with Sarah: how he had met her, and how long he had known her.

"Aye, a bright lass she was," he said, "I'd never met the like of her, nor will I again. A man at my age is not often so lucky."

"At what point did your relationship evolve into something more than a professional association?" I asked, and I felt as though I were prying, even though it was my job to do so.

He shook his head sadly. "She was young enough to be my daughter, and don't I know it full well. But what a mind! The lass was brilliant, and the conversations we had utterly changed the way I approached my work. She was always coming up with new problems and methods for solving them. My last article— why, I couldn't have written it without her." He looked at us mournfully. "I know it sounds as though I'm talking of my work, but what I'm really saying to you is—that she became necessary to me. To be with her was as simple and natural as breathing. Our habits of mind were so at home with one another, it was as though our age difference were nothing."

"But the academic world wouldn't have seen it that way," I gently reminded him. "Is that why you were so secretive?"

"Bunch of benighted hypocrites," he said, his blue eyes glistening with restrained tears. "We kept our relationship secret at my insistence. If she wanted to make a reputation in her own right, she needed to do so before we married. The lass had enough problems being taken seriously; people would have said I'd given her my research and ideas. Absolutely preposterous. It was just a matter of time before she'd have outshone me."

"And this did not bother you?" I asked. Now that I'd met

him, I truly could not envision the Scottish professor having killed Sarah Wingate. But the question of motivation had to be asked.

"Bah," he said. "I'm fifty-five and will turn fifty-six come January." Drawing himself up proudly, he continued. "I am a professor emeritus at what is arguably the preeminent department of mathematics in the world. I've published more books and articles than I can keep count of." He leaned forward. "What I'm saying to you is that my competitive days of needing to be the best and the brightest, the youngest man ever put up for tenure, are over. What I want . . ." He paused a moment and rephrased himself. "What I *wanted* was to be happy. Sarah made me happy. And seeing her do well made me proud." His last comment was emphatic.

"What about the other rivalries that must have confronted Sarah?" I asked. "Was there anyone—within the mathematics field or otherwise—who struck you as having particular jealousy or animosity toward her?"

But his answer was similar to what we had heard before. There were many who resented her success and challenged her at every turn. But in his view, he recalled no resentment so remarkable as to lend a suspicion of murder.

I was asking all the conventional questions, but given that the vicious circumstances of her murder pointed to Michael Fromley, my mind kept returning to whether Sarah had ever crossed paths with him. Impulsively, I pulled the photograph out of my wallet and handed it to Angus. "Have you ever seen this man?"

He shook his head. "Never. Why? Did he know Sarah?"

"That's what we're trying to figure out," I said, and promptly changed the subject. "How often did you see Sarah?"

"Usually twice a month," he replied. "She came to me; it was easier, as there was nothing to explain to her family, and my mother, who lives with me, served as a chaperone." His Scottish burr was evident with each *r* he pronounced.

"Why didn't she tell her family?" Alistair asked. "We understand why you would keep it from your colleagues, but obviously your own family knew. Why not Sarah's?"

"Further disapproval would be my guess," he said. "In their view, it was bad enough she pursued graduate work at all. It would have been even worse to learn that while doing so, she became involved with me. You see, I'm an old man with no social standing. And they wanted her to marry a young man from a well-connected family. They had money, to be sure. But they didn't have enough of the right friends or connections, as they saw it. Of course," he added, "Sarah was interested in none of that."

"Is there anything else we should discuss?" Alistair asked, and while the question ostensibly was for Angus, I suspected Alistair had implicitly directed it toward me. After Angus replied no, I answered as well.

"I keep trying to think of why and how Michael Fromley came to target Sarah. I simply cannot see it as a random whim. The murder was well planned and smoothly executed using knowledge of the Wingate family's habits and routines, and it occurred far from her home here in the city. I am convinced Fromley must have had some connection with her, however tangential."

"What did you say?" Angus asked, the moment he registered what I had said.

We merely looked at him in surprise, so he reiterated his question. "What was that name you just mentioned? Michael Fro . . . what?"

"Michael Fromley," Alistair replied, puzzled. "Do you know the name?"

"I've heard it," Angus said, and he seemed newly distressed. "I think . . . I can't be positive, mind you . . . but I believe it's a name she mentioned during my last conversation with her."

"In what context?" I asked, my mind racing.

"His name surfaced in conversation about a problem the lass was having, relevant to her work at the dean's office." His thick brow furrowed. "I can't quite recall—but she mentioned the name. I'm sure of it."

I looked to Alistair. "The dean's office? Could her position there have in any way brought her into contact with your research project?"

We knew that Sarah worked two afternoons a week for the graduate dean of arts and sciences in a clerical role. In light of Sarah's political activities and the way her mathematical genius had generated rivalries, her work for Dean Arnold had seemed to be the least controversial aspect of her life. Ostensibly she worked for extra money, but according to Angus, she had also done it to gain some administrative experience. She was worried she would be barred from teaching positions after obtaining her degree, as most women were.

"But I can't imagine how any administrative work for the dean would connect her to Fromley," Alistair said. "At our research center, we have absolutely no dealings with the dean's office, other than the usual requests for grants and funding throughout the year. While you might find Fromley's name in the text of a funding request, to my knowledge, he has never been to the dean's office or become acquainted with anyone there."

It made no sense, but then so little did.

After catching my train home to Dobson, I reviewed the paperwork in the case file until the wee hours of the morning, working through my exhaustion. I hoped Alistair was doing the same; he had promised me he would thoroughly review the Fromley files that night in search of any mundane references to Fromley's habits. I needed to know more about his lifestyle—for though he had vanished into the depths of the city, even someone like him couldn't disappear forever.

The missing women were our best hope, I decided. Tomorrow I would focus my efforts toward locating Stella Gibson and Clara Murphy—both of whom apparently had seen Fromley in the hours before their disappearance. Then I collapsed into a heavy, dreamless sleep that lasted until a pounding on the door and Joe's voice calling my name ushered in the next morning.

Thursday, November 9, 1905

CHAPTER 11

The sharp rapping at my door grew louder, almost matching the intensity of the pounding in my head.

"Late night?" Joe observed with raised eyebrows, after I managed to stagger to the door and let him in.

"Guess you could say that," I acknowledged uncomfortably. My voice, I knew, sounded raspy and tired. Odd how my body reacted to the combination of stress and sleep deprivation much in the same way it would a thoroughgoing hangover. I observed Joe sniffing my clothes, trying to be discreet but failing entirely, as he tried to ascertain any signs of a night spent drinking. Had he found them, I had little doubt but that he would have attempted to convince the mayor I was guilty of some dereliction of duty. I wondered if he would ever give up seeking excuses to get rid of me.

"Coffee?" I offered, heading toward my small kitchen to perform what was invariably my first task of the morning. The strong aroma of the fresh beans invigorated me as I turned my hand-crank grinder. Joe accepted, and I spooned the ground coffee into the filter of my metal press pot. After adding boiling water, I retreated to my bedroom to get ready for the day while the coffee and water steeped. Meanwhile, Joe sat on the small gray sofa in my sitting area, listening carefully as I shared the details of the previous day with Alistair.

Though he listened completely—and remarkably for Joe, without judgment—I anticipated his skeptical response. "That's quite a theory your new friend has expounded. I admit there's a logical reason to further investigate the Fromley boy, but I don't like all this twaddle about daydreams and fantasies. I'd feel more comfortable if there were even a shred of hard evidence to connect Fromley with the Wingate girl." And with that simple desire he succinctly voiced my own doubts.

"I know," I said. "But from the people we spoke with yesterday, it's clear Michael Fromley is both violent and deeply troubled. When you put that together with the remarkable coincidences that Alistair claims, then the implications are unsettling. Besides," I reminded him, "we have no evidence pointing to a different suspect."

"Well, there was some progress here yesterday," Joe said. "We got the results from those fingerprints you took at the Wingate home. They were viable prints that did *not* match those of anyone within the Wingate household."

I looked at him sharply; since Joe was so adamantly opposed to fingerprinting, I had expected to have to call the laboratory myself to learn the results.

"If I can locate a personal item we know to be Fromley's," I said, "then it will show whether the prints are a match." It would be a relief to have a solid evidentiary link between Fromley and this murder.

"Also, I spoke again with Miss Abigail. She believes the money you found under Sarah's mattress belongs to Mrs. Wingate."

"But she's not sure?"

Joe sighed. "Apparently Mrs. Wingate is in the habit of hiding money all over the house, then forgetting all about it. Miss Abigail finds money everywhere—in clothes pockets, in between the pages of books, even underneath cups in the china cabinet. There's no reason to believe the money under the mattress is any different."

No reason, except that a young woman had been brutally murdered within four feet of it. As such, it was evidence I did not want to discount—at least not yet.

Joe was primarily worried, however, on a different count: When he had left the Wingate residence late yesterday, their housemaid Stella remained missing. "The girl probably learned of the murder, got spooked, and ran away to be with friends or family," he said. "But Miss Abigail insists something is seriously wrong."

"It's possible Stella witnessed the murder itself," I said.

"Sure," Joe said. "But then why didn't she say anything to the Wingates about it? She just disappeared."

I shrugged. "People who have witnessed terrible things sometimes behave completely out of character."

I did not mention that I, too, urgently wished to find Stella. But with that goal in mind, we would speak with Mrs. Virginia Wingate first thing this morning.

Virginia Wingate sat ramrod straight on a wooden chair, her niece hovering protectively in the rocker next to her.

Abigail Wingate had opposed this interview; worried as she was about Stella's disappearance, she was even more concerned about her aunt's fragile mental state.

"You don't understand," she had whispered into the telephone when I rang to let her know we would be coming. "She is coping with Sarah's death by simply *refusing* to acknowledge it. She pretends Sarah is still alive, certain to return again to visit in just a few weeks. Yet she won't go upstairs, even for bed, which tells me she knows perfectly well what happened up there— though she won't admit it. She sleeps nights in the parlor room, and spends all day on the front porch, despite the cold." She sighed, plainly vexed.

"But it can't last," I said. "Plans will be made for a funeral—"

She cut me off. "In Boston—and my aunt will not go."

She had eventually submitted to the necessity of our talking with her aunt, and in return I had promised—to the extent it was possible—that I would not overtly reference Sarah's murder.

"And how will you explain our being there to question her?" I had asked, dubious as to how Abigail's odd request could be accommodated.

"I won't need to," she assured me. "If it occurs to Aunt Virginia to wonder why, then she will make up the reason herself. You'll see. Her mind is an absolute marvel of invention these days."

Thus forewarned, we all gathered on the front porch where

we exchanged a few awkward pleasantries and confirmed that there had been no word from Stella. It was Mrs. Wingate who captivated my attention as we talked. I had remembered her hair to be gray, but in the morning sunlight, it glistened pure silver. The effect was heightened by her skin, which was so pale as to be almost translucent. She was not unlike a piece of fine china: beautiful, fragile, and treated carefully in the hope she would not break.

"Mrs. Wingate, I understand you are quite close with your niece Sarah. She visits you often?" I was careful to phrase the question in the present tense, in deference to Abigail's request.

"Oh, yes." Mrs. Wingate nodded primly. "Sarah is a devoted niece. She never misses a birthday or holiday. And she often visits to take advantage of the peace and quiet available here, as she did this past weekend."

I watched her intently, observing her eyes. They were clear blue and watery, but unflinching as they met my own. I observed no sign of self-conscious pretense, and I began to realize Abigail Wingate was right: Some trick of the mind was working in a strange way to protect the elder Mrs. Wingate from the disturbing truth about her niece that she could not—or would not—face.

"During her visit this past weekend, did she seem upset or worried by anything?"

Mrs. Wingate pursed her thin lips, and then turned to Abigail. "Abby, would you say Sarah was out of sorts?"

"No," Abigail said. "She seemed a little tired, that was all."

"Mrs. Wingate, when did you last see Sarah?"

"Lunchtime Tuesday," she said. Her tone was crisp, even tart. "Then she went to do her own work, and I did, too."

"And Stella was helping you all afternoon?"

She nodded. Joe had remained uncharacteristically quiet, but now he broke into the conversation and asked Abigail to accompany him during a search of Stella's room. I was happy to see Abigail leave, however briefly, for I believed her anxious presence was making my interview with Mrs. Wingate more difficult. Once Abigail no longer fiercely hovered over her, Mrs. Wingate visibly relaxed.

"Would you care for some tea, Detective?" After I accepted, she rang the bell beside her chair and a heavyset, ruddy-faced woman appeared. I recognized her as Maud Muncie, their housekeeper. Mrs. Wingate asked, "Maud, would you be so kind as to bring two cups of tea? And some scones, if we've any left."

I pulled out my notebook and pencil. "I understand Stella has been working for you since August?"

"That's right," she replied.

"Does she have friends or family in the area that you are aware of?"

Her answer took me by surprise with its bluntness. "Why is that any of your business?"

"Because I need information if you want me to investigate her disappearance." My response was equally sharp, for I was not accustomed to being openly challenged.

"You're right." She sighed wearily. "I apologize. I am tremendously concerned." Her voice grew high-pitched. "Stella just went away," she said, leaning in toward me. "We were working together in the garden when she got up suddenly and ran toward the house. I didn't know why, and she never came back. I haven't seen her since."

"When was this?" I asked, as I tried to integrate this information into the timeline.

"It was around half past three," she replied.

"Is that a guess, or are you certain?"

"I am certain." Her response was firm. "I had checked my watch at a quarter past three, and this was some minutes later. I was keeping my eye on the time because I wanted to finish my gardening well before four o'clock so I would have ample time to dress for dinner."

My thoughts raced through the many different interview reports I had read, as well as Abigail Wingate's own statement to me. Many people in the area had reported hearing a loud sound around half past three. A loon, Abigail had said—though there were no loons in these parts. An owl, Mr. Dreyer across the street had said. A strange screech, the Braithwaites had described it. Could it have been Sarah screaming? Put into context with our timeline, it made perfect sense, for Sarah was last seen by Abigail Wingate around three o'clock. It was important because it placed Sarah's killer firmly in the house at three-thirty. So if Stella had left Mrs. Wingate at that time, then it was probable she had seen—and possibly even confronted—Sarah's murderer.

I asked her to clarify. "And you haven't seen Stella since?"

"No," she replied.

"Yet, at the time, you were not concerned enough to check on her?"

"Of course I was," she said. "I went in after her, when she did not return after several minutes. But the moment I entered the kitchen, Abby began insisting I call Dr. Fields. Dr. Fields, mind you! I am usually attended by Dr. Whittier. But Abby insisted it had to be Dr. Fields—and then she fainted dead away. Between trying to revive her and reach Dr. Fields by telephone, I had my hands full."

That explained, at least, why we were told nothing before Dr. Fields's message reached us near five o'clock.

Maud returned with two cups of hot tea and a plate of warm apple scones. After Mrs. Wingate murmured her thanks, I said, "Mrs. Muncie, before you leave, I have something to ask you."

She turned and stared, hands on hips, as I helped myself to a scone. "I've already told the policeman who interviewed me everything. Tuesday was my shopping day. I wasn't here."

"I understand," I said, my tone placating, "but my question is about Stella. Were you friendly with her?"

Maud grunted in reply. "I work here. I don't talk much with the others, if that's what you're asking. Stella was a bit of a girl, but she did her part. I had no complaints about her." She rearranged her apron, implying she was ready to return to work.

"What I'm asking is whether there is any place you can think of where Stella may have gone? Any friends she may have sought out?"

"I wouldn't know about that, Detective. Like I told the other policeman who came, I don't go in for small talk. Stella was a nice enough girl. But I can't say more than that."

"And you, Mrs. Wingate?" I asked, cradling my cup of warm tea in my hands. There was enough chill in the air that its warmth felt comforting.

After Maud returned to the house, Mrs. Wingate was quiet for some time. Then she said, "You might check Stella's whereabouts with a woman named Mamie Durant on West Thirty-eighth Street."

"Mamie Durant." I repeated the name, almost to myself, as I tried to place where I had heard the name before. "Isn't she—"

I articulated the question a split second before the thought fully crystallized in my mind.

"Yes," Virginia Wingate interrupted, seeming to intuit what I was thinking. Her watery blue eyes did not falter as they met my own. "She owns and manages a high-class gentleman's club, catering to wealthy clients."

I could only stare at her, dumbfounded. The club run by Mamie Durant was not the sort of place a well-bred lady like Mrs. Wingate would ordinarily know about, much less mention in polite conversation. *Gentleman's club* was a fine euphemism, but what went on there was prostitution—plain and simple. And Mrs. Wingate had broached the subject as matter-of-factly as though she were talking about a popular ladies' tearoom.

"How do you know Mamie Durant? Or rather, how does Stella—?" In my attempts to be discreet with Mrs. Wingate, I could not pose the question. The right words simply did not exist.

She cut me off calmly, amused by my embarrassment. "Mamie Durant was Stella's previous employer. She provided an excellent reference to the organization that found Stella for me. You see, she fully supported Stella in making a fresh start."

I was shocked to find her so unemotional about the subject— one which ladies of her social class did not discuss and usually pretended did not exist. I stammered lamely, "Does Miss Abigail know about Stella's background?"

"Of course she does not," Mrs. Wingate said, sitting up straighter. "No one here does." She took a sip of her tea before continuing. "Stella became quite ill during her last months at Mamie Durant's, and when she recovered, she began to do the laundry and light housekeeping there. Mamie herself apparently told her if she was happy enough with that sort of work, she should find respectable quarters to do it in. Housemaids in private homes often find husbands and marry; those in gentlemen's clubs do not."

"You said an organization placed her with you?" I asked.

"Yes," she confirmed with a nod, "it was one of those ladies' home committees in the city. A friend involved with their work sent Stella to me for an interview, knowing my views were liberal enough to take her." She smiled slightly. "Plus, I have no husband or sons in my household to worry about." After another moment, she shrugged. "It was really quite simple. She wanted a fresh start; I decided to give it to her."

I knew many people who would have given her a dozen reasons why it was a bad idea, but clearly Mrs. Wingate had considered such concerns unimportant.

"Thank you," I said, "you have been very helpful. If you think of anything else that may be important, will you let me know?"

"Of course," she said, rising to say good-bye. "I know where to find you. And do"—her voice caught—"*do* try your best to find her. I should like so much to have things back, just as they were."

As she stood before me in her wrap on the porch, I looked at her with pity and thought that she suddenly looked very old and frail. "Of course," I said gently, and bid her good-bye, thinking that no matter what tricks of mind Virginia Wingate might employ, not even the best of imaginations could ever make things just as they once were.

"Joe?" I called out from the foot of the stairs. "Are you ready to go?"

There was no answer.

"Joe?" I called again, more loudly this time.

Miss Abigail's pale face appeared suddenly at the top of the stair railing. "Come up now," she said, her voice filled with worry. "He's behaving strangely. Something is wrong, but I don't know what."

I bounded up the staircase, taking three steps at a time, and Miss Wingate quickly ushered me into a small bedroom where Joe awkwardly hugged the back of a rocking chair.

"Ziele." He uttered my name and took a step toward me, but his left leg buckled the moment he put weight on it. His large frame collapsed onto the floor and he looked up at me with unseeing eyes. "So dizzy," he murmured.

"Help me get him onto the bed," I said to Miss Wingate.

Once he lay flat, he continued to complain that he could not see, nor could he feel anything in his left leg. I cradled his head against the pillow and felt his pulse. "Don't worry. Just be still for now."

"Please go call Dr. Fields," I whispered to Miss Wingate, who stood helplessly next to us. "Immediately!" I called after her, when she left the room rather too slowly. "We've absolutely no time to waste."

CHAPTER 12

By early afternoon, Joe was resting at home, and I was suddenly on my own in this investigation. "Apoplexy" had been Dr. Fields's diagnosis. "He's had a bad stroke," the doctor had said. "I think his vision may return; I'm less hopeful about the movement he has lost in his left leg. But rest can work wonders for one's health, so let's wait and see." While Joe recuperated under the care of his industrious wife Anna—who had vowed to make all the preparations she thought appropriate for an invalid in the house, including vast quantities of soup—I stopped by the office to check for messages.

No good news awaited me. Mayor Fuller was unhappy about our apparent lack of progress. And there was no word from Alistair—odd, given that he had promised me an update.

Fortunately, the information I had requested from my former partner Mulvaney had arrived. I had asked him to locate the police records for the housebreaker who had previously victimized Sarah Wingate. His name was Otto Schmidt, and his arrest record described him as a recent immigrant with no visible means of support and a long history of arrests on charges of vagrancy and disturbing the peace. But the incident involving Sarah Wingate was his first arrest for theft. It was likely, of course, that he had stolen before and simply never been caught.

It took only a few moments to scan through the relevant facts. On September 15, 1904, at nine o'clock at night, he had been arrested for breaking into Mrs. Gardiner's boardinghouse for young ladies on Riverside Drive. Several items belonging to Miss Sarah Wingate had been taken. After Schmidt was convicted on that charge, he served six months in jail before disappearing during the confusion that followed a jailhouse fire. He had not been located since, and it was questionable whether anyone had even attempted to find him. Many offenders considered far more dangerous had escaped during the same fire, and Otto Schmidt was, by comparison, not worth the effort.

As always, Mulvaney anticipated my next request; his note indicated he would determine whether Otto Schmidt could be located, in hopes of ascertaining whether he was even in the New York area at the time of Sarah's murder. To be honest, I did not believe Otto Schmidt bore any relation to the murder; despite his long criminal record, the man's history was that of a petty thief, not a violent murderer. But his prior criminal connection with Sarah Wingate placed him under suspicion—a suspicion I would need to clear, particularly if only circumstantial evidence continued to connect Fromley to the case.

Reassured that Mulvaney would handle that angle of the

investigation for me, I headed back into the city for the day. I planned to follow up on Stella's disappearance by visiting Mamie Durant's place of business. The Wingates were anxious about her, and I believed it was possible—probable, in fact—that Stella had witnessed something that would help break open this investigation. I stopped by Columbia first in the hope I would find Alistair there, but he was not. Undeterred, I decided to take the subway downtown alone. It was still early enough in the day that I should find Mrs. Durant unoccupied and her place relatively quiet.

I had just reached the 116th Street station, about to descend underground, when I heard Isabella's voice calling to me. I was so pleased to see her that, before I quite realized it, she had determined to accompany me on this particular interview. I immediately regretted the situation, but it was too late: She was already seated beside me on the subway, talking excitedly about what she had managed to discover from some of Sarah's classmates. Together with Alistair, she had interviewed Lonny Moore briefly; he was the student who had lodged the complaint that Sarah's work was not her own. "But he has an alibi for the time of Sarah's murder," Isabella explained, "at least to the extent we can trust the word of his friend John Nelson."

"How good of a friend?" I asked.

"Apparently a close, longtime friend," she said, her voice flat.

I would find that fact more worrisome if Lonny Moore were our likeliest suspect. But it seemed a far more dangerous killer was still at large—a killer I hoped Mamie Durant could help us locate.

After we exited the subway, I saw a solution to my dilemma with Isabella in the form of the Rismont Tea Room. Isabella might wait there during my visit to Mamie Durant. While unaccompanied women could not dine alone in restaurants—in fact, they were routinely asked to leave should they enter—they were welcomed at the city's many tearooms, which catered to women out shopping. Yet when I proposed this idea to Isabella, she would have none of it.

"Don't be ridiculous—of course I'm coming with you. You didn't object before," she reminded me, her brown eyes flashing.

"Yes, but I've thought it over, and it isn't quite proper for me to take you," I said. "It's not the sort of place a lady should visit—especially accompanied by a man with whom you have just become acquainted." My voice was stiff and forced, betraying my awkwardness.

She merely laughed. "I am not going to sit in some teahouse while you do this, Simon," she said.

It was the first time she had used my given name—and she had done so without thinking. It was an odd sensation, for it had been months since anyone else had done so. Not since first Hannah, then my mother had died.

With some effort, I refocused my attention on Isabella, who was continuing with her argument.

"I'm no longer an eighteen-year-old debutante worried what others may think, and I have every intention of accompanying you on what may well be your most interesting interview to date. Remember," she added more gently, "I am exposed to far worse through Alistair's research than the woman we will be meeting today."

"But you may feel uncomfortable," I added feebly, thinking mainly of my own discomfort, "and you should consider your reputation."

"Simon, I will be perfectly comfortable and my reputation

will survive." She touched my arm lightly. "I do not count those who would hold such things against me among my friends."

And so it was settled, much against my own better judgment.

The door to the limestone town house on West Thirty-eighth Street looked like any other on the street: heavy wood with a burnished brass knocker. It was answered only moments after we knocked by a girl of no more than thirteen or fourteen, wearing a black dress and white apron. It was probably standard policy that visitors should not be made to stand for very long on the stoop outside where they might be recognized. But immediately on the other side of the wooden door was a large entry hall leading to another door, this next one made of imposing steel. It had no exterior handle, but three heavy-duty locks lined the door's edge. Unwanted visitors would clearly have a difficult time gaining admittance.

At the center of the door was an opening that resembled a mail slot. The maid explained we should submit a note explaining the purpose of our visit. I paused, pencil in hand. "Police Investigation" seemed unlikely to gain us admittance. I settled on: "We represent concerned friends of Stella Gibson."

After the housemaid passed it through the slot, we waited in silence. The girl stared at Isabella in a way that made her flush, despite her earlier protestations. In response, I offered Isabella a jelly candy from the small tin in my pocket so as to make clear she was with me. Isabella accepted, and the girl looked away.

After what seemed an eternity, but was probably five minutes, the metal door creaked open and we were ushered into a private parlor where, on the table, I noticed a stack of calling cards. *MAMIE DURANT, FACILITATOR OF SOCIAL INTRODUCTIONS.* It was a tasteful way to describe the services she offered, I had to admit. From an investigation some years ago, I was familiar with her general background. I knew she had done well for herself; she owned the town house outright, and today I could see that its interior was opulently furnished. The furniture was upholstered in a thick red velvet material that complemented the gold draperies, and each side table featured a marble top with gold leaf scrolling. A gleaming black grand piano dominated the left side of the room.

I recognized her as she entered the room, for I had seen her picture in the newspapers as well as our police files, but she was even more striking in person. She was a tall, solid woman with full red lips that were almost—but not quite—the same brilliant red as the hair piled in high curls atop her head. I was certain the color was henna, since I had never seen a woman's hair naturally achieve such a vivid red-orange hue. She wore a rich purple and gold dressing gown, and I suspected, despite the afternoon hour, that she had only recently awakened for the day. Her husky voice drawled in the honeyed tones of her native South, albeit in an exaggerated fashion that I suspected was cultivated to complement the persona she had created for herself.

"Good morning," she said. "So sorry to keep y'all waiting for me. I understand you came here to see me today because you're concerned about Stella Gibson?"

In answering, I made the necessary introductions and explained the situation, admitting that we were searching for Stella as part of a police investigation. I made clear that she and her business were in no way implicated. Rather, it was our hope that Stella might have contacted her or one of the girls in recent days.

Mamie did not appear surprised in the least. I supposed that, through the years, she had often heard this kind of request—through private inquiries, if not formal police investigations. And I suspected that, in framing her answer, she regularly asked herself whether the missing girl in question wanted to be found. Accordingly, I stressed the fact that Stella could be in real danger.

Her reply came after a moment's reflection, but it seemed candid.

"Oh, yes, Stella Gibson. Now she was a real nice girl; everyone here always said the sweetest things about her," she said. "But no, can't say as I've seen her around—not since she left us last August."

"She left on good terms?" I asked.

"She did," she said. "She was sweet and pretty, though a tad bit too shy to suit most gentlemen, so she didn't get on as well as she might have. Reminded them too much of the gals back home, if you ask me." She paused a moment as the door opened, and a different maid brought in a teapot with three cups. "I'm having a cup," she said, "so you may as well have one, too." She busied herself serving it until the woman was gone, and then resumed talking. "I thought it was good for her to move on, so when she wanted to, I pointed her in the right direction. I sent her to one of those do-good Christian reform places run by spinster ladies with too much time on their hands. I heard they set her up in a situation north of the city, probably with a self-righteous old lady who got to feel good for having rescued Stella from a sinful life." Her voice dripped with sarcasm.

Knowing what I did about Virginia Wingate, I stifled a smile at hearing these imagined traits. Mrs. Wingate was a spinster, to be sure, but I felt she would have more than shared Mamie's sentiments about self-righteous do-gooders.

"Was Stella particularly friendly with any of the girls here?" Isabella asked. If she was in any way uncomfortable, she did not show it.

"Well," Mamie said, and paused a moment. "I'd say she got on best with Cora Czerne; seemed like they were always good friends."

"Is Cora here now? Could we talk with her?" Isabella was momentarily excited.

"No," Mamie said, "she's already moved on, the way the more successful gals do. Found herself an even richer fellow than the last and moved to a new apartment far uptown. I can give you the address, if you want to try her there."

Of course we agreed.

If the rumors I'd heard were true, Mamie might have been speaking about her own history as easily as Cora's. I knew Mamie had been the mistress of a handful of men, each more successful than the last, whose lucrative gifts had generated the savings from which she started her current business venture.

She walked over to a drop-front secretary desk and unlocked its cover with a key that hung around her neck. Nothing in this house, apparently, was left unsecured. After consulting a small book, she wrote something on a piece of paper.

"What about family—do you know if Stella has any in the area?" I asked after she had rejoined us. Mrs. Wingate had led us to believe Stella had no family, but I was curious whether Mamie knew anything more.

But Mamie was of the same opinion. "Oh, no family living, I'm sure of it. Her father brought her here to New York, but they had no sooner moved here than he died. Heart failure," she said, sighing deeply. "I'm sure Stella would have gone back home then, if there were any family to take her in. Instead, she came here in desperation, and I took care of her."

I felt a flash of empathy for Stella, for I had seen many girls in my old neighborhood face similar, difficult choices. When some change in life circumstances forced them to support themselves, and they lacked training or skills, there were few good options. Some might secure a job as a seamstress or factory worker—but the long hours would not generate enough income to pay for food and a modest rent. Some found the easy money made as a prostitute on the streets to be initially more lucrative. But only the hardiest survived that life for long; they fell victim to illness and violence the longer they stayed on the street. Somehow, Stella Gibson had found her way here and established herself under Mamie's protection. I could not help but wonder how. But that question probably had no simple answer, and I only hoped whatever ingenuity Stella had used then would continue to serve her now.

I was about to thank Mamie and say good-bye when I had one final thought. "Mrs. Durant, I know you must be discreet regarding your clients, but we *are* investigating a murder. Bearing that in mind, we would like to ask you about one particular suspect."

Mamie chuckled with a deep-throated sound as she shifted her position on the sofa. "Now, you all wouldn't be so naïve as to think the gentlemen who come here actually use their real names?" She laughed again. "You'd have to describe him to me awful well, or show me a picture."

I obliged, taking out my wallet and thumbing to where I had placed Michael Fromley's picture.

We were fortunate that Mamie had not outright refused

even to look. That she was highly successful was largely the result of her habit of being exceptionally discreet. By all accounts, she was a savvy businesswoman who operated by exercising the utmost discretion.

But after she had taken the photograph and looked at it— first casually, then more intently—I noted the change in her face: Her features froze despite her best intentions.

Silence followed.

"His name is Michael Fromley," I added.

I could hear her sharp intake of breath. I leaned forward, saying no more but willing her to speak.

When she spoke at last, her voice was like steel.

"I'm afraid I can't help you, Detective." She did not look at me. She was already up, heading toward the door.

"But Mrs. Durant," I said, quickly moving to block her path. "We suspect this man has committed a murder—a particularly vicious killing involving a young woman who knew Stella Gibson. If you are familiar with him, we need to know."

We were checkmated: I did not budge, and neither did she.

"Mrs. Durant," I said, "I gave you my word when we first arrived that you would not be implicated by my investigation. But I was presuming your cooperation. You recognize I have the power to bring you in for official questioning."

Nothing but silence.

"If I take you in for questions, you may end up in the Tombs. And in the Tombs, one never knows what may happen. It's very unpleasant, I hear—especially if one stays for an extended period of time."

She was unmoved. "Do what you will. I have no more to say to you."

She raised her dark green eyes to mine, and there was no

mistaking their determined look. And then she was gone, leaving us to see ourselves out.

Outside, I seethed with frustration, pacing angrily back and forth. "She knows something—something substantive that she refuses to tell us," I said. I had threatened her with everything I could, and she still defied me. The reasonable explanation—the only possible explanation—was that she feared Fromley more than me. And I resolved to find out why.

Isabella tried to be optimistic. "Perhaps it was just the shock of it," she said. "She may come around. She will know how to contact you."

But Mamie Durant would not contact me. Of that I was certain, from the way her face had hardened with some bitter, private resolve upon seeing Michael Fromley's picture. I could punish her by bringing her to the local police station for questioning. But to do so would accomplish just that and no more; it would not yield me the information I sorely needed.

Suddenly the door to Mamie's home opened and a skittish girl hurried outside. "Mamie said to give you this, sir"—she pressed a piece of paper in my hand—"but not to bother her no more. She don't want your questions."

As I glanced back at Mamie's town house, I thought I saw a curtain move behind the third-floor window. I looked down at the paper. Scrawled in blue ink was an address on West Forty-first Street near Eighth Avenue and a number for a landlady named Mrs. Addison. *Fromley's address.*

It was the address I had wanted, had been searching for so diligently the past two days. But I felt a surge of anger that I was expected to take this scrap of information and be thankful, when she obviously knew so much more.

That was apparent from the fact that she was in possession of Michael Fromley's current address—when even Alistair and his aunt Lizzie were not.

It would be several days before we finally learned the reason Mamie refused to talk about Fromley.

And the truth, when we learned it, would be even worse than I imagined.

CHAPTER 13

It was difficult to shake the frustration Isabella and I both felt as we left Mamie Durant's home; we judged indefensible the fact that Mamie obviously had information that she refused to tell us. I was grateful for Fromley's address, assuming she had given me his most recent one. With luck, it would lead us to the man himself. But her reasons for not sharing all she knew mattered little to me; whatever they were, they paled in comparison to the importance of solving Sarah Wingate's murder.

The landlady, Mrs. Addison, was at home when we arrived at Michael Fromley's rented rooms on West Forty-first Street. She confirmed the identity of her boarder when we showed her his picture, but she was adamant that he had not been around since mid-October. Her description of his habits was sketchy, but at least she willingly granted us access to his room. Her young housemaid escorted us up to the third floor.

"This is as far as I go," she announced when we approached the top landing. "He gives me the shivers, that one does," was her brief explanation—and when we pressed her for details, she merely retorted she had brains enough "to stay far away from the likes of him." She was gone before we could ask anything more.

Isabella reached for the brass doorknob of Fromley's room, but I placed my hand over hers before she opened the door. "What if he's inside?" I whispered.

"Oh," she said and backed up, her eyes suddenly large as she noticed my left hand clenched around a Colt revolver.

Isabella retreated several feet down the hall, and I proceeded to turn the doorknob. The door swung open with a loud creak. I gingerly stepped into the room and ascertained the space was empty. That much was a relief, so I poked my head back into the hallway and indicated Isabella could enter.

"What a horrid place," she said, recoiling from the room's musty smell as much as its dingy appearance. Orange floral wallpaper was tempered by stained green curtains, which were drawn shut. It took a moment for our eyes to adjust to the darkness, even after we opened the curtains. When I could see again, I immediately located a wash table near the bed with a small mirror above it. After putting on my lint-free cotton gloves, I placed the shaving bowl and brush into a clean bag; these items were certain to have a number of Michael Fromley's fingerprints on them. I would turn them over to the police laboratory in Yonkers before the end of the day in anticipation of a match with the fingerprints I had taken earlier from the Wingate home.

This task accomplished, I took a closer look at our surroundings. There were no photographs or personal items on display, not even a book or magazine. Did he really spend much time here? I could not help but wonder, as I reflected how the room appeared peculiarly empty and neglected. Yet the wardrobe was filled with clothing, of differing sizes and condition. Fromley was apparently a pack rat, reluctant to part with any article of clothing that was outgrown. Isabella began searching the wardrobe, as I checked the drawers in the nightstand and the suitcase hidden under the bed.

Just as I was about to suggest we leave, Isabella spoke, and her voice was agitated. "Simon, you need to take a look at these. They were hidden underneath a pile of shirts."

She handed me a stuffed folder, and looked away as I took it, pacing nervously near the window. But Fromley's room faced an air shaft that provided little light or air. Turning, she crossed the room and threw open the door. And after another moment, still unable to bear the stifling atmosphere of his room, she retreated into the hallway.

I sat on a hard wooden chair and placed the folder in front of me. What Isabella had discovered was a file overflowing with photographs—disturbing photographs in light of what we knew about Michael Fromley's obsessions. Each one pictured a woman, invariably young and attractive. Some appeared to be taken at random, of women standing or sitting on the subway, the trolley, or the ferry. Had they known he was photographing them? If so, had he posed as a photographer? Even if he had one of the new folding Kodak cameras I had seen advertised, they were bulky enough to be noticed.

Alistair had said something about how those women Fromley encountered on the streets or on public transport seemed particularly to arouse his interest. It had sounded like theory and nonsense at the time, but as I began to count . . . twenty, thirty, forty . . . there were photographs of well over fifty such women collected here. Had Alistair known about Fromley's photography habit? And how had Fromley gained the cooperation of so many women?

Even more sobering was the second type of photograph included in this odd collection: cadavers laid out, as was typical at most morgues. I shuddered involuntarily, as I skimmed through picture after picture of cadavers—all women, each bruised or maimed in some way. There were only ten photographs of this sort, but even one would have been too many.

I put aside the question of why he would want to possess such pictures. Instead, I pondered how he could have gained access to them. They were of the kind one would find in a police file, even a mortician's record. But ordinarily no layperson would be able to obtain such photographs.

I tucked the file into my satchel silently and left the room, joining Isabella in the hallway. She looked anxious and wan. I could think of nothing comforting to say, so I simply touched her arm and escorted her out of the house to the street below, where we hailed a hansom cab to take us downtown, back toward Tin Pan Alley and Clara Murphy's flat.

In searching for Stella, we had learned a good deal about Fromley—albeit not the kind of information I had originally envisioned. Hopefully in locating Clara, I would find Fromley himself. The folder of pictures, heavy in my bag, served as a reminder of why it was absolutely critical to do so.

While in the cab, Isabella slowly came to herself again. The pictures we had just seen illustrated Fromley's disturbed habits of mind in a way she had never encountered at Alistair's center.

While she had often reviewed Alistair's typed transcriptions and case observations, she had never attended an interview session and only rarely seen Fromley himself.

She shuddered. "Seeing those photographs makes him seem more real, somehow. They show us something of how he views the world around him. I never would have imagined confronting it would be so upsetting." After a pause, she added, "I knew he dreamt and obsessed over horrible, evil things. But encountering that on the written page is a far different thing than seeing photographic evidence of it."

"But remember, he is nothing more than a man," I said with a reassuring smile. "That's how I view it. Because I can't fear him. The moment I do, my resolve to catch him might waver."

I don't know if she believed me, but she pulled herself together, explaining how the photographs we had found were consistent with Alistair's larger presumptions about Michael Fromley.

"In some ways, Alistair has prepared me for this," she said. "He always claimed that Michael's fantasies and daydreams fueled his violent actions. That was why Alistair—and Fred Ebbings, too—worked to help him humanize the people around him. They believed the more Michael learned to recognize the thoughts and feelings of others, the closer he would be to a full rehabilitation."

I said nothing to Isabella as we approached our destination on West Twenty-eighth Street, but what we had just discovered made me concerned about Clara Murphy. I hoped Clara would be able to help us locate Fromley. But most of all, I hoped we would find her in her flat—alive, unharmed, safe from whatever violent impulses motivated this man. The fact that she was last seen in his company made me uneasy about her well-being.

As opposed to last night, when the place had been deserted and most residents out for the evening, this afternoon the lobby was filled with a cacophony of sounds: a woman belted out scales in her most operatic voice; the tinny jingle of a piano sounded out "My Gal Sal." The place was crowded, noisy, and teeming with life—the perfect antidote to our mood after visiting Fromley's rooms. We went to apartment 432, where—just as I had done last night—we knocked several times with no response.

"Still not at home." I sighed in frustration. "We'll have to try back later." I turned away from the door and decided to find the building's custodian, who might know something of Clara's schedule and habits.

"Wait a moment," Isabella said. "We should say something first. She may be here, simply not answering because she is afraid."

If that were the case, I could not imagine what I could say to persuade her to open the door. Variations of "Police, open up" never seemed to work. But perhaps Isabella would fare better.

"You try," I urged. "It may sound better coming from you."

She shrugged in agreement, and called out softly but clearly. "Miss Murphy? Are you there? My name is Isabella Sinclair. A friend and I were hoping to have a word with you. We only need a few minutes of your time."

We waited a moment, and as we heard the chain lock being undone from inside the door, I once again appreciated Isabella's gift for striking just the right tone.

The door opened only a crack at first. A single eye peered out, taking full stock of Isabella before finding her acceptable.

Then the door opened wide enough for us to enter.

It was dark inside, just as it had been at Michael Fromley's.

And it was filthy—the bed rumpled and unmade, the washbasin unemptied. The stench of urine from a chamber pot permeated the room. As my eyes focused, I also noted faded pink wallpaper peeling off the wall. This particular flat was among the more squalid I had seen.

Once she had let us in, Clara Murphy retreated to the sole chair in the room—a bare wooden rocker—and eased her body into it gingerly. Isabella and I noticed her injuries at about the same time, but Isabella reacted first.

"Miss Murphy, you're badly hurt!" she exclaimed. "You must see a doctor straightaway."

Clara Murphy was clearly taken aback by the idea. And when she understood Isabella was serious, she rejected the proposal out of hand.

But she had not counted on Isabella's persistence. "At least allow us to call a nurse to come to you here."

"Thanks, but I'll be fine," Clara said again, her speech slurred by a swollen mouth. "I just need some rest," she added wearily.

I had no doubt that was true, for she looked as though she had not slept in days. Or eaten, either, I suspected, as I noted her bruised face and jaw. As my eyes better adjusted to the dim light, I began to register the extent of her injuries. Her face was covered with multiple lacerations and bruises; her left arm hung limply in a way that suggested it was broken; a patch of hair from the left side of her head was missing, and from the way she had lowered herself into her chair, I suspected additional injuries lay hidden under her clothing.

She offered living evidence of the extreme violence of which Michael Fromley was capable.

"Miss Murphy," Isabella continued, "my friend is with the police. Would you allow Detective Ziele to call someone in your local precinct? They could help you to press charges against whoever did this to you."

Clara's laugh was a hoarse cackle.

"Miss," she said, "I know you mean well, but you need to stop. Never mind my injuries. And forget about the police. No one's going to listen to what the likes of me has to say. Now what did you come here to talk with me about?"

She was right, though I felt ashamed to admit it. Police resources were limited, and scant attention was paid to the complaints of women like Clara Murphy. "Likely brought it on herself staying out too late in the wrong company," most officers would say. The underlying presumption, of course, was that ladies didn't get themselves in trouble. But no one deserved the abuse Clara Murphy had taken, and I resolved to order a nurse's visit and groceries after we were done, despite Clara's earlier protestations. If nothing else, her arm would give her a lifetime of trouble if she didn't get it set soon—and properly. I for one knew that.

Sensing she wanted us to leave her alone, I began my questions at once. "We don't plan to take up much of your time, Miss Murphy, so I'll get straight to the point. What can you tell us about Michael Fromley?"

Although she blanched, she answered promptly. "Well, I know he's the man that did this to me." She used her good arm to indicate her more obvious bruises.

Perhaps I should have offered some sort of expression of sympathy, but in truth, it was all I could do to stay focused on my questions, for the room's stench was terrible to endure.

Isabella must have felt the same way. She asked, "Miss Murphy, may we open your window for a few minutes? The fresh air would do you good."

This earned her a dubious stare. "It's November. It's cold out."

"Yes, but the sun is out. We'll only crack the window, and not for long." Isabella's compromise won Clara's grudging agreement, and I breathed in relief the moment I felt the fresh air enter the room.

"We're searching for Michael Fromley in connection with a recent murder," I said. "We understand you were well acquainted with him."

She stared at me with a blank expression, and for a moment I wondered if she had not heard me. Then she spoke again. "Mind telling me who he killed?"

"We believe he has murdered a young woman north of the city," I answered carefully.

"He stabbed her?"

"Repeatedly. The official cause of death was a slash to her throat, but she suffered many additional stab wounds." I hoped she would ask no more. I typically never divulged case details to potential witnesses. But I sensed that giving her some information would encourage her to cooperate with me.

She seemed to be thinking, deeply. "Disgusting animal," she finally said, just under her breath. We simply waited a moment for her to compose herself.

She began to explain. "I noticed Michael early last month when he came to my show. I was in the chorus of *Little Johnny Jones*, though I got fired the same night I met him. The director complained I was always late to rehearsal, but it's not like they paid me enough, was it? I had to work the extra jobs that always made me late."

She paused a moment before continuing. "That's of course

when *he* showed up, when I was down on my luck. I'd just picked up my last paycheck from the office, and there he was, all smiles and flowers, ready to take me to dinner."

I asked her to clarify. "But you had seen him before?"

She shifted position, and her movement was slow and difficult. "Yes, I'd seen him before," she acknowledged. "He came to show after show, flirting with all the girls. He wasn't my type at all—too pleased with himself, too aggressive. Don't think I'd ever have agreed if I hadn't just been fired. But that doesn't matter now."

She went on to outline their short history together, giving dates and places as best she could remember. Michael Fromley had behaved the perfect gentleman their first several dates, squiring her sometimes to uptown dinners and shows, other times to downtown clubs. One evening, early on, he had been drunk and slapped her when she refused to invite him up after such an evening. She wished she had heeded that warning. But after ignoring his apologies for a week, she had agreed to see him once more; she went out with him to the Fortune Club on Saturday the twenty-first, as we had learned from Izzy. It was that same evening that Fromley had put knock-out drops in her drink, taken her to a deserted river warehouse, and brutally assaulted her. When she regained consciousness, he was gone; she made her way back home, where for the past two weeks she had subsisted more or less in the state we found her.

The man she described was mercurial. Sometimes he flashed large sums of money and was in a wonderful mood; other times he was broke and easily angered. But when he had money, he spent it on entertainment at the city's seedier restaurants and barrooms, not its finer establishments. Large portions of each evening's cost were for alcohol. "I knew he was too fond of the liquor," she said mournfully, "I just didn't know his problems went so far beyond that."

Before we left, we obtained a list of each place she recalled Fromley had taken her in the past month. She had been under the impression he was a regular customer at three or four of the restaurants, so we would visit those first.

In parting, I let her know we would send a nurse by. "I'm telling you so you'll know to expect her, and not be frightened," I said. "It will be no expense to you—it is the least we can do to thank you for talking with us. And it looks like you've a broken arm that needs to be set."

She continued to protest, even as we shut the door behind us.

We stayed on Twenty-eighth Street, crossing the stretch between Broadway and Sixth Avenue that was home to most music publishers. Isabella and I did not talk; it would have been impossible to hear each other, anyway, over the cacophony of sound. Each music publisher employed song pluggers to adver- tise their newest offerings—sometimes even on the sidewalk outside. We had just passed Paul Dresser's Publishing when my attention was distracted by a singer and piano player perform- ing a catchy ragtime riff. I had no warning before I was tack- led, sent sprawling to the ground by a man who came at me from behind.

I landed—hard—on my bad right arm, gasping in agony as pain shot up into my shoulder.

My attacker was all hands, one moment reaching for my leather satchel, the next trying to gouge my eyes. I wrenched my head away and saw Isabella had been knocked down, but was mercifully alone. We had only one attacker—the one on my back, pinning me to the sidewalk. Then I tasted something salty I knew to be blood. Before I could succumb to my usual weakness, pure instinct kicked in. I elbowed and kicked with all my might, my bum right arm useless for anything other than maintaining an iron grip on my bag. He continued to pummel my ribs to force me to let go of it. Through gut-wrenching pain, I focused on elbowing the man, dimly aware of Isabella screaming for help as I struggled to fight against the rain of blows.

Help came in the form of the two ragtime song pluggers. The singer, a large African man, lifted my attacker from me with an ease that I envied. His partner, a wizened older man, occupied himself with helping Isabella before he joined the singer in pinning the assailant to the wall.

I got up and went over to Isabella. Apart from the dirt stains on her coat, I saw no obvious injuries. She seemed shaken, but otherwise all right. "You're not hurt?" I asked.

With a brave smile, she answered, "I'm fine. Thank you— both of you." The latter was directed toward our rescuers.

I took stock of my own injuries. The whole incident had lasted no more than a minute or two, but my assailant had landed several key punches. I had scratches on my face, and bruised ribs I was sure, but nothing was broken. I pulled out a handkerchief to dab the bleeding from the worst scratch near my left eye.

"Do you know this man?" the singer asked. His speaking voice was also a deep baritone.

A large crowd of onlookers now surrounded us. I stared at my assailant, now wedged between the brick wall and my rescuer. The culprit was a large man nearly six feet tall with a hefty paunch. His face was puffy and rough stubble covered his balding head as well as his chin. Though I searched my memory, especially for past cases, I had never seen him before.

I shook my head. "I take it you don't know him, either?" I asked Isabella.

"No, I don't," she said.

"What's your name?" I asked as I approached the attacker.

"None of your business," he said—but the response earned him a sharp jab in the ribs from the singer.

"Think you'd better answer when a gentleman asks you something. Try again." The singer glared down at the man he had pinned to the wall. If my attacker was about five feet ten or eleven inches, then my rescuer easily towered over him by another half foot. Plus, he was in excellent shape, I could tell.

"Hal Jones."

It didn't ring a bell.

"And what business you got attacking this gentleman?" My rescuer seemed as determined as I was to get to the bottom of this.

"None." He stammered, growing more nervous as he seemed to realize the situation he was in.

"So you're telling me you're the kind of fellow who attacks gentlemen and ladies for no good reason? I don't believe that for a second," the tall singer said.

"Are you aware you have attacked a police officer?" I added, looking at my attacker sternly.

Now he was wide-eyed with fear. "He didn't say anything about that. I just did it for the money."

"What money? Someone paid you?" I asked, observing him closely.

"I got paid ten dollars," he said. "A man approached me not

half an hour ago as I came out of Moretti's. I'd lost a bundle and I really needed the dough." He glanced first at me, then at the singer. "Maybe you could put me down. This isn't comfortable."

"Nah," the singer replied. "You'll do as you are. Now pay attention to the officer's questions."

"He gave you ten dollars up-front?" I asked.

He nodded. "Yeah. And he said if I got your bag, he'd find me and give me something extra."

I looked around at the crowd surrounding us. Had Fromley been watching?

"What did he look like? And how did he describe me?"

He smirked. "He didn't describe you, except for saying you'd be the man coming out of *that* building"—he pointed to Clara's apartment building on the block behind us—"with a real peach." He pointed to Isabella. "He looked—you know, ordinary. Brown hat, brown coat. Medium build. I didn't see his face. He never looked at me directly."

"Is this the man?" I showed him the picture of Fromley that we carried around.

"Maybe. I can't tell. Look, mister, I needed the money. It wasn't anything personal."

At that moment two policemen from the Tenderloin precinct barged through the crowd and immediately made for the singer and his accompanist, brandishing their bully sticks.

"Let go of that man, now! And hands in front, where we can see them."

Their prejudice was obvious—and I felt bad for my rescuers, who wore a look on their faces suggesting they were accustomed to this treatment.

I stepped in front of the officers and pulled out my own identification. "You've got it wrong. Those men are to be commended for helping me. You need to arrest this other man." I gestured to the pudgy man still pinned against the brick building. "For attacking a police officer."

"You sure?" The more senior officer looked around at the crowd, searching for anyone who would contradict me.

"We're certain," Isabella said, gazing at him with level eyes. "Everyone here who saw it will tell you the same."

"All right." The senior officer still looked suspicious, but he directed the singer to bring over my assailant, whom he promptly cuffed. "You'll be pressing charges then?"

"Absolutely," I said.

After once again thanking the men who helped us, Isabella and I followed the two policemen to the Nineteenth Precinct station house, where we made the statements necessary for the assault charges. From there, we walked to the subway station on Thirty-third Street and hopped on a northbound train headed back to the research center, where I hoped we would finally meet up with Alistair. I desperately wanted to talk with him tonight.

I was preoccupied by all we had seen today, from the disturbing photographs hidden in Fromley's closet, to the violent injuries he had inflicted on Clara Murphy, to the attack he—for it had to be Fromley—had orchestrated against me. It hadn't been a random attack. As my mind raced through possible scenarios, I decided he must have followed us after we visited his rooms at Mrs. Addison's. Then, while we were in Clara Murphy's building, he had plotted the attack and bribed Hal Jones to help. It had involved a degree of planning and foresight I had not expected, given what Alistair had said about him.

I wanted to hear Alistair's thoughts on the matter—because what struck me as important was that the attack had been designed to do more than just scare me. The man had tried to steal my bag. Assuming Fromley were responsible, he had gone to great lengths to recover and destroy the evidence I'd obtained—evidence that included the photographs, the glass I had taken for prints, even my case notes. It was a stroke of luck that the glass had not broken during the fracas. Was it possible he knew what I had taken? I supposed it was, if he had surveyed his room after we left.

A troubling thought lingered at the edges of my mind, just beyond my reach.

Could it have been anyone other than Fromley who orchestrated the attack this afternoon? I had enemies from old cases in the city, to be sure. But the timing alone made Fromley a suspect. We had visited his home and interviewed his last girlfriend immediately before the attack. And who else would have wanted my bag?

Probably what troubled me most was the fact that the man we wanted to locate had instead found us. It was an uncomfortable sensation.

With these thoughts weighing on my mind, I felt a renewed sense that Alistair was right: Michael Fromley must indeed be the killer we sought. I had been foolish ever to doubt it. And I would be even more foolish if I did not do my damnedest to find him straightaway.

CHAPTER 14

I would have preferred to take Isabella straight home, for she was clearly disturbed by the day's events—but she insisted on returning to the research center. I suspected she also wanted to talk with Alistair. And she had left her dog uptown and would not hear of going home without him.

"You must at least eat something," I said as we arrived at Alistair's offices.

"Will you ask Mrs. Leab to prepare something? I don't care what." Her voice was weary.

I had learned yesterday that Alistair maintained a kitchen in the building for his meals, managed by Mrs. Leab, a capable woman he had brought over from England for light secretarial and housekeeping duties at the research center. When Columbia first moved uptown, it had been a necessity, given the few amenities available in the neighborhood. Now that the area around Columbia had begun to attract restaurants and coffeehouses, it was simply convenient.

Alistair's office was empty, but I found Fred Ebbings down the hall, working with Tom Baxter.

"What happened to you?" Tom asked, noticing the scratches on my face. I filled them in on the day's events, which they agreed were not in keeping with behavior they might have anticipated from Fromley.

"I'd have expected him to go to ground," Tom said. "He was the type to run and hide, not hover on the fringes of this investigation. I wonder if he thinks you really have evidence incriminating him?"

"But if so," Fred added with a sniff, "why does he care? Michael never thought of the future. He lived moment to moment. That's why this attack against you, for instance, seems out of character to me. It involves a fair amount of foresight and planning—skills I always thought he lacked."

I disagreed. "He used roughly half an hour to plan and execute the attack. That's not a lot of time. And how much planning does it take to find someone in the Tenderloin who will take a swing at a stranger for extra cash?"

No one answered. Switching topics, I asked, "Have you seen Alistair?"

"He was here earlier," Fred said, shrugging. "We were reviewing our interviews with Fromley from August of this year. I just reread the transcript of one session in which he discussed a recent dream. It was remarkable—in the dream, he first killed himself and then worked to dispose of his own body." He lifted his head with pride. "I had thought it an excellent sign at the time, proof that he was transcending his old self."

I stared at him in disbelief; it sounded like half-baked nonsense to me. Did he honestly believe this sort of case review would help me track down Michael Fromley?

"Yes, you read him as destroying and burying his violent impulses—quite literally," Tom said smoothly as he changed the subject. "Look here, Ziele, you've had a wearing day. Give me the list Clara Murphy gave you of the restaurants Fromley frequented and let me check it out for you tonight." He put his arm around my shoulder and walked out of Fred's office with me. "And ask Mrs. Leab for some dinner, if you haven't already. She made a terrific vegetable soup today."

And indeed, by the time I rejoined Isabella, Mrs. Leab had brought a tray of bread and soup into the meeting room for us.

"Thank you," I said, gratefully accepting it. "Has Alistair left for the day?"

I broke off a piece of the bread—a delicious sourdough. Mrs. Leab had warmed it with the soup.

She chuckled. "You just missed him. He's out for a fancy dinner and a night at the opera. Gone to his regular box, he has. He said Caruso's singing tonight was not to be missed."

"Any message?"

She shrugged. "Not that he left with me. Sorry."

What had Alistair been doing all day? I had not spoken with him today, not once—even though he was supposed to be providing me with extensive help in this case.

"It's Alistair's working style," Isabella said, looking at me as though she understood. "He is a loner at heart, especially when he is mulling over a difficult problem. When he figures it out, he resurfaces. I've seen him do it time and again. Besides"—she smiled—"he did lend you me for the day."

"True enough," I said. Isabella had been very helpful—although she had joined me only by accident, if we were to be accurate about it.

"Simon, you're hurt!" Isabella's expression had changed, and she was staring aghast at my right arm.

I looked down and saw nothing unusual. Then I realized she had never before had reason to notice my injury, for I had always worn a jacket or overcoat. They had hidden the injury—or at least made it less readily apparent. But in my shirtsleeves, it was obvious that my right arm hung at a slightly odd angle and had limited movement.

"It's an old injury," I hastened to reassure her, "though I admit it's feeling worse than usual after my skirmish this evening."

"How did it happen?" she asked as she blew on her spoon to cool the soup.

"Malpractice," I said dryly. "The bone was crushed in one place, fractured in another, and the doctor who attended me set it incorrectly. He didn't notice until it was too late. Not wholly his fault, of course. He was overwhelmed by so many patients—" My voice grew rough and broke off. "It's done now anyway. I have an arthritis-like pain that sets in worst when it's cold and damp, and I've lost what strength I once had in it. But I manage all right most days."

"Surely it can be fixed—or at least improved?"

"Of course, with surgery. But surgery costs time and money, with no guaranteed outcome. I get along all right as I am. Luckily, I'm left-handed." I smiled and tried to make light of it—but she seemed to intuit that there was a darker history involved than I was ready to tell her.

Her brown eyes probed my own as she asked, "You were injured on the job?"

Someone knocked at the door.

"Something like that. It's a story that must wait for another time, I think." I got up, crossed the room, and opened the door to admit Horace Wood.

"Just dropping off some notes for Professor Sinclair. I thought he was in here with you," Horace explained. "They're my write-up of what I found out about Sarah's political activity from the college paper as well as some of her classmates." He looked uncertain. "Maybe you'd rather see them instead?"

"Please," I said. Given what Mrs. Leab had said, Alistair was otherwise occupied tonight. I, on the other hand, would have plenty of time to review the materials on my train ride home.

After Isabella again declined my offer to escort her home, I left the building with Horace beside me. To ease the awkwardness, I felt compelled to make conversation.

"You're heading home?" I asked.

"Not yet. I'm going to an important rally tonight held by the Municipal Owner's League," said Horace, his voice clipped and hurried.

"Who?" I asked.

"The independent party Hearst founded." Horace was appalled I hadn't remembered. "Tonight's rally is meant to show that reform-minded people won't be intimidated by Tammany."

"I haven't had much time to follow the election news given

the investigation," I said to placate him. "But I saw the headlines around town. Everyone seems to agree Tuesday's contest was crooked."

It was true. Even William Randolph Hearst's archenemies supported him. Hearst, as owner of the *Journal*, was neither liked nor particularly respected among his competitors. But his main rival, the *World*, and even the conservative *Sun* conceded Hearst had grounds to contest the official vote tally.

"Blatant thievery is what it was!" Horace was indignant. "You saw what happened to me Tuesday." He gestured to his purple bruise. "It was even worse for working-class voters downtown. I can't believe there's even a chance that cheat McClellan may stay in office." He practically spat as he spoke.

Seeking more congenial ground, I ventured, "Is your fiancée also involved with tonight's rally? I believe Isabella mentioned you were to be married next summer."

But I had asked the wrong question. Angry and hurt, Horace explained his fiancée had recently broken off their engagement.

I cast about for a different topic, for Horace's agitation was becoming stronger the more we talked along these lines.

"How long have you been helping Alistair with his research?" I asked.

"Almost seven years. I was here as an undergraduate, too, and my biology advisor briefly partnered with Professor Sinclair. He dropped his association a couple years ago, but I stayed on. The work satisfies my fellowship obligation without my having to teach."

Recalling my own days in college, I could well imagine why Horace preferred to avoid the classroom. With his unkempt appearance and nasal voice, he would have been disrespected; the typical student would have made his classroom a misery.

"It has been an education working for Professor Sinclair. Sometimes I learn more than I want. You see, when the professor gets caught up in his own research, he can forget about what's most important."

I assumed he meant Alistair forgot important things like eating lunch. Good-naturedly I replied, "But he has Mrs. Leab on his staff to make sure none of you forget to eat."

Then I looked and saw Horace was serious.

"No," he said, "I've learned things that trouble my conscience and keep me from sleeping at night."

I nodded sympathetically. "I can see why learning too much about criminals like Fromley would give you nightmares."

"Well, the professor himself—" Horace stopped himself.

But he had piqued my interest more than I would have liked to admit.

I baited him, hoping he would say more. "I'm sure you're mistaken. Ridiculous to think Alistair could be responsible for giving anyone bad dreams." I managed to sound amused, which had the effect I intended: He grew frustrated that I had misunderstood him.

"That's not what I meant. The professor himself is responsible." He withdrew again. "But I shouldn't say too much. It's not my place, and he's been good to me. Generous with recommendations and assignments, and a couple times he's helped me out of a real jam." He shoved his hands in his pockets, looking steadfastly at the sidewalk below us.

I tried a firmer approach to encourage him. "Alistair is helping me with an important murder investigation. If there is anything you think I should know, I'd say it's your duty to tell me."

"Well—" He was reluctant, but after another moment, he began talking. Horace was concerned about Alistair's methods as they related to larger political goals. He was bothered, apparently, that Alistair would use his learning to "let criminals go free." While that was not what I understood to be within Alistair's concept of rehabilitation, Horace was adamant in his belief.

"He takes his research to court and testifies about the criminal as a *person*. He describes the defendant's background, outlines why he behaves as he does, and interprets what that behavior means. He predicts the criminal's entire career path, whether he will become a habitual offender or can be rehabilitated. And in the professor's view, they *all* can be rehabilitated. He talks in circles until the judge and jury have entirely forgotten about whatever heinous act brought the defendant to trial in the first place. And if that doesn't work," he continued, sounding pained, "he resorts to other, less traditional methods. Believe me, there's nothing the professor will not do to advance his own research."

"Surely you exaggerate," I said. But I was listening with no small measure of concern.

"Ask him about Moira Shea sometime—then you'll see," Horace said knowingly. "Mention her name just once and see what he says. It will surprise—no, it will shock you, the lengths he has gone to in the name of scientific progress. And you will understand why you should think twice before you trust him." His tone was now hushed.

I looked him full in the eye, not knowing what to make of him. I accepted that Horace was opinionated and unmannerly, but now he was making a serious allegation against the man who employed him and supported his graduate research. To his credit, he seemed almost ashamed by it.

"I don't have time for riddles now," I said. "We are in the

middle of a difficult murder investigation. Either you have something to tell me—or you don't."

"You're right." He drew himself up. "You should know it,
and you may as well hear it from me. Moira Shea is the first girl
Michael Fromley murdered. He stabbed her fourteen times. It
happened two months before the attempted-murder charges he
faced in Catherine Smedley's case. The police never connected
him to the Shea murder. But Alistair Sinclair knew—and did
nothing. He aided and abetted Fromley by covering it up, when
justice should have sent Fromley to the electric chair."

He paused a moment to let this information sink in. "Ask
him why during the Smedley case, Hogart, the most experienced prosecutor at the DA's office, was replaced with a rookie
just before trial. It has even been rumored"—he bent toward
me confidentially—"that the professor bribed Judge Hansen, a
close family friend, to lean on the prosecution. The charges were
dropped abruptly—and the case dismissed. I'd like to think
what I'm telling you isn't true. But the facts raise a lot of questions."

I was silent. Horace gave me a final, embarrassed glance.
"Better be careful, Detective."

As soon as he said it, he was gone.

And I was left standing alone at the corner of Broadway
and 114th Street, stomach churning, completely aghast that this
allegation could have any truth to it.

CHAPTER 15

I began to walk briskly, my feet keeping pace with my turbulent emotions. My anger seethed red-hot, and as I made my way over to Riverside Drive, the peaceful sight of the Hudson glistening in the moonlight did nothing to assuage the raw emotions that had taken hold of me. By instinct, I walked downtown. The shock of betrayal stung sharply: My anger toward Alistair intermingled with disgust at my own failure to recognize his duplicity. If Horace were right, then I had been lied to and taken advantage of in a manner that was completely self-serving. And worse, Alistair had been derelict in duties both ethical and professional. Why hadn't I questioned him more? Had I been so blinded by his learning that I forgot every instinct I usually followed?

After some twenty blocks, my rage had calmed and cold logic prevailed. The allegations Horace had let slip were serious— and before I could evaluate them, I needed to look Alistair in the eye and hear his response. He was at the opera tonight, Mrs. Leab had said. And for Alistair, attending an opera was a social event as much as a musical one. He maintained a box there, which he had no doubt filled with society friends this evening. It was a tangible reminder that he had been born into a strato- sphere of class and wealth I did not fully understand. That, I accepted. But had it created in Alistair a sense of entitlement, of being above the law? That, I could never abide.

I walked back to Broadway and grabbed a cab down to Thirty-ninth Street where the Metropolitan Opera House was located. Fortunately, I arrived just prior to the first intermission— for though the flash of my police credentials yielded information about Alistair's regular box, it did not persuade the recalcitrant house manager to let me enter during the performance.

"If it's not a matter of life or death, I can't do it. Especially during Caruso's solo—Mr. Conreid would have my job," the man said stubbornly, referring to the general manager at the Met who was notorious for indulging his newest star. "You'll have to wait."

I could have forced the issue, I supposed, but it did not seem worth the fight. From the lobby, I listened to Enrico Caruso's full-throated tenor as it reached the solo's crescendo, and found myself hoping that Horace Wood had been mean-spirited or grievously mistaken. Anything but right.

The moment the curtain fell and the lights came up, I made my way to Alistair's box, pushing against the crowd of well- dressed patrons making their way to the bar. Alistair, luckily, was still seated, casually sipping a glass of champagne as he chatted with a woman wearing a green gown and glistening jewelry. He did not notice me until I interrupted him.

"Alistair. It's urgent that I speak with you. Please come downstairs with me." My voice sounded false and oddly formal, even to my own ears.

"Ziele! What on earth are you doing here?" he said in surprise as he rose halfway out of his seat. "Is something wrong?"

"I need to talk with you," I said again. "Outside, where we can speak in private."

"I'll be downstairs in a moment, then—I'll meet you outside the lobby. I need a minute here."

Turning to leave, I overheard Alistair as he made his excuses.

"Valeria, can I get you anything while I'm up?" He addressed the woman beside him.

"Alistair," she said, pouting, "must you leave right now? With that ill-bred man? Why, he came storming in here, not even dressed in appropriate evening clothes! But I suppose I'll forgive you if you'll be so good as to bring me another champagne when you return." The peal of her flirtatious laugh was the last sound I heard as I left the box.

I had never liked society women. At least, what I had seen of them; after all, I had never known any of them personally. But the ones with whom I had crossed paths, however obliquely, seemed to be stiff and artificial. This lady was certainly no exception.

"Well, Simon," Alistair said, sounding jovial as he joined me downstairs. "What is so important that you had to pull me away from good music and company in such dramatic fashion?" His cheeks were tinged red from the champagne, and I reflected he would have done well to refuse his last drink.

"Moira Shea," I said, and the name was an accusation. "I want to hear what you have to say about Moira Shea."

He flinched ever so slightly, but his tone when he replied remained smooth. "Where did you hear about her? She died over three years ago, and her death has no relevance to our present case."

Our case indeed. I resented him more for reminding me of how closely we had partnered together these last crucial days.

"It doesn't matter where I heard about her. And on this subject, I alone decide what's relevant to my case." The words came out even more forcefully than I intended, and he looked at me in surprise.

"Come." He gestured toward Fortieth Street where fewer people were congregated. "I believe we require more privacy for this conversation."

Halfway down the block, we ducked into a small Irish pub by mutual agreement. We found a small table in the corner, far from the crowd at the bar. Alistair promptly ordered two pints of stout that neither of us wanted.

I stared at him, waiting for him to begin, and trying to ignore the sick gnawing sensation in my gut.

"I had hoped never to tell you this," he said. "I have kept what I'm about to say secret from all but my closest associates at the research center. Which of them told you?" His expression was grim. "I assume it was Horace, who is notoriously loose-lipped. Besides, I cannot believe Fred would have betrayed my confidence."

I did not even acknowledge his question. "I need to know about Moira Shea," I said.

He moistened his lips and, with his napkin, wiped away some foam from the beer that had got onto his mustache. "When

I came to you this past Wednesday morning, I told you some background about my decision to work with Michael Fromley."

"Yes, I believe you said you facilitated a plea bargain that released him to your custody because he had not yet 'crossed the line,' so to speak. Despite his violent tendencies, he had not yet committed murder. That was the single reason why I understood you to believe that your research, particularly your work with Fromley, was so important. But that wasn't the truth, was it?" My eyes bored into him as I waited to hear his answer.

"You gave me a hard time then, because you didn't see much distinction between attempted and actual murder," he said. "Yet I came to you because I had heard about the way you responded to new ideas. My contacts in the police department said you had quite a reputation for it, and were willing to learn in a way more seasoned members of the force would not. I felt you would be capable of understanding why the things I wanted to learn from Michael Fromley were so important."

"Yes," I said, impatient with his flattery. "But I would never sacrifice justice for the sake of knowledge. And I would never endanger the life of another human being for it. Tell me that is not exactly what you have done here!" I knew I sounded judgmental and I could not help myself. "Tell me the truth about Moira Shea," I demanded, "the full story, with nothing omitted this time."

He banged his fist on the table in response, jostling our glasses of beer. "Simon, don't be so damned single-minded. You have the capacity to see and understand the moral complexities here—I know you do, because I chose you for it."

"What do you mean, that you 'chose me' for it?" I demanded. "You couldn't possibly have chosen me for anything. A young woman had the misfortune to be murdered within my jurisdiction. You contacted me only some hours after the murder. If you had relevant information, then you had no choice but to deal with me."

Yet the thought occurred to me: Was it possible the man had manipulated me to an even greater extent than I already recognized?

Alistair was adamant. "Absolutely not true. For a man with my contacts, a couple of hours were sufficient to learn all I needed to know about you. I could have gone to Chief Healy, though his suspicions of me are probably worse than your own. And given my contacts in Yonkers—a larger jurisdiction than yours that has aided you with the case—I could certainly have handpicked someone there. But I chose you. Because I was told you had the intellectual capacity to understand the importance of my work. And my work is not so far from your own interests. Why, our paths might have crossed naturally, had you not had to leave Columbia."

I simply stared. I had no idea how he had managed to learn of that part of my life, and I resented him the more for knowing it. Somehow it seemed a double betrayal: that he had taken advantage of me both professionally and personally by withholding information he knew to be important.

"Yes," he continued, "I know all about how your father gambled away everything and left your mother. You had to leave college to support her and your sister, didn't you? Pity—it was a damned waste of a fine opportunity, if you ask me." He took another sip from his beer. "I even know what happened the day of the *Slocum* steamship disaster. You had business uptown at the Thirty-fourth Precinct. When the call came in, you joined a group of police-commandeered rescue boats. I hear you helped rescue many survivors. But your fiancée didn't make it; she was among the thousand who perished."

It was private information he should not have had, and I felt myself shaking with rage as unwanted flashes of memory distracted me. Alistair was partially right; I had been meeting with another officer from the Thirty-fourth Precinct to discuss a rash of robberies that spanned our jurisdictions. An officer walking his beat had called in with news of the burning steamship. I joined a number of others who sped to the waterfront near 138th Street to help. We had saved a number of people, but I had pushed to get closer and closer to the burning ship. Pushed too hard, those with me said—because I risked destroying our boat and the lives of everyone on it.

I took a series of deep breaths and forced myself to refocus on the present. Alistair wanted only to distract me and change the subject—something I would not allow.

"Enough of this talk. Either tell me about Moira Shea now, or I will go straight to my old precinct and find out from them. And I will be sure to share everything I have heard tonight about your role in suppressing information you obtained about her murder."

It was not an empty threat, and he knew it.

He drummed his fingers on the table, glancing over toward the crowd at the bar as if to ascertain whether anyone was listening. But the assorted men gathered there had taken little if any notice of us; they were fully occupied in singing various Irish tunes in even more varied keys.

I looked at Alistair, waiting expectantly. After a moment, he cleared his throat and at last began to tell me what I wanted— yet dreaded—to hear.

"You must believe me, I didn't know about Moira Shea

when I first made the arrangements for Michael Fromley in the Smedley case. When I spoke with Fromley's half brother Clyde Wallingford, when I argued that the prosecutor should drop all charges, and even during our first few months working with Michael—I never heard a word about Moira Shea. The Catherine Smedley case was weak, and the other crimes of which he had been accused were minor."

"Did you bribe or otherwise influence the judge in the Smedley case?"

"No," Alistair said heatedly. "Who told you that lie?"

"Judge Hansen is a close friend of yours, however," I said.

"Our families have known each other for years but that does not mean I acted unethically. The attempted-murder charge was dismissed because it was weak. And Michael's plea on the lesser charges—the plea that released him to my custody—was perfectly aboveboard."

I persisted. "I understand the original prosecutor was removed from the case against his will." I looked at my notes. "That would have been Frank Hogart, with a stellar record of convictions and a reputation for tenacity. I believe you found the second-year rookie from the DA's office to be more amenable to dismissing the major charge."

Alistair looked at me with a pained expression. "The district attorney's office shuffles schedules all the time. Personally, I think for all his bluster and complaints, Hogart didn't *want* the case. Had it gone to trial, it might have blemished his perfect conviction record, for the evidence simply wasn't there. And it would have hurt his tougher-than-nails image if he himself permitted the dismissal."

He sighed deeply. "Michael did not confess to the Shea murder for nearly a year. He told Fred during a session in October

1903. Fred came to me at once, worried about the legal implications for us." He leaned in even closer to my ear. "If we believed his 'confession,' then we were concerned we may have had an ethical obligation to report it."

"*May* have had?"

"Yes," Alistair repeated firmly, "*may* have had. It is difficult to explain without going over the entire case history, but Michael Fromley is a young man who maintains a very fragile distinction between fantasy and reality. Just because he says a thing, why should we believe it? How could we be certain that what he confessed to us about murdering Moira Shea was the truth—and not simply another instance of his active fantasy life?"

"Is a dead body not certainty enough?" I said. "All *you* needed to determine the truth was to consult whatever police 'source' was so forthcoming about the Wingate case in Dobson. The source could have confirmed whether a murder victim named Moira Shea ever existed."

"And I did just that," Alistair said, defensive now, "but what you fail to grasp is that such knowledge did not resolve the issue. Of course, I consulted the police. And I reviewed the crime logs of the *Times* and the *World*. There was nothing the police told me—and nothing Michael told me—that was not also public knowledge, reported in the pages of every press in the city. A girl named Moira Shea had been slashed to death in an empty warehouse by the river. And she had last been seen getting onto the subway. Were these circumstances in keeping with Michael's disturbing fantasies? To be sure. And yet"—he leaned into the table again, his voice dropping as he realized he had been talking rather loudly—"how could Fred and I say with any certainty that Michael had not simply borrowed his confession from the pages of the *Herald*? He was constantly feeding his imagination with clippings from the newspapers and magazines. Could we be sure he had actually committed this crime? Or—had he merely *wished* he had done so, *imagined* he had done so, because it so perfectly complemented his fantasies?"

"How about physical evidence?" I was angry now, too. "Or witnesses. Anything that may have placed Fromley at the scene. The police might have figured it out, had you properly reported what you knew."

"Please," Alistair said, "give me some credit for thinking through these issues. When he confessed to us in October 1903, it was well over a year after Moira Shea was killed in August 1902. You know perfectly well how ill preserved most crime scenes are, even a day after the crime occurs."

He was right. The time span was a long one, and the lack of interest in physical evidence had been my greatest frustration at the department.

"But you might have given it a chance," I argued. "There may have been other physical evidence to link him to the crime that was preserved. It could have been reexamined in light of what you knew."

"You are missing an important point," Alistair said, going on to explain. "There were discrepancies between Michael's account and certain details about the Shea murder. He convinced us of his motivation, and certainly Moira Shea's death was consistent with his choice of weapon. But he kept changing the details: the time of day the attack occured; what Miss Shea was wearing. These are important details the murderer should have known. It was established that she had taken a one o'clock train, and she had worn a yellow shirtwaist and dark skirt. Michael should have been clear about these details—and yet he was not. That led us to doubt the veracity of his confession."

But it was Alistair who missed the most important point. I said, "So you were reluctant to act because Michael's confession may have been false. Still, it was not your call to make; didn't it occur to you to speak with the police? Or even your old friend Judge Hansen might have reminded you of your responsibilities. To keep quiet was nothing short of obstruction of justice."

He flushed ever so slightly. "My other concern involved the importance of our work. To make an issue of Michael's guilt would be tantamount to throwing away significant research that could do tremendous good. To risk that was virtually unthinkable." His tone was firm. "At first, I was despondent, believing all our work had been for naught. We had believed Michael was a criminal-in-the-making, not yet fully formed, which offered us a chance to test rehabilitative measures in a way never before done. Suddenly, our research risked being invalidated—for if Michael had crossed the line and committed murder, then what good was our research? Our efforts had been directed toward preventing him from acting on his violent fantasies."

He paused a moment, and then continued with growing excitement. "Then it occurred to me: It was only our research *premise* that had to change. We could begin with the assumption that Michael Fromley may have been a murderer when we commenced work. How much more impressive, then, if we rehabilitated him! We would have every prison program in the country clamoring at our door for information about rehabilitation. Every psychologist would come to consult Fred about what treatment approach worked. Every jurist would analyze the implications for sentencing. Sociologists would be able to reframe questions about how the criminal is shaped, and economists might begin to analyze the cost savings to society of lower crime rates. We might have achieved something truly groundbreaking, if only—"

Here, I interrupted with my own sentiments. "If only you hadn't lost track of this confessed murderer and let him loose on an unsuspecting public. How could you think, even for a moment, that your research was more important than such a risk to human life?"

He replied quietly, "Of course I did not. I never expected it to come to that."

"And putting aside your decision to keep quiet when you first learned of Michael's confession, you didn't even report the danger he posed when he went missing two weeks ago."

"We sincerely believed he was on his way to a successful rehabilitation. We did not think he posed a substantial risk."

I shot back, "But you were worried enough that you contacted the police each day, simply to reassure yourself that no criminal incident in the police blotter could be attributed to him. You did that much, yet you could not sound the alert that would have required the police to search for him and perhaps keep him out of trouble in the first place."

"If you're not going to listen to reason, there is little point in continuing this conversation," he said.

"I am listening," I said. "Listening attentively, and with a great desire to understand. But the choices you've made strike me as so reckless that it is difficult to do so."

Both of us sat in silence, thinking. We were at an impasse.

"I need to know just one more thing," I said quietly. "Had you known about Moira Shea from the beginning, would you still have facilitated the dismissal of charges against Michael Fromley and accepted him into your custody?"

His answer was important to my judgment of him, for in my mind, the question of his intent was crucial. Had Alistair made reckless decisions along the way because he had been blinded by the importance of his research? Or, was his hubris so large that he believed his own intellectual pursuits were all-important, and the rest of the world be damned?

There was a long moment's pause as I waited for his reply.

Finally, he looked at me, and I saw both honesty and fear reflected in his eyes as he replied, "I do not know." He seemed to collapse in the chair. "What do you plan to do now? Are you going to proceed as we have been doing? Or are you going to sound the alarm, and circulate this information?"

My response perfectly echoed his own.

I looked at him squarely. "Like you, I do not know."

CHAPTER 16

It was half past eleven by the time I returned to Dobson that night. Despite the late hour, Joe was awake, reading in the front parlor that had become his convalescence room. He preferred that room, with its view of the street leading down to the train station and factories, to the second-floor bedroom that would have isolated him from the daily rhythms of life in the village. As a result, the sofa had been converted into his sickbed, and a bookcase brought in with all manner of reading material. After I peered in the window and confirmed he was up, I tapped at the glass, and then let myself in through the front door at his signal.

Joe greeted me with surprise and pleasure. "Didn't expect to see you again so soon, Ziele. Thought you had a murder to solve."

"How are you feeling?"

He shrugged. "Okay. I'm getting old. I don't recover from ailments as fast as I used to."

"This wasn't just an ordinary 'ailment,'" I reminded him. "A stroke is a major illness; you shouldn't expect too much of your body, too soon."

"Bah." He waved me off. "I wasn't made for the sickbed. I'll lose my mind, as well, if my body doesn't heal soon."

"You like to fish?" I changed the topic, after noticing Izaak Walton's *The Compleat Angler* was bookmarked on the table beside him.

"Fly-fishing," he confirmed. "Just hope I'll be back in shape by April, when the spring season starts."

"I'm sure you will be," I said. "I brought something to drink. Do you have a glass?"

"You'll find them in the corner cabinet in the dining room."

I returned a moment later with two glasses and placed them on the table nearest Joe. Then I pulled out a bottle of brandy, a favorite I had just purchased.

"I assume Anna's safely in bed?" I raised an eyebrow toward the upstairs before I poured him a stiff glass. Joe's wife had definite ideas about what convalescing patients needed, and I strongly suspected liquor would not meet with her approval.

He chuckled. "Nearly two hours ago. The woman is worn out tending to me. She's very thorough. I'd frankly trade some of that care for a bit more freedom."

More soberly, he added, "I want to stay involved in the case. I can still manage Mayor Fuller and his complaints. And I can still supervise all the work done by those helping us from Yonkers."

"Agreed." I raised my glass and toasted him. "To your health—and a speedy recovery."

"Aye," he said.

He savored the aroma for a few moments before he spoke again, his tone matter-of-fact. "You're in a dark mood. And why should that be? The last I checked, you had use of both legs and all your wits. In my opinion, a man that can say that has no worries." Joe's words were full of jest, but his eyes were serious and searching as he looked at me.

"Actually, I may have lost my wits," I admitted, the fingers of my left hand tracing circles around my brandy glass. "I placed my trust where I shouldn't have."

"You mean with that Columbia professor and all his cockamamie ideas?"

I nodded, and filled him in; I left out no detail as I described what I had uncovered as well as what Alistair had said in his own defense. "I think what troubles me most," I said, "is my sense that Alistair is still hiding something. I am convinced he has not yet told me the full story of the Fromley matter."

"Now you're being smart again," Joe said. "But the real question is: What are you going to do with what you know? How does it affect solving Sarah Wingate's murder?"

"I'm tempted to bring the city police into the case. I could do so in an instant if I shared what Alistair told me," I said. "But the drawback would be the political infighting that would result. And the press would be all over it, the way they cover any story with a hint of scandal or impropriety. Taken together, those are two complications that could potentially hinder the investigation more, on balance, than additional city resources would help. So much attention would send Fromley permanently underground." I sighed deeply. "I also know the scrutiny could well destroy Alistair's reputation."

"And why do you care about that?" was Joe's rejoinder.

I was unsure, and I admitted as much to Joe. The press would seize upon Alistair's currying of personal favor and disregard for police authority; they would sensationalize it into the sort of scandal that sells newspapers. And while in my angrier moments I thought that was exactly what he deserved, I knew that to punish him would not help me solve this case any faster.

"Alistair's admission underscores the danger Fromley poses," I said. "We need to find him. That's really the only priority, but chasing him is like chasing a ghost. Wherever I look, I discover places he has been and people he has hurt. But I cannot find *him*."

"Then maybe you need to think more like a ghost," Joe suggested, only partly tongue-in-cheek. "In other words, where does a man like him go when he needs to disappear? If you can figure that out, then you might better your odds of finding him. And you, of all people, should know the places a man can disappear in the city."

It was the first time Joe had alluded to knowing anything about my personal history; but then again, this night had been full of surprises. And while most of them had been unpleasant, Joe's company had been unexpectedly good-natured and helpful. In the aftermath of his stroke, the petty awkwardness between us was gone. After I bid him good night, I returned to my own bed and a fitful sleep in which I dreamed of my own father and his innate ability to disappear into the fabric of the city whenever he fell deeply in debt. I thought of all the hiding places I had known him to choose. Which of them would appeal to someone who wanted to disappear permanently? If I could answer that, then perhaps I would be much closer to tracking down the elusive Michael Fromley.

Friday, November 10, 1905

CHAPTER 17

Joe and I had reached an agreement last night: He would continue to manage the Dobson end of the investigation from home, and I would focus on whatever was required in the city. Unsurprisingly, Alistair was not in his office when I looked for him the next morning. I had come here, however, in hopes of consulting with Tom Baxter. Earlier, he had impressed me as levelheaded and pragmatic; I could not imagine he would have countenanced Alistair's decisions about Fromley had he known of them, and I was interested to hear what he would say now. I found him at his desk, almost buried among several piles of papers.

He greeted me with some surprise. "Good morning, Ziele. I didn't expect to see anyone else here so early this morning." He waved his hand over his desk, explaining, "Just trying to get some midterm exams graded. I'd hoped to return them to my students this week, but I'm making such slow progress, I fear they will be disappointed."

I returned his greeting and then waited a moment as Tom paused uncertainly, looking at me as though trying to divine what I wanted before I told him.

"Sit down," he said finally; "you look as though you've got something on your mind."

"You might say that," I said with an ease I did not feel. I claimed the chair across from him. "Actually, I need to speak with you about a matter that occurred two years ago in October 1903. While I believe that is before you came here, Alistair may have told you something about it."

I explained the relevant details I'd learned the previous evening, leaving out nothing of importance. As I suspected, he had known nothing of Fromley's purported confession, and seemed only slightly less appalled than I had been to learn of the cavalier way Alistair and Fred had chosen to conceal this information. As his brow furrowed in concentration, I allowed him to digest the problem for a few moments before I mentioned that I wanted to examine any relevant case files.

"A capital idea," Tom said, swinging around in his chair energetically. "Surely the files can help with some of the information we're missing." He glanced at his watch; it was already nearly nine o'clock. "Mrs. Leab should be in by now—I'll ask her to bring them to us."

In addition to light housekeeping and cooking duties, Mrs. Leab kept appointments for all three professors, typed their letters and formal reports, and engaged in limited filing duties. Tom returned with her after just a few moments, each of them

carrying a stack of thick files. CASE NOTES / OCTOBER 1903"
read the label on each, with sublabels designating the more specific material contained therein. Though unsurprisingly, there
was no overt reference to Michael Fromley's confession. Tom
divided the papers into two stacks. We each read silently, trad-
ing papers as we finished them, until we had digested the material contained within. The body of material primarily consisted
of Alistair's case notes, but observations by Fred Ebbings, copies of police reports detailing the circumstances of Moira Shea's
murder, and newspaper clippings covering the same were also
included.

I have a terrible memory for criminals themselves. Unless
there is anything particularly unusual about a criminal's personality or the crime itself, the facts of one case blend together
with the others in my mind. And yet, I remember each and every victim with a clarity that astounds me. Each haunts me—
and Moira Shea began to do so that morning, the moment she
assumed shape and form from the scant facts I gleaned about
her in the reports. She had recently trained as a nurse at the
Bellevue Training School for Nursing and was working her
first job, as a private nurse for an elderly woman on East Sixty-
first Street. She occasionally volunteered at Miss Wald's Henry
Street Nurses Settlement. One police officer speculated that her
murder was premeditated, committed by someone she had encountered while working in poor neighborhoods. This struck
me as unlikely; the nurses who tended to the sick were so badly
needed in the roughest of areas, they were welcomed, never
hurt.

The pictures in Moira Shea's file showed a woman with
strong features. Her hair was piled high atop her head and she
wore glasses with simple frames. From her expression alone, I

could imagine she had not easily succumbed to her killer. That was confirmed when I found the coroner's report detailing the significant number of defensive wounds she suffered; she had fought her attacker vigorously.

Moira Shea was twenty-one when she was stabbed to death in a vacant warehouse near the East River in August 1902. The autopsy report indicated there was no evidence of sexual assault, although some of her clothes were missing when her body was found. As Alistair had mentioned last night, Moira was last seen traveling downtown on the Second Avenue El by witnesses who came forward later. Those on the car near her described a man oddly dressed; he wore a brown trench coat despite the summer heat. His behavior had attracted attention, too; he had mumbled to himself and stared at each woman on the El intently. He had gotten off at Moira's stop, following in her direction, yet apparently keeping his distance. Witnesses could say nothing more; several were alarmed they had not intervened or at least taken him more seriously at the time.

After thoroughly reviewing this evidence, I turned my attention to Fromley's confession. I saw immediately that Alistair had been right on at least one count: Fromley's story was full of troubling discrepancies. According to the police report, Moira had been stabbed fourteen times; yet Fromley stated he "couldn't remember" if he had stabbed her more than once or twice. Her stab wounds were about the face, hands, and chest; yet Fromley claimed to have beaten her with his fists, then slit her throat. The coroner had estimated her time of death as around six o'clock in the evening; Fromley maintained he killed her near midnight, after "enjoying her company" for the evening. That was a euphemism for the sort of sexual violation the coroner's report explicitly ruled out.

In evidentiary terms, Alistair was right to be less than entirely convinced by this confession. Had I been the police officer in charge of questioning Fromley, so many discrepancies would have raised real questions in my mind, as well. And yet, that was precisely the point: Alistair had taken it upon *himself* to make that judgment call. And to make that decision alone was neither his responsibility nor his right.

But if Fromley's confession was lacking in terms of hard, logistical details, it was nonetheless filled with exceptionally lurid details to describe his motivation for murder. "I didn't like the way she avoided me," he had said. "She looked right past me— as though I were nothing." According to his notes accompanying the confession, Fred Ebbings had suggested to Fromley that perhaps, like all well-bred ladies, she had been cautioned not to interact with strangers. But Fromley refused to accept that possibility. Instead, Fromley believed the woman was purposely ignoring him; he grew angrier and angrier that she did so; then he decided he would make her regret it. The more he looked at her, the more he wanted to make her see him. "I kept staring at her face," he explained, "and looking in her eyes. When she didn't look back, I decided I'd have to *make* her look." His confession continued along these lines, detailing his determination to make her appreciate his true power. He claimed to have followed her and subdued her by the abandoned warehouse where the actual murder took place.

So what was the truth of it? I wondered. Was it possible that Fromley's confession was merely conjectured fantasy? His own fictionalized version of a real murder he had read about in the papers? Or, was he guilty of this crime—and we simply could not verify it because his confession was riddled with flaws? Perhaps the details of the murder had become irretrievably confused as they intermingled with his fantasies. I found myself as much at a loss to make this judgment as Alistair had claimed to be.

"So what are your thoughts?" I asked Tom after I finished. We looked at each other uneasily.

"Well," Tom said, "Fromley was nothing if not a trouble-maker, and he certainly appears to be the man you want for murdering Sarah Wingate. But the Shea girl?" he said, and frowned. "Not a shred of hard evidence points that way. Not even the boy's own confession, since I personally believe Fromley would have better remembered the details of what was supposedly his first murder."

He paused a moment before he continued. "What you may not realize, however, never having met Fromley, is how sharp he is. Fred maintains Fromley is a psychopath." He paused for a moment, observing my reaction before going on to ask, "Are you familiar with the term?"

"I assume it is an academic term for a crazed murderer," I said dryly.

"Sort of," Tom acknowledged with a rueful smile. "It actually designates a specific kind of personality. A person who is considered psychopathic lies just for the fun of it. Fromley often did; he may have given us a false confession just for his own amusement. You'll also recall from what we have told you that Fromley was both impulsive and aggressive, so he was often involved in fights. What would be considered psychopathic about this behavior was that he never felt remorse for what he had done. If he hurt or mistreated someone, he was completely indifferent to their pain, because he had previously rationalized why they deserved their mistreatment."

Tom looked at me intently, as if wanting reassurance I had

followed him. I recognized it as a teacher's habit; he wanted to be sure his listener had understood one point before he ventured on to the next.

"I understand," I said, anxious for him to continue.

"I explain this so you don't lose sight of how intelligent he is. So you don't forget how easily and expertly he lies. I would not put it past him to have fabricated the entire confession simply to put Alistair in the very position of indecision and uncertainty in which he found himself. Fromley would have enjoyed watching Alistair squirm as he wrestled with his doubts. And," he added, "I also do not discount that if he were guilty of Moira Shea's murder, he may have contrived to riddle his confession with so many errors it could not be deemed credible. That way, he could both claim credit for the crime and yet remain safe from punishment, since reasonable minds would doubt his culpability."

"Then why bother confessing at all? Why do you claim he needed 'credit' for having committed the crime?" I asked. Tom was persuasive, but this part of his analysis made no sense to me.

"Because Fromley wanted Alistair to appreciate his criminal plans—both real and imagined," Tom said. "Alistair's research with Fromley, whatever benefit it might produce for scientific advancement, created a troubling effect upon Fromley's ego. He came to feel self-important as a result of having educated men hanging upon his every word, working full-time just to try to figure him out."

"I suppose that makes sense. But since we cannot conclude beyond a reasonable doubt that Fromley did—or did not—kill Moira Shea, I have a dilemma regarding Alistair." I looked at the mass of material that fully obscured Tom's desk. "There's not enough hard evidence here for me to tell the city police and expect to be taken seriously—especially since it involves a killing that occurred over three years ago."

Tom's mouth formed a grim, hard line. "And it would destroy Alistair's reputation. I'm sure you're aware of that."

I said evenly, "My only concern is what will best help us solve the Wingate murder—and prevent another one like it. If I report Fromley's link to a past crime, within the city's jurisdiction, the detective bureau would at least offer us additional resources. But we would also have to deal with political posturing and the press—both of which may hinder our ability to track down Fromley."

We debated the issue for the better part of the next half hour, back and forth, until at last we came to a resolution. Tom remained concerned with protecting Alistair's reputation—a view he frankly acknowledged to be self-interested, given his own affiliation with Alistair and the research center. But together with my own concerns about third-party involvement, we reluctantly agreed to keep the matter to ourselves, at least for now.

"This is only because I think undue attention to Alistair's lapse in judgment would undermine our efforts in the Wingate case," I said. "Yet, to what extent do we continue to involve Alistair?"

"You mean you would consider ending the association?" Tom seemed genuinely shocked, despite the matters we had just discussed.

"Absolutely," I said. "I do not trust him. From reviewing this evidence"—I gestured toward the stacks of paper on Tom's desk—"I know the allegations involving Fromley are questionable. The Fromley confession is of dubious value, and Alistair strenuously denies using undue influence in the Smedley case.

But it doesn't change the fact that Alistair put his own research above and beyond all other concerns. Can you honestly tell me otherwise?"

"That judgment is one only you can make," Tom replied frankly. "I believe the ethical line Alistair may draw is different from your own. But such differences, while hard for you to understand, may not be unethical. I have no doubt that compelling evidence would have convinced Alistair to turn Fromley in. But lacking that, he chose to continue as before." He paused a moment. "You know, he's not as unsympathetic to your priorities as you seem to think."

Something about his tone was odd; I looked sharply at Tom. "What do you mean by that?"

"Alistair has been a criminal law professor for his entire career. But it was simply that—a career—for the longest time. It occupied his days, earned him the respect of family and friends, and"—he smiled slightly—"permitted him free time to pursue more social interests. Criminology did not become his passion— his obsession, really—until his son Teddy was killed."

"Killed?" I asked sharply, recalling how Isabella had stiffened at the mention of Teddy's name. "I had heard only that Theodore Sinclair died tragically while traveling in Greece."

"Not exactly," Tom said. "He was killed during a robbery. Teddy, just like Alistair, believed he was invincible." He added, "When he was robbed, he fought back. He might have lived otherwise. The loss—and some unsettling circumstances surrounding it—affected Alistair profoundly."

And Isabella, I thought, feeling a surge of sympathy for her. Some people would say a young man who died too young was simply that—no more, no less. But I knew better. Murder was different.

"After Teddy's death," Tom continued, "Alistair became driven to understand *why*. He wanted to learn everything he could about the motivation and point of view of people who commit crimes, especially those who kill. On a personal level, he needed to know; and intellectually, he also believed that if we learned more, then the disciplines of sociology, psychology, and law could do more to prevent the criminal mind from developing in the first place. Or, at the least, we might arrest the path of the criminal mind's development early on and redirect it. Rehabilitate it, in Alistair's terms."

Tom paused a moment to let me digest this information. "I tell you this much, to help you understand, but this is Alistair's story. If you need to know more, you must ask him. There are other complications . . ."

I nodded thoughtfully. "Understood." I suspected those complications were somehow related to Isabella's odd silences, perhaps even to Mrs. Sinclair's permanent separation from Alistair. But I was not like Alistair. He had felt compelled to uncover my own secrets; I was content to let his lie.

We were interrupted by Mrs. Leab's brisk knock at the door. "Detective, you just received a message by courier."

I thanked her and read it quickly. "It's from Joe. The Yonkers police lab where I sent Michael Fromley's shaving bowl and brush for fingerprint analysis has confirmed they were *not* a match with those prints retrieved from the Wingate home."

I sighed deeply in frustration. Just like Fromley himself, hard evidence linking him to this crime continued to elude me. The lab report proved neither his guilt nor his innocence, since the prints from the Wingate home could have been left by anyone. But the lack of a tangible link was disappointing.

As I got up to leave, I noticed a page from the Fromley materials that had dropped under my chair. It was a page that had been appended to Moira Shea's autopsy report. It looked insignificant, having only to do with burial instructions, but I scanned it nonetheless. As I read the final notation, an electrifying jolt ran up and down my spine, and my hands began to tingle. I read it once more, to make sure I understood it.

On August 22, 1902, just before the body was to be released to Potter's Field for a pauper's burial, a woman claiming to be Moira Shea's mother had come to retrieve the body for a proper funeral.

That woman's name was listed as Mrs. Jackson Durant, a widow who was a resident of New York City. But she had signed herself *Mamie Durant*.

My thoughts raced as I wondered how to make sense of it. Was this connection to Moira Shea the reason why Mamie had terminated our interview so abruptly?

And just as suddenly, came the more unsettling thought: If no formal, public evidence had ever officially linked Michael Fromley to Moira Shea's murder, then why did Mamie Durant react so strongly to the mention of Fromley's name? She had also known exactly where he lived. She must have felt he was to blame for the murder, but how could she have known? It was yet another unsettling reminder that Fromley and his uncertain past affected this case in ways I had yet to comprehend.

CHAPTER 18

"There you are, Ziele!" Alistair's voice was full of relief. He had just entered the building and begun bounding up the stairs, two at a time, when he caught sight of me. "Listen, I need to speak with you for a moment and clear the air from last night." Although his energy was as boundless as ever, he looked at me anxiously and taut lines of worry etched his brow. For the first time, he showed some sign of the strain of the past few days.

"No need," I said, clearing my throat. "I reviewed your case files this morning with Tom, and I understand your difficulty somewhat better. Not that I agree, mind you. But I think we need to put our differences aside and concentrate on solving this murder case."

"Why, of course." He grinned broadly, his usual confidence

and enthusiasm suddenly returned to him. "My thoughts exactly. There has to be some connection between Michael Fromley and Sarah Wingate that will establish solid proof and lead us straight to Fromley; we've only got to keep working and we'll find it."

I had begun to explain my next step when we were interrupted by a high-pitched cry of shock—immediately followed by the sound of Isabella's dog Oban furiously barking. We raced toward Alistair's office where we found Isabella, shaken and appearing small in Alistair's chair; Oban, agitated and running in circles; and Mrs. Leab, dumbfounded, staring blankly at a large cardboard box that sat open on Alistair's desk.

Alistair charged into the room and, seeing no one was hurt, pulled the box toward him. After he saw its contents, he reprimanded Mrs. Leab roughly. "Why did you allow Isabella to open this? You should have saved it for me."

"But it was addressed to her, Professor. Not you."

Alistair flipped back the box lid to confirm it, and there it was: *Mrs. Isabella Sinclair, The Center for Criminological Research.*

"But why would he address it to me?" Isabella asked. Now that the initial shock had receded, her curiosity had returned.

As I peered inside, my stomach lurched when I recognized the long braid of blond hair, smattered with bloodstains. I realized its significance with a start: It was Sarah Wingate's missing hair from the crime scene.

"It came through the regular mail?" I asked, examining the outside of the box carefully for any sign of a postmark; there appeared to be none.

"I found it on the steps outside," Mrs. Leab said. "It was

there when I came in this morning." A look of anxiety crossed her face. "I'd like to go wash up."

Alistair excused her, suggesting she return to her own work. She was ill at ease, disturbed that she had touched the package that contained such awful things.

I pulled on my white cotton gloves. "Has anyone looked at this?" I lifted out a yellowed envelope that had been nestled under the braid. It contained no markings and was not sealed.

Isabella shook her head.

I carefully removed the note folded inside and moved closer to show it to Alistair. Written on heavy white paper it read:

> *Your move, Professor. Here's a little remembrance in case you miss our regular chats. Maybe your daughter-in-law would like to spend some time with me.*

Below was a messy scrawl, a signature I could not decipher. But Alistair recognized it immediately as that of Michael Fromley.

Alistair frowned deeply, holding the paper up to the window to examine in the light. "This is unlike him," he said, looking intently at the paper, and tilting it first one way and then another. He turned to his large file cabinet and, after searching for only a minute, he pulled out a large file that apparently contained writing by Michael Fromley. He laid out one sheet for comparison, and we compared the dark, heavy strokes of black ink.

Alistair said, "It certainly *seems* to resemble his handwriting."

"But?" I sensed that he remained troubled.

Alistair put down the letter and repeated his earlier comment. "It is not like him. I would never expect him to admit his own guilt, and certainly not in this way." He was emphatic.

"But perhaps you do not know him as well as you believed." I thought again of the unwarranted trust Alistair had placed in Michael Fromley. "None of you do."

He chose to ignore me, replying only, "Tom has a good eye for evaluating handwriting—it is something of a hobby for him. We can leave it for him to examine. Meanwhile, I think this incident, taken with the attack on you and Isabella last night, must lead us to refocus our search."

We were interrupted by Mrs. Leab; her voice thick with worry, she informed Alistair that there were people congregated downstairs wanting to speak with him.

"People?" he asked.

"I think they're newspaper reporters."

I accompanied Alistair downstairs, and we had barely opened the door when a stocky, balding man armed with a notebook accosted us. With barely a glance at me, he quickly set upon Alistair. "Professor Sinclair—we're hearing reports that you pulled political strings to let a murderer loose. Is that true?"

Suddenly Alistair was surrounded by reporters from four local newspapers. They had materialized from nowhere to circle around him, and their questions came in quick succession.

"This is Sheffield with the *Tribune*," another voice announced. "I understand your family is closely connected with Judge Hansen, who dismissed attempted-murder charges against Michael Fromley and approved releasing him into your custody as part of a plea for lesser charges. We have a quote from the initial prosecutor on the case, Frank Hogart, alleging that bribery was involved. Do you care to comment?"

Yet another man, this one short and pudgy, shoved his way to the front, wielding an umbrella like a scythe to cut through the crowd. "Yoder here with the *Times*. Is it true that this same man whose release you negotiated has now embarked on a murderous rampage just north of the city?"

Alistair backed into the vestibule, shut the door partway, and looked at me in stunned disbelief. "You?"

"No, Alistair," I said. "I've discussed the matter with no one outside our circle."

"Maybe the Wallingfords, then," Alistair muttered, "trying to deflect attention from their family." He sighed wearily. "Well, now that they're on the scent of this, they must be dealt with. If you'll excuse me . . ."

As he moved outside onto the stairs, he began to address the throng of reporters. "Gentlemen, it seems you have some questions—and some grave misunderstandings—pertaining to a research project we have been conducting here at the Center for Criminological Research." His demeanor and voice rebuked them sharply. "I know each of you adheres to high standards of journalistic integrity, and no one wants to publish unsubstantiated rumors that will lead only to a libel suit." He paused to let the warning sink in. "If you'll bear with me a moment, I will be happy to explain this project and its background for the benefit of your readers."

I managed to make my way through the crowd, and Alistair's voice trailed off as I moved farther away from the stairs. Obviously Alistair was handling himself well, but the unwanted questions and unwelcome attention were exactly the sort of distraction I had hoped to avoid.

Suddenly I became aware of Isabella at my side, slightly out of breath from having run to catch up with me. "Simon, wait," she said. "Haven't you heard me calling your name?"

"Why, no," I said, caught off guard. "What's wrong? Alistair appears to have the reporters well in hand." I could see she was agitated and I assumed her concern related to the aggressive newsmen who had pigeonholed Alistair.

"No, no—it's not that," she said impatiently. I noticed her right hand was clenched around a yellow piece of paper. "Alistair's friend McGinty from the coroner's office just telephoned. There's a dead body that may relate to our case, so McGinty thought . . ."

My heart sank. We were too late. I felt an all too familiar frustration that our efforts had not been enough. Alistair's prediction had proven true: Fromley had killed again. We should have managed to find him before now.

"Who is she?" I barely managed to breathe the words. I was not ready to confront another victim like Sarah Wingate.

"I don't know. McGinty didn't say." Isabella looked stricken. "He mentioned only that a body had washed up from the Hudson River. A man walking his dogs discovered it; apparently information found nearby links the corpse to Michael Fromley."

"Where is the body? Have they taken her to the morgue yet?" I asked.

"Not yet. McGinty called right after they got word at headquarters. The coroner's still on site where her body washed up, near Seventy-ninth Street." She handed me the paper where she had written the address.

"Then that's where I'm headed," I said. "You'll let Alistair know?"

Of course she would have anyway. I was simply trying to give her something to do that might distract her from asking to come with me. I did not want Isabella's company, not for this. Not when I felt such a strong sense of failure—and when I knew what horrors most likely waited down by the riverbank.

CHAPTER 19

The Hudson River loomed cold and gray before me. There was a biting chill in the air that seemed to sharpen my perception of everything—from the trees that displayed their few, last, withering leaves to the hulking black barge that roiled the water downstream. Odd how cold temperatures can generate an effect that is uniquely visual.

A group of policemen huddled together by the riverbank near Seventy-ninth and Riverside. They were obscured by the coroner's wagon, a rickety contraption that had somehow managed to lumber over the rough, rocky earth all the way down to the river. I suspected they had not wanted to risk carrying the body far in light of its condition, for even just a few hours in the water badly decomposed a corpse.

I quickly recognized Jennings, the coroner with whom I'd had many dealings in the past. He was a short man, overstuffed and unevenly shaped. But I had seen him at work on the autopsy table and, in complete disproportion to the rest of his body, his hands moved swiftly and expertly, as did his keen mind.

The officer in charge, a strapping Irishman with a shock of red hair and strong accent, was addressing a group of young men who were obviously rookies. "Okay, lads, let's get to work. We need to search up and down the shore, the whole perimeter." One young man looked positively green with nausea, and all were decidedly uncomfortable. I suspected few had ever seen a dead body before. This was not to say that those of us more familiar with the sight never felt ill—I could already sense my own stomach beginning to churn—but I liked to think we veterans learned to disguise it better.

The officer waved his hands broadly, gesturing up and down the waterfront. "And remember, anything that may be relevant, just bring it to someone's attention. Anything at all."

I approached Jennings, greeting him in a louder voice than usual, for his hearing seemed to grow worse with each passing year.

He looked up in surprise. "Ziele, why, I thought you were working upstate now."

"Not upstate—I'm just north of Yonkers, in one of the river towns," I said, accustomed to this sort of comment. It was all a matter of perception, and not long ago, I would have thought of Dobson in exactly the same way. Even our current location on the Upper West Side was considered to be very far north by many.

"I've got a case in Dobson that brings me back to the city," I said.

For a moment, I thought even more explanation would be

necessary; the redheaded officer came over to question me, but retreated after noticing that Jennings seemed to know me quite well.

"It may relate to your business here." I indicated the large covered corpse Jennings had been working over. "What have you found out?"

Jennings cleared his throat. "River dumps are tough cases, you know that." It was an admonishment, one I well understood. When a corpse was in the water even a short period of time, much of the evidentiary information a coroner might obtain was destroyed.

"I do," I said. "But I also know that you still have opinions." I continued in my most persuasive, reasonable voice. "I won't hold you to anything until you've done the full autopsy."

Somewhat mollified, Jennings grunted; then began to speak slowly. "Here, we're relatively lucky that the cold, moving water of the Hudson helped slow the body's decomposition."

He trudged over to the side of the wagon where the corpse would be more accessible, and I followed. Though it helped that we were outdoors, I could already detect the distinctive smell of rotting flesh. We approached the form covered by a thick black blanket, and I watched with trepidation as Jennings lifted its edges and pulled the blanket to expose the body's head and upper torso.

I staggered back in shock. It couldn't be—and yet, there was no mistaking what I saw before me.

"This is a man," I managed to say. The words caught in my throat.

Jennings looked at me in amazement. "Well, of course it is."

"I expected a woman," I said, aware that I now sounded idiotic.

Jennings dignified that only with a grunt. "As I was about to explain," he began, "this is a river dump, so—"

I cut him off. "I need you to back up a moment. I understood there was evidence connecting this corpse with Michael Fromley. How is this man connected to Fromley?"

Now it was Jennings's turn to stare. "This man isn't connected with Michael Fromley," he said in exasperation. "We believe this man *is* Michael Fromley."

Silence followed—and time stood still.

I regarded the misshapen mass of flesh and bone in front of me. The man's features had been rendered unrecognizable by his time in the water. Was it really him—the man we had hunted and almost despaired of finding?

And by slow degrees, the logical conclusion dawned on me: If it were Fromley, then this case might be over. Sarah's killer would be present and accounted for, his guilt sealed by circumstantial evidence. It would be a phenomenal end to the case.

But first, I needed some confirmation from Jennings. "May I see the identification you found on him?" I asked, gesturing toward the pile of soggy personal effects.

Jennings shrugged. "Fine with me if it's okay with Bobby." The short, square man snapped to attention upon hearing his name and nodded. Like most rookie policemen, he was slightly intimidated by Jennings.

"What do you have?" I asked him. He stepped aside to let me examine the things.

"Mainly soggy odds and ends, sir," he replied. He was right. There was a sock, as well as a thick bundle of cloth that I determined to be a coat. Some papers fished from its pockets had been carefully laid aside to dry. And there was a small pile of rocks—pebbles, really—next to the papers.

"Those rocks were in his pockets and mouth, sir—probably intended to weigh him down," Bobby explained. "Didn't work particularly well; whoever wanted him to stay down should have used heavier ones."

I recognized a couple of theater tickets and what appeared to be a pawnshop receipt. But there was no wallet or ring—in short, nothing that might identify the corpse. "Why do you think this corpse is Michael Fromley?" I asked, puzzled. "I see nothing to indicate it here."

"Sorry, sir." The young man flushed with embarrassment as he pulled a watch and chain from his own vest. "It's because of this, sir. They told me to keep it safe, and I'd forgot I put it in my own pocket to do so."

I cradled the gold pocket watch in my hands. On the back was clearly etched an inscription: *Michael J. Fromley, 8–11–98 from your loving Aunt Lizzie*. I did not yet allow myself to feel more than initial relief. Watches were often stolen or borrowed; only a proper autopsy would firmly establish whether this was truly Michael Fromley. I dared not hope just yet.

"Any other identifying information?" I asked.

"Not yet," Jennings replied. "They'll have already contacted the family for dentals, as this corpse has got a gold tooth. If that matches Fromley's dental records, then I'll have no trouble making a positive identification during the autopsy. But now all I've got is that watch. And of course, the fact that Fromley has been reported a missing person."

So the Wallingford family had filed an official report. My one-time meeting with Clyde Wallingford had left me skeptical as to whether they would do so. Wallingford had seemed to believe Michael Fromley was entirely Alistair's responsibility.

"Tell me how he died," I said, returning to Fromley's

corpse—for I had begun to accept that it probably *was* Fromley's body that lay exposed on the coroner's wagon.

"He was killed before he went in the water," Jennings said as he put on his gloves. He motioned for me to come closer to the corpse's head. "First, look at the eyes." He pried open one of the dead man's eyes and explained something I did not quite follow about lines. "Furthermore, see how his head is rotated all the way to one side?" he instructed. "You never see that position in a drowning victim. His head got that way because rigor mortis set in while he was still on land."

"Any sign of violence to the body?" I asked, knowing from my quick glance at the swollen, discolored remains how difficult a question I was asking. If the river had not erased signs of foul play, it may have actually created them. Underwater branches and rocks could take a toll upon whatever came near them.

"You're in luck there." Jennings's eye glinted as he looked at me slyly, proud of himself. "We think he was a gunshot victim. I'll know more when I do the autopsy, but there were holes in his clothes consistent with a gunshot wound to the chest. Including on the coat you examined over there." He gestured to a pile of effects that had been pulled from the river.

My mind raced with possibilities. If this were indeed Fromley, perhaps he had committed suicide, as his mind became unhinged by the murder he had committed and the gruesome fantasies that haunted him night and day. Or had he been killed in the heat of a fight? It had been clear that his volatile temper repeatedly got him in trouble. If this proved to be Fromley . . .

"What's your interest in him, anyway?" Jennings asked.

I opted for the truth, knowing I could count on Jennings to be discreet. "Actually, he's the prime suspect in a murder I'm

investigating—that of a young woman in Dobson this past Tuesday."

"Tuesday?" He looked at me sharply, standing up straight.
"You surely don't mean Tuesday of this week?"

"Yes," I replied, and wondered why he seemed so surprised.

"Well, if this corpse is indeed Michael Fromley"—he returned to the disfigured body in the wagon and removed the
blanket entirely, revealing the corpse's full state of decomposition—"I'd say you can clear him of that suspicion."

The corpse was a grotesque mass of black, with little remaining semblance of humanity.

Jennings continued to talk. "Look at the protruding eyes
and tongue, the distended abdomen, and the extensive skin mac-
eration. This bloke's been dead, by my guess, for at least two,
maybe even three weeks."

It was impossible.

And yet, as I gazed at the dark, mottled, distended corpse in
front of me, I knew Jennings spoke the truth.

And if so, I realized with dizzying certainty, then everything we had learned and thought about the case up to this
point was utterly, stupidly, and senselessly wrong.

CHAPTER 20

Dead for at least two weeks. I walked north on the riding path along the Hudson River with no particular destination in mind; I simply needed to walk. Maybe Jennings was wrong. Maybe the corpse wasn't Fromley. Maybe it was some poor sod murdered so Fromley might fake his own death. Until Jennings's autopsy was complete, I could believe it was possible. But the pit in my stomach told me not to pin my hopes in that direction.

Quite literally, I had been chasing a ghost—and that must have been the real killer's plan. As long as we tracked the long-stale movements of a dead man, the real killer remained safe. What had foiled his plan was the unpredictability of the Hudson waters, which had washed up Fromley's corpse too soon. Only a few more months in the water, and—if it were still possible to identify the body as belonging to Michael Fromley at all—it would have been impossible to determine an accurate time of death. We would have continued to blame Fromley as the killer for lack of other evidence.

I lost all track of time as I continued to think. I considered those whom we would now treat with renewed interest as suspects. Angus MacDonald, who had devoted his life's work to the Riemann hypothesis, only to have a young female graduate student beat him to the solution, immediately came to mind. I wanted to believe the older man's attestation of innocence, but now we would need to revisit the possibility he was involved. Lonny Moore, the student who had tried to sabotage Sarah Wingate's academic success, was also a likely suspect—along with any of the other men at Columbia who had resented Sarah's feminist agitation. One of them might have managed access to Fromley and the research center without much difficulty. I would need to discuss that with Alistair come morning.

Whichever culprit I sought, somehow Fromley remained the key. It had to be someone with access not only to Fromley's thoughts and murderous fantasies, but also to Fromley himself—assuming the confession letter sent in the box to Isabella proved to be Fromley's real handwriting. So Fromley remained important: no longer as a suspect to be tracked down, but as a guide to the real killer. The murderer we sought had the ability to kill—but more important, he had the ability to frame a murder scene that had deflected all our suspicions to Fromley.

That thought led me unavoidably back to two uncomfortable suspicions. The first involved Mamie Durant and her mysterious connection with Michael Fromley. She had known where he lived—when even Alistair and the Wallingfords had not. Why? The second involved Alistair, whose own secrets were now inextricably connected to this case. I could no longer consider Fromley without examining Alistair's methods at the same time. What information was he still withholding from me? And how did it bear on this strange twist involving Fromley?

I sat down on a bench and gazed blankly at the river, watching the interplay of light and dark cast by the shadows of early-evening dusk. I reached into my pocket, pulled out the locket Sarah had worn, and stared at her picture. Who had killed her? And why?

I would find the answer only once I had uncovered the oddest triad of connections: among Sarah Wingate, Michael Fromley, and the real murderer himself.

Saturday, November 11, 1905

CHAPTER 21

The autopsy results came swiftly the next morning and they were definitive. Dental records confirmed that the washed-up corpse was indeed Michael Fromley. And, by measuring the extent to which it had decomposed, Coroner Jennings was confident that Fromley had spent at least two to three weeks in the river. Together with the bullet fragment found lodged beneath the corpse's sternum, which suggested Fromley had been shot before his body was dumped into the Hudson, this information placed us firmly back at square one. It did not matter that Fromley had died within the city's jurisdiction, and thus, technically speaking, was not ours to investigate. His death called into question everything we thought we had discovered about the Wingate murder.

I delivered the news confirming Fromley's death to Alistair personally at his apartment on West Seventy-second Street and Central Park West. He lived at the Dakota, a sandstone and yellow brick building with some Gothic features. The low iron fence surrounding it, which was decorated with grotesque human and serpentine figures, made it seem particularly uninviting this dismal Saturday morning, as cold rain poured from dark clouds that all but obscured the daylight. Alistair proved equally unwelcoming; the moment I told him the news, he skulked away to his library in silence.

Isabella—who must have heard voices in the hallway from her apartment next door—came almost instantly to Alistair's apartment to offer me coffee and breakfast. At her request, Alistair's housekeeper, a matronly woman named Mrs. Mellown, put on coffee, eggs, and toast. I ate as Isabella tried to raise my spirits.

"This is a setback, of course," she had said. "But the things you have learned in the last few days will help you, I'm sure of it."

"We owe Sarah Wingate nothing less. But this case was going to be tough—potentially unsolvable—from the very beginning. It was the information Alistair brought to the table that made it seem possible. I've no solid leads of my own."

Her tone had been adamant. "Then you will keep looking. You have seen for yourself that Alistair's experience and intellectual breadth will not solve your case. Focus upon what you know, and let your own common sense and instincts lead you."

Yet, what Isabella and others called my "good instincts" actually was something I considered more akin to dumb luck. It was a sudden flash of understanding when all the pieces of a puzzle came together in a pattern that made perfect sense. But with every case, I worried that my luck was about to run out. And this case was certainly no exception.

Disheartened and frustrated, Alistair finally emerged from his library a half hour later. He looked as dejected as I felt, the heavy bags under his eyes attesting that he, too, had passed a night of sleepless anxiety and worry. We needed the strong coffee in front of us as we retraced our steps to figure out where we had gone wrong. We finished breakfast in silence, as the rain pounded its steady drumbeat against the windowpane.

"I suppose we've still a case to solve," he said, offering a weak smile. "Shall we begin?"

"Everything I need is uptown. Should we head to the research center?" I asked, though the thought of returning outside into the pouring rain was decidedly unappealing.

"Nonsense. It's all right here. Come."

We followed Alistair into his dining room, where Mrs. Mellown had already laid a crackling fire. It was a large room, painted in tones of gold and white, and decorated with treasures accumulated during his travels to the Far East. Tapestries, gold vases, and even a pair of samurai swords were placed in different areas of the room. Two piles of folders were stacked at one end of Alistair's eight-and-a-half-foot dining room table, for Alistair had brought home the most relevant files. As Isabella set to work organizing them in chronological order, I was reminded of all we had lost: Our efforts of the past four long days had been for nothing.

"Fromley, of course, remains the key," I said. "Though we now know he is not the killer himself, he remains the link to the murderer. The real killer *wanted* us to think he was Fromley. He framed the crime scene to resemble Fromley's handiwork.

He sent the package to Isabella containing evidence and a confession in Fromley's own writing."

Alistair shook his head in disbelief. "How could the killer have known so much? The Wingate murder scene was a perfect match to the scene Fromley had fantasized about. He had described it to me in vivid, breathtaking detail—not just once, but time after time."

I ran my fingers along the side of the table, thinking aloud. "As you say, the question is *how*. I can think of a few possibilities. The first is that Fromley liked to talk. If he described this fantasized murder scene to you, then he may have just as easily described it to someone else." I added, "From what you say, it appears he took a positive delight in sharing his revolting thoughts."

Alistair caught my train of thought. "So the question becomes, which person or persons would he have shared this murderous fantasy with? Someone who, in turn, had his *own* motive for murder—and decided to coopt Fromley's sick vision in order to frame him."

"Exactly," I said. "Someone who is a copycat; he wants his crime to appear as though it were done by a different, known killer, so the investigation will proceed in the wrong direction. Just as our investigation did."

"So we must continue to focus upon those persons Fromley was in contact with," Alistair said, "on the theory one of them is the real culprit."

"Which means we look closely at anyone who had access to him or his files." I watched Alistair's reaction carefully. Clearly, he was displeased by the suggestion—but to his credit, he responded rationally.

Though he raised an eyebrow, he said, "I see your point. All of us at the research center have had unfettered access to From-ley. But not one of us knew Sarah Wingate, much less had a mo-tive to kill her."

"That we know of," I said.

"Fine. Let's consider the matter in practical terms, then. You have eliminated the possibility that the killer is a woman, which clears Isabella and Mrs. Leab. I cannot fathom Tom or Fred in the role of the killer. Tom is as upstanding and honest a man as you'll find. In physical terms, Fred is too thin and frail to have managed it. And, while he is an odd duck, I can't see Horace as the killer, either." Alistair paused as he searched for the right words. "Horace is awkward and bumbling, whereas the killer was highly sophisticated, able to manage a complicated copycat scenario. And Horace has been distracted lately by personal disappointment. His fiancée called off their engagement quite recently, and he does little but sulk about. Because of it, his work has been irregular of late, though he has continued to come in as scheduled."

"What about his gambling?" I asked. "You said he was in debt. The pressure of debt—especially if it's owed to less-than-understanding bookies—can be tremendous."

"I don't doubt it," Alistair agreed. "But plenty of young men get into a spot of trouble, are helped out of it, and never have is-sues again. I was one of them, once. I've helped Horace with his debts and I can assure you he is a small-time gambler who has been clean of late. He hasn't asked me for money in at least two months. Besides," he added, "we can't seriously think Sarah Wingate was killed for money, can we?"

"You did find a significant amount hidden under her mat-tress," I said.

"True, but you told me about Mrs. Wingate's habit of hiding

money throughout the house. It was probably hers, not Sarah's—and besides, it wasn't taken. Nothing in the house was disturbed. I don't believe money is the motive responsible here."

I tended to agree with Alistair's assessment. "What about other people? How easily could another professor or student have gained access to your files, or even Fromley himself?"

Alistair looked uncomfortable. "Well, we don't have any special safeguards in place. We haven't really needed them. We rely on an honor system of sorts, where if someone borrows a file, they sign it out. And certainly anyone who wanted could have visited Fromley. We had him under bodyguard protection until recently, but he was free to come and go as he pleased. Though I don't recall anyone ever visiting. People were afraid of him; they avoided coming to the center because of it."

"So we can eliminate no one," I said, sighing. It was as I suspected, but I had hoped that better precautions were securely in place.

It was my nagging sixth sense, convincing me there was something he still had not told me, that led me to try once more. "Is there anything you can tell me that you have not already?"

"Ziele, old boy," he said, "I assure you, I am an open book in terms of anything you need to know."

He managed to look crestfallen, but I still did not trust him.

"Then," I continued, "from this point on, I am running a traditional investigation in which everyone is a suspect until I identify the killer. I want to focus anew on our victim and her circle of acquaintances and friends. Someone wanted Sarah Wingate dead—and for a reason that became urgent here." I tapped the calendar, looking at Tuesday's date. "Why Tuesday, November seventh? Some particular set of circumstances came to a crisis around this day, making the killer feel he had to take

Sarah's life. If we look hard enough at the people surrounding her, perhaps we can determine the answer. The connection with Fromley—and some hard evidence—should then fall into place."

I picked up a pen and grabbed a clean sheet of paper, drawing a large point near its top. "Our focus is on our victim." I wrote the name *Sarah*. "But we cannot lose sight that the manner in which she was killed implicates Fromley." I drew another point, much lower down, and wrote *Fromley*.

"Fromley was a special case," I continued to explain, "because his desire to kill came from pleasure, from fantasies he enjoyed. He would kill because he liked it. But our real killer"—I drew another point across from *Fromley* and wrote *Copycat Killer*—"had a specific motivation to target Sarah." I linked *Copycat Killer* with *Sarah*. "And a specific connection to Fromley that he took advantage of." I finished by connecting *Copycat Killer* to *Fromley*. I stepped back to survey the large triangle I had created. "Something connects these three people—but what?"

Alistair traced the word *Killer* with his right index finger. "Did any of your suspects have reason to know both Sarah and Fromley?"

"Lonny Moore could have," I said. "He, Sarah, and Fromley were each regularly on campus at Columbia."

We thought in silence.

"Mamie Durant, as well," I said. "We know she has some connection with Fromley. And she is connected with the Wingate family, if not Sarah herself: Stella went directly from Mamie's employ to that of Mrs. Wingate."

"And what about Dean Arnold?" Isabella asked.

Alistair and I both stared at her. Isabella had spoken with Dean Arnold on Wednesday, but nothing of importance had come out of the interview. Sarah's work in his office was ordinary, routine.

"I read your notes after you spoke with Angus MacDonald." Isabella paused for a split second to gather her thoughts. "He thought Sarah was upset by something relevant to her work at Dean Arnold's office. Do you recall? And I was struck by his belief that Sarah even mentioned Michael Fromley's name during their last conversation."

She looked at me expectantly, under the impression she had noticed something important. But I didn't think so.

"Yes, I remember," I said, "but think of it logically. For her to have mentioned Fromley's name, especially in the context of her work, makes no sense." I spread my hands wide. "When Alistair and I discussed the matter, we decided that MacDonald must have been mistaken. The man was thoroughly grief-stricken, you see. How can we consider him a reliable source on this point?"

Isabella was clearly unconvinced and she began shuffling through the files with a peculiar expression. What could she be looking for with such urgency?

Alistair did not seem to notice her behavior, for he had moved on to his own concerns. "Well, that all sounds very reasonable. But I believe we might use what we know about criminal behavior to narrow down where and how we search for your unknown killer."

I cut him off sharply. "We don't have time for esoteric theories, Alistair—"

He responded quickly, before I could interrupt again. "I offer you a practical theory, of the exact sort you already use. During one of our earliest conversations, you told me you didn't think a woman could have murdered Sarah because, quite simply, her murder was too brutal. The typical woman doesn't commit that sort of crime, you said; she would prefer poison to the knife." He became animated, in his element once again. "I can help you refine that kind of theory in a way that may help you."

"Okay," I agreed. "Then tell me, in practical terms."

Alistair spread out several more sheets of paper and began making a list of traits, though he spoke faster than his hand could keep up. "You tell me you believe the murderer is a copycat killer. That, I tell you, means he is also highly intelligent and organized. Can you guess why?"

"Absolutely." I immediately understood where Alistair was headed. "A killer who aims to copy another's type of crime must be smart enough to learn another criminal's habits as well as organized enough to carry them out. In our case, he carried out his plan so well we were completely fooled."

"Intelligent. Organized." Alistair mulled these traits. "Our killer commits the crime believing he is capable of deceiving and frustrating the authorities, right?" After I nodded in agreement, he added, "This belief grows, the more time that passes without the killer being caught. Or questioned. Or even suspected."

Alistair began pacing the room, his energy too irrepressible to permit him to stay in one place. "Moreover, I believe Sarah's killer is motivated chiefly by control. We see it demonstrated throughout the crime scene. He first, chiefly, needed to control the victim. We can now make sense of the chloroform that was in Sarah's system—remember how our first instinct was that its presence was an anomaly? We can now explain it. Whereas Fromley would have relished the torture of a victim who remained alive until the very end, and the thrill of seeing her blood,"

Alistair explained, "our *real* killer required perfect control. He subdued her with chloroform. Once she was unconscious, he took her life quickly, with one stroke of his knife. And then— only then—did he begin to frame the crime scene as Fromley would have done."

I picked up where he left off, adding my own conclusion. "It also shows the killer did not murder in the manner he did because he enjoyed the brutal attack or the display of blood. He simply needed the murder scene to fit the Fromley prototype." I paused to look at Alistair. "The positive side of this, I suppose, is that we have less cause to worry the real murderer will kill again."

"It's true that he has killed for a different reason," Alistair said, thinking aloud, "but what troubles me is that he has involved himself so closely in our investigation. He monitors us— and that implies he has concerns that are unsettled. Killing Sarah may not have resolved his problems in the way that he hoped."

"Or possibly our investigation is creating new ones," I said, adding, "I'm sure he counted on our not discovering Fromley's body for some time."

"The real killer is unlikely to know we found Fromley's body," Alistair said thoughtfully. "That may give us some time. I am concerned he may react poorly when he discovers his best laid plans to frame Fromley have not worked."

Alistair and Isabella both looked uneasy. "React poorly, how?" I asked. I felt as though they had noticed something I had not.

"You're going to say this is like the Sid Jones case, aren't you, Alistair?" Isabella looked worried.

"Well, similar," he acknowledged. "Especially in this one last point." Alistair's voice was suddenly cautious. "A person for whom this degree of control is paramount sometimes also manifests that control by keeping close tabs on the investigation. That was the case in the Jones matter Isabella just mentioned. Jones had murdered someone, and he posed as a news photographer covering the case—simply so he could stay abreast of the investigation. And the closer the authorities came to discovering him, the more he panicked, and the more violent he became. So we must be alert to anyone who takes . . . well, what we might characterize as an undue interest in our work."

Now I was confused. "But we've had no real news coverage of the case until yesterday. You suspect one of the reporters who approached you?"

"No," Alistair said, and his disappointed frown made it clear I had missed his point. "I mentioned the Sid Jones case only as an example. Control and interest can take many forms. In one case, the killer pretended to be a police officer—and proceeded to interview every witness in the case. But in our case, the killer's interest is evidenced in the attack he orchestrated against you as well as the package he sent to Isabella. The real killer meant not only to mislead us, but also to taunt us and revel in his ability to frustrate us."

Alistair paused, and something about the way he was obviously holding something back caused a chill to run down my spine and I involuntarily shuddered. "So how does your point about the killer's possible interest in our investigation help us to find him?"

Alistair's answer did not reassure me. "You are too pragmatic, Ziele," he said. He smiled at first, but then his tone became ominously sober. "I mention this last point not because I believe it may further our investigation. I mention it to warn you, both of you"—here he looked sternly at Isabella—"to be extremely careful. It is likely—in fact, it is almost certain—that our actions are being monitored. And it may be by someone closer to our investigation than we might imagine."

CHAPTER 22

"You're a tough man to track down these days." My old partner
Mulvaney had managed to locate me at Alistair's apartment late
Saturday morning, after telephoning several other places without success. "Joe says this investigation practically has you living in the city again."

It was true. All leads pointed here, and Joe was managing
everything in Dobson from his sickbed. Not that there was
much to manage in Dobson. No substantive leads had materialized there, and both the mayor and the public were less worried
by the murder. The victim, after all, had been a visitor—not
quite one of their own.

This morning, Mulvaney had run across two additional
leads to pass along. First, Otto Schmidt, the vagrant who had

robbed Sarah Wingate, had been found begging for change outside an East Side saloon, too drunk to be coherent. The police
would hold him until he sobered up and could be questioned.
Mulvaney's other news held even more promise: some items,
potentially linked to the Wingate murder, had been found overnight in the trash at Grand Central Station. A janitor there had
discovered a carpetbag containing a bloodstained lead pipe bun-
dled with some clothing—a fur hat, shirt, trousers, and a woman's petticoat and handbag. Mulvaney's memory was sharp, for
he had recalled the details I had shared about the man seen in
the woods the day of Sarah's murder. But what specifically tied
the bloodstained clothing to my case was the ticket stub found
in the trouser pocket, dated for November 7, a return from Dobson, New York.

"How do we know this clothing is associated with Sarah
Wingate's killer?" Alistair asked.

"We don't," I said. "But what are the odds that, on the same
day Sarah was killed, someone *other* than her killer traveled on a
return ticket from Dobson to Grand Central Station, depositing
a bloodstained weapon and bloody clothing in the garbage? It's
possible. But circumstances would seem to suggest a connection."

"Just as circumstantial evidence suggested Fromley was the
killer," Alistair said wryly.

"That's right," I said. "Circumstantial evidence is not
foolproof—but sometimes it's all we have, and when we can
weave it into a seamless chain of events, it can be persuasive."

"Where were the items found?" Alistair asked, as we hustled
down to his lobby and waited for the doorman to hail us a cab.
Isabella trailed behind us, fiddling with an oversized umbrella

she would not need. While the day continued to be gray and dismal, the morning's heavy rain had stopped.

"A janitor found them in the garbage at the north construction site down at the depot," I said, then corrected myself. "I mean the station." The old Grand Central Depot had been renamed recently, and like most people, I hadn't yet grown used to its new name. It had been under renovation for years now. First, the building had risen three stories higher and gotten a new façade. Now construction was under way for an even more ambitious expansion, with literally hundreds of buildings just north of Forty-second Street being demolished for a new Park Avenue underground approach. It was in the midst of that chaos where we soon found ourselves.

"It's huge," Isabella said, "much larger than I would have imagined from the newspapers."

"And filthy," Alistair said, brushing soot off the shoulder of his fine woolen coat.

They were right. The sight before us blended nature and industry in a way that was uncanny: The maze of railroad tracks, trains, and construction equipment was barely visible through what appeared to be a dense fog, but was actually a mix of smoke and soot. I saw both Alistair and Isabella had covered their mouths with scarves, so as to protect themselves from the foul air. I had no real difficulty breathing, but the noisy din was another matter entirely; I suspected that the clanging of metal rails as workers welded them together would ring in my ears for hours after we had left the rail yard.

A tall figure walked toward us out of the dust. "Are you Ziele?"

I could not make out who it was, for all I saw was the black of his coat. "Yes," I hollered loudly to confirm. My voice sounded unusually hoarse, as smoke caught in my throat.

"Mulvaney said you'd be by. Come this way." He motioned to an area past a row of train tracks and we followed slowly, watching our step. Alistair assisted Isabella as she lifted her heavy skirts high above muddy ground and slippery rails.

"This is Will Porter," the man in black said, "the janitor who found the items you wanted to see. I've gotta take the evidence back to the precinct, but you can have a few minutes to look it over. If you got any more questions, I'll be over by track nine."

He turned and was gone. I had not caught his name, or even got a good look at his face.

Will Porter was a wizened man with leathery skin, a slight build, and a hunched back. He eyed us suspiciously, and seemed to raise an eyebrow when he noted Isabella's presence, but he made no comment.

"You got questions for me?" he said, impatiently shifting his feet. "I gotta get back to work."

I was no more anxious for a lengthy interview than he was. "Can you tell me how you found these items?" Given the dust, soot, and grime that surrounded us here, I could not fathom how the man had managed to notice anything particularly unusual about them.

"Well," he said, shifting his weight as he answered me. "It was when I got back to the incinerator room that I saw what was there. I was putting garbage in the fire when I saw a carpetbag stuffed full of things. I opened it and right on top was a woman's handbag. So I got curious to see what was in it."

He looked at us, clearly wondering if we were going to question him further about this admission. I understood immediately and made a calculated decision to let it pass. The man had no doubt hoped to find money in the handbag; that was why he had examined it more closely. I did not ask whether he had found anything; I'd rather he responded to more important questions.

"Go on," I said.

"I noticed the handbag had a peculiar stain." He paused, then continued, "And that made me look to see what else was with it. I saw the lead pipe, inside the hat, wadded up in some woman's petticoat with dried blood all over it. That was then I realized the stain was also blood. That got me spooked, so I called the police."

"And the rest of the clothes?"

He shook his head. "You can take a look. It's all in there. I didn't touch nothing else. After I saw all that blood on the lady's petticoat, I got scared maybe there was a dead body here somewhere. So I called the police, and they sorted through the rest of the stuff."

"Everything is this way?" Alistair asked.

"Yeah, in the incinerator room." Will gestured toward the stairs behind him to our left.

I motioned to Alistair to wait. "And do you recall exactly where you found the carpetbag?" I scanned the length of the train yard. It was massive.

"See those six cans lined up against the eastern side wall over there? It came from one of them," Will said. "I've still gotta do those others"—he pointed to the opposite side of the yard— "once you guys finish with me."

I nodded. "Did you happen to notice anyone in this area behaving strangely, in the last few days?"

Will looked at me blankly. "Whaddya mean, behaving strangely?"

I tried to be more specific. "Did you see anyone who looked like he didn't belong? Perhaps in an area where strangers don't normally venture?"

He cackled, showing us a mouth riddled with missing teeth. "There's strange people here every day, mister. Men with suits inspecting this or that rail, talking about building plans. And the men working construction get paid by the day. Sometimes they're here, sometimes not—depends how much they need the money that day. It's backbreaking work, it is. Lucky it's not my job."

"Any other janitors with you out here?" I asked.

"Nah, just me." He grinned. "There are others inside the terminal, but out here, it's all just a big trash heap anyways. I only gotta take care of what trash makes its way into those cans. The rest takes care of itself."

We thanked him, and before he returned to his work, he again pointed us in the direction of the incinerator room. It was a relatively small room, and it seemed even smaller because of the large trash bags that lined each wall from floor to ceiling. The incinerator itself was merely a small opening in a brick wall, covered at the moment by an iron door. There was a rusted metal table to the back where the suspicious clothing lay, guarded loosely by a policeman with instructions to return the materials to his precinct captain once we had taken a look.

"Sir, you're the detective Mulvaney sent?" After I nodded, he ushered us into the room. "Please disregard my own things over there," he said, pointing to a coat, hat, and scarf at the far end of the table. "Had to take them off. It's beastly hot down here." Beads of perspiration dripped down his face, even though now he wore only his shirt.

"True enough," I said, as we all removed our own coats. "Let's make this quick." Alistair and Isabella offered no objection.

The carpetbag itself was on the far left end. A leaf pattern of reds and oranges must have once been visible, but it was now worn and covered with soot. I examined it and noticed nothing unusual.

Isabella approached the table, as well, and we watched as she gently fingered each item of clothing. She picked up the handbag that had attracted Porter's attention. "Could this have have been Sarah's?" She gingerly lifted it. It was flat and black, obviously well-worn; the thick black straps showed signs of previous repair. Her fingers grasped the small gold fastener to open it.

"Ma'am, we put the contents from inside it over here," the young officer said.

She put the bag down, and we all moved over to the pile indicated. I first noticed a small handkerchief, a black leather notebook, and a silver hand mirror.

"S.W.," Isabella whispered. The initials on the handkerchief, presumably, stood for *Sarah Wingate*. It was our first obvious link between the items and her murder.

"Look. This address book has had all its pages ripped out," Isabella said, thumbing through a derelict paper booklet with a worn black leather cover.

"What else is there?" I asked Isabella, who was going through the rest of the items.

Isabella frowned. "A small change purse, empty."

I thought of Will Porter and could not help but wonder if the change purse had been empty before he found it. But I pushed the thought out of my head; the money did not matter to our investigation, and Sarah no longer needed it.

"That's all?" I was incredulous. Apart from what money may have been there, it seemed hardly enough to have warranted carrying a handbag at all, much less stealing it. "Why did he bother even taking these things from her?" I asked in frustration. "It makes no sense."

"Fromley liked souvenirs to fuel his fantasies. Maybe the real killer decided to take some random items to make it look more like Fromley," Alistair said. "This handbag could have been lying about in Sarah's room. If so, it would have been easy to take."

"But then why discard everything?" Isabella asked.

"Why risk keeping everything?" I countered.

Alistair shook his head and held up the fur hat. "And how could he have worn this for any part of his journey from Dobson to Grand Central without attracting someone's attention?"

I shrugged. "Plenty of people in this city dress strangely but attract no attention. And the hat would partially disguise his head and facial features."

We each regarded the fur hat. On closer examination, despite its dark brown color, we could identify sticky markings of blood. It was likely the man had discarded it as soon as he no longer needed it, putting it in the bag where it had rubbed against the bloodstained clothing.

"The woman's petticoat looks as though it were used to wipe something clean. Maybe even this lead pipe," I said.

"The weapon responsible for her head injuries?" Alistair asked.

"Very likely. Dr. Fields believed they were made by some kind of metal object."

"What about any other clothing?" Isabella asked. "If his shirtwaist and trousers"—she held up two garments mottled with blood—"are so stained, then presumably everything else he wore would be bloodstained, as well. What about his coat? His boots?"

"He may have removed his coat," Alistair said.

"And also," I said, "I suspect this carpetbag only attracted Will Porter's attention because it was stuffed to capacity, and he hoped to find something of value in it. If the murderer split up the items he wished to dispose of, then other items may have gone unnoticed." I turned to the young officer. "Will you ask that all other garbage bags that may have been deposited here in the last week be examined before they are incinerated?"

As the man agreed, Alistair began combing through each pocket, using a pair of white cotton gloves we had brought for the purpose. He wordlessly handed another pair to Isabella, and she quickly pitched in to help.

Meanwhile I examined the return ticket stub already found in one of the pockets. Under the name *New York Central and Hudson River Railroad*, it was stamped November 7. On the back, the conductor had punched a hole next to Dobson to indicate fare paid. While we could question the conductors and ticket takers who had worked Tuesday afternoon, it was doubtful any would remember, given the thousands of passengers who passed through the terminal each day—and this had now been four days ago. Assuming this clothing proved to belong to Sarah's murderer, I was struck by the oddity—really, the brazenness—of his choice to travel by train, immediately following the murder, to the most crowded train station in the country, counting on no one noticing anything amiss with his clothes, his hair, or even his behavior. There was anonymity in numbers, people said. I supposed that was true.

"And what do we make of this? Is there a particular place

that sells them?" Alistair picked up the fur hat and looked at it quizzically.

I shrugged. "Not that it would be of help to us. He could have bought it at any of a dozen places here in the city. Any neighborhood with a large Russian immigrant population." That meant the Lower East Side or Williamsburg in Brooklyn, where the largest groups had settled.

Isabella was worrying with the handbag again.

"Are you ready?" I asked. "We have other leads to pursue."

"Just a minute," she replied, "I want to check something."

As we watched in amazement, she turned the handbag inside out, revealing a small zippered compartment almost hidden in the side of the bag. "There's something inside," Isabella said, feeling the contours of the pocket. "Paper, I think."

Flipping it another turn, she was able to unzip the hidden pocket and draw out a paper envelope, mottled with bloodstains. "A letter," Isabella said, "sealed shut, and not yet postmarked," and she opened the envelope and scanned its contents.

I waited a few seconds but soon grew impatient. "Who is it from?"

She handed it to me before she had entirely finished reading it.

"We've made a wrong assumption—this isn't Sarah Wingate's bag at all! Or perhaps it is, and she planned to mail something for Mrs. Wingate's housemaid." She looked up at us, eyes wide with astonishment. "This letter was written by Stella Gibson on November 6. It was never posted. And look at the addressee. Based on this," she said, "if Stella is still alive, we may have a good lead as to her whereabouts."

Stella Gibson. The Wingates' missing housemaid, who had disappeared in the hours just after the murder.

"My dearest Cora," the letter began. *"It was so good to hear the news of your last letter, for I have been deeply concerned. . . . "*

My eyes scanned the letter's contents, taking in its larger subject matter rather than its small details. Stella's confidences were immaterial; what mattered was that she and Cora were obviously on close terms. After allowing Alistair to take a look, I shoved the letter into my coat pocket and we quickly made our way out of the incinerator room and back to the main terminal entrance.

"I'd say we owe Cora Czerne an overdue visit." I felt a pang of guilt as I said it. I had hoped to interview her Thursday, right after Mamie had given us her address. But investigating Fromley's own quarters had taken priority, and what we discovered there had spawned other, more pressing concerns.

We would know more answers soon, I vowed, as our cab raced up Fifth Avenue into the East Nineties, well north of the fashionable East Side areas where the Vanderbilts and Astors had built their opulent mansions. But along the way, I found myself thinking not of Cora Czerne, but of Mamie Durant. I could not shake my suspicion that she would play a role in unraveling this case. But probably not a willing one.

CHAPTER 23

"Mrs. Ralph Noland? Do we have the wrong address?" Isabella's voice reflected her bewilderment as she read the name listed near the large brass knocker on the door of the rowhouse at number 135 East Ninety-first Street. According to Stella's letter, we could expect to find Cora Czerne here. The house was a plain brownstone, marked only by the presence of two grimacing gargoyles above the front door. Alistair pretended to examine them with great care, leaving me to explain about Mrs. Noland.

I rapped the knocker. "I expect it is merely an alias she uses, to make everything all right with the neighbors."

"Oh," Isabella said, blushing, "of course."

While not fashionable, the neighborhood in which we stood

was occupied primarily by upper-income families. An unmarried woman would attract attention—and ostracization—should
anyone notice an unrelated man making visits. Cora Czerne's
alias allowed her to pretend to be married; she no doubt explained her husband's absences with complaints about his frequent business travel. The pretense was all that mattered; it was
the way in which many a mistress assured herself a respectable
existence.

In just a few moments, the door opened, and we were greeted
by a young housemaid with carrot-red hair drawn tightly back
into a bun. She appeared to be no older than sixteen, and judging from her thick brogue, I guessed she was straight off the
boat from Ireland. We presented my card, for overt references
to police work often made people reluctant to talk.

We waited in the entry hall a few moments while she presented the card; then the same girl ushered us into a small front
parlor. Knowing we would have little other chance of nourish-
ment for lunch today, we accepted her offer of tea and biscuits.
As we waited in uncomfortable high-backed blue-patterned
chairs, I observed the many small wildflower prints that were
framed against blue toile wallpaper. Unlike Mamie Durant's
sitting room of colorful purples and reds, this room was a model
of traditional propriety.

The biscuits arrived right away; we had just polished them
off when Cora came into the room. She was an attractive woman,
with olive skin, dark eyes and hair. She greeted us politely
before sitting down, though she regarded us with a wary expression.

"Why are you here, Detective?" she asked. "Frankly, I can't
imagine what business you have with me." She smoothed her
plain blue skirt.

"Actually, our interest is not with you," I said, after I introduced the others, "but with an acquaintance of yours—a friend, I believe." I paused a moment before continuing. "We are searching for Stella Gibson. We believe you may be able to help us locate her."

She stiffened slightly, but asked only, "And what leads you to believe I know anything about this woman? What did you say her name was, again?"

While I was unsurprised that she feigned ignorance, I had little time to waste. I went ahead and played my hand.

"Even before we located this letter," I said, pulling the letter Stella had written out of my pocket, "Mamie Durant had told us you and Stella were friendly with one another."

I placed the letter on the small coffee table between us. Cora simply stared—first at me, then at the small bloodstained envelope. After a moment, she picked it up and read it carefully before placing it back on the table. Her fingers slightly recoiled from the dark bloodstains and I realized she was repulsed but otherwise untroubled by the blood. It was a reaction that suggested she knew Stella was safe.

"I see." Cora breathed in sharply as she stared out the window, absorbed in her own thoughts.

Alistair opened his mouth to say something, but I indicated he should not, with a slight shake of my head. I did not want to rush Cora; it seemed that she required a few minutes to compose herself and determine what to say.

"We need your help to find her," I urged finally, after some time had passed. "The family for whom Stella has been working is quite worried. We believe she may have witnessed a murder, and if so, that fact places her in great danger."

She looked at me, and her tone was scornful. "And I suppose

you can protect her? Who are you, exactly? A small town detective working with the Wingate family, I presume? Your primary concern is with the Wingate girl's murder, which means you cannot fully appreciate how your interference may itself endanger Stella."

We had not mentioned the Wingate name or that a young woman was the murder victim. But it had not mattered; Cora already knew.

My voice held steady. "I am a detective with several years' experience in the city, though now I am with the police in Dobson, New York. The Sinclairs are private citizens assisting me." I showed her my identification as proof, then continued, "I believe Stella may have information that will help us catch Sarah Wingate's murderer. Only when he is caught will everyone—including Stella—be safe."

"I can protect her," she responded with stubborn defensiveness. "*You* are the ones with little understanding of what she faces. You haven't got the faintest idea of what my life, or Stella's, is like." She paused, eyeing Isabella, who sat gracefully, her composure unruffled. Then Cora continued. "I know how this city works and how to make my way in it. No one will look out for Stella better than I can."

"Miss Czerne, you are a young woman of what—twenty-three? Twenty-four?" I hazarded a guess. "I take it you are helping Stella to hide somewhere in this city. You've been doing so for exactly four days. Do you really think you're prepared to keep it up when four days stretch into ten, then thirty or forty? Stella is not earning money if she is in hiding, and her costs—and yours—will only grow. It's no way to live for either of you." I leaned in closer to her chair and my eyes locked on her own.

Cora smiled condescendingly. "I think you misunderstand

both my position and wealth. It is true that men like Mr. Noland don't marry girls like me. But he will not marry elsewhere any time soon; he simply can't work himself up to it. He meets suitable girls who are pretty and whose company he enjoys. Yet he's never quite certain they're pretty enough or amiable enough to be his wife. So while he wallows in indecision, he spends time"— she paused—"and money"—she emphasized—"on me." Her eyes narrowed sharply. "And I know how to save what money I get."

Had I ever doubted it, I now recognized Cora as a protégée of Mamie Durant's. Cora had just articulated her mentor's model for achieving financial independence—and perhaps also her habit of looking out for those who aroused her sympathy. I thought of the murder victim Moira Shea, whose body Mamie Durant had claimed and buried for still-unknown reasons.

I tried a different approach, hoping to make her see reason. "You are aware you place yourself at risk by helping Stella. Did Stella tell you anything about how Sarah was killed? It was a brutal murder—one that no other young woman should suffer."

She shrugged. "As I just said, I take care of myself all right," she said. "And I look out for Stella because she needs it. She's the kind of girl you think can't possibly make it here. She's too frail, in both body and spirit, especially since the attack. But she has nowhere else to go, so while she's here, I'll look out for her."

"Which attack?" Alistair asked abruptly. "Are you referring to Sarah Wingate's murder this Tuesday, or to a different incident?"

"Well, the first attack, of course." Cora looked at us incredulously. "But I suppose when you confront the same attacker again, it doesn't make much difference, does it?"

She seemed positively annoyed that we were so dense.

For our part, we were thoroughly confused. But Cora had

used the words *same attacker*. While it was possible she had misunderstood Stella, it certainly implied Stella might be able to identify Sarah Wingate's killer.

"Our apologies, Miss Czerne," Alistair said, "but we had not heard that Stella was victimized by an earlier attack, much less by the same man she may have seen on the day of the Wingate murder."

She regarded us with a look of amazement. "How is that possible?" she said. "I thought you said you had spoken with Mamie Durant. Surely Mamie told you about the attack on Stella?"

Seeing only our blank faces, she sighed deeply. "Well, I suppose she wouldn't have wanted to cast herself in a bad light. Not for the attack itself, mind you—but in the aftermath, the coverup . . . she certainly might have handled things better than she did. A lot of us thought as much."

Cora went on to give us the details of the January night almost two years ago when Stella had left Mamie's establishment on a quick errand. A man had followed her, overpowered her on a deserted street, and then forced her into the basement of an unlocked brownstone. Stella had recognized the man by face though not by name; he had visited Mamie's establishment some months prior. At the time, she had thought him spoiled and overbearing, but not dangerous. She had been wrong. As Stella later described it, she was lucky; her screams brought help fairly quickly, and her life was saved. But she spent months recovering from a brutal assault, afraid to venture outside.

At first, Mamie Durant would not even admit the young man's attorney to the house. She helped Stella through the process of pressing charges; anything less was, at least initially, unacceptable. But pressure was brought to bear from the man's family and their influential contacts; money exchanged hands; and in short, Mamie prevailed upon Stella to drop all charges. It had seemed a godsend when the Wingate job materialized away from the city and its terrible memories. Mamie had been anxious to be rid of Stella, probably because of a guilty conscience more than anything else.

"Personally," Cora said, "I don't think Mamie would have done it just for the money. But the man's family was well connected. They could bribe the right people better than she. Their contacts threatened to shut her down entirely. I'd like to think," she added, more soberly, "that she felt ashamed of herself afterward. She took an interest in placing Stella with the Wingates that was uncharacteristic for her. I think she simply couldn't face Stella any longer after what she'd done. Or rather, what she'd failed to do."

None of us knew quite what to say when Cora had finished talking. Alistair, in particular, seemed to be struggling with what to make of this new information.

"But you have no recollection of the man's name?" he pressed.

"No," she said, "Stella never told me."

"And you never heard the name Michael Fromley mentioned?" he clarified.

She seemed annoyed. "If I have, I certainly don't remember."

But Stella would know. And Mrs. Durant, too. And somehow this was all connected to Mamie Durant's dismissal of us the moment she saw Michael Fromley's picture. Even if Michael Fromley had not been Stella's attacker—and he could not have been if Cora were right about "the same person" murdering Sarah—then he was still involved somehow. I was sure of it.

"You mentioned that Stella recognized the attacker as the

same, in both incidents," I said to Cora. "You understand it makes our need to talk with her that much more urgent."

"No," she said decisively. "She is someplace safe. I will not jeopardize her safety. And I also won't force her to talk about those things that she is better forgetting."

"I doubt Stella can forget, no matter how she avoids the subject." Isabella spoke gently, in her most persuasive tone. "But she could ensure that no other young woman suffers by the hand of this man."

Alistair echoed Isabella's entreaty. "Where is she, Cora? If you don't tell us, then you must see how many people you put at risk. You disapprove of Mamie Durant's handling of the first incident. Just think how different things might be today had she encouraged Stella to press charges. Stella would not be in hiding today. Sarah Wingate would still be alive. And the man who did this to both of them would be safely behind bars, incapable of harming another soul."

Cora was stubborn and silent.

"Take us to her," I said. "Or—arrange a meeting, if you prefer. Whatever you like. But we need to see her."

It seemed as though a long time passed before she finally looked at us, without any trace of emotion. "Tomorrow morning at nine o'clock. A brief meeting. No more than, say, fifteen or twenty minutes." Her lips compressed into tight lines of determination. "And at a public place—Bethesda Fountain at Central Park should be good."

It was not the most convenient arrangement I could think of, but I was in no mood to argue. "Why not earlier?" I asked. "Surely you could arrange getting Stella to Central Park later this afternoon?"

"No." She shook her head, then looked at her watch. "I

have an appointment this afternoon. One that I will not re-schedule."

She had done all she was willing to do, and would not hear of another plan, so we found ourselves back on East Ninety-first Street walking toward Fifth Avenue and Central Park.

"In the interest of saving time, I suggest we split up," I said. "It's near three o'clock. I'll go downtown to interview Otto Schmidt, who has no doubt sobered up by now. Why don't the two of you return to Columbia and speak with some people there?"

Alistair agreed. "I suppose you'd like us to speak with Lonny Moore, if we can."

"Yes," I said, "and we have the names of two women who worked closely with Sarah on women's voting rights—Jenny Weller and Ruth Cabot. You might speak with them, if they are at home."

"What about Dean Arnold?" Isabella asked. "Remember what Angus—"

"I know," I said, cutting her off. "By all means speak with Dean Arnold—assuming you can find him anywhere near campus on a Saturday afternoon."

Isabella smiled. "I'll find him."

"Then we'll all meet for dinner and compare notes," Alistair said. "How about Chinese? I know a wonderful place on Pell Street off Mott. They call it the Chinese Delmonico's."

Delmonico's on Fifth Avenue was one of the city's most elegant restaurants, and they probably did not appreciate the comparison. Given his love of fine dining, I had no doubt Alistair was a regular at the original Delmonico's. At first his desire to visit Chinatown seemed surprising. But as he continued talking, raving about their menu, I realized his adventurous palate was prompting his request.

"What time?" I asked.

"An early dinner," Alistair said. "Six o'clock should give us enough time."

Alistair and Isabella hailed a cab, while I turned to pick up the Third Avenue El downtown.

"Number 24 Pell," Alistair called after me.

But I barely heard him, for my thoughts had returned to Otto Schmidt and the investigation still before us.

It took me the better part of an hour to locate Otto Schmidt, for he had been moved to an Upper East Side station house due to overcrowding. I traveled to the Oak Street station downtown, only to have to catch the El back uptown once again. It was a ridiculous waste of time. When I finally arrived at the correct station house, I was directed to a holding cell at the far end of the hallway from the main office. I expected the officers on duty had wanted to distance themselves as much as possible from Schmidt, for his clothes reeked of alcohol and vomit.

He was a wiry, thin man with a gray stubble beard. He sat in a plain metal chair in the far corner, gripping a thin, threadbare gray blanket tightly around his chest. His wild-eyed intense stare immediately bored into me as I entered the room.

"Get away," he called out. "Now, I said. Get out!"

He fidgeted violently, as though trying to disappear into the chair. After a particularly strenuous twist, he appeared to hurt his right arm, and began to writhe in pain.

"Otto Schmidt?" I asked as a courtesy, though there was no real indication the man was paying attention.

After grunting once more in pain, he closed his eyes tightly, now refusing to look at me. "I said go away. I will not talk with you. I promised to leave and talk with no one. I swore to it."

Then he opened his eyes again and looked forward, wild-eyed and crazed.

While he had earlier been drunk, his behavior now smacked of something different. It wasn't the alcohol that made him belligerent. It was fear.

Speaking more loudly, I addressed him again. "Mr. Schmidt, are you aware of why you are here?"

He shook his head. "I swear I was about to leave, just like I promised. But the pain was so bad. I just needed a little something to kill the pain. I intended to go after that, but they came and took me. That's why I didn't keep to my promise. Because they came and took me."

"Who came?" I asked. "The police?"

"Yes," he said, and nodded vigorously. "That's why I couldn't leave. I can't talk with you. You need to go."

"Mr. Schmidt, where were you going, before the police picked you up?" I asked.

He stared at me blankly. "I hadn't decided yet. Maybe Baltimore. I had friends there once. He didn't care, so long as I left New York."

"Who didn't care, Mr. Schmidt?" I asked. "Who made you promise to leave?"

"I don't know, I don't know," he replied weakly. "I'd never seen the man before. But he hurt me"—he pulled the blanket tighter around him—"and made me promise to leave and talk with no one."

"Mr. Schmidt," I said, trying to keep my tone calm and my words simple, as though I were talking with a child, "I can help you leave. I can help protect you from the man who hurt you. But first, you need to tell me what happened."

"No, no," he repeated, in a frenzy of panic. "He said you'd

say that, and I'm not to talk. Just leave." His eyes darted around the room.

I sighed in frustration, for this conversation was spinning in circles, leading nowhere.

"You have been arrested at my request," I said, "and I have the ability to release you. I will give you train fare to Baltimore. But I can do that only if you cooperate with me."

Otto Schmidt looked at me for the first time, still fidgeting. "You promise you'll help me leave? And you won't let that man know I talked?"

"I promise."

And in that fashion a loose agreement was reached, and I procured the details we needed. As I more or less already knew, Otto Schmidt was not the man responsible for Sarah Wingate's murder. He had no recollection of her—only the items he had stolen from her, which had landed him in jail the first time. It had been a crime of opportunity; Sarah's room had been the first unlocked door he had found after entering Mrs. Gardner's roominghouse. Since his escape from jail, he had spent most of his time in Boston, returning to New York only within the last six months, where he found work he liked well enough in the kitchen of a German restaurant in the Bowery.

To hear him tell it, all was well until early this morning, when a man had accosted him and ordered him to leave town. He had been thoroughly scared by the brutal encounter, but could share few details about the man: only that he was heavy-set with brown hair, wore an odd hat, and had beaten Otto Schmidt with a metal pipe. Otto had no idea why the man wanted him to leave; the man had threatened him if he talked to the police or anyone else. I had little doubt but that Schmidt would have made his way out of town immediately, had he not wanted alcohol to numb the pain of the beating. Ironically, had he not made a spectacle of himself begging for liquor so early in the day, we might never have located him.

I pulled money out of my wallet, but did not give it to Schmidt. "I promised you train fare," I said, "but I don't want you to spend it on drink. The man who will release you will take care of buying your ticket."

He was insensible again, and I got no response.

"Get the man a doctor," I said to the clerk on duty as I exited past the main office. "I believe he has a broken arm and requires medical care. You can send the bill here." I left Alistair's card behind. And I handed him an envelope with Mulvaney's name on it, containing a note and money for Otto Schmidt's train. "Will you see that Declan Mulvaney gets this? Thanks."

I would follow up with Mulvaney later to let him know that, for our purposes, it was okay to release Schmidt. I trusted him to put Schmidt on the train.

I boarded the Third Avenue El yet again, this time bound for Chinatown. I had wasted much of my afternoon in transit, and though it was not rational, I found myself irritated that Alistair had chosen such an inconvenient spot for dinner. Yet I was the one who had agreed, largely because it would have been so convenient to the Oak Street station where Schmidt was originally held.

Schmidt's situation continued to perplex me. How had Sarah Wingate's killer known Schmidt was on our list of possible suspects? The only scenario that made sense was that the killer wanted Schmidt to disappear so we would be unable to talk with him. That was important—not because Schmidt knew anything, but precisely because he did not. If Schmidt remained unavailable to us, then we could not formally clear him of suspicion in Sarah Wingate's murder. It was a calculated way to ensure our investigation remained hindered by many suspects we could not eliminate.

But Schmidt's attacker had found him even before we did. How was that possible? I supposed that once Mulvaney began asking around in an effort to find Schmidt, a lot more people had became involved. Too many people, frankly. What troubled me was Alistair's warning that the killer was likely monitoring our progress—either on his own, or through the guise of police or journalistic efforts. Whoever he was, he seemed always to be one maddening step ahead of us.

CHAPTER 24

I got off the El at Chatham Square and walked along the Bowery toward Doyers Street and Chinatown. It was Saturday evening, and throngs of people made their way in and out of import shops, meat and vegetable markets, restaurants, and some of the more dangerous saloons. On Doyers, Jimmy Kelly's Mandarin Club was already packed and, across from it, the Christian Mission house had a decent turnout. Turning onto Pell Street, I saw that Mike Saulter's place teemed with customers, as did a typical restaurant called the Oriental. I was in the heart of Chinatown, where all manner of vices, religions, and foods coexisted.

Mon Lay Won—or, as Alistair had described it, the Chinese Delmonico's—was on the upper floor of an import house, so I climbed narrow steps that led up to a small dining room with red carpet, rice-paper decorations, and a handful of tables. After the chaos of Chinatown's streets, it was a surprising oasis of calm.

Alistair and Isabella were already there, waiting for me at a front table. Apart from his fondness for Chinese food, I could see why Alistair chose this restaurant: It was a quiet place with very few tables, where we might talk undisturbed.

"We should order family style," Alistair said. "Their chop suey is excellent, and the boneless stuffed chicken wings are the best I've tried outside of Hong Kong."

I glanced at the menu. At a cost of $2.50—the most expensive item on the menu—I expected them to be.

"I'm also partial to the fried lobster in rice," Alistair said.

Our waiter appeared at our table to take our order.

"We'll begin with a pot of Lin Som tea," Alistair said, "and the water nuts along with egg drop soup." He went on to order a variety of dishes, thanking the waiter at the end in Chinese. Once he was out of earshot, Alistair went on to lament that there were not more Chinese restaurants in the city beyond Chinatown. "I suppose people are afraid the vices they associate with Chinatown would follow the restaurants."

It was too bad for all concerned. I knew the police had shut down a Chinese restaurant near Union Square earlier this year in response to neighborhood complaints. After a two-week investigation, they learned that the restaurant had served food, nothing else. But the two weeks of lost income had bankrupted its owner.

"What did you learn this afternoon, Simon?" Isabella asked, as she poured each of us a cup of the hot Lin Som tea that had arrived.

I filled them in, and, as expected, Alistair's primary concern was that Otto Schmidt had been threatened and assaulted.

"This killer overreacts every time we make progress—no matter how minor," Alistair said, grim faced. "It suggests he remains nervous and far too invested in our investigation. I don't like it."

"Nor do I," I said. I drank my cup of tea before asking, "How did the two of you make out today?"

Alistair was animated as he began to recount their interview with the suffragists. "First," Alistair said, "I found Jenny Weller at home. She and Sarah were not close friends at Barnard, but both were involved in the suffragist movement there." Alistair shuddered. "She was a dreadful woman, by the way. She had too much nervous energy and no sense of humor whatsoever. I was on edge our entire conversation. But I learned a few things of interest from her. She confirmed Sarah was active in the suffrage movement, a great worker. She also recalled an incident two or three weeks ago when she saw Sarah arguing with a young man near the 116th Street subway stop."

He used chopsticks to help himself to the plate of water nuts that had arrived. Isabella also handled her chopsticks expertly. I, on the other hand, seemed to be all thumbs.

"Simon, a lesson in chopsticks before the lobster and chicken arrive," Isabella said, laughing. "It's very simple when you know what to do. Place your thumb like so and your forefinger here." She proceeded to demonstrate the technique until I had picked it up—and if I was not as expert as they were, soon I at least exhibited basic competence.

Alistair continued his story. "I then spoke with three other former classmates of Sarah who board upstairs from Jenny Weller—Caroline Brown, Tillie Maddox, and Ruth Cabot. Caroline does the thinking for all three of them; the other two rarely open their mouth unless she asks them to. So I have to give extra significance to something Ruth Cabot told me. They last saw Sarah at a ladies' committee meeting at a Mrs. Llewellyn's home. It was on"—Alistair pulled a black notebook from his jacket pocket and found his notes—"Wednesday, October 18. It was a meeting to discuss the reform platform for the mayoral election; I gather they planned to pass their concerns along to Hearst." He finished the last water nut and moved on to the egg drop soup, which Isabella and I had already begun. "Ruth noticed that Sarah was upset, not participating in the discussion as she usually did. And she looked terrible that night, her eyes pinched up as if she had a headache. When Ruth asked about her, Sarah responded that she intended to quit her position at the dean's office as soon as the term ended." He paused to take another spoonful of soup.

"Go on," I said, impatient.

"Sarah claimed she was wrapping up one last project— something no one else could finish as easily—before she quit. And then she told Ruth not to worry."

"So just like Mary Bonham and Angus MacDonald, Ruth believed something happened in the days leading up to Sarah's murder that deeply troubled her," I said, thinking aloud. "Perhaps Isabella is right and there *is* some connection to Sarah's work with Dean Arnold. Did Lonny Moore make any additional complaints through the dean's office?"

"Not that we're aware of," Alistair said. "But let me go ahead and tell you about my conversation with Lonny. He's well connected, Ziele. If he becomes your prime suspect, you'll do well to remember that. His father is a high-level banker with J. P. Morgan and has influential friends throughout the city. I know some of them."

What Alistair meant was that Lonny's family counted them-

selves among the working rich, and they maintained connections with the truly rich and powerful through service professions
like law and finance.

He continued to explain Lonny's background. "He lives
alone in a single dormitory room in Wallach Hall overlooking
the quad. His friends—Isabella and Horace spoke with them
earlier, you recall—live on the same floor and have provided
him with an alibi during the time of Sarah's murder. They say
he was in Sam Baker's room with the rest of them, playing cards.
But alibis provided by close friends sometimes crumble." Alistair
leaned back in his chair, flexing his fingers. "And Lonny did
have an acrimonious relationship with Sarah—both before and
after his complaint about her organic chemistry performance.
Since you'll want to speak with him and judge for yourself, I
told him to be available tomorrow around eleven o'clock, following our appointment with Stella."

I was silent a moment, thinking. Then I asked Alistair, "Do
you think he is the man we're looking for?"

"I can't judge as of yet," Alistair said. "He is smart enough
and angry enough to be. And he is apparently in perpetual need
of money—which may prove important, as Isabella will explain
in a moment. You'll have to keep your own counsel tomorrow
morning. One more important thing, however. Lonny may not
prove a murderer, but he has already proven to be a thief. Sarah's advisor, Caleb Muller, was with Lonny when I arrived. The
young man apparently submitted an article Sarah had drafted
to a leading mathematical journal. He was hoping to pass the
work off as his own."

"That's certainly interesting," I said. I would make my own
judgment in the morning. I turned to Isabella. "You learned
something from Dean Arnold, I hear."

Isabella's excitement was apparent, but she poured more tea before she began talking. "Dean Arnold was in his office this afternoon, taking advantage of the weekend to catch up on paperwork with the help of his secretary, a young man named Samuel Cohen," she said. "I learned that Sarah began working for them last January, and came in on Wednesday and Friday afternoons from one o'clock until five."

"Did he say what sort of projects she worked on?" I asked. With my chopsticks, I picked up one of the boneless stuffed chicken wings and had to admit Alistair was right—they were extraordinary. The flavor was a unique blend of spices that were new to my unadventurous palate.

"She helped with the dean's meetings and appointments; she checked completed dissertations for proper formatting; and she worked with budgets and grants. The dean's office manages the budget requests for individual departments as well as grant requests from the dean's discretionary fund." Her eyes lit up. "The dean himself noticed nothing, but Sam—he remembered Sarah was bothered by something two or three weeks ago. In other words, within the same time frame everyone else has mentioned."

"Did he know what?" I asked, growing eager because Isabella's excitement was palpable.

"He did not," she said, "but he recalled she was working on recent budgets that included Alistair's research center. So he loaned me the papers she was working on to review, which I did once I was back at Alistair's office."

"And?"

"The short version: Someone has been stealing Alistair blind," she said. "The long version, as I'll explain, is somewhat more complicated." She pulled some notes out of her bag for me to see. "First, you need to understand how the budget for the Center for Criminological Research works. Alistair essentially funds his own work—but through the university, not his own bank account."

"Why not through personal funds?" I asked. "It would be simpler, no?"

"It would be simpler," Alistair said. "But not as good for the university. My affiliation with Columbia provides me with many benefits, so it is something I can do to help them. Essentially I funnel money to my research center through the dean's discretionary fund so it may count as a donation. Their annual fundraising figures are improved, which then helps them attract even more donors, since people like to donate to successful causes."

We were interrupted by the proprietor, a Chinese man who had taken "Jimmy" as his English name. He wanted to make sure we had enjoyed our meal—as well as to push his after-dinner tobacco offerings.

"We have fine new cigars. You try?" he asked. He passed out a menu with FINEST QUALITY OF CIGARS & CIGARETTES written on top in all caps.

"No, thanks, Jimmy—not tonight. We're a bit pressed for time, you understand," Alistair said.

"Then I bring you dessert." Apparently we had no choice in the matter.

He motioned to a waiter, and in an instant, dessert was on the table. "Star fruit, lichee nuts, and moon cakes," he said, adding, "Be sure to look for the secret fortune inside. It's Chinese tradition from Ming dynasty."

Alistair broke his moon cake in half, exposing the small slip of paper inside. *"Your past success will be overshadowed by your future success.* Let's hope so. Ziele?"

I read it aloud. *"The first step to better times is to imagine them."* I tasted a bite of the moon cake. The texture was odd; I preferred the fruit.

Isabella laughed and added hers. *"Grand adventures await those willing to turn the corner.* If only it were so easy."

I moved our conversation back on point. "I follow what you are saying about why Alistair's financing of the research center is done through donations. Now what?"

Alistair shrugged. "The money stays there, earmarked for the research center, until I put in a formal request."

"That's something Mrs. Leab has traditionally done," Isabella added, "with Alistair dictating the request and signing off on it. The problem is that huge sums have gone missing over the past year from Dean Arnold's earmarked account. Checks were disbursed from the account made out to the research center, but they never made it to Mrs. Leab. Someone else managed to cash them by forging Alistair's name."

"You never noticed missing funds?" I asked Alistair.

Alistair looked embarrassed. "Apparently not. We are talking about funds I never requested. Whatever I asked for, I received. There seemed no reason to inquire about what was held in reserve for later."

"How much money, exactly, do you donate every year?" I asked. It seemed inconceivable that someone would not keep tabs on what was obviously a large amount of money. But Alistair's relationship with his money was different from that of most people. Because he had more than was ample for his requirements, he had no reason to keep close track of his funds. His answer made that clear.

"I'd have to ask my accountant," Alistair said. "For the university as a whole, I donate my annual salary back, several times over. But we are talking about a portion of that earmarked for my research."

Isabella cradled her cup of tea as she leafed through the dean's papers, which included a series of budget memoranda from various academic departments. "Sarah caught the problem because anyone who receives money from the dean's discretionary fund is required to document exactly how it is spent, supported by receipts or canceled checks. This is done on a quarterly basis," she explained. "What Sarah discovered was that large sums of money sent to the research center—totaling nearly fifteen thousand dollars—were never documented."

She pushed her plate aside to make room for the papers, prompting a waiter to appear from nowhere to clear the table.

"My first question has to be whether someone from the research center could have put in for the checks, then intercepted and taken them?"

"I thought of that, too," Isabella said. "But look"—she pushed a paper in front of us—"I compared this requisition request for $2,000 against all of our handwriting—Tom's, Fred's, Horace's, even Mrs. Leab's. It's not a match for anyone."

"Someone might have disguised their writing," I said.

"Maybe," Alistair responded, "but most of us academics aren't in the profession for the money. We're motivated by a passion for our field. So it's hard to see greed leading any of my associates to concoct this sort of scheme."

What Alistair said was no doubt true. But I could not help but reflect that Alistair's associates were not independently wealthy, either. Their perspective might be different.

"You mentioned Lonny was perpetually in need of money, so there's an avenue to explore," I said thoughtfully. "Our best bet will be to contact the bank on Monday morning. The check was cashed, so the money went somewhere. By tracing the canceled check, perhaps we can generate additional leads."

Alistair pushed his dessert plate aside. "The important issue for now is what the discovery of this scheme may have meant for Sarah Wingate. She may well have identified the person who stole these funds. But everyone described her as upset. Theft . . . money . . . budget discrepancies . . . these strike me as annoyances, not something that would have upset her to the degree Angus MacDonald and Ruth Cabot suggested."

"Especially since no one stole the money from *her*," Isabella added.

"Also, let's not forget that the person who stole from my fund may have no connection to Sarah's murderer," Alistair said. "The theft and the murder may be wholly separate crimes."

"Remember the money you found at the crime scene under Sarah's mattress?" I asked Alistair. "It was roughly the same amount that was requested here." I indicated one of the missing sums Isabella had referenced. "It's an odd coincidence that she possessed in cash the same amount that she recently questioned in that accounting. Maybe she *was* killed for money. But not her own money—Alistair's money."

None of us knew the answer. Abigail Wingate, after all, had been convinced the money belonged to her aunt. But I was relieved that we were finally doing solid detective work, following up each lead to make sure we understood every aspect of Sarah's life as thoroughly as possible. I felt we were inching closer to building a case as we reviewed each detail of her life.

One question nagged at me: Where was the Fromley connection in all this? For I did not forget—no, not for a moment—that the perpetrator we sought was linked both to Sarah Wingate and Fromley.

"And now," Alistair said, beginning to gather his things, "I do apologize, friends, but I must be off. I have tickets to see *Wonderland*, the new musical at the Majestic." He put down money on the table that more than sufficiently covered our dinner. "Ziele, would you mind accompanying Isabella home? I'll see you in the morning at Bethesda Fountain in Central Park."

"We're near Ferrara's, one of my favorite coffeehouses. Would you like to stop by before I take you home?" I asked her.

"That sounds lovely, Simon," she said.

"It's just four blocks up on Grand Street between Mott and Mulberry. They have the best coffee in the city."

As we walked up Mott, the lanterns and jostling crowds of Chinatown yielded to Little Italy with its multitude of restaurants and music. We passed one restaurant where the strains of a violin playing "O mio babbino caro" swelled into the street. We reached Ferrara's Bakery and Café before I knew it, and after surveying glass shelves filled with cookies, pastries, and other delectable confections, we took a table by the front window where we could watch pedestrians go by. I ordered an espresso, Isabella preferred tea, and we decided to share a large cannoli. Her brown eyes drifted behind the counter over to the espresso machine that puffed, gurgled, and then shot steam straight up in the air.

Noting her interest, I said, "No one makes espresso like they do here. I think Ferrara's was first in the city to acquire an espresso maker. There's an art to making a good cup; the ground beans and steam must be managed perfectly."

"You must be careful, or you'll become a gourmand like Alistair," she said, laughing.

"For food, never. But coffee—well, good coffee is my weakness."

The waiter brought our order, and Isabella gazed into the concentrated shot of dark coffee.

"You'll be up all night," she warned.

"I'm up most nights during an investigation, anyway," I said lightly. Sleep came, when it came at all, in intermittent spells. However much my body might crave rest, my mind refused to unwind.

"Do you have family here?" she asked.

"Not anymore," I said, tasting the cannoli. "I'm all that's left." I explained how my mother had died last winter, and my sister had long since married and moved away. I did not bother mentioning my long-absent father; he could be dead, too, for all I knew.

"And no sweetheart or Mrs. Ziele with whom to spend your Saturday night?" she asked. Her voice was light, teasing. "I'm assuming there's not, or you would not be spending the evening with Alistair and me."

"There was." I drained my espresso shot. "She's dead." The words came out more harshly than I intended.

She grew somber. "I'm sorry." Then she paused. "What was she like?"

So I told her about Hannah. I told her about Hannah's quick wit and infectious sense of humor. How on warm summer nights, we had sat and talked for hours on her building's narrow stoop—and how she'd seemed to understand everything about me. And how I had planned to marry her and take her away from the Lower East Side, as soon as I'd graduated Columbia and become a lawyer. But none of that had happened. First, my father had deserted our family after a night of uncontrolled gambling, dashing my own dreams of finishing college. And then, shortly after I had been promoted to detective and begun to save enough to think of marriage, Hannah had been taken from me during the horror of the *Slocum* disaster.

"People say, of course, that the grief becomes easier with time. It has." I looked at her soberly. "What I have trouble letting go of is the blame."

"But who do you blame, Simon?" she asked curiously. "Of course I read the newspapers, and I know they say the *General Slocum* crew mishandled things awfully."

"Not the crew, though they were useless in helping to save anyone. I blame those who had the power to avert this disaster, but were blinded by profit and under-the-table payments. They murdered her," I said with bitterness, "though any one of them might have saved her. Lundberg, who inspected the ship, could have cited them for having defective life preservers or unusable lifeboats. Barnaby, the owner, could have invested in the latest safety equipment. And the captain, Van Schaick, had countless chances to run a safer ship. But I doubt the district attorney will be able to make even one of them pay for what they did. Lundberg's third trial this past May ended in another mistrial. And I've given up hope Van Schaick will ever face a jury."

"And would it make you feel better if any one of these men went to jail?" she asked. "It wouldn't bring Hannah back."

"No," I replied honestly. "But when others have lost so much, those responsible should lose something, too."

We sat together in silence for some moments, then I said, "It was another passenger who killed her in the end. She must have jumped. Maybe she was close enough to swim for it. Or maybe the flames were too close, their heat too much to bear. But someone jumped right after her, too close behind. It was the force of his weight that knocked her unconscious, ensuring she drowned."

She barely whispered it. "You can't know that, Simon. You weren't there."

But of course I had been there. I'd been one of several policemen who had raced toward the burning ship. As we had approached, falling timber from the *Slocum*'s decks rained into the East River. The water was filled with people: some screaming for help, others frantically trying to swim to shore. They jumped off the boat in groups—sometimes two or three persons together, other times ten or twelve.

Hannah had worn red that day—a new dress that warmed her skin and lit up her auburn hair. I had barely been able to breathe through thick, smoke-laden air as our boat came closer and closer, pulling up more survivors on the way. I helped them all, barely noticing, for I was vainly searching the waters for Hannah. Closer, closer, I had urged the helmsman, directing him toward the front bow of the ship where a young woman in red stood pressed against the ship's rail. I couldn't make out her face . . . couldn't tell whether or not it was indeed *her* . . . and as we came close, all went black in a wall of fire.

I later learned that burning lumber from the *Slocum*'s collapsing upper deck had broadsided our boat, and we had been lucky to be rescued ourselves. I spent two days in the hospital before I got out and retrieved her body from the large, makeshift morgue. Well-meaning neighbors had told me about Hannah's final moments, in properly vague terms, and assured me that there had never been a chance for her. But I knew better. I would forever be tormented by my mind's image of the girl in

the red dress—the girl who may or may not have been Hannah—
the girl I had tried, and failed, to reach.

"I was there, only too late." My voice was grim as I admitted it to Isabella, explaining everything.

She reached toward me and opened her mouth to speak, but
I cut her off. "Don't say it." I pressed her hand quickly. "I understand." I disengaged my hand just as rapidly.

I couldn't bear to hear the words she almost said—not yet,
not from her.

"Your husband died, as well." It was a statement, not a question.

"Two years ago," she said, nodding. "He was an archeologist.
He was part of a team working in Greece who made an impor-
tant but controversial discovery involving artifacts of great value.
But then Teddy and his partner were murdered because of it."

Her face closed down and I decided to change the topic.
Tom had said there were unusual circumstances surrounding
Teddy's death—and I didn't need to know them now.

"What I can't figure out," I said, "is why you are so interested in Alistair's work. For the past two years, your work has
centered on a man as depraved as I could imagine."

Her eyes met mine. "I think evil is less threatening if one
understands it. I have never shared Alistair's optimism that it is
possible to rehabilitate a man like Fromley. But when I understand more about him and why he behaves and thinks as he
does, then I don't fear him. Or those like him," she added, "including the men who killed Teddy."

In her own way, she was like Alistair then: Her desire to
understand the criminal mind had been a method of dealing
with her grief following Theodore Sinclair's violent death.

"But what about you?" she asked. "Your life's work is spent identifying and arresting criminals."

"I don't do it because I want to understand criminal behavior," I replied thoughtfully. "What I understand are the victims. Once they are gone, no one is left to look out for them—"

"No one except for people like you," she said softly, finishing my sentence. "You are a good man, Simon."

We continued to talk about lighter topics, and I managed to enjoy the evening and forget some of my frustration with the case. But after I saw Isabella safely home to her own building, and settled onto the train bound for Dobson, a dark gloom settled over me once again. I began to face up to the possibility that, despite our best efforts in this murder case, we might still fail. This case could prove unsolvable. And while that would certainly amount to a personal failure, what made the idea unbearable was the image of Sarah Wingate—whose life, like Hannah's, had ended too soon.

Others might say it was the effect of the coffee, but I knew better: The two of them, and the circumstances of their untimely deaths, haunted my thoughts throughout the night, refusing me peace.

Sunday, November 12, 1905

CHAPTER 25

I read the *Times* as the train whisked me back into the city Sunday morning to meet with Stella Gibson in Central Park. The day's headlines continued to focus upon Tuesday's mayoral election debacle, informing me that Hearst's challenge to Mayor McClellan's victory was headed to New York's Supreme Court, though the *Times* editorial believed his chances were slim. Other news was also dismal: Stock markets in New York and London were in turmoil due to alarm over the violence in St. Petersburg and Odessa; and Emil Greder, a baritone with the Metropolitan Opera, had attempted suicide because of money he owed to loan sharks.

The last story returned my thoughts to Isabella's discovery from yesterday. Someone had known enough about Alistair's money habits to realize his donations were so large he would not miss the withdrawn amounts. And the thief had known enough about the dean's disbursement fund that he was able to request— and intercept—the money he wanted without raising suspicion. But his error had been to think funds drawn from the dean were essentially blank checks that would never need to be justified. None of our present suspects seemed to fit that profile— unless Stella offered us new information.

I walked from Grand Central Terminal to the park, energized by the crisp chill in the air, and found myself at Bethesda Fountain before anyone else. Though the park was far from where I used to live, I'd taken many walks there, especially in the early days after Hannah died. This place in particular, with the statue of the Angel of the Waters presiding over the fountain, had always struck me with its serene grandeur.

Alistair arrived shortly after me, the dark bags under his eyes suggesting he also had slept little.

"How was the theater?" I asked.

"Forgettable. I should have seen *Peter Pan* instead, judging by recent reviews. But Kitty—well, never mind. I was just trying to please the others in my party."

"Isabella isn't coming this morning?" I asked.

He shook his head. "She went to the research center instead. She wants to review more of our financial records. Fred and Tom plan to come in this afternoon to assist."

We stopped talking as two women appeared on the upper terrace and made their way down the stairs toward us. The shorter woman of the two was Cora; Stella towered over her in a way that surprised me. Both the Wingates and Cora had emphasized Stella's emotional frailty in describing her to me, so I had pictured her as diminutive. But she was tall, with a face marked by strong features, including a sharp, aquiline nose, and unusual pale coloring—blond hair that was almost silver, and eyes of robin's-egg blue. Her movements were those of a skittish colt, startled by each nearby sound and movement, and I immediately remembered something Cora had mentioned earlier: How after she was attacked in January, Stella had not wished to venture outside. She seemed uncomfortable, even now, in this open public space.

She came over to us with a wan smile and spoke shyly. I recalled she was from near Boston the moment I heard her speak; most of her words were missing their *r*'s. Cora acknowledged us with merely a nod, as she hovered protectively beside Stella.

"It's good to see that you're safe," I said. "The Wingates have been very worried about you."

A flash of guilt crossed her face. "Please let them know I'm fine. I didn't mean to make them worry."

"We were worried, too," I added, "especially after we found a bloodstained ladies' bag with your unmailed letter to Cora at Grand Central."

She was confused for a moment. Then she said, "That must have been Miss Sarah's bag. She offered to mail the letter for me when she was in town early last week. I wonder why she didn't? It's not like her to forget a promise."

But no doubt Sarah had something weighing on her mind that distracted her.

"I'm sure you know why we wanted to meet with you," I said gently. "We need to know what you saw the day of Sarah's murder."

She nodded. Her tale unfolded gradually, and with each detail, we came to realize the true horror of what had happened at the Wingate home that Tuesday afternoon.

"I was in the garden helping Mrs. Wingate when I heard a sound that made my blood curdle. It almost sounded like a cat-fight, to my ears—except it came from within the house and we don't have cats." She took a deep breath, and shoved her hands in her pockets. "So I told Mrs. Wingate I'd got to check on something, and I went into the kitchen to make sure nothing was wrong. I knew Miss Abigail was walking the dogs, but Miss Sarah was inside working."

She stopped, looking at the ground and kicking a stone with the toe of her black button boots.

"Go on," I said to encourage her.

She swallowed hard. "I don't know why I didn't call up to her, but I didn't. I was at the foot of the kitchen stairs when I heard an odd gurgling sound. I got worried Sarah was sick, so I started up the kitchen stairs to the second floor." She grabbed at her blue scarf and wrapped it tight around her. "I suppose I knew something was wrong halfway up the stairs. I heard more strange noises, awful gasping sounds." She shuddered involuntarily. "I knew better, but I couldn't stop moving up the stairs. I needed to see what was going on." Her voice grew quieter until it was no more than a whisper. "I'd reached the second floor when I heard a man's grunts. They were regular—every couple seconds or so—and there was a thudding sound, too, like when Maud and I beat Mrs. Wingate's carpets outside."

She paused. "I was quiet as I moved down the hall. I kept to the side, and I was ready to hide in the nearest room the second I heard the grunts stop. I made it to the guest room doorway and looked in. And that's when I realized what a terrible mistake I'd made."

Several moments of silence followed.

Finally, she drew a deep breath and described the scene that represented her worst nightmare come true. "There was blood everywhere—on the wall, on the bed, all over the floor. I've never seen so much blood in my life. And still he wouldn't stop. He kept striking her, over and over and over with some kind of metal pipe."

For the first time she looked at us directly. "I only saw his back. But I knew it was him. I recognized his broad shoulders and thick neck. He was doing to her exactly what he'd threatened to do to me. That day he took me, he told me he would take every ounce of blood from my body and paint the room with it. He said I had been a pretty girl but no one would recognize me when he was done. And that he would not grant me death—those were his very words, grant me death—until I had suffered enough."

She trembled, biting her lip. "But Sarah was dead already, I saw that. And I was so scared. I had to force myself to move, just inside the linen closet across the hall. It's a shallow closet and I didn't quite fit—I couldn't close the door all the way—but it was the best I could do. I just couldn't *move*, you see." Stella's breathing came fast now. "It seemed an eternity before he was done. I heard sounds that made me think he was stuffing something in a bag, and his footsteps came close as he left the room. If he'd turned left, he would have seen me. And I thought he was going to for a moment. He stood outside the guest room door for a long time, listening—and I got scared I was breathing too loud, so I held my breath until I thought I'd pass out. Then he finally turned, and I heard him go down the stairs. When he was gone, I went to my room on the third floor, grabbed my coat and some money, and ran all the way to town and the next train."

She fought back tears. "I should have warned Mrs. Wingate,

I know. All I could think about later was that maybe he'd hurt them, too. But I was so scared, I just had to get away."

"But you never saw Sarah's killer's face?" I asked her to confirm.

She had not.

"I recognized him, though," she said, adding, "he was the same man who attacked me last January. I could never forget him. His name was Michael Fromley." Her voice was soft but unwavering, leaving no room for doubt.

But it couldn't be; it was impossible.

The pit in my stomach grew larger as I felt my control over this case begin to slip. The dead ghost of Fromley had once again resurfaced to confuse us, making us doubt everything we had learned.

When we explained that Fromley's involvement was out of the question—that Fromley himself had been dead by the time of Sarah's murder—she was initially disbelieving.

"Impossible," Stella insisted. "Sarah's murderer did to her exactly what he intended to do to me. And I know it," she said, "because that monster described exactly what he wanted to do the day he assaulted me. He liked seeing how much his words scared me."

I could only imagine.

It was only after we explained the autopsy results, and how definitive they had been, that she finally accepted the truth.

"Jesus, Mary, and Joseph," she swore softly, finally understanding. "But how could anyone else have—"

"Have possibly known?" I finished her question for her. "That is our question, too. As well as this one: How do we explain what you saw?"

It was Alistair who supplied the most logical explanation

why Stella believed she had seen Michael Fromley on Tuesday. She had seen only the man's back. The crime scene had embodied his previous threats. Then her imagination—fueled by terror and fear—had supplied the rest.

"Do either of you," I asked, turning to Cora, who had been hanging back during our conversation, "have any idea as to who else might know the details of Stella's assault last January?"

The two women looked at each other. "Perhaps one of the girls at Mamie's place knew," Stella said. "I think most of them were aware of what happened, though only a couple knew me well enough to hear the details."

"Actually," Alistair said, "we would be more interested to know whether any patrons knew? Perhaps one of the girls spoke too freely about it?"

I divided our well-thumbed stack of suspect photographs in half, passing some to Cora and the remainder to Stella.

Cora stopped abruptly when she passed over one particular photograph. "Why do you have a picture of Lonny in here?"

We had clipped it from a recent Columbia yearbook.

"You know him?" I asked.

"Of course," she replied cautiously. "He used to stop in regularly; at least, he'd go through periods when he did. Then he'd disappear for months at a time."

I was almost relieved to hear of a connection with Lonny, whose animosity toward Sarah was well known. He certainly had the strongest known motive for wishing to harm Sarah.

"Would he have been there around the time you were assaulted?" Alistair asked.

"I don't know," Stella finally answered. "I don't remember many details from that time."

"Would there be any record at Mamie's?" I asked.

Cora's response was immediate. "Oh, no, Mamie never would keep records. It would be the end of her business."

Alistair offered another idea. "But is it possible he was there and one of the girls told him about it?"

"Possible, but doubtful," I said. "To so perfectly replicate Fromley's crime fantasy, I would think he would need to see— or hear—a greater level of detail than a secondhand account could provide."

"You know, perhaps Michael and Lonny were acquainted," Cora said. "They both came to Mamie in recent years. And they were cut from the same cloth, I'd say—too much money and neither one right in the head."

It was one possible explanation.

"What about Mamie herself?" I asked. "Obviously she knew the details. Could she have shared them with the wrong person?"

Cora laughed. "Not Mamie. You don't know Mamie if you think that. She has no close friends. No confidants. She keeps her own counsel, makes her own decisions."

"It sounds like a lonely sort of life," I said.

"Maybe," said Cora. "But it protects her. She trusts no one. And honestly, no one trusts her, either."

Given Mamie's dealings with us, I could understand why.

"Are we done here?" Stella asked. She appeared exhausted and no doubt wanted to return home.

"Miss Gibson," I asked, "may we help you in any way? Until this case is solved, we can offer you a measure of protection. We can even help you leave the city if you like."

She thanked us, but declared herself perfectly comfortable with her current arrangement. "I've got a room on East Seventy-third Street that suits me fine."

I watched her walk away, her blue scarf catching in the breeze behind her. From what I'd been told, Stella's life had not been an easy one even before Michael Fromley terrorized her last winter. What she had now witnessed was undeserved. I could only hope that with time—and the care of friends like Cora—she could once again live a normal life.

We headed back uptown, talking over the new information we'd uncovered, and I considered a new angle: Had it been possible we were looking in all the wrong places—first, for Michael Fromley, and then for Sarah's unknown assailant? We had been searching for connections to Sarah, connections to her world at Columbia. But my nagging suspicion that Mamie Durant somehow played an important role in this case had intensified.

That also raised a new possibility we had not yet considered: What if the killer had come to Dobson with Stella as his intended target—and encountered Sarah instead? If so, we would need to alter our approach to the investigation. I mentioned as much to Alistair as we descended into the Seventy-second Street subway station.

"It strikes me," Alistair said, "that Sarah's murder was carefully timed during a moment when she was alone in the house. If the killer's target were truly Stella, it would have been even easier to isolate her during one of her household errands—to the ice house, to the basement, even alone in the kitchen or outdoors." He paused a moment. "What troubles me more is the fact that Lonny Moore so little resembles the man Stella and Abigail had both described seeing the day of Sarah Wingate's murder. They described a stout, heavyset man of medium height, whereas Lonny is short and pudgy."

I had a different view.

"Though I'd like to think otherwise," I said, "I fear neither

Abigail Wingate nor Stella Gibson are the most reliable of witnesses. Abigail's memory latched on to the only man she had seen that day. And as for Stella, until just a few minutes ago, she was convinced that the man she saw in Sarah's room during the murder was Fromley himself."

There were no strong leads. But based on what evidence we had, Lonny Moore seemed the most likely suspect. He had hated Sarah, and his jealousy had prompted him to steal her work. Either at Columbia or at Mamie Durant's, he might have crossed paths with Fromley. There would be much to talk about with him, but after the ups and downs of this investigation, I would not pin my hopes on Lonny—at least, not yet.

CHAPTER 26

Upon our return to the research center, Alistair was greeted with sobering news: Two of the major papers—the *Tribune* and the *Post*—planned to run a story on Monday about possible improprieties on the part of Judge Hansen in the Michael Fromley case. Alistair's name was as yet unmentioned. But that was only, Alistair maintained, because he had so thoroughly cowed yesterday's reporters with the threat of a libel suit should they report the wrong facts. I wondered whether it was possible that a generous bribe had also worked to keep Alistair's name clear of the story. It was understood that many news editors were not averse to such persuasion, especially when scandal was involved. With his personal reputation at stake, Alistair began to telephone his more influential contacts. But given what I knew about

the yellow sensation newspapers, I doubted even Alistair's connections and money would be sufficient to keep his name out of
the spotlight for long.

With Alistair otherwise occupied, I met with Lonny alone.
Sullen and scowling, he glared at me as I entered the second-
floor meeting room. He was dressed nicely, even expensively, in
a green cashmere sweater and heavy brown tweed pants; I also
noted the gold pocket watch draped from his vest, which he
made a point of checking the moment I came in. While he affected the manner of a man who has been delayed for an important meeting, he reminded me more of a schoolboy brought in
for a reprimand. Did he truly understand that I was interviewing him on suspicion of murder? And how reasonable a suspicion was it? I wondered, as I searched his pale blue eyes for any
sign of a man both violent and intelligent enough to have committed this particularly brutal murder.

Once our initial greetings were dispensed with, we got
down to my true business. "Could you tell me your whereabouts
this past Tuesday afternoon, November 7?"

"Don't you talk with your colleagues? I already told the
professor working with you. I had a card game going over at
Sam's," he said, annoyed that he had to repeat the information.
"That would be Sam Baker, one of my friends. He and the others there can vouch for me from two o'clock until well past dinner."

"Policemen like me tend to recheck people's alibis multiple
times," I said easily. "It's our way of determining whether you're
telling the truth. I will need the names of the other persons in
Tuesday's card game."

His response was belligerent. "You've got nothing on me."

"I had understood from Professor Sinclair that you wished

to cooperate. That you were interested in helping us in this investigation," I said.

He glared at me a moment, then thought of something. "Say"—he leaned forward, eyes gleaming with curiosity—"I've still not heard how she was killed. Was she strangled? Shot? Stabbed?"

"I ask the questions here; not you," I said sharply. His question left me cold. Either he had wished her dead so fervently he now relished the details of it—or worse, if he *were* the murderer we sought, then he wanted to hear me recount the details. Either way, I had no plan to indulge him. "I'm sure you understand all details of a murder investigation are confidential."

Disappointed, he sank back into his chair.

"A number of people have mentioned your name in connection with Sarah Wingate," I said. "How did you know her?"

"My name in connection with her?" He practically spat the words. "I had no connections with that woman."

"No?" I arched my eyebrows, feigning surprise. "From what I've been told, I understand that she was your classmate in at least two courses." I looked through my notes to ensure I had the right facts. "Those would be organic chemistry and an advanced mathematics course. In fact, you were sufficiently familiar with her and her work, or thought you were, to challenge her grade in organic chemistry."

If possible, Lonny's face turned an even brighter shade of red. It was anger; not embarrassment or even frustration. The mere mention of the incident seemed to rekindle a long-nursed animosity.

"That was not a connection," he said, sneering. "That was how I tried to get decent treatment for the rest of us. She had the professor fooled into thinking she was brilliant, so she could steal what was rightfully someone else's, take credit for it all. I tried to tell them, and they just didn't listen. They bought her side of the story, hook, line, and sinker." He glowered darkly.

"Did your interaction with Miss Wingate ever extend beyond the classroom?"

"No, I never saw Sarah Wingate outside of class. I met her in the chemistry class you just mentioned. We were classmates, nothing more." Then he tried to turn the questioning. "Who else are you interviewing from her classes?"

"Why do you want to know?" I asked.

"Because if you haven't been talking with certain people, I can point you in the proper direction. Have you spoken with John Nelson?"

"Why would it be important to speak with him?" I asked coolly. I remembered John Nelson had been mentioned previously as one of Lonny's close friends.

"He knew Sarah Wingate for what she was," Lonny said. "He wrote an article about her and her rabble-rousing friends last year for the *Spectator*, exposing their conspiracy to disrupt the campus. What about Cyril McGee?"

I recognized the name from the list Professor Muller had given us. I pulled out my notebook and wrote the name down, as well as a memo to myself to review those articles from the campus newspaper that mentioned Sarah Wingate. When I finished, I looked at Lonny expectantly.

"You'll see he has useful information, too," Lonny said, in answer to my look, beginning to feel self-important.

"What about the name Michael Fromley?" I said. "Do you know him?" Cora had suspected they were acquainted, and I was curious whether he would admit it.

"Is he a suspect, too?"

I pulled out his picture and showed Lonny. "Do you know him?"

He shook his head.

"Think harder," I said, "maybe you saw him someplace. Here at Columbia, perhaps. Or farther downtown, at Mamie Durant's."

His eyes widened.

"It is my business to know these things, Mr. Moore," I said. "Did you think you would be able to keep that quiet?"

"But how did you find out?" he whispered.

I ignored him and repeated my own question. "How long have you known him?"

He shrugged. "Ran into him a few times, that's all. I don't know him well enough to recognize his name. Michael, you said?"

I didn't believe a word of it.

"Where else did you see him beside Mamie's?"

He had grown red in the face and was breathing hard. I had clearly struck a sore point. "Also at a gaming house," he finally said. "But only once."

"Which one?"

"The House with the Bronze Door. On West Thirty-third."

I wrote down the name of a place I knew well by repute. It was an upscale gambling establishment that catered exclusively to gentlemen. For those with the money and social connections to gain admittance to the game, the house offered a high-class experience. They guarded against cheating, lavished patrons with food, drinks, and cigars, and kept all identities safe by practicing the utmost discretion.

"You and he have rich tastes," I said. "When did you last see him there?"

I knew Fromley had been hard up for money, even black-balled at the lower-class gambling houses according to my friend Nicky. It was likely Fromley's behavior and financial problems had extended into the upper-class houses, as well. Not that it mattered anymore in terms of Fromley—but in terms of evaluating Lonny's connections with Fromley, it might.

Lonny thought a moment. "I think it's been at least a year since I saw him there. I only saw him once or twice. That's the result of my habits, though, not his. I lost a lot one night, and when my father helped me out, he forbade me ever to go there again." He sighed. "It was the best place I ever played. But he said we weren't rich enough for such high stakes."

I suspected there were other reasons, as well. Alonzo Moore Sr. would have had no choice but to answer for his son's debts at a place like the House with the Bronze Door. Its clientele must have overlapped with his business clientele—and for a son to renege on obligations within that world would reflect badly on the father.

"How does a student like you have money to gamble?" I asked. In reality, I knew the answer to this question, given the easy credit found in the hundreds of gambling houses operating in the city. But I was looking for a reason to connect Lonny with the funds diverted from Alistair's research center.

His voice took on a mean, hard edge. "I've got more in the bank than you'll make in five years. At least, it'll be mine as soon as I turn twenty-one. Why is this any of your business?"

"Just need to be thorough," I said, keeping my tone mild. "Other than the incident you mentioned at the Bronze Door, have you had to ask your father for money?"

"Nah. I've been lucky of late. Haven't lost much—not more than $25 to $50 a night."

Not much money, indeed. The sums he mentioned were large. Why, $25 would easily finance the monthly rent on a middle-class apartment in a decent neighborhood. Still, if he were telling the truth, these numbers were on a far smaller scale than the thousands taken from the dean's fund.

There was a sharp rap on the door and a man with silver hair, wire-rimmed glasses, and a dark suit rushed in before we answered. "I got here as quickly as I could. Lonny—not another word more. And you"—he fixed me with an angry stare—"who are you and what business do you have with my client?"

I stood up without extending my hand. "Detective Simon Ziele. And you are?"

"John Bulwer, criminal defense attorney. I've been retained by Mr. Moore's father to represent him."

"How does my father—" Lonny began, looking ashamed.

"Young man, you're lucky you have friends who were concerned enough about you to make the call you should have made yourself," the lawyer said sternly. He went on to explain that Lonny's friend Sam Baker, upon learning this morning about Lonny's meeting, had telephoned Alonzo senior at once.

I was impressed by one thing: Late on a Sunday morning, it had taken Lonny's father no more than an hour to secure Mr. Bulwer's services and arrange for him to come uptown.

The lawyer turned to me. "Now, what business do you have with Lonny?"

"Lonny was acquainted with a young woman—also a student here at Columbia—who was murdered earlier this week within my jurisdiction in Dobson, New York. I have some questions for him; he has been kind enough to agree to answer them." I tried to sound as pleasant and nonthreatening as possible.

"Is he under arrest?"

"Of course not, Mr.—" I pretended to have forgotten his name.

"Bulwer. John Bulwer." He grimaced. "So if Lonny's not under arrest, then he is free to leave anytime."

"Absolutely." My words remained pleasant, but my tone turned more severe. "Of course, I could compel him to come to Dobson's police station for questioning. But Lonny may prefer to continue answering my questions here. It is certainly more convenient and probably more pleasant."

John Bulwer looked displeased but did not object to continuing. "What have you discussed so far?"

I glanced at my notes. "Let's see. We reviewed Lonny's alibi for the time of the murder. We talked about his relationship with both the murder victim and the man who was once our prime suspect. And I was about to ask him about one more issue." I reached for the file Alistair had left me containing the materials Lonny had stolen from Sarah. I presented the contents to Lonny and his attorney. They included several pages of handwriting in neat, perfectly formed letters that in no way resembled what I knew to be Lonny Moore's scrawled hand. Certain phrases stood out: ". . . symmetric about the critical line $Re(s) = \frac{1}{2}$. . . . The unproved Riemann hypothesis is that all of the nontrivial zeros. . . . distribution of prime numbers. . . . definition of $\zeta(s)$ to all complex numbers s."

"Is this your work, Lonny?"

He looked at Mr. Bulwer, who was quick to respond. "You don't have to answer that."

"What about this letter?" I leafed through several more pages of notes and proofs, then pulled it out. Addressed to the editors of the *Bulletin of the American Mathematical Society,* the letter stated that a proof for Riemann's hypothesis, accompanied by an expository article, was available for immediate publication if they were interested. It was signed "Alonzo Moore Jr."

"I take it the letter is yours. But I believe this work"—I touched the stack of papers lightly—"belongs to the late Sarah Wingate. She had apparently finished the proof not long before she was killed."

Lonny's face went white and he slumped deeper in his wooden chair.

"Don't say a word, son," Mr. Bulwer warned, his voice stern.

"You have a long history of hostility toward Sarah Wingate." I leaned in close to him. "And this letter clearly shows"—I tapped it with my finger—"that you planned to pass her work off as your own."

Lonny stared at me, wide-eyed. "You—you've got it all wrong," he stammered. "I didn't kill Sarah."

"You stole her notes and proofs, and were planning to publish her research as your own," I said. "You expect me to believe that you stole from her, but did not otherwise harm her?"

"We'll be leaving now." Mr. Bulwer stood up and tried to pull Lonny along with him. But Lonny pushed the lawyer's hand away and gripped the sides of his chair so tightly that his knuckles shone white.

"No—I'll answer this one." Lonny turned to me. His demeanor had changed; now, he was scared.

"I swear to you I didn't kill her. I did steal her papers. But that wasn't something I planned. I was in the library when I heard she had been killed. So I checked her library carrel to see if she had left behind anything interesting. That's when I found all those notes. And I figured if she's dead and not using all that research anyway, then why shouldn't I get something out of it?"

The three of us stared at each other in silence.

I finally said, "But your professors would have known the work was not yours. They would have known you for a fraud."

Lonny shook his head. "Maybe, maybe not." He repeated himself again. "You have to believe me. I admit I stole her work, but I didn't kill her for it."

I stared at him. He had given me enough to build a circumstantial case against him—one that provided me with a tangible answer to the question of why Lonny's hatred of Sarah had erupted into murder *now*. She had obviously just finished the proof, one that he intended to claim for his own. He had been acquainted with Fromley, so I could argue he had reason to know about Fromley's criminal fantasies. And while two close friends had supplied him an alibi, I had been suspicious of that alibi since I first heard it. It seemed too convenient. Time and again, I'd seen the testimony of friends crack during questioning.

I thought some more.

While I had nothing on him in terms of the money stolen from the dean's fund, that could yet come—or, as Alistair had said, prove a coincidence unrelated to Sarah's murder.

I didn't like Lonny Moore. And watching him now, I wanted to believe he was the killer responsible for Sarah's death. It would be an easy solution. And yet something about it didn't sit right with me. So I didn't arrest him. In fact, I let him go with a stern warning to stay in town and prepare for more formal questioning.

After seeing Lonny and Mr. Bulwer out, I checked each office to see where Isabella was working. I couldn't find her.

"Have you seen Isabella?" I asked Fred, who was leaving the first-floor kitchen with a cup of tea in hand.

He shrugged. "She was here earlier. But she brought the dog with her today. I think she mentioned taking him for a walk."

I decided to look at the financial records myself when Tom raced down the stairs, stopping short the moment he saw me.

"What's wrong?" I asked. "You look as though you've seen a ghost."

It was true. Tom's skin was ashen and he uncharacteristically appeared at a loss for words.

"There's been another murder." Tom's face was anguished.

"Who?" An uneasy chill ran down my spine, and I knew I didn't want to hear the name Tom would say.

"Stella Gibson. Cora just called to tell us—actually, to blame us. She believes you were followed earlier today, and that is why Stella is now dead."

I stood still, dumbstruck by the news. We had seen Stella just hours before, alive and well. But also afraid, I acknowledged with a sharp pang of guilt, remembering her anxiety.

"How?" I asked, still almost refusing to believe it.

"She was shot once in the head."

CHAPTER 27

"Shot once in the head." Tom's words echoed a refrain through my mind as the two of us made our way to the nondescript limestone building on East Seventy-third Street where Stella had found the briefest of sanctuaries.

We had taken the subway downtown to Seventy-second Street, but now we needed a crosstown cab. I raced toward one waiting a block away, and Tom puffed heavily as he tried to keep up with me. He had not wanted to come—but with Alistair nowhere to be found, I had asked Tom to assist me. I had no idea what we would find at the crime scene, and an extra pair of hands could prove useful.

I was racked with guilt. Had Cora been right? Had Alistair—or had I—unwittingly been followed as we met with

Stella? If so, then we had led Stella's killer right to her. While I did not want to leap to conclusions, my pangs of conscience were unrelenting. Almost worse was my sense of failed professional responsibility. Another young woman had died because we had been too slow to identify Sarah's killer.

Our cab made its way through the park, the horses' hooves drumming a steady beat. Tom looked pale with tight lines drawn around his face. Nerves, I supposed. His experience with crime had been limited to studies, statistics, and the occasional interview. Today he faced the real thing.

When we reached East Seventy-third Street, I was struck by the activity in the neighborhood. While the area was not crowded, there was regular street traffic as well as an occasional passerby. Only a block away from Stella's building, a large church was finishing its late morning services. This killing had been audacious. His method this time—by gunshot—had been loud enough that it should have attracted someone's attention. Yet he had risked it, which made me fear that our initial inability to catch him had emboldened him.

Stella's death also made me wonder anew whether she—and not Sarah Wingate—had been the killer's intended victim all along. Or had she been killed because she witnessed Sarah's murder? Both possibilities seemed reasonable at this point. And my list of potential suspects was wide open once again, for the timing of Stella's murder had exonerated Lonny Moore; I myself could vouch for his whereabouts.

Stella's building near Third Avenue teemed with city police, or so it seemed the moment we entered. There were six men outside, and another four in the basement, where the cramped space was stifling. I scanned their ranks in search of a familiar face.

When I recognized Roy Goodman, I breathed a sigh of relief that might have been audible. I knew him from his days as the evidence-room secretary downtown. Most of the department found him to be intolerable and gruff, but those officers who complained about him were generally the same ones who mishandled their evidence. He reserved a gentler manner for those who respected protocol. He was now in the field, which meant he had gotten a promotion since I last saw him. But I had no doubt he still approached his work with the same care.

He was examining a bloodstained object between white cotton-gloved fingers as I approached him. Behind me, Tom flinched, his eyes darting around the room.

"Ziele," Roy acknowledged without surprise, as though it had been three days and not three years since we had last seen one another.

"It's been a while, Roy," I said. "You in charge here?" I doubted it, since it was unlikely he had advanced through the ranks that quickly, but it was always better to be politic about these matters.

"Malloy is. Think he's outside." Roy gestured above us to where the other group of police officers had congregated outside the building.

But I made no move to leave. I remembered Timmy Malloy, an oafish lieutenant who delighted in exercising whatever authority he had, and I would get better information from Roy. So I introduced Tom and explained how Stella Gibson's murder might be closely related to my investigation of a killing in Dobson earlier this week. With some remorse, I omitted mentioning (at least for now) that we had spoken with Stella just hours earlier. If Cora had told them—something I doubted, given her mistrust of the police and her penchant for secrecy—then they would ask me about it. Until then, I wanted to learn more information before I shared any.

"So what have you found here?" I asked, eyeing the leather pouch in Roy's hands, brightly discolored with fresh blood. My stomach lurched as I breathed in the unmistakable smell of it.

"The coroner took her body not ten minutes ago," he replied. "She'd been shot once. The bullet entered through her left temple. Must have killed her instantly."

I felt a stab of guilt and wondered again whether we had been unwittingly responsible for leading Stella to her death.

Roy was saying, "The killer either had impressive aim or a stroke of good luck. She probably felt nothing, not for more than an instant." He eyed us for a moment. "You got gloves on you? Your friend knows not to touch anything?"

"Of course. I have gloves," I said, putting on the pair that was always in my satchel, "and my colleague will simply observe." I glanced at him. Tom looked calmer, with full color returning to his face. I suspected it had been a relief to learn Stella's body was already gone.

"She was killed over there." Roy motioned to an area by the massive furnace still marked by a pool of blood. "We assume he forced her down here, to the basement."

"But no one heard anything?" I asked.

"The only person at home other than Stella was her landlady, Mrs. Logan. She lives on the first floor and rents out rooms on the second and third floors. She claims to have heard nothing until she heard the gunshot. And by the time she made it down here to see what had happened, the killer was gone."

"Can we talk with her?"

"Too late," replied Roy. "She's been taken to the hospital

with chest pains, from the strain of it all, she says. You didn't miss much; when we spoke with her, she prattled on but had little worthwhile to say." He cleared his throat before continuing. "I gather you've spoken with Cora Czerne, the victim's friend. She showed up with some groceries and supplies after Mrs. Logan found Stella's body. We questioned her briefly." He shot me a pointed look. "She mentioned that she and Stella had been assisting you on a different case."

I admitted it. "They were, but I am at as much of a loss as you at the moment. I was interviewing my most likely suspect in the Dobson murder when Stella was killed. Assuming both murders are connected," I added lightly, "I find myself in need of a new prime suspect."

Satisfied by my explanation, Roy turned to offer me the bloodstained pouch he had been holding.

"This is the most interesting thing we found at the scene," he said. "It's part of a whole set." He showed me how to open the case to reveal a collection of barber's shaving blades. I heard Tom's sharp intake of air; it was just the sort of murder weapon we had theorized about that first day, when Alistair had been utterly convinced of Fromley's guilt. Sarah's throat had been slit, and her body slashed, with just such a sharp blade.

"And this paper was with it," Roy continued, showing us a diagram that he had found on the ground, near the shaving blades.

"Step-by-step instructions for defiling a corpse," Tom commented in amazement. "Look at this." He showed it to me.

"This more or less mirrors the exact condition of Sarah Wingate's corpse when we found it. You know Fromley's handwriting. Is this it?" I asked. The script was in pencil, slanted to the right, written with heavy pressure that made dark lines.

He shook his head in amazement. "I'd say so; as you can see, his handwriting was quite distinctive. So the murderer was either given it by Fromley, or it somehow made its way into the wrong hands."

"Who is this Fromley you are talking about?" Roy asked, exasperated. "Is he a suspect I should be aware of?"

"No," Tom said. "He's a dead man who nonetheless continues to play a key role in the case we are investigating."

"But Stella was shot. These knives were never used?" I wanted to clarify that point.

Roy nodded affirmatively.

"I don't understand it," Tom said. "Fromley's dead. Why would the killer continue to copycat a dead man?"

"But the killer may not be aware we know Fromley is dead," I said, hazarding a theory. "It's possible." And it was, though I realized it was also unlikely. The real killer had always been a step ahead of us, showing he knew nearly as much as we did. "The diagram and the blades do suggest he intended to model Stella's death after Sarah's. But something happened to make him abandon that plan, so he settled for killing her fast."

"The landlady, Mrs. Logan, was in the kitchen when he forced Stella down here. She must have been banging around with her pots and pans," Roy said. "Maybe there were others around, too, and he couldn't take the time."

"I also suspect he didn't intend to leave these notes and blades behind. He may have been startled by something or someone," I said. "It's positive proof for us. Without these, we would suspect the killings were connected given the remarkable coincidence—but we would not be positive." I paused a moment. "What puzzles me is how the murderer ended up with Fromley's written plans. It seems only two possibilities are plausible: He either stole the notes from Fromley himself, or he stole them from your case files at the research center."

Tom raised his eyebrows. "I don't recall ever having seen anything like this in Alistair's case files."

We spent another twenty minutes at the crime scene, gathering what information we could. The officers formally assigned to Stella's case needed to complete their jobs. I thanked Roy for his help, and gave him instructions for how to contact me. A day or two more, I promised myself, and I would tell Roy all we knew about Stella.

As we made our way back uptown, Tom asked, "How did he—whoever he is—manage to find Stella? Didn't you check to be sure no one was following you?"

I shook my head. "The park was quiet this morning. I saw no one except for Alistair, Stella, and Cora," I said. "If we were followed, I missed it. But her killer had to be following us. How else would he have known we planned to meet Stella?"

"He's keeping close tabs on us," Tom said.

That was exactly what Alistair had warned me, the moment Fromley was confirmed dead. The real killer was close—watching us and disrupting our progress whenever he could. But why? Because he delighted in feeling he outwitted us? Or because we were beginning to threaten him, forcing him to lose control?

"The real question is, why kill Stella?" I asked aloud. "If she was killed because of Sarah, then why did he perceive her as a threat? She had not seen his face; in fact, she had mistaken him for a dead man."

"But how was her killer to know that?" Tom reminded me. "You didn't until early this morning. I think we should assume she was killed because of what the killer presumed she knew."

"Unless she was the killer's target all along," I said, "in which case the true reason may lurk in Stella's background."

"If I did not know Fromley was secure in his grave, then I should have no doubt of the man we are looking for," Tom said.

"But that is the point—to confuse us," I said grimly. "So we must disregard it, as much as we can. Alistair may never be convinced of it, but murder is not always about method and conditioned behavior. In the end, what counts is motive. That must remain our focus: Who had the motive and the means to kill both of these women?"

Yet my voice was filled with much more confidence than I actually felt. I did not like the way in which the dead Michael Fromley continued to shadow our case everywhere. And our lack of progress, even as this other killer spiraled out of control, was infuriating.

"She's not with you?" Alistair was lying in wait for us as we returned to the research center, and there was no mistaking the panic in his voice.

Tom and I froze, staring at Alistair, who was wild-eyed and agitated.

"Who's not with us?" I asked. But my stomach had gone hollow; I already knew the answer.

Alistair's voice was unnatural and high-pitched when he said her name. "Isabella. She's gone missing."

CHAPTER 28

Panic is a contagious thing. Its danger lies in its ability to spread quickly, without warning. It had taken hold of Alistair already—and he needed to regain his sense of control before he undermined all of our efforts.

He repeated himself. "She's missing. She ought to be here but she's not."

I tried to be reasonable. "Perhaps she went for a walk," I said. "Or even finished up here and returned home."

"No, no. Fred said she took the dog for a walk, but that was hours ago. Oban is back; she should be, as well."

Oban materialized at once upon hearing his name, his golden tail thumping as he ran from one of us to another. When my eyes met Alistair's again in startled realization, my concern rose to a level that must have almost equaled his own.

"That's right," he said. "Isabella would never have left for this long without him. At least, not without asking me or Mrs. Leab to take care of him."

He paced back and forth. "She had something to tell me. I was on the telephone with one of those infernal reporters, so I put her off. Now she's gone."

"I've not seen her, either," said Mrs. Leab, wiping her hands on a dishtowel. "The professor called me to come in around eleven. She wasn't here then."

"Why are you so worried, Alistair?" Tom asked. "I certainly don't mean to make light of your concern, but you don't normally keep such close tabs on your daughter-in-law. I understand, of course, that Stella Gibson's murder has unnerved all of us. But I see no cause for alarm."

Alistair froze—and in that instant, I realized it was the first he had heard of Stella's murder. After I filled him in, he began pacing wildly.

"When was she last seen?" I asked.

Alistair's reply was anguished. "Fred saw her just before eleven."

"Where is he?" I asked.

"He left a few moments ago to look for her," Alistair said.

I turned to Tom. "Did you see her at any point this morning?"

He frowned. "No, I didn't. But when I came in at half past ten, the light was on in her office."

We hastened down the hallway to the small room where Isabella and Horace shared a small office with two desks and a file cabinet.

"Has Horace been in this weekend?" I asked, surveying the papers strewn across his desk.

"No," Alistair said, adding dryly, "Horace isn't exactly one for weekend appearances."

I ignored his comment. Our only focus now needed to be on Isabella. I flipped through several of the pages atop her desk. "Check Horace's desk," I directed Tom.

"All these papers appear to be hers," Tom said. "I expect she spread out, using all available desk space."

I began to examine more thoroughly the pile of documents Isabella had been reading.

Alistair paced the length of the room. "Where could she be?"

"She's not in danger, is she?" Mrs. Leab asked, and her voice betrayed a sharp edge.

That was the last I really heard of what they were saying. Isabella was a diligent record keeper, and I had located some notes she must have jotted down this very morning. On one page, in her clear, rounded handwriting, I saw she had meticulously tabulated all moneys allocated to Alistair's research from Dean Arnold's discretionary fund. Funds supposedly earmarked for Michael Fromley's case. Funds signed for and spent with forged signatures. Next to the list was a name—the Golden Dragon— one of Chinatown's most notorious gambling joints.

There were hundreds of gambling houses throughout the city, but they were not created equal. When we had examined the recreational habits of first Michael Fromley and later Lonny Moore, names like the Bronze Door and the Fortune Club had surfaced. The former was a high-class gentleman's establishment; the latter was a workingman's entertainment hall. But the Golden Dragon was of another species entirely. Run by a man called Lou "the Bottler" Oaks, it was a gambling house of last resort, patronized by only the most desperately addicted. Any vice—be it gambling, opium, prostitution—could be indulged at the Golden Dragon.

What set the Golden Dragon apart even from rough joints like Saulter's was its credit system. Loan sharks were on hand, ready and willing to loan money on the spot so patrons might lose even more. A loan from the Golden Dragon came at a steep cost, and most customers who took advantage of it paid dearly, with interest rates so high a $100 loan quickly became a $1,000 debt. And anyone unfortunate enough to miss their installments would pay first with their limbs, then with their life. It certainly placed the large sums taken from Alistair's funding in an understandable context. If Isabella had somehow figured out who had taken the money and why, then her discovery may have placed her in danger.

Yet—unless she'd questioned someone about the matter—how could anyone else have known of her recent discovery? She had wanted to speak with Alistair, presumably about what she had learned. Failing that, what had she done next?

The pit in my stomach deepened, and I looked at Alistair with trepidation. He had been less than forthright with me throughout this investigation and I did not wholly trust him. But I knew he would not risk Isabella.

"Isabella may be in grave danger," I said. "It's imperative for us to find her right away."

"Why is she in danger? Ziele, this kind of talk is completely unhelpful if you cannot also tell us where to look!" Alistair was becoming overwrought with worry.

"Isabella wrote down a name, the Golden Dragon," I said, going on to explain what that meant. "She didn't dream it up; she found it somewhere in the papers she was examining."

"Then let's split up these papers and take a look," Tom said.

But soon we had finished scanning through each stack to no avail.

"Whatever she found," I said, "she must have taken it with her." Agitated, I tapped my fingers on the desk.

Alistair was despondent. "That makes it almost impossible to figure out where she went."

Tom did not complain, but he rubbed his forehead as though he had a terrible headache.

"There's no reason to dwell on what we don't know," I said. "We need to focus on what we do know—and what we can find out. But I need you to think hard, Alistair. Stop panicking and think."

I walked over to the blackboard that lined one wall of the small office, and I redrew my triangle showing Sarah Wingate, Michael Fromley, and the unknown killer. Under each name, I abbreviated everything we knew. For example, Sarah had discovered funds gone missing. Michael Fromley had frequented Mamie Durant's as well as numerous gambling joints until he found himself blacklisted because of his behavior. For the killer, I wrote that he had access to Fromley. That he owed significant sums of money and likely had stolen from Alistair's fund to cover his debts. That he had increasingly managed to threaten our own investigation and the well-being of those helping us. "What else?" I tapped the chalk against the board.

When Alistair said nothing, I pressed on. "You must focus more intently than you've ever done before. Think about everything you've learned because now you need to put it to use. This isn't about understanding a criminal type who interests you. It's not about tracking a killer after the fact. It's about saving Isabella. She doesn't have much time—if it's not already too late."

Alistair looked at me uncertainly and swallowed. "Our killer is unraveling." His voice was rough, so he cleared his throat. "Each day, he grows more desperate and acts with increasing violence. Based on what you tell me about the Golden Dragon, and assuming Isabella was correct in identifying the killer's connection to it, I would guess the killer suffers from an addiction, probably to opium. If his supply is exhausted—or he cannot gain access to the increasing amounts he needs to satisfy his craving— then he becomes increasingly agitated and desperate."

"So his erratic, violent behavior may be the result of drug withdrawal, in addition to the pressure of our investigation?" I asked.

Alistair nodded.

"We can't discount a gambling addiction, either," I said, explaining why. People were less familiar with the symptoms of gambling addiction, but many were the same as symptoms of drug addiction: the restlessness and anxiety, sometimes so severe the person experienced sweats, chills, or both. The constant lying. The need to spend more and more money to support an increasing habit. For where once $1 or $10 bets satisfied, only $50 bets would do. I knew the symptoms well.

"Whoever this killer is," I said, "he's no longer trying to intimidate us through ten-dollar bribes and boxes of evidence. He killed Sarah Wingate. He just killed a witness to her murder. And he won't hesitate to kill Isabella unless we can reach her and stop him."

"What are the chances of that?" Alistair asked. He ran his hands over the taut lines on his face, looking suddenly old.

"No chance at all unless we try." I waited. "He's close to us. He's been watching our every move. That means we're close to him—even if we don't know it."

Alistair picked up a paper from Isabella's stack of notes and reread it. As I looked over his shoulder, my mind began to race in multiple directions until it led me to a single promising idea. I grabbed the list of money sums Isabella had compiled and excused myself.

"Keep looking for anything that may help. I've got to make a telephone call," I said, muttering the last words. I didn't want their questions.

"Declan Mulvaney, please." Impatient, I waited for my old partner to pick up. It seemed an eternity—but was probably only a few minutes—before I heard his familiar, reassuring voice on the other end of the line.

"Ziele, how are you, old boy?"

"I've been better," I said, my voice strained. I explained the urgency of the situation before moving on to the purpose of my call. "Do you know the Golden Dragon?"

"The gambling den?"

"That's right."

"It's one of the toughest gambling joints in the city." Mulvaney didn't mince words. "Why?"

"Do you have any influence over the owner? I need information." I waited.

Mulvaney's silence was long and studied.

It was an open secret that the police and the city's gambling joints were partners in an unusual arrangement. When protection money was regularly paid to the governing police precinct, then the police ensured those gambling dens were not raided. As long as the payoffs arrived on time, the police would turn a blind eye to whatever illicit activity went on. But if the payoffs were late, then the house would be raided, trashed, and closed down.

"The place is up to date, Ziele," he finally said. "If you could wait until next month's payment is due, then I could try. But I've got nothing on them right now."

"And no contacts?" I asked. I was desperate now. "Anyone with a good relationship who could ask them some questions?"

"They're tough customers, Ziele. I can't help you there."

"How about some advice, then?" I asked, explaining my situation: that I needed to locate the name of a customer who had borrowed—and still owed—large sums of money. I didn't know the customer himself. But thanks to Isabella's careful comparison of Sarah's notes with new evidence she had somehow discovered, I had the dates he had borrowed money and a list of amounts owed to the Golden Dragon.

"What about Nicky at the Fortune Club?" I took a deep breath after I said it. "Would he have the connections to get the man's name?"

Mulvaney chortled. "Only you, Ziele, have the imagination to think of that—finding a man based on an amount of money. Only you." Then he grew sober. "I think Nicky could do it. You're right on that count." There was a long silence. "If you go that route, you know what you're risking, right?"

"What do you mean?" I asked. I was on guard now.

"Nicky's always taken care of you because of his deep regard"—he drew a breath—"the affection, even, he held for your mother."

He waited for my reaction, but I gave him none. I was not unfamiliar with the rumors that had swirled around Nicky Scarpetta and my mother. But I had never dignified them by acknowledging them, and I would not do so now.

After a moment, he continued, saying, "Be careful, Ziele.

You deal with the devil, it's only a matter of time before the devil wants his due."

"Nicky is not the devil," I said, objecting strongly to his characterization.

"No," Mulvaney said, adding sagely, "but Nicky's favors are not free. Not for most people. And when he wants payment, it won't come cheap."

"You think I should be concerned?" I asked, taking him more seriously now.

He thought a moment. "Yeah, I do. But then again, you want to save the girl, right? There are worse things you could do. You got scruples about this, maybe you ought to have been a rabbi or a priest. They're the ones that get to have scruples in this life." He considered what he had said. "And I'm not even sure about them."

And so our conversation ended. I thanked him and replaced the telephone receiver on its hook.

I stared at it for another few seconds. Then I took a deep breath and picked up the receiver once again. "Four-seven-six Franklin," I said to the operator—and waited for someone at Nicky Scarpetta's Fortune Club to pick up the telephone.

I explained my plan to Alistair and Tom while I waited for Nicky to call back with the information I needed. He had agreed to follow through, just as I had expected. "Yeah," he had said, "The Bottler owes me a favor. I got no problem calling it in."

We waited in agonizing silence, but Nicky was quick to call back.

I picked up the phone, my anticipation high.

"I got the name for you," Nicky said without delay.

"Who is it?" My heart seemed to be beating loudly enough for everyone to hear.

"Theodore Sinclair," he said. "No doubt about it. Your dates and amounts made a perfect match."

I sighed in exasperation. "It's not his real name. Theodore Sinclair was the son of one of my colleagues. He's been dead two years."

Alistair, overhearing, dropped his head into his hands.

"Can you get me something more?" I asked Nicky. "Like a physical description, maybe the address where he lives? If this guy owes thousands of dollars, as the list I've seen suggests, then the Bottler's men know exactly where to find him."

We waited some more.

"It's almost as if he's out to destroy you, Alistair," Tom said. "Whoever he is, he is stealing from your fund; assuming the name of your son; and taking your daughter-in-law. You really have no idea who he may be?" Tom was careful with his last question, but it needed to be asked.

"I—" Alistair was cut off by the telephone's ring.

I answered it on the first ring. "Ziele here."

"All right," Nicky said, "I got the address and description. The description ain't much help. Customer looks like half the fellas in this city. But you'll get him from the address. You ready?"

"Go," I said. I had a pencil in hand, and with Tom and Alistair watching eagerly, I first wrote the physical description: brown eyes/hair; medium, stocky build; square jaw; visible injuries.

Nicky explained, saying, "He got roughed up last week when he didn't pay up."

Then the address: I wrote down 508 West 112th Street, apartment 5B.

Thanking Nicky again, I hung up.

Alistair and I looked at each other. His face was ashen.

"You know who it is?" I asked.

But his ice-blue eyes reflected confusion. "I'm hoping I'm wrong."

"We've got his address. Let's go find out," I said, my voice grim. Almost as an afterthought, I asked Tom, "Will you wait here in case she returns?"

"Wait a minute," Tom said. "I still don't understand. Who is it?"

Alistair looked away, then walked out of the small office, leaving it to me to answer Tom's question.

"These words describe a lot of men in this city," I said, tapping the piece of paper I carried. "I'm hoping my own suspicions are wrong."

Alistair and I each kept our own counsel as we headed south on Amsterdam Avenue to 112th Street. My own mind filled with disparate images that, though once unconnected, now came together in rapid succession and assumed larger significance. The purple bruise he had suffered when I first met him. Our half glimpse of him in the Bowery, when we had convinced ourselves we were mistaken. His restlessness. His lies. His profuse sweating. These individual images, one by one, linked together until they formed a picture and I saw him whole.

He had the means: he'd been trusted with ready access to everything at the research center, from files and financials to Fromley himself. He had also been in a unique position to monitor and hamper our progress, even as he pretended to help us. And he had the motive: enormous debts resulting from an addiction to drugs or cards, I had not yet determined which. While his connection to Sarah Wingate remained unclear, the rest of it made perfect sense. And the image in my mind was confirmed by the name next to the doorbell at 508 West 112th Street.

Horace G. Wood.

CHAPTER 29

"You must have suspected him, the moment I told you about the Golden Dragon. You thought you saw him outside Nicky's that first day, remember?" I made the comment in a bland enough tone, but I had to admit I was curious. I had met Horace just five days ago, but Alistair had worked with him for seven years. How could he have been so blind?

But of course, it was precisely because he *had* known Horace that he missed seeing it. We never scrutinize the familiar in the same way we do the unknown.

Alistair seemed to have retreated into a private world of his own. His face was wan, etched with lines of worry. He commented only that "the address confirms it."

My heartbeat accelerated as we approached the door of Horace's apartment.

"We don't know that he has her," I said, "but it makes sense that he does." I rapped sharply on the door. "She was working at his desk this morning when she discovered the connection between the stolen funds and the amounts owed to the Golden Dragon. She may even have asked Horace about it." I rapped again, and this time when no one answered, I pulled a thin metal file out of my pocket.

Alistair raised an eyebrow. "My understanding of the Fourth Amendment and police procedure may be rusty, but don't you need a warrant for that?"

I shook my head. "It's okay." I applied more pressure to the pin tumbler lock. "If we were breaking in to look for evidence only, you would be correct. But when someone's life is at risk, as Isabella's is, then we're completely justified."

I didn't tell Alistair, but for Isabella, I'd break through this door even if the law didn't sanction it.

The pin stack lifted and the lock turned. "Got it." I gave Alistair a grim nod and he followed me inside.

"Isabella? Horace?" I called out their names, but there was no answer.

Horace's apartment was a railroad flat, which meant one room connected to the next like the cars in a train. We passed first through the room he used as an office or living area, then the kitchen, and finally entered his bedroom. The place was messy and strewn with papers, but I noted nothing out of the ordinary.

"I'll search his front rooms; you try the ones here in back," I said. While I had little hope we would find Isabella here, surely something in the apartment would lead us to wherever he had taken her.

I was searching through a mass of papers covering one corner of the living room when a crashing sound startled me. I returned to the back of the apartment, where Alistair stood in the midst of shattered glass and broken bottles. He had apparently ripped Horace's medicine cabinet right off the wall and thrown it onto the adjoining bedroom floor, smashing it to bits.

His explanation seemed wrenched from somewhere deep within. "I've known him for years, given him every opportunity. I loaned him money. And look how he repays me." Alistair's throat was choked with emotion. "He has betrayed me personally and committed unforgivable crimes."

His anger spent, he sank onto the bed and dropped his head into his hands.

After a moment, he looked up, and I was struck by the despair in his eyes. "You can't believe he would harm Isabella. He knows her."

My own gaze did not waver. "I know Horace's betrayal has come as a painful shock. But you cannot let it dull your thinking. Isabella needs you too much right now."

I bent down and began to sort through the contents of Horace's medicine cabinet. "Now help me think."

Alistair began stacking different medicine bottles onto Horace's nightstand. "In retrospect, I suppose his behavior these past few weeks should have made me suspicious. He's been restless. And despite the cool weather, he sweated constantly."

"But you never noticed anything that suggested a criminal tendency?"

His response was dry. "You may not believe it, Ziele, but I don't sit around and speculate about my associates and their propensity for crime."

I picked up the jagged remains of two medicine bottles. Their names were still visible. "He has a number of opium products here." I passed Alistair the glass fragment that represented the remains of Greene's Syrup of Tar. "He also has Soothing Syrup, Gray's Cordial, and some laudanum—liquid opium."

Alistair shrugged. "Ordinary stuff, typical of most people's medicine chests. If he is addicted to opium to the extent his debt would suggest, then he needed far more than this. He needed the sort of fix you can find only in an opium den."

"Let's move on and search the other rooms," I said. We worked in silence for several moments until Alistair shouted out that he had found something.

"What is it?" I asked, rushing into the kitchen.

"His appointment book," Alistair said. "Look—he had four meetings with Sarah Wingate in the weeks leading up to her death." He shook his head. "If she knew he had stolen the money, why didn't she report him and be done with it?"

"I don't know. They were negotiating something, perhaps." I studied the appointment book carefully another moment. There were other meetings, as well, in the weeks before her death, but they were coded with initials. *F.A.E.* was each Tuesday. And each Friday night was marked *H.R.E.* I put the book in my pocket to examine later. Any evidence that did not point us to Isabella would have to wait—even the evidence that would certainly seal Horace's fate in front of a judge and jury. We found a shoe box by his desk, containing deposit slips for the checks embezzled from the dean's fund.

"I see why he had little trouble depositing them," I said. "Although they're made out to Alistair Sinclair/Center for Criminological Research, look how he signed and deposited them: *'Make payable to Theodore Sinclair.'* The alias made it easier for him to manage your money. As though you had given it to your son."

Alistair seemed to ignore me, but there was a greenish cast to his complexion that concerned me.

"You all right?"

"I'll be fine," he said, brushing off my concern.

In the same shoe box, we also found copies of IOUs he had signed for amounts in the hundreds of dollars. There was no formal name to show to whom he was indebted, but each paper had an odd symbol on its back. The Bottler's mark, I supposed.

"We now have plenty of evidence of wrongdoing," I said, placing the papers back in the shoe box. "But we've still no idea where he's taken Isabella."

I sat on the sofa in Horace's front living room. Resting my chin on my hands, I gazed at Alistair. "You know the criminal mind better than anyone, Alistair. And you know Horace Wood. Help me. Where would he have taken her?"

"He's comfortable in this neighborhood, where he lives and works," Alistair said, thinking aloud. He sat in a drab floral armchair next to the sofa.

I caught his train of thought. "Yes. So he's taken her someplace nearby. Someplace private—where it will be quiet and deserted on a Sunday."

Alistair got up to pace the length of the room. "Yes, and someplace he can feel in control. He will not want to be interrupted."

"What about the administrative building?" I asked. "No classrooms in it—only offices. And closed all weekend."

Alistair shook his head no. "Not likely. The administrative building is quite secure; they even have their own key system, designed to protect the academic and financial records kept there."

"What about a classroom building, like the science or humanities buildings? Many students choose empty classrooms to study in the evenings."

"Good idea, but it doesn't offer certain privacy. Where else?"

"The chapel," I said. "It's always open for anyone who needs it."

"That sounds more promising. It fits what I know—what I think I know—of Horace," Alistair said. "Is there any other place?"

We thought a moment. The setting sun cast a brilliant beam through the window, illuminating something shiny on the armchair. I leaned over, reached down, and picked up a woman's earring. *Isabella's.* My voice rising with excitement, I said, "She was here, Alistair—look. This is her earring, isn't it?"

"I think so." There was doubt in his voice, but it didn't matter—because I was certain. I could recall her clearly as she had been at dinner last night, wearing this exact earring: a small ruby set within a gold petal's embrace. I shuddered to think what may have become of her now, but I forced my mind once again to focus. I would be of no use to Isabella if I could not think straight.

"So if he had her here earlier today," Alistair said, "he will not have gone far."

I offered another suggestion. "We're near Morningside Park."

He shook his head. "Too open and public."

I looked out the window. Horace had a perfect view of St. John's Cathedral's rising stone arches—though admittedly it was still more a construction site than a functioning place of worship. It was now near dusk, and in the glowing pink sunset, St. John's was beginning to cast a shadow over—

That was when I realized it. Of course—*St. John's*. It was just across the street and would be deserted this Sunday evening.

It made perfect sense, and Alistair agreed.

"Hurry," I said as we raced down the stairs. "We should pray we are not mistaken—and not too late."

CHAPTER 30

There was no sign of light within the Cathedral of St. John the Divine. We moved quickly but watched our step, for even the surrounding sidewalks were littered with rough stones and the odd mason's tool—tangible evidence of how J. P. Morgan's recent donation had enabled work to resume on our country's grandest cathedral, designed to rival the best in Europe. It was hard to imagine such a future for the pile of stone and dirt and wood that had yet to transform itself into anything resembling a building, much less a cathedral.

We were on Amsterdam Avenue approaching the main entrance when a hunched, dark figure rapidly approached us, taking us by surprise. I recognized him with a start, but it was Alistair who spoke first.

"Fred, thank God it's only you." Alistair breathed a sigh of relief. "You gave us a scare, coming from behind like that. I take it you've not seen Isabella. We have an idea she may be here."

Fred gave us a skeptical look, but he agreed to join us. With him in tow, leaning heavily on his wooden cane, we entered the building. At first, the *clop clop* of Fred's cane was all that we heard. On the stone floor, it sounded even louder than usual.

"We've made a mistake; no one's here," Alistair said.

We passed under the massive arches of the cathedral's crossing, following handwritten directions meant to assist worshippers in locating the single finished room where services were held.

"I think this may help us," I said, grabbing a lantern from where it sat against a wall. "Do you have a match?" Alistair did—but once lit, the lantern illuminated a three-foot radius around us, little more.

We followed the signs directing us toward a small chapel.

Clop clop. Fred's cane and our own footsteps together made a loud drumbeat that echoed throughout the cavernous stone halls.

"Shh . . ." I signaled for Alistair and Fred to be quiet.

It took a moment for us to ascertain that the sound we heard was actually a human voice, for our ears had to adapt to the strange echo that bounced from walls to floor and back again. I felt the tightness in my chest ease slightly as I registered the voice to be that of a woman crying for help.

Isabella.

She had heard us. And her own voice was a welcome sign that she was still alive, that we were not yet too late.

"This way." I motioned for them to follow me into a tight narrow stairwell leading down into the netherworld of the crypt, just under the crossing. It was the only portion of the cathedral completed to date. I forced all superstitious thoughts out of my mind, reminding myself that the space we would enter was as yet a crypt in name only. It was too soon for anyone to be buried there. *But not too soon for anyone to die there*, was the thought that immediately followed, unbidden and discomforting.

We reached the bottom of the stairs. The space in front of us was a jumble of the same stone, wood, and dirt that had marked the exterior areas above us. It also seemed to be a workman's storage area of mortar, stone, and even two elaborate stained-glass windows, yet to be installed.

I did not see Isabella right away. My eyes were first drawn to the straight rows of wooden chairs that filled the room. Now empty, they normally accommodated a handful of worshipping congregants.

She whimpered, and then I saw: She sat on a wooden chair at the front of the room, her hands and feet bound together with rope. A small table was beside her, where six small candles glowed. I opened my mouth to speak to her, but before the words had left my mouth, a whoosh of air swept the room, she let forth a chilling cry—and what light there had been was suddenly extinguished.

Which meant he was nearby.

He would be agitated. Nothing happening now was proceeding according to his plan. He would not have expected to be caught at all—especially not now.

With greater confidence than I actually felt, I spoke up in the darkness. "Horace, it is finished. I am placing you under arrest for the murders of Michael Fromley, Sarah Wingate, and Stella Gibson." I paused. "Release Isabella now, and you will avoid making your situation worse than it already is."

Silence followed.

I heard no sound that would indicate where he was. My fingers circled my Colt revolver in preparation.

At my side, I was aware of Alistair as he fumbled for a match. He finally managed to relight the lantern that had been extinguished just moments before.

In its light, we saw Isabella again, though now the dark figure of Horace Wood loomed over her, pointing a gun at her head.

I issued a stern order. "Drop the gun now, Horace."

He stared at us, unmoved.

I stepped forward and showed my own weapon. "I'm a far better shot than you, Horace. Be sensible and drop the gun."

"Not so fast." That voice came from behind us.

I turned to see the barrel of a Smith & Wesson revolver held by Fred.

Horace laughed—a wild, terrible cackle.

I will always remember the terrible sadness in Alistair's face as he, too, turned to face Fred and said, "I don't understand."

"What's not to understand, old boy?" Fred cocked his head and made a crooked half smile. "That you've been bamboozled? Or that I have aligned myself with—well, let's call it a better-paying job opportunity, shall we?"

Alistair stifled his shock enough to whisper a single word. "Why?"

Fred shrugged. "No need to be so surprised, Professor. You think you're the only one who craves the good life? Who wants the luxuries that money—and I mean a good heap of money—can buy? Of course you're not. Horace has his own reasons, but mine, I tell you, are quite simple."

"You did it because of vile greed." Alistair's voice seethed with condemnation.

"Let's just say Horace and I agreed that the resources of your trust fund were not being put to their best use," Fred responded lightly. "Why spend all that money on a depraved sociopath when we could envision far better purposes?"

Alistair's face reflected a steely resolve now that he had begun to understand the gravity of our situation. He drew himself up and issued a command. "Horace. Fred. You must both put your guns down now."

I winced, for though I admired his fortitude, it was the wrong approach. The knowledge and training Alistair might normally bring to this situation were compromised by his emotions. He had been cruelly betrayed by two of his closest associates. And it was not an anonymous hostage they held; it was Isabella.

"Still trying to give me orders, Professor?" Horace replied with a belligerent sneer. "Look around. I don't think you're in charge right now."

Horace was agitated, sweating profusely despite the frigid chill of the stone vault where we stood.

I had little experience with hostage situations, but everything I had learned suggested we needed to keep both men talking and feeling in control. Once that was accomplished, we might turn them against each other, which would improve our chances of defending ourselves.

I interceded calmly, as if there were no danger at all. "You're right, Horace. Alistair is most certainly not in charge here. You are." I put my gun away and began to walk toward him, slowly, with my hands in my pockets so I would appear relaxed and at ease. "It's a painful symptom, the restlessness, isn't it? It keeps you from sleeping at night. And the sweats that come and go must be rather embarrassing." I lowered my voice and took a few more steps toward Horace. "But the worst part of all must be how badly you want it."

Another step forward and my voice took on a sharper edge. "What has you hooked, Horace? Is it the drug?" I paused. "Or is it the game?"

Horace glared and jabbed Isabella with the gun. "Move another inch and she dies now."

I turned to Fred. "Did you know he needed to feed a terrible habit when you joined him in this scheme?"

Fred smiled wickedly. "My dear boy, if it hadn't been for Horace's unfortunate addiction to cards, he would never have contrived such a plot. It was his inspiration, truly."

"And you?" I asked.

"Merely an innocent bystander who happened to notice both Horace's problem and his unique method of solving it." He let out an exaggerated sigh. "It seemed unfair for Horace to share the spoils of Alistair's riches by himself—especially when they were ample enough for two. So I suggested a partnership."

"You mean," Horace interrupted, "that you began blackmailing me for half the proceeds."

There it was: a rift in their partnership that I could exploit. Interests in this kind of pairing were never perfectly aligned.

I made a calculated decision. "I'll bet," I said to Horace, "that he didn't even help you last week when goons from the Golden Dragon showed up to demand payment—and took it out of your skin."

Horace merely grunted in reply, but he appeared less agitated than before, so I continued. I was developing this theory as I talked, but as I listened to myself, I knew my reasoning was sound.

"No doubt it started innocently enough. Playing for money made the game more fun. And then the next step, playing in a gambling parlor, made the game even more exciting."

Fred interrupted. "Horace got hooked on faro, the current favorite of all the gambling houses. When it got too expensive, he discovered its cheaper, Lower East Side version: penny stuss."

"But playing for pennies must have been unsatisfying. Only larger bets gave you what you craved," I said. "So that's when you discovered some Lower East Side houses actually extended loans—on terms favorable to them, of course. You borrowed money from a ruthless loan shark and fell behind in your payments. You must have been desperate for money to pay off your moneylenders and get back in the game. With no legitimate way of doing that, you began to explore other means. Clearly, you already knew that Alistair funneled significant sums from his vast wealth into university funding for his research center. So you hatched a scheme to take advantage of that."

"But I gave you money, time and again," Alistair said to Horace. "I'd have helped you."

"Your help would have come with conditions, though," I said quickly before Horace could respond. "You'd have wanted him to stop playing."

Fred added his own interpretation. "It was an interesting psychological study to observe. Horace was destroying his own life. He more or less abandoned his thesis, drove his fiancée to break off with him, and fell thousands of dollars into debt. And still, he thought of nothing but gambling. To sit at the table and place a bet gave him a rush of power. It was so intoxicating that theft led to more theft. And then one day, it led to murder."

I was familiar with the storyline. I'd seen variations of it destroy many lives, including that of my own father. Always desperate for money to stay in the game, he usually found help in the form of a woman. But those without my father's charm and good looks turned increasingly to crime, like Horace.

"So it was Horace who killed Sarah?" I asked, my voice quiet.

Neither answered.

"Why don't you both walk over there to the wall?" Fred waved his weapon in Isabella's direction.

We needed to stay apart until I had a better plan. I caught Alistair's eye and he followed my lead: a few baby steps to suggest cooperation, but no real movement.

Alistair cleared his throat. "Horace may have killed Sarah, but Fred must have planned it. Horace simply isn't bright enough."

Horace grumbled, though his words were unintelligible.

I picked up where Alistair left off. "Yes, parts of the plan were quite brilliant. For example, your coercing Michael Fromley to write that letter confessing to Sarah's murder was excellent planning. You must have forced Fromley to write the letter just before you shot him. When you mailed it in the box with real crime-scene evidence, it was utterly convincing. Then you dumped his body in the Hudson River, and assumed you had successfully created the perfect scapegoat for the next crime you intended to commit: the murder of Sarah Wingate. Framing Fromley was easy; you knew so much about him. Taken together with the signed letter of confession, Fromley's guilt would appear certain. Yes, you were remarkably smart in your planning. But I assume Fred takes all credit for that."

"He certainly does not." Horace contested the idea hotly.

"No?" I continued talking, moving ever so slightly closer to Horace. "Then tell me, which of you missed the obvious flaw in your planning? One of you didn't foresee the risk that Mother Nature would wash Fromley's corpse ashore so quickly. You probably counted upon him staying underwater the entire winter. By springtime, the body would be so thoroughly decomposed that even an expert autopsy would not be able to pinpoint his time of death."

"Come now," said Fred in protest. "The plan was a stroke of genius, undone only by the whim of nature and your own foolish persistence. *Most* detectives"—he emphasized the word—"would be pleased to wrap up a case so satisfactorily. After all, Fromley was scum of the earth. The world is a better place being rid of him."

"Maybe so," I said, agreeing, "but it wasn't your call to make. And what about Sarah Wingate? And Stella Gibson? They certainly did not deserve to be killed."

"Yes," Fred said, "that was unfortunate. But the Wingate girl had become a problem, hadn't she, Horace?"

I took a deep breath and moved yet another few steps closer. "Why, Horace? Why did you have to kill Sarah? Because I know you did. Fred doesn't have the physical strength. And while Fred was happy to partake in the money, I'm not sure he was as motivated to kill for it. He doesn't share your need—or your sheer desperation."

Horace was seething with anger as he looked at me. His voice choked as he said, "She didn't know it was me taking the money—not at first. Her coming to me was a gift, a stroke of good luck. She'd noticed the budget discrepancies. How signatures didn't match. How funds requests were unsupported." He circled the back of Isabella's chair, drawing closer to me.

"Imagine," he said, his face twisting at the irony, "she asked for my help. I agreed, said I would take care of it, talk it over with Alistair for her. I promised to see that the proper forms were submitted. But stubborn girl, she wouldn't take my word for it. She kept checking into things. And to this day I don't know how, but she managed to figure out that I was the one embezzling the money." He gave an exaggerated sigh. "That's when I realized I would only be safe—and free to continue as before—if I could make her go away. So I decided that, for once in his life, Michael Fromley might serve a useful purpose."

"But when Fromley washed up dead, ahead of schedule," Fred added, "Horace panicked, and has been making a mess of things ever since."

I inched another step closer.

"And Stella was simply part of the mess?" I asked. "Is that how you saw it?"

"Isabella telephoned me this morning, asking troublesome questions. And she mentioned you were meeting Stella in the park. I went to find you there, and I overheard parts of your conversation," he said. "I couldn't take the risk that Stella might later remember something important."

"I doubt she would have. She thought you were someone else," I said lightly. "So you've shed blood this morning for nothing." Another inch closer. "But it's over now. And you have to let Isabella go. By holding her, you only make your situation worse."

Horace laughed. "Nice effort, Ziele. But—" He put out his arm as if to halt me, and his voice was suddenly harsh and serious again. "Stop right where you are; don't come even a single step closer." He jabbed the gun into Isabella's back, and we recoiled as she winced in pain.

"You won't shoot her," I said. "Or else you already would have done it."

"Nonsense." His face contorted into a sinister grin. "She's alive only because I was unavoidably delayed when Fred first secured her down here in the crypt." He brandished his gun. "Foolish girl. She went rummaging through my desk and found evidence of my large debts. From the moment she put two and two together, her fate was sealed. I'll do whatever is necessary to stop all of you from destroying me." Now he was livid, speaking quickly.

Horace grimaced, then steeled himself. "I know what you want. You want to misconstrue everything I've said into a confession," he continued, waving the gun toward us, "but it would be nothing but your word against mine."

I made a quick calculation and could only hope it would pay off.

"I cannot see any difference, Horace, between you and Michael Fromley. Except possibly that you've outdone him. You've killed three people, whereas—as best we can tell—he only killed one."

"That's disgusting," he said. "You think I am anything like that animal? I didn't even use all the money I embezzled for myself. I donated some of it to good causes."

"Yes," I said easily, "the Hearst election. You used that quite nicely to distract us from the truth. We all thought you were distressed about the election. You were beaten up by the Bottler's toughs. But you had ready the perfect lie: You were hurt at the polls while voting for the wrong man. And now, you try to persuade us there was something noble about your theft, because you gave some money you stole to a politician."

My fingers circled my revolver—imperceptibly, I hoped.

"There is nothing noble about stealing or killing. No matter how you try to justify it." I took two steps closer.

He pointed his gun directly at me. "You are placing blame on the wrong person. The question you should be asking is, what moral right did *he* have"—he gestured wildly toward Alistair—"to use the school's good money toward the most awful of purposes—a depraved criminal. A man like Fromley didn't deserve to live. I did a good thing by killing him."

A long pause followed in which none of us said anything; we were almost afraid to breathe.

"You may as well cooperate with us now, Horace," Alistair said finally. "Just let Isabella go. If you know nothing else about me, you at least know I can help make it easier for you with the authorities. I have influence, friends in the police and judiciary. Let her go, and I will help you."

Horace's laugh was wild and maniacal. "Yes, Professor. Maybe you can study me then, like you did Fromley. I can be your new research pet." Then his eyes grew cold. "I am no project. And there will be no authorities. I am not some common criminal you can manipulate as you like." He gathered more confidence. "Here is how this will work, instead. You will both go over there." He gestured toward the stone wall behind Isabella. "You will get on your knees with your hands above your head, facing the wall, and begin to count slowly from one to one hundred. Do it now," he said, jabbing the gun once again at Isabella's head. "Or else she dies."

Alistair and I glanced at each other wordlessly and I saw that we both understood the situation: Horace was prepared to kill us all, and Fred was unlikely to interfere.

Where was Fred? Out of the corner of my eye, I saw him behind us. He had his gun in his left hand and his cane in his

right hand. Fred was right-handed, I recalled. His most dangerous weapon was in the wrong hand.

Horace was the real danger.

We had to act now.

"Let me see your hands!" Horace said in a menacing tone.

Just then Isabella stood up, throwing her weight against the
ropes that held her, dislodging Horace's gun as she fell, toppling
her chair. Her action gave us the split-second element of surprise that we needed.

Alistair and I both ran for Horace. Alistair lunged for his
arms. I grabbed hold of both legs with the intent of pulling him
down.

It was then that a crushing blow hit my back, sending me
rolling backward until I was pinned under a chair. Searing pain
along my right side rendered me almost immobile.

Through my agony, I realized Fred's cane had hit me from
behind. How had the old man managed to put so much strength
in his swing?

Fred materialized from nowhere, and used the toppled chair
to restrain me, my good arm pinned behind me. Only my useless right arm was free.

Where was Horace? I couldn't move my head, for the chair
pressed too deeply against me.

I heard footsteps—but whose? And was that Isabella crying?

From nearer than I expected, I heard Horace's voice saying,
"Let's finish it now."

He was by Isabella. I had to do something.

I closed my eyes and focused every ounce of strength I had
left in me toward my bad right arm.

Up, up, I thrust my arm against the chair with great effort.

I pushed with all my might though the pain nearly overwhelmed me. The chair toppled, but Fred fell on top of me.

No matter—my left arm was free. In a fluid movement, the result of years of practice, I grabbed my own gun, shoved it under Fred's arm, and took clear aim at Horace's own arm.

I missed.

Everyone ducked as the bullet ricocheted across the room.

Alistair lunged again, but Horace was too fast. He side-stepped Alistair's grip easily and aimed his gun at Isabella's head. We heard a click.

Alistair and I screamed, "No," in unison. I shoved Fred out of my way and he fell, striking the stone floor headfirst with a loud thud. I aimed once more for Horace. This time, I hit my mark. The bullet pierced his right leg, sending him crashing to the floor.

I was there in an instant, managing somehow to pin Horace's stout frame under me.

But I was a second too late. Horace's shot rang out with a deafening blast.

Alistair caught Isabella before she slumped to the floor, and I watched in horror as a red stain spread over her chest.

Fred lay senseless in the corner. Horace moaned in pain, clutching his leg, as I secured him with the rope that moments ago had bound Isabella. It was only a flesh wound that I had given him. Then, I joined Alistair in working to stem the swell of blood that came from somewhere within Isabella's ribs.

"You saved her, Ziele," Alistair breathed. "He was shooting to kill. The gun was pointing directly at her heart."

But as Isabella's blood continued to flow freely, I was consumed with worry. I hardly noticed the throbbing pain in my own arm as I ripped my shirt into strips for Isabella's wound.

With Horace secured and Fred unconscious, Alistair went to get assistance, and I waited in an anxious silence that was broken only by Horace's whimpering and Isabella's staggered, hoarse breathing.

Don't let her die.

I prayed the words without being entirely aware that I was doing so.

That plea was never far from my lips, even several hours later when Alistair forced me into the guest bedroom of his apartment.

The news was reassuring. "The doctor said she will make it, but she requires sleep and quiet. The bullet missed her vital organs, so there is no immediate danger." Alistair's eyes were filled with empathy as he said, "Why don't you stop your vigil and get some rest? You'll be of no use tomorrow otherwise."

Because I lacked the will to object, I obliged—and promptly fell into a fitful sleep haunted by images of Isabella, Horace, Fred, and a faceless Michael Fromley. It was a relief to wake the next morning to hot coffee and an appointment for Horace Wood's arraignment downtown, where he would be formally charged with three counts of murder and one count of attempted murder.

Fred had yet to regain consciousness. He was now in the hospital under police guard. He would be charged as an accessory to murder when his health permitted.

It should have been a moment that gave us satisfaction. Justice, it seemed, had been done. Isabella would heal, Fred would pay for his wrongdoing, and Horace would find himself permanently behind bars, if not in the electric chair—a fate which, as Joe commented when I telephoned him with the news, was no better than Horace deserved.

But as I thought of Sarah Wingate and Stella Gibson and even Michael Fromley, I felt only emptiness, struck by how meaningless such justice would be. We had worked tirelessly to find our man; now that he was found, we would work to bring him to trial and ensure that he faced up to the crimes he had committed. It was the best we could do. But it could not bring back those who had been lost.

Perhaps that is why the news we heard late that morning changed nothing. Just before we were to leave for the arraignment downtown, we got word that Horace Wood had cheated society of whatever justice a court may have fashioned.

It was the fault of the night guard, who had forgotten to remove the prisoner's suspenders.

Horace was dead.

He had hanged himself in his cell overnight.

Wednesday, November 15, 1905

CHAPTER 31

For what could well be the last time, I stepped out of the elevator onto the eighth floor of the Dakota building and crossed the hallway to number 8A. I would see Alistair shortly, but first, I hoped Isabella was well enough for a brief visit. Alistair had mentioned by telephone that she was recuperating as well as could be expected from her gunshot wound.

A tall, severe woman with black hair pulled into a tight knot answered my knock.

"You are?" She regarded me with cold disapproval. No doubt she was the nurse attending Isabella.

I forced a pleasant smile. "Detective Simon Ziele. Is Mrs. Sinclair at home?"

She shook her head. "Mrs. Sinclair is not receiving company.

The police already took her statement. Multiple times, despite her condition." The nurse gave me a baleful look.

When I spoke again, my voice was authoritative. "Please give her my name. I'm not here on official business."

She glared, but permitted me to enter. After disappearing a moment, she directed me to follow her into the front parlor room where Isabella waited.

Isabella brightened and greeted me with a warm smile. "It's good to see you, Simon." She sat on a small sofa under a quilt, looking thin and pale, surrounded by books, magazines, newspapers, and of course her dog. He wagged his tail when I approached but did not leave her side.

"You, too." I took the chair opposite her, easing myself into it, for my own body was heavily bruised from Sunday night's altercation. "You're feeling better?"

"I am." She wrinkled her nose. "I'll be even more so when Nurse Cabot's duties are finished. She's competent, but too heavy-handed for my taste." She regarded me solemnly. "How are you?"

"Good. I have a couple days off, now that this case is finished."

That had been Mayor Fuller's doing. His congratulations on a job well done had been exaggerated and insincere. But Joe had explained it, saying, "The mayor's just relieved the case is solved, the killer wasn't a local man, and we didn't screw anything up."

"I see our case made the news." I picked up her copy of the *Herald*. The main headlines continued to focus on the mayoral election scandal, but at the bottom of the first page I read: *LOOSE CANNON IN THE IVORY TOWER*. The *Times*, resting on her coffee table, proclaimed, *RENOWNED CRIMINAL LAW PROFESSOR HARBORS KILLER IN OWN RESEARCH LAB*. The irony in the title did not escape me; the headline might have referred to Michael Fromley as easily as Horace Wood. I did not blame Alistair for misreading the danger Horace posed, but I had yet to forgive him his reckless behavior regarding Fromley. Alistair had brought Fromley to the research center knowing that he likely had blood on his hands. For Alistair to pretend otherwise was disingenuous. No matter how unreliable the evidence, Alistair had chosen to disregard it rather than investigate it. He had thought only of his own research goals and taken a risk—one that Horace and Fred had exploited for their own purposes.

I gave her a quizzical look. "How is Alistair taking all this?"

"You can ask him yourself." Alistair flashed a wide smile as he walked into the room and greeted me. He leaned over and poked at the *Herald* in my hand with his index finger.

"A poor excuse for journalism, that's what it is. The story is riddled with loose speculation and factual error."

I looked more closely and saw what he meant. Dates, Fred's name, and even Horace's cause of death had been botched in the write-up. Alistair would no doubt obtain a retraction of the more egregious charges. But such a remedy, buried in the fine print on page twelve of tomorrow's news, would do little good if enough damage were done today.

"Will the research center survive?" I asked, trying to gauge the extent of Alistair's concern.

His response was edgy. "It remains to be seen; the decision depends on the Columbia trustees. Unfortunately, the papers are fascinated with the story, and they find new angles to explore every day." He sighed deeply. "I suppose, while embarrassing for us, what they sensationalize is less damaging than it might be. After all, they could have dug up far worse had they stayed on Fromley's trail. The accounting scandal and Horace's suicide have made for more interesting news than speculation about whether a dead man did—or did not—have murder on his conscience."

Alistair didn't mention the rumors alleging he had curried judicial favor to secure a murderer's release into his own custody. Fortunately for him, they had died a sudden death. Alistair made a few sizable political donations to the right people, they in turn had made the right phone calls, and Alistair's suspected breach of ethics was quashed at the editorial level. In other words, no reporter who expected to be paid for his efforts would waste time on that story.

"We'll weather this," he was explaining. "It's professionally embarrassing, but muckrakers like this"—he swatted at the paper again—"ultimately will not destroy the work we do. In a matter of months, it will blow over."

"Fair enough," I said. "What about Fred?"

Alistair shook his head. "Nothing new. He hasn't regained consciousness since Sunday night. He may never do so; apparently with each day that passes, his chances of recovery grow slimmer." He thought for a moment. "It's strange. I don't harbor the same anger toward him that I do Horace. I suppose it's because Fred was less calculated in his intent. He jumped at the opportunity to steal when it presented itself, but he didn't seek it out."

I raised an eyebrow. "I'm not sure I agree." I returned the newspapers to the coffee table. "But tell me, what bothers you more: their betrayal, or your not having seen it?"

Alistair's response was immediate. "It was being caught unawares that stings most deeply. I suppose the experience offers a valuable reminder of how truly difficult it is ever to know and understand another person."

We were silent.

"Isabella, I have a gift for you." I reached my hand into my pocket and pulled out the ruby and gold earring we had found at Horace's apartment. "It's yours, I believe," I added gently.

She took it and looked at me in amazement. "How did you— I mean where?"

"We found it at Horace's apartment. It's what tipped us off that you had to be nearby."

Her fingers closed around it and she murmured something to herself. It sounded like "for luck."

"Excuse me?" I asked.

For the briefest of moments, her expression was one of intense sadness. But then she smiled and spoke with an air of nostalgia. "Teddy gave these to me when we were first married. For good luck, because red is the color of happiness and good fortune."

"Perhaps he was right," I said lightly. "You survived a very close call Sunday night."

Alistair looked at his watch. "We should go."

"Of course," I replied. Alistair and I planned to attend a memorial service that morning for Stella Gibson.

Isabella gave me her hand, pressing it into mine warmly. "Simon, you must keep in touch. Perhaps you'll come to see us? You could even join us for Thanksgiving."

As she waited for my response, I noticed Alistair looking at us oddly. Embarrassed, I stammered some sort of noncommittal reply before making an awkward exit.

She was a widow of not two years—and Alistair's only son's widow at that. It would be unseemly to strike up too close a friendship with her. And yet as I thought of her deep brown

eyes and infectious smile, I was well aware of how easy that
would be to do.

The sky outside was starkly gray with the promise of snow—the
season's first. As I walked with Alistair down Central Park
West, he began to speak in fits and starts. His basic point was to
ask whether I would join him at his research center. "I have a
couple of openings now," he said with a rueful smile, "and you
could finish your degree."

It was a generous offer, and for a moment I was tempted by
the thoughts of what I'd once wanted—a college diploma, then
on to a law degree. But my answer came with sudden clarity, for
those dreams had long passed. It wasn't that I was too old,
though at thirty I was no longer young by the standards of the
day. But time and experience had changed me. There was no
going back to the man I once was, even if I wanted to.

Alistair seemed to understand, though he still handed me a
bag containing three books.

"What's this?" I didn't look as we continued to walk.

"Three books you should read: a translation of Enrico Fer-
ri's *Criminal Sociology*, W. D. Morrison's *Crime and Its Causes*, and
Hans Gross's *Manual for Examining Justice*."

Hans Gross had been Alistair's former mentor, I recalled.

"I don't think further reading will change my mind," I answered him as I accepted the books.

"That's not why I'm lending them to you," Alistair said,
stopping to allow a carriage to pass before we crossed Colum-
bus Circle. "You have a gift for reading people and understanding their behavior. If I didn't know it before, I saw it clearly
Sunday night when you managed both Fred and Horace. I know
you'll say it's only a matter of understanding basic motives, but

believe me—it's something more. You should develop it, and these books may help you. And besides, you will need knowledge to advance your career in the city."

"I have a new career in Dobson, in case you've forgotten," I said.

He grinned. "I don't think you were made for life outside the city, Ziele. This present case excepted, I'm not sure Dobson will offer you the sort of challenge upon which you thrive."

We turned left toward the Church of St. Ignatius and he continued talking. "We need more police officers like you. Just as we need better educated lawyers and judges, sociologists and psychologists. Our knowledge of the criminal mind lags sorely behind where it should be. Because people consider criminals, especially murderers, to be so vile, it is almost impossible to overcome their moral concerns to do what we need to do toward real scientific achievement."

"But all the same, you won't stop trying," I said.

He looked at me with a wry expression and laughed. "Very true, Ziele. Very true."

Guilt was paramount in my mind when I walked slowly up the gray stone steps to the small midtown chapel where Stella's memorial service was held. Light snow now fell steadily; it collected on the grass and trees, though the streets were kept clear for now by passing cars and carriages. Alistair and I brushed the snow off our hats and coats before taking a seat in a pew toward the back of the sanctuary.

The memorial was surprisingly well attended, with at least forty people filling the room. We had not expected a memorial service at all, but Cora Czerne had insisted and, together with the elder Mrs. Wingate, had made all the arrangements and covered the cost. It was odd seeing such an eclectic group of people gathered together. Mrs. Wingate was seated between Abigail and Cora in the first row, appearing fragile but sitting up straight. All of those from Stella's past jobs were in attendance, too—from Maud, Mrs. Wingate's cook and housekeeper, to a group of young women idly chatting toward the back, whom I took to be from Mamie Durant's. To an outside observer, however, they would have raised no eyebrows; in the uniform of black mourner's garb, they appeared the epitome of respectability.

The service proceeded smoothly, with the priest making the usual remarks: Stella would be missed tremendously by those who had known her; it was a tragedy that her life had been cut short while she was so young; and yet, none of us here should despair, as Stella had found peace in a better place now. It was the sort of thing people said to make those of us still living feel better, but such platitudes seemed insufficient to assuage the dark emotions stirred by a vicious murder like Stella's. I looked around the room and wondered if the priest's words really imparted meaning to anyone listening. Were they insincere and hollow only to me? Perhaps I was the only one in the room who was forever haunted by thoughts of the dead. I could never seem to let go of what might have been, if only the story of their final days could be rewritten.

I noted Mamie Durant's arrival some twenty minutes late. Dressed all in black, save for a red scarf that poked out from beneath the collar of her woolen coat, she attracted no one's attention. She sat silently until the service concluded, and no doubt would have preferred to leave without saying a word to anyone.

But after a hasty good-bye to Alistair, I managed to buttonhole Mamie as she was leaving. "Mrs. Durant? Might I have a word with you?"

"Why, if it isn't the detective," she said. "I can talk for a minute or two, but I don't see how I can help you. Stella is dead, and from what I read in the newspapers, her murderer was someone entirely different from the suspect you were originally looking for. Too bad you weren't faster on the uptake, or perhaps Stella would still be alive." It was an insult meant to serve as a warning; clearly she did not want to entertain too personal a conversation.

"I just have one question. A loose end, so to speak," I began.

"Go on," she said, though she looked at me with a guarded expression as she directed me away from the main throng of mourners toward an area of the churchyard where we might find greater privacy.

"There was a girl called Moira Shea. She was probably murdered by Michael Fromley in August 1902. I saw her autopsy report in the course of my own investigation and something puzzled me. Just before her body was to be released for pauper's burial, a woman claiming to be her mother came to retrieve it. That woman was you." I paused to catch my breath, but not for too long, lest she interrupt me before I finished. "What was your relationship to Moira Shea that you couldn't bear having her sent to Potter's Field?"

When she didn't answer, I went on to explain, saying, "I'm asking this personally. Your answer will not go any further. I give you my word."

The pause that followed seemed interminable.

"Give me one good reason why I should tell you, Detective," she said, challenging me in a dubious tone.

I smiled, trying to appear friendly. "A detective's compulsion to tie up loose ends?"

She snorted. "You've got a lot of loose ends, from what I've seen. I'll chalk it up to pure curiosity. You detectives don't like it when there's something you can't figure out." She looked at me hard. "Anything I say stays between you and me?"

I nodded in the affirmative.

She walked even farther away from the area where other mourners had clustered, wanting to ensure we would not be overheard.

"Moira *was* my daughter," she offered, "at least—the closest thing to it I will see in my lifetime. Her mother worked for me before she got sick; she died of tuberculosis when Moira was just three years old. I was her guardian, though I never got around to adopting her formally. I guess I felt I didn't need to— it wouldn't have changed the way I felt about her." She shrugged. "You see, we all make our own families, Detective. However we see fit."

Her breath caught sharply. "While she was alive, I lived with her across town where no one knew me. I wanted the best for her. Better than what I had; better than what her mother had had." Her voice began to shake, charged with a fury that seemed undiminished by three years' passage of time. "What right did *he* have to take her from me? From everyone. And your police made a royal mess of it; they never even managed to put together enough evidence to arrest him. Their failure made it seem Moira died for nothing at all."

I waited a moment. "How did you become suspicious of Michael Fromley? The police never suspected him with respect to Moira's murder."

"Blundering idiots," she said. "I hired my own private investigators. They came to the same conclusion in Moira's case that the police did in the Smedley girl's case: There was plenty of suspicion but not enough proof. So I kept them on payroll to watch him." Her eyes narrowed as she looked at me. "It wouldn't have mattered what your professor did or didn't do. If that researcher of his hadn't murdered Fromley, in due time I'd have arranged it myself. That brute had no right—no right whatsoever—to keep breathing after my Moira was gone."

Yet Mamie had helped Fromley evade justice after he attacked Stella—persuading the girl not to pursue charges, once again allowing Fromley to walk away from his crime scot-free.

I challenged her. "Then why didn't you?"

Her response was as cool as ice. "I did arrange it, actually. Fromley was on the verge of getting exactly what he deserved when he was arrested for Catherine Smedley's attempted murder, and your professor entered the picture with his strange desire to study that creature. That's when I called it off." She laughed, and it was a harsh, guttural sound. "Your professor thinks it was all his doing that he got Fromley in his clutches. He thinks someone like me can't pay a bribe, call in a favor? Pay off a judge?"

She stood up straighter, speaking with fierce pride. "It cost me $500 to deliver Fromley to Alistair, free and clear of the jailhouse and the electric chair. You see, above all, I wanted to know *why* . . . some explanation as to why he killed my Moira. And I thought maybe your professor could give me that, if I gave him the chance." She added darkly, "I could always have Fromley killed later, which was to my advantage anyway. Too soon after Moira's murder, suspicion might have fallen my way. But after a few years? By then, my relation to Moira would have been all but forgotten."

So Alistair was cleared—or was he? The fact that Mamie had intervened didn't necessarily exculpate Alistair from blame.

And even if Mamie was solely responsible, I was certain that I would never tell Alistair—for his own sake, as well as my promise to Mamie. I didn't want Alistair to feel absolution for his part in all that had happened. He needed something on his conscience to counterbalance his near-blind devotion to his research.

Disappointing, too, that Alistair had kept his relationship with Mamie from me. "I'm an open book," he had lied.

"Did you ever get the answers you wanted from Alistair?" I asked.

"Oh, I spoke with the professor often enough, all right." She made a noise of disgust. "I must say, I expected more for my money. He learned nothing at all that I could tell. He didn't know why the lout picked Moira. He couldn't even adequately explain why Fromley was driven to do the things he did."

But I knew that no answer Alistair could have found would satisfy her. Knowledge could fill many voids, but not a loss such as hers.

She paused a moment before drawing herself up as she prepared to leave. "Good day, Detective. I hope our paths do not cross again." And she was gone, her black coat and umbrella disappearing into the thickening snow and the jostling crowds along Broadway.

CHAPTER 32

It was time to go home. A somber mood had taken hold of me following Stella's memorial service, and I keenly felt an empty sense of purpose. Snow was now falling fast, with a couple of inches on the ground and more expected tonight. On impulse, I ducked into a coffee shop that was bright and warm, its aroma of freshly ground beans pleasurably inviting.

"Biscotti and a double espresso, please."

I placed my order with the short Italian man behind the counter who spoke no English, but appeared to make an excellent espresso—at least according to the customer in front of me. Then I settled into a small table overlooking the street and began reading my newspaper. Unable to focus, I put it aside, and turned instead to the note I had received last night.

Ziele,
Nice working with you, kid. I'll be in touch.
—N.S.

Mulvaney had been right. "The devil always demands his due," he had said.

In that instant, I was thrust into the underworld of illicit favors I had worked so hard to avoid. But the Lower East Side and its influences seemed to drag me back, whenever I thought I had succeeded in leaving.

Then again, what choice did I have? When she left the research center to seek out Horace, Isabella had taken with her the proof that might have led me to him. Without Nicky, I could never have identified Horace so quickly. I could never have saved Isabella. The alternative was unthinkable.

And Nicky himself was not the devil, even if he was a major player in the city's system of money and favors—one that operated in all classes of society. Alistair traded well-placed donations for favors and bribed newspapers to sit on stories he didn't want printed. The difference was that Alistair had a fancier name for it—*quid pro quo,* to borrow a lawyer's turn of phrase. And he had shown me its danger: How the ease of manipulating others made it simple to go too far. Had Mamie's admission of bribery absolved Alistair? Not necessarily. After all, a judge who took one bribe might have taken two. I didn't know, and I decided it didn't matter.

What mattered was that I was made of sterner stuff—at least, in that respect.

There were no simple choices. But I was resilient, if only through sheer determination and stubbornness. I would be able to handle Nicky and whatever new complications crept into our dealings with one another. We would cross paths again only if I chose to return here.

Was Alistair right that I craved the excitement and challenges of the city in cases I'd encounter only here? Maybe. Or maybe not. There was no need to decide now.

The espresso's warmth invigorated me as I drained my cup and ordered another. Someone put a record on the gramophone in back, and the music of a violin concerto swelled over me as I sat, enjoying the experience of being here, one of an anonymous crowd, this moment on a snowy November evening.

I waited a long time before I got up to leave.

As I shoved Nicky's note back into my coat pocket, my fingers brushed against something else. I pulled out a scrap of paper. It was my fortune from Saturday night's moon cake, which I had shoved into my pocket and forgotten.

I placed it in front of me and smoothed it out, visions of Isabella filling my mind—for I would forever associate memories of that night in Chinatown with her.

The first step to better times is to imagine them.

I traced the slip of paper with my finger.

It called to mind a pleasant memory, nothing more.

I put it with the other papers I planned to toss—then reconsidered, folded it carefully, and placed it in my wallet.

And I ventured once more into the storm, where glowing billboards from nearby theaters cast half shadows of silver and blue onto the snow-covered ground, ghostly images that danced alongside me as I walked down the street and into the night.

AUTHOR'S NOTE

This is a work of crime fiction grounded in a particular historical time—New York, 1905. Because it is a story first, I have taken liberties with historical fact wherever the story was improved by it, while striving to remain true to the spirit of the times. Of the many wonderful resources available, I turned most often to the holdings and helpful staff at the New-York Historical Society; the New York Public Library; the Hastings-on-Hudson Historical Society; the archives of the *New York Times*; Luc Sante's study of the seedier side of old New York; Kenneth Jackson's comprehensive history of New York, always an informative starting point; and Ric Burns and James Sanders's illustrated history. I also found helpful a number of sources on criminology, including *Criminals and Their Scientists: The History of Criminology in International Perspective*, edited by Peter Becker and Richard F. Wetzell; *Inventing the Criminal* by Richard F. Wetzell; and *Fingerprints: The Origins of Crime Detection and the Murder Case that Launched Forensic Science* by Colin Beavan. I consulted the above as well as contemporary accounts to frame the criminal himself; I am indebted to John Douglas in *Mindhunter* for his discussion of the role fantasy can play in the criminal act.

A few historical side notes are worth mentioning. In reading both turn-of-the-century and modern accounts of killers and criminal scientists, I am struck by the fact that in both eras, scientists turned to violent criminals themselves to learn about the criminal mind. Modern criminal profiler John Douglas has detailed how interviews with notorious killers yielded the knowledge that became the foundation of the FBI Behavioral Science Unit. But a century before him, the French criminologist Alexandre Lacassagne completed a similar project, albeit on a smaller scale. My fictional Alistair Sinclair follows their example. The earliest criminal scientists were limited by people's fear that understanding the criminal mind would lead to excusing criminal behavior. Still, by the turn of the century, ordinary police officers had begun to work with criminal experts to organize and synthesize information about criminal behavior. Their uneasy alliance presages the relationship in this novel between Simon Ziele and Alistair Sinclair.

Moreover, the mayoral election held on November 7, 1905—the day this novel begins—really happened, as did the incidents of ballot box destruction and voter intimidation alluded to in the novel. Even by the looser standards of the day, this election fraud was so egregious it led to major reforms. And finally,

Sarah's research topic, the Riemann hypothesis, was taken from David Hilbert's famous list of problems expected to be important in twentieth-century mathematics. Though he considered it to be one of the easier on his list, it remains unsolved as of this writing.